# MY HOME SWEET HOME

*(A LIFE OF COMMITMENT WITH CONTENTMENT)*

*To Wanda & Robert*

*" Enjoy "*

# MY HOME SWEET HOME

## (A LIFE OF COMMITMENT WITH CONTENTMENT)

*Author*
*Maxine E. Derr*

*Pen Name*

## GALA WAKEN

*Gala Waken*

| Library of Congress Control Number: | | 2013922096 |
| --- | --- | --- |
| ISBN: | Hardcover | 978-1-4931-5076-2 |
| | Softcover | 978-1-4931-5075-5 |
| | Ebook | 978-1-4931-5077-9 |

Rev. date: 12/06/2013

To order additional copies of this book, contact:
Xlibris LLC
1-888-795-4274
www.Xlibris.com
Orders@Xlibris.com
138345

To my children,
Jack, Daniel, Cynthia and in memory of Mark.

This second book is dedicated to my children and all my grandchildren and great-grandchildren. They have been filling my life with joy and peace—my fringe benefits! The children have had faith to go to other states to live and make their home sweet home, giving me the freedom to visit in many places throughout the USA. Maxine's son Mark's life is woven throughout this story as a remarkable miracle of God's will be fulfilled and Maxine's belief. "There is a God, and no one will ever make me believe there isn't. Heaven is the final destination for those who believe."

# TABLE OF CONTENTS

# CHAPTER ONE

## *CARRY ON*

Commitment is a serious and willing trust made to one another in a marriage ceremony: "To have and to hold, from this day forward, in sickness and in heath, for richer, for poorer, for the rest of my life, so help me God." It is only by the grace of God that a married couple can fulfill their commitment to one another with unselfish love.

Joy was serious and willing to make her marriage succeed. She had tried so hard in her own strong will, but to no avail, realizing it takes both partners to be committed with trust and working together for the same reasons. She gave up after years of abuse—abandoned, helpless, heartbroken, and with no spirit left of any hope for the future.

God sent a neighbor, Grace Atkins, to listen to Joy's plight, who told Joy, "Christ is the only answer." After, this realization entered her mind: "That's what I need!" She told Grace that she realized that and wondered what she should do. Then Grace invited her to go to the church services that evening, September 1961.

Joy walked to church that evening, taking baby Gale—she was three months old—and Clark, who was seven, went to his class that he faithfully attended each week. Joy timidly sat in the last pew, with Gale in her bassinet, at the back of the college auditorium.

Services were being held here because the new church was under construction.

She listened to the sermon intensely. The altar call was given, and Reverend Paul Davis announced, "To those who are seeking God, come forward and pray." The organist played while the congregation sang "Just as I Am." Joy stood up and stepped out into the aisle, and she felt the weight of the world came off her shoulders as she (it seemed) flew down the aisle to the altar. She rededicated her life to Christ, committing her life to trust in Jesus Christ, witnessing to others about how the power of God's love transforms even the worst of sinners into a new creature in Christ, a new creation, acceptable to be called a child of God. Joy, hope, and peace filled her heart once again.

*Thanks be to our God,* Joy thought.

After trying to make amends with her husband, she was once again disappointed in his behavior, and the family was abandoned once again. He had been gone for over a year and came back to visit and see how the family had been doing.

"I'd like to come back here to live, can I come back?" he asked Joy.

"No!" she replied. "You told me you wanted your booze and your freedom, when I told you that your drinking would come between us, you said to me, shaking the bottle in my face, 'Looks like the bottle won, good-bye, it's been good to know you.' Now you go and enjoy them. You have abandoned us one too many times."

Dean said, "Then give me a divorce."

"No, I don't believe in divorce, and I will not give you one. For over seventeen years, you were always number one. Now there are four children, and they outnumber you, four to one. They need peace without your drinking and conflict they have had for so long," she said, with intensity of the truth.

"I deserved that," Dean said as he left.

A few weeks later, October 26, 1963, he stopped in to see the family but didn't stay long. He said, "I am going to see a friend that lives close by." A couple of hours later, this friend came over and told Joy, "Dean has been seriously injured and is in the hospital in Carlson, Michigan, and there was also an eighteen-year-old boy that had been killed instantly by a drunken driver at the same time. They had been in the middle of the road when the car hit them." Dean passed away two days later. The doctor told Joy that if Dean hadn't abused his body with cigarettes and alcohol all his life, he may have survived.

Widowed with four children—another challenge for Joy to overcome, but now she had the Lord to guide and direct her in the right direction. He was Lord of her life now. He said, "I will never leave you nor forsake you" (Hebrews 13:5), and He never will. Committed, trustworthy, faithful to the end, a comforter, and a prince of peace as no human could ever be. We all fall short of the glory of God, but He gives us the power to overcome sin when we are committed to Him, doing His will, not our will. Trials and tribulations through the years were many, but by the grace of God, this family triumphed through them and learned many lessons along the way guided by the Lord.

2

From housekeeping for others, Joy was given the opportunity to accept an office job by one of the ladies she had been cleaning for. She was so thankful that someone had faith in her that she could learn and do something besides housework.

Another new year had arrived and with it the experience of attending business school to prepare Joy for her office career, which she was excited about. The Thompsons were giving her the opportunity to work for them in the office four days a week, and she would also continue to clean their home once a week. During this time, her neighbor Lana Reed babysat for Gale, her youngest child. Lana and her husband, James, had two boys, John and Ricky. This gave Gale someone to play with and learn about sharing and getting along with others, a blessing before she started school in the fall. Joy was contented knowing her daughter was being cared for by someone she knew and who lived close by.

Studying was hard; caring for the family and keeping her housework done, Joy was afraid she wouldn't finish her homework, but with determination and late hours, she seemed to get done what was required of her in time. Sometimes remembering what her mother had instilled in her—"Can't never tried"—gave her the incentive to keep trying no matter how hard or time-consuming it was, praying faithfully for God to help her.

Time waits for no one, and it went by. Before she knew it, summer was here and the children were out of school for the summer. Joy had finished her courses for this semester and was working in the office now, doing the payroll for the construction company. She had to learn the difference between cranes, bulldozers, front-end loaders, excavators (all sizes) to determine which wage scale the men received; also, the truck drivers and laborers all had different wage scales, and their benefits had to be reported to the different unions. My goodness, this seemed like a different world than she was used to.

Making mistakes was a learning process, a long hard one; Thorne Thompson got upset whenever he heard about it and was about to fire Joy, but Teressa stepped in and asked him to give Joy another chance. She told him she would spend more time to help teach her to recognize the differences of the machines, drivers, and wages.

Teressa Harrison had been their secretary for many years and was the one who suggested they pay for Joy to go to business school in order to get the basic bookkeeping knowledge she needed, then hire her to learn on the job about the equipment and contracting business because Mrs. Thompson didn't want to work in the office anymore. Teressa was a Christian and a sweet person to everyone. She and her husband, Bill, didn't have any children, yet they loved everyone else's. In her desk, she had a drawer full of all kinds of candy. Whenever children came into the office, they got to pick which kind they wanted and usually left with a bagful. They all knew where the candy drawer was and waited patiently for her to ask if they wanted any. Mr. and Mrs. Thompson's son, James, was in charge of all the crews on the jobs and getting the bids ready for any new jobs coming up for bid. James and his wife, Joan, had four daughters. The Thompsons had a daughter named Carla; her husband, Philip Arnowski, worked in the office, keeping the garage crew operating smooth, ordering parts and dispatching the equipment operators where they were to go.

Philip and Carla had two boys and a little girl. The Thompsons liked to be called Darla and James. They were very plain and down-to-earth, treating everyone with kindness and hospitality and yet very business minded. Darla would go sit on the doorstep of a client if they wouldn't pay their bill. Until she got paid right then, she wouldn't take any excuse.

The summer of 1964 was another year of trials of faith and trust for Joy as a parent of the four children and their wills and dreams.

Darwin came to her and said, "My buddies and I are going to California to see one of the guys' girlfriend and go to Disneyland." Knowing there wasn't any question that he had already made up his mind to go, there was no sense of discussing whether he could go or not. She told him, "I really don't like the idea because it is a very long way for three teenagers to be going by themselves without an adult along."

Although Joy tried her hardest explaining how many things could happen to them.

Lyle Casey was anxious to go see his girlfriend; he wanted Darwin and Leonard Brown to go with him. He was the oldest of the three and said, "We will be taking a Greyhound bus, and I am sure it will be safe for us all together." Joy found out later they took the bus to St. Louis, Missouri, and hitchhiked the rest of the way.

Darwin called a few days later to let her know. "Mom, I wanted you to know we arrived and we are all doing fine, and I will call you again later, bye and I love you."

She had no clue of the details of the trip except when Darwin called her and explained, "We ran out of money, and Lyle already flew home, his parents sent him the money. Could you please send us some money for the bus?" Joy replied, "I am glad to hear you are safe, and all right, yes, I will send some money by Western Union. Be careful, and I will be happy to see you back home."

After arriving home, she learned that Darwin and Leonard hitchhiked from California because they needed the money for food. They got in an argument, and Leonard stayed in Oklahoma, and Darwin came back the rest of the way by himself, very upset with him.

"Thank You, Lord, for keeping him safe and his return back home to us." This trip was taken between his junior and senior year of high school in 1964; he was sixteen years old. *Another trial to strengthen my patience to help raise children by myself. Only by the grace of God am I able to cope with everything one at a time,* Joy thought.

This year, Donald, Joy's eldest son, was married to Lacy Carlson. Their beautiful wedding was at the Free Methodist church in Springdale. Darwin, Clark, and Gale were all in the wedding party along with Lacy's brothers. Joy was happy for the newlyweds and enjoyed being mother of the groom, and contentment filled her heart.

Joy's eldest brother, Karl Junior, took all the wedding pictures after the ceremony and gave them a set as a wedding present, and he gave Joy a set also.

The year went by fast—Thanksgiving, Christmas, and New Year's. Darwin graduated and was working for a building contractor to be able to afford a race car and go to different racetracks, winning many trophies for coming in first. He repaired his car, working many long hours learning more and more about how motors run and go faster.

He met a young lady, Annabelle Barton, and had been dating her; she was the eldest of ten brothers and sisters. She was a sweet and kind young lady, especially to little Gale.

Joy had bought their home the year before, after the settlement with the insurance company and searching for a banker who would let her borrow the money for a mortgage. Darwin had been working for a building contractor and decided it would be a good investment to reconstruct the garage and back room into an apartment to rent for extra for Joy's budget.

She agreed with the suggestion, and he went to work on the project, working evenings and weekends until it was completed. It was a lovely apartment and soon was rented to a newly married couple. They kept it very clean and paid their rent on time. Renting was no problem, and it was nice to have extra income.

Joy was able to buy a new car; her old one wasn't reliable anymore. Driving back to and from work was twenty miles each way. It was good to feel secure, and she didn't have to worry about the old one breaking down on the highway. She felt like she drove on a wing and a prayer every time she drove the old one out of the driveway.

Work was going along smooth by now. Joy could tell the equipment apart and was getting the paperwork completed in good time. She was feeling more confident of herself. She was able to relax and enjoy working with everyone in the office, even Mr. Thompson when he and Darla were in town, usually during the summer months. By this time, Joy was working in the office five days a week.

Donald and Lacy had a baby girl on November 29, 1965, Debbie Marie, Joy's first grandchild. Just think, she had married in 1945, twenty years ago. My, where had the time gone? So many memories, good as well as bad ones—they are all behind. Now life has a new meaning, and the future looks so promising for all the family. God had blessed this family and has provided for them a new hope and a stronger love to give.

Joy taught two-year-old children in a Sunday school class since Gale was two and was amazed to see how much these little ones could learn during the year they spent in class. They were like little sponges, soaking up all they could, learning the songs, listening to the stories, and doing the activities. Joy felt blessed as she continued to teach the children. Being able to get down to their level seemed hard for some people, but "being as a little child," as Jesus said, faith is believing they too can be taught the truth. As the time went by, Joy took her granddaughter, Debbie Marie, when she turned two years old, and a little friend named Lori asked to go also, so Joy picked her up, and they were in the same class. What a joy these little ones were, so willing to listen. When they were about three years old, they would come up with question after question about Jesus and God. They wanted to know for sure that Jesus loved them and all the little children in the world. "How could He love everyone at the same time?" they asked.

One Saturday Joy was going to bake a cake, and she needed something from the store. She asked Clark if he would to go to the store for her. It was only a couple of blocks away.

He lowered his head and said, "I can't go in the store anymore."

"Why in the world can't you?" Joy astonishingly asked.

"Because Brent and I stole some candy, and Al Street told us to get out and stay out and don't ever come back in the store again."

"Clark, you go in your bedroom and get enough money out of your bank that would pay for the candy you and Brent took, then you go up and tell Al you are sorry for what you did," Joy said with anger in her voice.

So Clark got the money and took it to the store to see Al, but he was back in just a few minutes, crying, and said, "Al wouldn't let me in and told me to leave."

Joy telephoned Mr. Street and told him, "Al, this is Mrs. Godman. Clark told me about the candy he and Brent took, and I made him take money out of his bank to bring to you and ask you to forgive him, and you wouldn't even give him a chance to tell you. Why didn't you call me and tell me when Clark did that? As Christian brothers and sisters, aren't we supposed to go to one another and discuss these things?"

"Mrs. Godman, I have called other parents, and they won't believe me when I tell them what their kids have done," he said.

"Well, I am not other parents, I want to know when things like these happen. I know what kids will do, I had five brothers, and I was a kid once too," she replied.

"You send Clark back up here, and I will accept his money and his apology," he said.

"Thank you very much. I am trying to raise my children right," Joy told him.

Joy's granddad, Hank Wilson, had been in the rest home for some time and kept saying, "I want to go home and go over the River Jordan, there is nothing here for me anymore."

On August 4, 1968, he went home to be with God the Father. He was born on May 28, 1869. A time for rejoicing because he was ready and they all knew he went to heaven. His Christlike life was an example to behold, a gentleman's gentleman, if ever there was one. Grandpa Hank Wilson was her mother Betty's father. Betty passed away in 1959.

Darwin and Annabelle had been dating often and were getting serious. Darwin asked her folks if they would let him have her hand in marriage. They told him he would have to go to the Catholic Church to take marriage-preparation classes because he wasn't Catholic. Darwin agreed and took the marital instructions. He gave Annabelle an engagement ring and asked her to marry him. They were married on November 1968 at St. John's Church in Logan, Michigan. It was a large, beautiful wedding and reception. Annabelle was a beautiful bride and Darwin a handsome groom. In attendance was a maid of honor, the best man, many bridesmaids, and attendants; participating were some of her sisters and brothers. Joy's brother Karl Junior developed their wedding pictures after the ceremony and gave them a complete set for a wedding present; he also gave a set to Joy.

Joy's two older boys are married and have left the nest, starting their own families as God had purposed for man and woman to do.

The rest of the year seemed to go by fast, and another year was well on its way. What will this year bring for the family? God only knows. Keeping busy with everyday routine and church functions, the joy of the Lord was Joy's strength to help her carrying on with all her responsibilities, loving her family and trusting in the Lord to supply all her needs.

It was April 1969, springtime now; the snow was gone. The tulips were blossoming and so beautiful. It was good to see new life bursting all around. But this joy didn't last long because Joy received the news that her brother Karl Junior had passed away. This was a shock because he had been so careful with his health, actively jogging and dieting right. Karl Junior was only forty-nine years old; that seemed so young and so surprising to everyone.

Karl Junior and Darla, his wife, had three children: Linda, Alex, and Shirley. The doctors said that a blood clot hit his heart. He had been jogging that morning and went back home and told Darla, "Call the emergency, I don't feel well," and he then just dropped to the floor and died. It was too late for any help. Death is so hard to accept, realizing your loved one is gone and won't be around anymore. We all wonder why. He had been such a good brother and had done so much good for others in his life. God only knows why, and we have to go on with life as best we can with God's love and compassion.

Pastor Gilbert Shorn came to visit Joy and her family to see if they needed anything and to comfort her. She thanked him and began to cry, tightly holding Gale in her lap with one arm. With the other she hit her hand very hard on the arm of the chair and said, "There is a God, and there isn't anyone who is going to tell me there isn't!"

"Yes, Joy, I know," Pastor Shorn said with an astonished look on his face.

"My brother was such a good man, Pastor," Joy said, and she cried and sobbed much harder. Pastor Shorn waited quietly for a while until Joy was calm.

"Will you be all right if I leave now?" he asked.

"Yes, I will. The boys should be here soon. Thank you so much for coming. I needed this cry and outburst, letting it out, I couldn't hold it in any longer."

"I understand, Joy," he replied.

Joy had to find another renter for the apartment, and she placed an ad in the paper. A woman came to the door and said she was a relative of a friend of her son Donald and would certainly take good care of the apartment and pay the rent on time. So Joy believed her and rented it to her. Things were pretty good at first, but after a month or so, Joy noticed that there were cars coming and going late in the night and early in the mornings, so she confronted the lady with it and told her she wouldn't allow men coming and going all hours of the night. So it stopped for a while, and Joy warned her that if it went on, she would have to move because she didn't allow "night crawlers" coming and going. Then she wouldn't pay the rent, and Joy had to ask her to move, and she wouldn't move. Joy's brother Franklin hired a lawyer, and they had papers served on her, and after three months, she finally moved, never paying the back rent.

The next couple that rented the apartment were very good renters like the first couple. She was pregnant, and the baby was due in four months, and they were good neighbors doing all they could to help around the yard or to babysit Gale if Joy needed her.

The boys were working and providing for their families and enjoying different activities on the weekends. During hunting season, they would go hunting for rabbits and pheasants, and during the deer season, they usually went up north in Michigan.

This fall, Joy's three sons went up north, deer hunting, and while they were gone, Joy got her deer; she was on her way to work one morning, and she heard a *thump! Thump!* She felt something hit her car and looked in the rearview mirror and saw a deer lying in the road. She backed up and saw that the deer was dead. A man stopped and got out of his car and asked her if she wanted him to call the Fish and Game and report this, and she agreed that he should. As she waited, she looked at the car to see how much damage it had done, and to her surprise, there was not even a scratch. She was astonished and thought, *Thank God.* The officer came and asked Joy if she wanted to keep the deer, and she said yes.

He said, "You need to get it someplace and have it cut up and frozen as soon as you can." Then he helped her put the deer in the trunk of the car and took all the information on how it had happened, and then he said, "You are sure lucky it didn't do any damage to your car." She totally agreed with him.

Joy laughed and said, "My three sons went up north, deer hunting, and I didn't even have to leave home, and I got one."

He also laughed and said, "Yours is a sure thing, you didn't even have to buy a license."

She had to call the office and tell them she wouldn't be in that day because of the deer. They too were surprised and happy for her.

When the boys got back from their trip, they were all disappointed. No one shot a deer; they were all skunked. Then Joy told them about her experience with the deer, and they said, "It is pretty good. We all bought licenses, and not one of us got a deer. Mom stays home and goes to work, and she is the one that gets a deer without a license and doesn't even fire a shot. Not only that, it didn't even dent her car. Talk about providence."

Joy said, "God always provides."

That was the big laugh around the neighborhood for some time. "The three Godman boys went up north hunting and came back skunked. While their mom was on her way to work, she bagged a deer."

Darwin had built a home a few miles from Joy's, and it was good to see them invest in a home for the future with Darwin's talents and determination. It was a lovely home, one they could be proud of and where they would be ready to raise a family in the future.

Donald and Lacy were living in the mobile home they had bought when they were married, and he was still employed at Crowley's Factory, which was close to their home. Debbie Marie was five years old now, and they were expecting another baby. The time had come for the baby to be born, and Donald took Lacy to the hospital in Atwood, a little town not far from their home. It was in the evening of the twenty-ninth of December 1970. Donald called Joy to let her know they were at the hospital if she wanted to come and be there when the baby arrived.

Just as Joy arrived, Misty was born, and the nurse lifted her up wrapped in a blanket for Joy to see, and she yawned as if she was bored with this *ole* world already. Tears rolled from Joy's eyes down her cheeks as she thought, *Thank You, God, You are so good! New life—Misty is life everlasting, a part of Donald and Lacy, a part of my husband Dean and I, a new generation living on with new hope and abundant joy. Although with the death of our family's loved ones, Satan tries to control our spirits with depression and sorrow setting in to discourage and take the hope away, it is only by the grace of God we are saved through faith in our Lord and Savior, Jesus Christ, who died, was buried, and arose again, defeating death. He lives in our hearts eternally so we may love those who are living by telling them about life everlasting. He is the Way, the Truth, and the Life, and no one comes to the Father except through believing in Him.*

The year had ended with a new baby in the family, and joy continued to fill Joy's heart, and with the expectations of the new year coming for her and the family, she always remembered to thank God for never leaving nor forsaking her and for all He had done for her by giving His Son, who died on the cross to take her place.

# CHAPTER TWO
## *A MIRACLE*

## LIFE

A miracle itself, of which no man can perform.
A gift from God, our Creator, Himself did form.
It's taken lightly by some folk,
And others think life as a joke.
God asks nothing in return to Him, except to praise and answer Him.
When He calls for us to do according to His will,
To all we now know, keep praising Him still.
And let some folks know that He is God,
And cares for us no matter where we trod.
Our spirits may be low and gone,
But God is there; we are not alone.
He is anywhere we seek to find.
Just call and believe in Him; He is kind.
He'll answer your prayer and will revive
And let you know He is still alive.
He lives in our hearts, you know,
Although some people don't let it show.
He is in the kind words we say,
And the little deeds we do each day.
Life has fruits to behold,
These are more precious than silver and gold.
From life's budding vine we may find
Love, joy, meekness, peace of mind,
Faithfulness, and courage to behold,
Of which no man has bought or sold.
They are the free gifts from heaven above.
Our Father gives in return to love.

His Son, He gave for us to know
Salvation for the world below,
Life everlasting for all to have,
His healing love, a soothing salve.
They hung His Son. His life did take,
But God had plans; the earth did quake.
He rolled back the stone, and Christ arose.
Life again, God restores to those
Who will believe and seek to find
The answer that God had in mind.
That Christ should die and live again,
To redeem us all from the power of sin.

For those who will seek to find the answer,
Which Christ Himself is the master.
His love, to them He will give,
And the Spirit within He will live.
A life with Christ they will find
And have a perfect peace of mind.
Our sins are washed away for good,
Revived for life, and live as we should.
According to our Father's will,
Life everlasting. To love Him at our will.

Written by Joy, April 1971.

## GOD SPOKE

God spoke everything into existence
His *word* is powerful beyond all distance
Yet so close the *word* will penetrate
Into our hearts as we concentrate
Upon the *truth* and the *way*
I ask *Him* in my *life* to stay.

Jesus said, "I am the WAY the TRUTH and the LIFE, no man can come to the Father except through Me" (John 14:6 KJV).

It was good to see the flowers blooming in many varieties and colors. Spring is always so beautiful with new life and the birds singing each new morning to cheer the soul. Seeing, hearing, smelling, and touching the beauty God gives each and everyone freely, along with the warmth of the sunshine after the long winter of cold and cloudy days.

The children were happy to get out to play without all the winter clothes to put on, and they had so much energy to wear off. Gale was almost ten years old now and eager to romp and play. Climbing trees was one of the things she liked to do. Although Joy would warn her about being careful not to fall, she did fall hard and broke her arm. They took her to the hospital for an x-ray. Dr. Knecamp set and put a cast on. She was strong—didn't complain too much for a child. The doctor advised her to be very careful now.

Summer months were very busy for construction workers, and Joy kept busy at the office every day, concentrating so she wouldn't make mistakes, and now she had the problem of finding a different babysitter for Gale. This was going to be something she had to concentrate on—finding someone she would be able to trust. Joy asked some of her friends if they knew of anyone who would take care of Gale, and Rita Street, her friend, offered to take care of Gale for the summer. Joy thought, *Thank You, Lord, I didn't know what I would do.* Although, Gale wasn't too pleased about that arrangement; she and Rita didn't get along very well. Joy didn't have much choice because she couldn't find anyone else after a long search.

Clark helped Mr. Richmond at the church with small chores and with lawn work at his home. He raised beautiful flowers every year and sold them. Mr. Richmond was a kind man; he liked Clark and guided him in many ways, a good father figure for Clark. This gave Clark spending money, and he saved most of it to buy a bicycle. He still loved to go fishing and up to the college gym with Ronny Slate to play when he wasn't working.

This year, 1971, Gale turned ten years old in June, and Darwin's wife had her first baby. They named her Desare. She was born on October 7 (a day before Joy's birthday.) Clark turned seventeen in November. It didn't seem possible; the years had gone by so fast. *The holidays will be here before I know it,* Joy thought.

It was sure fun to Christmas-shop for the three granddaughters along with Gale's and Clark's gifts too. *What a blessing these children are. God is so good to me,* Joy thought. She began to wonder what she would do for the

Christmas program with the two-year-olds she was still teaching at Sunday school. Then she remembered the birthday cake they used (an artificial one) when they sang the "Happy Birthday" song to the children on their birthday. She then taught the children what to do when they were in front of the congregation for the program. When it was their turn to do their part, the children followed Joy down the aisle as she carried the cake with one large candle burning. In front they lined up and sang "Happy Birthday, Jesus" and then tried to blow out the candle, but it wouldn't go out (it was one of those candles that won't blow out), and Joy said, "This light is like the light of Jesus, it will never go out." The children were so sweet, and the congregation told Joy they didn't think two-year-olds could do much in the program. Joy answered, "It took some thinking to come up with it, and God knew I wanted them to be in the program."

Joy received the news that Donald and Lacy had separated; he left Lacy and was dating Sherry Long. This was a shock to Joy because she believed everything was going well with them. She had been taking Debbie Marie and Sherry's daughter, Lori, to church with her on Sunday mornings. Sherry and Bart were separated and were getting a divorce. They also had a son named Brad. She had no idea there was any trouble between Donald and Lacy. This almost broke Joy's heart because she had gone through so much trying to make a success of her marriage, but she had to accept it. She realized she couldn't live her children's lives for them, and now she would open her heart to Sherry and her children.

The holidays were over now, and all the trimmings were put away; the house was back to normal. The children were back to school and back to their routine schedule.

Gale had joined the Girl Scouts, and Joy was a den mother helping with the girls work on their badges. This gave Joy more time to spend with Gale.

While Gale was staying at Rita's, she met a friend, Patty Gilmore, who stayed at Rita's once in a while. She also belonged to the Girl Scouts. Joy met her mother, Ina Lee, one day when they went to pick the girls up at Rita's house, and they became friends. Ina Lee's husband had passed away also, and she was raising Patty by herself.

On May 13, 1972, Saturday morning, Joy and Gale were making cookies for her scout meeting, and the phone rang; a lady said, "Now don't get upset, just listen to what I have to say. Your son Clark has been in an automobile accident and is on the way in an ambulance to Mondale because the Logan hospital wouldn't take him, his injuries were too severe."

"You get someone to drive you over to Mondale, don't you even try to drive yourself. Do you have someone who can take you?" she asked.

"Yes, I have another son who lives close by, he will take me," Joy answered.

Thinking when she hung up the phone, *Darwin raced cars, he will probably get me there faster than anyone.* Joy called Rita and asked her if Gale could come and stay with her and told her why.

Rita said, "Yes, and I will be down to pick her up."

Darwin came as soon as he could, and they were on their way, both of them were worried and wondered how the accident happened. Joy couldn't understand why Darwin wasn't driving faster, but he was going the speed limit and didn't want to get a ticket. It seemed like they would never get there, and it seemed like it took so long. Arriving at the hospital, they checked in and were escorted to the floor where Clark was being operated on, and a nurse took some information she needed and said one of the doctors would be out and talk to her soon. Joy and Darwin were so nervous waiting for someone to come.

Then Pastor Shoren came in the door and said, "I came to see if there was anything I can do, if not, I will stay with you for a while to see how Clark is doing so I can tell the congregation. They are all praying for Clark. We received the message about the accident and the sequence that happened after. It was that a lady saw Clark's car roll over and over by the golf course and land. She stopped at Bob Klevin's King's Point gas station to telephone the police and for an ambulance that would be needed. At the same time, some men in a couple of cars stopped, got out, and raised the 1965 Triumph convertible off Clark's head and turned his head to the side so he wouldn't choke on his own blood [one of the men had first-aid training]. These acts of compassion and concern definitely saved Clark's life."

Then finally the doctor came over to Joy and said, "Your son has been seriously injured. His head has been crushed, cracked across his temple from one side to the other, his cheeks are crushed, and his jawbone is badly broken. He has no right to be alive, his head is in bad shape. We are doing everything we can do for him. It will be some time before you will be able to see him, and when you do, be prepared to see a lot of swelling and black eyes, it isn't a very nice sight to see. And you can only see him for five minutes on each hour." He took Joy's hands and held them for a while and asked, "Are you going to be all right?"

And she answered, "Yes, I will."

Pastor Shoren asked if he could pray with Joy and Darwin, and they said yes. As he prayed, Joy's faith was strengthened, and she believed God would answer the prayer. Jesus said, "Where two or more are gathered together in my name, there I will be." He was there among the three of them, uniting them in prayer for the healing of Clark and giving them all the strength of endurance for the long days ahead. Joy felt the peace of God and His assurance Clark would come through, although it would take a long time.

Patiently waiting to be able to go in and see Clark, Joy, Darwin, and Pastor Shoren sat quietly. Joy was remembering when they were at the hospital in Carlson about nine years earlier when Dean was in critical condition after being hit by a drunken driver. He remained unconscious from Saturday evening until noon on Monday when he passed away. Memories flooded her mind about whenever they would go in and see Jack; he would lie so still for a while, and then he seemed to be wrestling from within, fighting with the will to live until death. This happened several times during their visits, and afterward Joy and the older boys would go to the chapel in the hospital and pray.

It was hard for Joy to accept his death, and she felt guilty because she wouldn't let him come back to live with them, but that was the past, and she now has to think about Clark and his future. She spoke, "Clark is very young and hasn't abused his body with cigarettes and alcohol like your dad did. His doctor told us that is one of the reasons why Jack didn't make it. Clark has a much better chance for his body to heal. God's will be done in Clark's life. I thank God we have the church praying for him."

One of the nurses came in and said, "You may go in and see Clark now for five minutes. Be prepared to see a swollen face, black eyes, many tubes inserted, and machines hooked up to him." As they walked in, Darwin took one look at Clark and almost fainted.

Pastor Shoren took hold of him and helped him stay on his feet and asked, "Do you want to stay here with your mother?" and he answered, "Yes, I will be all right now." The shock of seeing Clark like this was overwhelming to them all, and it took a while to adjust to the reality of how serious these injuries were.

Tears filled Joy's eyes as she looked at Clark lying there. She was crying on the inside and praying, "God, please let Clark live, don't take him away from me. I have had enough people I love taken away." Pastor Shoren could see Joy's tears and put his hand on her shoulder to comfort her. By this time, their five minutes were up, and they had to leave the room. It would be another hour before they could go back in to see Clark again.

Rita Street came to the hospital to help and to stay with Joy while the family took breaks. Joy would not leave the hospital; she stayed there for eight days, sleeping on the waiting room couch and washing up in the nurses' lounge. Rita brought her clean clothes each day and reported on how Gale was doing. Gale was staying with Rita and going to school from there. After eight days, Joy's boss told Joy she had to come back to work or lose her job, so she decided to go see Clark every day after work. The drive was approximately forty miles over to Mondale and fifty or more miles back to Springdale. It was a long day for her, but she made up her mind to go see him every day until he regained consciousness.

Clark showed signs of some brain function, but the doctors were very uncertain about the outcome, and they told Joy not to hope for too much, but she had faith in God that he would come out of this. One of the doctors told Joy, "We don't know if he will ever become conscious or not, and if he does, he may not even know his own name."

Joy looked up at this tall middle-aged doctor and said, "Someday he will come walking back in here, knowing his own name too."

The doctor replied, "I wish I had your faith. But after these nine weeks or more we have cared for him, we feel we have done all we can for him, and you will have to find a place for him to convalesce."

Now there was another hurdle to get over—trying to find a place for Clark in Logan, where it would be closer to home. Joy called many convalescent homes to see if they would take Clark in the condition he was in or not. Many said no, and others were reluctant and wanted to know more about how serious his injuries were and how much care he would require. Finally, Mrs. Grantor from the church told Joy she would take care of him at the rest home on E. Michigan Avenue she operated. What a relief for Joy. This would be on her way home from work, and she wouldn't have to leave

Gale so long and could spend more time with her. It had been hard on her since Clark's accident. She was eleven now. In fact, the only day Joy didn't go to see Clark in Mondale for over nine weeks was on Gale's birthday, June 5. Dean's folks went up to see him and spent the day with him. Joy took Gale to Cedar Point Amusement Park in Sandusky, Ohio, for her birthday. It was fun and relaxing to spend time with Gale.

July 12, 1972, after all the papers were signed, instructions given, and doctor's appointments made to take Clark back to Mondale for checkups and physicals as well as to see the neurologist, Joy was ready to have him transported by ambulance to Mrs. Grantor's Rest Home. The doctors and nurses who cared for Clark most of the time were lovely people and wished them well, and they hoped that Clark would fully recover.

What a blessing it was to be able to go see Clark for an hour or two every day and then go right home and get her rest after work. Over a month had gone by now, and it was about time to take Clark back to Mondale for a checkup. Joy had set a day and time for an ambulance to take Clark, and it was getting near that day when she stopped to see Clark and to tell the nurses to get him prepared to go. She walked in Clark's room, and he was sitting on the side of the bed with his hands on his hips and said, "Mother, get me out of here, that old man is driving me nuts." What a surprise— he had awakened for the first time to complete consciousness. Joy was overwhelmed with happiness and joy to see him so alert. The elderly man in the bed next to him had moaned and groaned all night continually until it broke through Clark's unconscious state to his awakened state of mind. With help from the nurses to get Clark in the wheelchair, he would be able to go to the Mondale hospital for his appointment.

What a surprise for the doctors to see Clark awake and knowing his own name when they arrived for the appointment. The neurologist just kept shaking her head every time she asked him a question and he was able to answer it, questions about things that happened before the accident and school problems, like math, spelling, and history questions. She explained to Clark, "What a lucky young man you are, others who are injured as bad as you were are not as fortunate. It is the short-term memory questions you weren't able to answer, and you will have to write things down in order to remind yourself because the part of your brain that controls the short-term memory has been damaged, and that will affect you the rest of your life. You are still capable of living a normal life by learning to cope with making a list of things you want to remember daily and permanently." Each time he went back to see her, she was amazed at the healing process taking place, his attitude, and how he was handling the handicap of the short-term memory loss.

Clark lost his sense of smell and had a drooping eyelid. The doctors operated on the eyelid and repaired it the best they could, and besides the trachea scar in his neck, he had no other visible signs resulting from the accident, which was a miracle that he even lived. As the doctor stated, "Your son has no right to be alive with the injuries he has on his head."

*But by the grace of God he is living, and I thank Him for that. As humans we cannot control life or death; only God has the power.* Joy thought.

Joy felt that Clark needed to continue having adult supervision after he was released from the rest home, so she rented their home and moved out to Michigan Center with her brother Louis. He worked evenings, and Joy worked days. Gale needed someone with her also after school. She had been with others since Clark's accident and needed to be with family. Although the change was hard on them all, it had to be done.

After the fourteen weeks of semi-unconsciousness, Clark's convalescence was like a child, learning all over again and needing full attention and teaching. He caught on quickly after repeating a few times then going on to another task.

After a couple of months and summer going by fast, Darwin and Donald called and asked Joy, "We are going to the lake for a picnic, and we would like to take Clark along and get him out in the sun and fresh air for a while, will it be all right?"

Joy replied, "If you are very careful with him."

"You know we wouldn't do anything to harm him, Mom, he is our brother," Darwin said.

"All right, you can come and get him, but please be careful," she replied.

The day seemed long with Clark gone most of the day. Joy had grown accustomed to looking after his needs and being assured he was comfortable. Late in the afternoon she began to check the clock several times, wondering, *Where are they? Is Clark getting tired?* Finally, they drove in. *What a relief to see them,* Joy thought as she went out to see them.

As they got out of the car, Donald said, "You will never believe what Clark did today, Mom."

She answered, "What did he do?"

"He water-skied all around Lime Lake without falling down," Donald replied.

"Oh my God." Joy added, "I am sure glad I wasn't there."

"That's why we didn't ask you and Gale to come along. We wanted Clark to get out and get some exercise and fresh air. When we asked him if he wanted to ski, he said, 'Yes, I can do it.' So we let him, we were very careful and watched him get up on the skis."

The time had come to take Clark back to Mondale for another checkup, and Joy was anticipating what the doctors would say when she told them about Clark water-skiing around the lake and how his healing process was coming along.

It had been about a month since they had seen the doctors and the neurosurgeon, who usually tested Clark for brain activity and memory evaluations, so when they entered the hospital floor where these doctors were located, some of the nurses recognized them and spoke with a cheery "Hello, how are you doing, Clark?"

Clark replied, "Just fine, I went water-skiing a week ago, would you believe it?"

"Really? You are kidding us, aren't you?" was the reply from most of them.

"I am not kidding, am I, Mother?" he replied.

"No, he isn't kidding, he really did, although I didn't know his brothers were going to let him do it when they took him on a picnic last Sunday," Joy explained.

They went away just shaking their heads in astonishment. The same reaction was apparent with all the doctors when they were told.

The neurologist said, "Clark, you were very brave to even think you could do that, let alone going all the way without falling once."

Clark explained, "My brothers came and got me because they thought it would be good for me to go with them to the lake and get some fresh air and exercise. They were all skiing, and I wanted to see if I could still do it, so they let me."

"You are certainly one very lucky young man to recover from that serious head injury you had and are able to do the things you are doing now," she stated.

Joy said, "God answered a lot of prayers, and with faith in God, I kept believing He would answer. Besides, when the doctor told me they had done all they could do for Clark and I would have to find another place for him and they didn't even know if he would ever come out of this even knowing his own name, I looked up at him and said, 'Someday Clark will come walking back in here.' And he replied, 'I wish I had your faith.'"

As the neurologist finished examining Clark, she said, "I want to see you again in about six weeks from now, and keep up the good progress you are showing."

The trip back from Mondale was beautiful, and Joy said aloud as they drove home, "Thank You, Lord, for all You have done for us, Your faithfulness is never ending. Every day new mercies we see, and Your provisions are always there for our needs."

Clark said, "You are right, Mom, God is good."


*Much credit is given to some of the doctors and staff at Mondale University Hospital (1972).*

Some of the doctors in Mondale were Dr. Stuebneu, Dr. Bosac, Dr. Burchfield (an eye doctor), and Dr. Aron Smith (a psychologist), many more and the nursing staff also.

God provides the necessary people at the right time in all situations for His will to be done. Providing the minds and hands of those dedicated to the preservation of life to be enjoyed and used for whatever choices that are made in their lives to live.

# CHAPTER THREE

## *ACHIEVEMENTS*

The summer months had passed, and the fall season was here. The hunting season was near, always one of the best times of the year for Donald and Darwin; they loved to hunt. So in 1972, they planned to drive to Alaska for moose hunting, along with a friend, Ned Hunter.

This trip lasted over five weeks, from Springdale, Michigan, through the western states, Canada, and the Alcan Highway. Their first hunting was in Haines, Alaska, where they hunted for mountain goat for several days, but no luck, except Donald shot a wolf. After that, they headed to the interior where they had planned to hunt for moose. Stopping at a small sporting-goods store in Tok Junction, they were informed by the proprietor, "If you do not fill your moose tags, you can use them for caribou." They thought, *Great, we won't have to worry about the money for another tag if we don't get our moose.*

They hunted moose in several places, backpacking in along the road system. Several small bull and cow moose were seen, but they were holding out for a sizable bull. No moose yet, but Donald shot a lynx, and Darwin shot a black bear.

Money was getting short, so they headed off to the Delta Junction area to hunt caribou. They were informed that all the caribou were miles off the road, so they checked at a fly-in service, but Ned decided he didn't want to fly to a remote area. This was all right with Donald and Darwin because they only had enough money for two people to take the plane. They had planned to use a credit card for gas money on the way back home.

They were flown in to a remote location and, for three days, hunted hard but saw no caribou. The pilot flew in to check and see if they had any luck, and they told him their fate. The pilot offered to take one of them up to look around. After flying around for thirty minutes, they finally located some caribou. The pilot then dropped Darwin off at the closest place he could put his Super Cub down and then flew off to get Donald and their gear.

The next morning, Donald and Darwin bagged two nice caribou bulls. They proceeded to butcher it, and they backpacked to the landing strip about two miles one way, and on their arrival from the third and final trip, they were greeted by a Fish and Game officer. Checking their license, he informed them that in order to use their moose license for caribou, they should have traded tags. He issued them a citation and said, "You have to turn over your guns." They both gave him their rifles, then he said, "I also want your handguns."

Darwin said, "We didn't shoot the caribou with our handguns, and you have no right to take them away from us and leave us here in the wilderness without protection."

A glaring stare contest between Darwin and the officer began and lasted for a couple of minutes until the officer finally backed down and said, "OK." Darwin has a strong and daring spirit when it comes to the truth of any matter.

They went to court and explained to the judge, "We thought we were legal, and changing tags was something we offered to do once we flew back to town." This didn't matter to the judge; he fined them $150 apiece, and Darwin spoke up and said, "You will have to put us in jail because we only have $75 between all of us."

"OK, your fine will be $35 each."

After finishing the court procedures, the guys got into the truck and pointed it toward home and headed out, happy to be on their way.

On their arrival at Bear Creek, the Canadian border check station, they were informed they needed at least $300 cash to enter Canada. Tempers flared, especially Darwin's. They were lucky they didn't get arrested. They drove back into Alaska, two hundred miles or more, and located a small thrift store and sold Darwin's aluminum flat-back canoe, ten-horsepower outboard motor, and a .41 Magnum pistol, and Donald sold his .22 Magnum pistol— all for $300. Driving back to the border check, they were not happy campers. The family was glad to see them arrive back home safe and sound, anxious to hear about the trip to Alaska.

The Thompsons decided to sell the business, and the new owners were four men from the Redmond Asphalt Company: Willard Barnes, Walt Parks, Davis Werner, and Glen Owens. This was quite a surprise to them. Teressa and Joy didn't even know if they would be employed by the new owners or not. But they wanted them to continue to work.

Louis was dating a lady named Velma, and she came over to his house and visited, usually on Sundays to get acquainted with us. They soon became serious and talked about marriage, and Joy thought it was about time she moved back to her own home in Springdale. Clark was able to care for himself now without anyone's help, and the new school year, 1973, would be starting soon for Gale to attend. She had been attending school at Michigan Center for one semester and missed her friends.

It was good for them all to be back in their own home, and the children were able to see their friends. The family could attend church, and the grandchildren could come over and stay all night; Joy had missed being with them. There is no place like home sweet home, and they were so happy to be there once again. They had been away for about a year and a half. Contentment filled their hearts as they all settled back into their routine. Being in Springdale, a small quiet community, was good for the children and Joy.

Although, unfortunately, one afternoon Gale was playing with her friends up by the fire department, and close by was a place (a large hole) where some old appliances had been dumped. The children were running and jumping back and forth on the appliances, and she fell and broke her arm again in the same place she had broken it before. Dr. Campnel was the same doctor who had set it and put the cast on her first break. He told her, "You had better start acting like a little lady instead of a tomboy, so be really careful now, you don't break the other arm."

Joy agreed with him and said, "When I had a little girl, I thanked God, because my husband wanted a little girl so bad, but he isn't alive to help raise her. I have been both mother and father to her for twelve years now."

Clark was going to rehabilitation classes to see what he was capable of doing, and the Salvation Army tested him for different types of jobs. One test they gave him was a large board full of nuts and bolts and he was to see how long it would take him to remove them from the board. So he started unscrewing the nuts from the bolts one at a time, then he realized that took too long and proceeded to run his hand down the line of nuts and bolts several times until they fell off, one row at a time. He went in the room where the instructors were and told them he was done, and they could hardly believe he was done. They said, "There is nothing wrong with your mind, you can surely figure out the quickest way to remove those bolts." The results of the test was he should be capable of working at most any manual labor, and they suggested that he should go to a technical school to learn a trade, so he tried being a cook and a truck driver, but his short-term memory loss was a handicap for him because he couldn't remember what he had read.

The year was a good one for Darwin. He took flying lessons and was enjoying them, adding many hours toward getting his pilot's license to fly alone. He was dedicated to his desire to reach his goal. When he finally received his license, he wanted Joy to fly with him, and she did and said, "It is a thrill to look down and see Logan from a small plane and proud of Darwin for his accomplishment." She was thinking, *Darwin has always been brave to try anything whenever he felt it was a challenge.*

The time was slipping by fast. Winter had gone, and the spring flowers were in bloom; everything looked so beautiful. Nineteen seventy-four, another year to be thankful for and enjoy to the fullest. She joined the American Business Women's Association this year with Teressa.

Clark attended a technical school to become a machinist. He had high scores in the testing for this type of work and was advised by his teachers to take up this profession. This was at a physical rehabilitation school located near Grand Rapids, and after six weeks of training, he could come home for a visit. This was very good for him to be more independent and to learn to cope with his disability. Clark got along very well operating the machines and learning this trade because he liked doing it and caught on quickly. It was repetition, and he was able to learn and perfect the operation of the machinery.

Six months later, the course was completed. He came back home to search for a job and was able to find a small factory located on the east side of Logan that hired him. This was approximately twenty miles from Springdale, and so he bought a motorcycle to ride back and forth to work. It is May 5, 1975, now, and another accident occurs.

One beautiful spring day, Clark was on his way home from work on his motorcycle, and a woman pulled out from a side street and hit him broadside, and he went flying into the ditch. He was taken to the hospital by the ambulance, with a badly injured hip. The hip ball went through the socket and tore it up, but the doctor was able to repair it so he wouldn't need a steel ball and socket to replace his own. The doctor said, "You are too young to have a replacement, and I believe, with healing, it would be some time before you will need a replacement." This was another nine weeks in the hospital in traction, with his leg lifted high with bars and pulleys while lying flat on his back.

Clark was thankful that so many friends and family came to visit him and cheer him up. After arriving home and on crutches, he walked up to the college each day to enjoy the beautiful weather and just to be outside once again.

Their home was close by a lake, and Clark would take a lawn chair out by the road in case any of his friends were going swimming. He would wave and stop them and ask if he could go along. They were happy to take him along and bring him back home. The doctor said it would be good for him to swim and exercise his hip.

There was a dock in the lake not too far from shore, and Clark would walk with his crutches to the dock and put his crutches on the dock, swimming out as far as he felt he was capable of doing and still be able to get back to the dock safely. Clark was content now.

Gale would be fifteen, and she wanted a horse for her birthday, and Joy told her they did not have any place to keep a horse and they cost too much to feed and care for. She was so determined to have a horse. She went to a farmer who lived up the road about a half of a mile, and she asked him, "If I get a horse, would you let me keep it in your barn and fenced in a corral?"

"Well," he said, "You have to water and feed it and clean up after it also."

"I will," she agreed to do it and came running home to tell me. "I do have a place to keep a horse," she said, so excited. "Now you can get one for me. I saw one in the want ads, 'A horse for sale, Tennessee Walker, very gentle.' Can we go and look at it, Mom, please, can we?"

Answering, "I don't know anything about horses. You will have to call Donald and see if he will go with you to look it over, he knows more about horses than I do." She called Donald and asked him if he would take her over to see the horse, and he agreed to do it.

He called and said, "It was a two-year-old and very gentle, a good horse for Gale, and it surely would be worth it. With the saddle, it was $150." She told him to let them know they wanted her. Her name was Shannon; she was all white and so pretty. From then on, Gale rode all over, free as a bird. She took to riding so easily and just loved to ride Shannon. She did take good care of the horse and shared her with friends, letting them ride too. Eventually she met another young girl who had a horse, and they rode together.

Summer was coming to an end, and it was time for school to start again, and Gale wasn't looking forward to that. She didn't like school because it was hard for her. She was in middle school now and was with the older grade level of children. She was very slow in her classes and got frustrated because she couldn't understand her lessons.

She found a friend who talked her into going home with her after school, Golda Kane. She called and let her mom know where she was so she could drive over to pick her up.

Golda's brother, Bruce, liked Gale and wanted to go with her, and he asked if he could, and Joy said, "No, she is too young." After that, Gale went over to the Kanes', not telling her mom, and she went to get Gale, and they lied and said she wasn't there.

Joy called the police, and they told the police the same thing—she wasn't there. By this time, she was getting very angry with the Kanes. The mother was always drinking, and their home was very dirty. Joy just couldn't understand why Gale would even want to go to such a place; her home was so clean and nice. This went on for some time until Gale met a really nice young boy, Alan. She was so thankful Gale was dating him. He liked her and treated her well. That didn't last long, and she started to go with Bruce again, and Joy was upset; she disliked him very much being with Gale.

"If you don't stop hanging around him, I will sell your horse to Donald!" Gale didn't care. Joy gave the horse to Donald because he wanted to ride her and breed her with his horse.

June 5, 1977, Gale turned sixteen and was pregnant by Bruce. Joy wasn't about to have a grandchild brought into this world without them being married. She believed it is hard for a child without mother and father being married. Gale was rebellious; she knew her mom wanted to give the child his name. *God only knows where I went wrong. I tried so hard to raise her to the best of my ability and was heartbroken when this happened. No matter how hard we try, we cannot live our children's lives for them,* she pondered.

The busy time with working, keeping house, and general responsibilities seemed to go by so fast. She enjoyed her Sunday school class, prayer meetings, and American Business Women's Association, they met once a month. It was a good organization to belong to. They earned money to give to young ladies for scholarships to college. She met ladies from all different professions. Teressa, her coworker, and she had joined in April 1974 and went to the conventions, meeting many ladies from other states and chapters. Through the years, they held offices like treasurer, secretary, vice president, and president.

June 8, 1977, Teressa was president and wrote a letter recommending Joy for Woman of the Year, and it was granted to her. This was an honor for a humble soul trying to do what a mother should be doing for her family, Joy thought.

Teressa Harrison
President of Apollo Chapter
American Business Woman's Association

## "WOMAN OF THE YEAR 1977"

Portraying the businesswoman of today, and a mother of four (4) children, who has come a long way through life, is my Gal Friday.

Let's start now from the beginning of my storybook, and I'll tell you why I believe she should become Woman of the Year.

Born right here in our city she received her education in the public school system. At an early age she became a member of the Park Side Baptist Church where singing in the choir. She became active in Girl Scouts, along with other activities of young girls. While she was still young, she suffered the heavy loss of losing her father, to whom she was very close. She had two younger and three older brothers, she and her sister had to take over many household duties and responsibilities to relieve her mother of strain. Working her way up through the school years, enjoying the school activities, she met and married her school day's sweetheart. At that time in her life she was very ambitious, and worked hard to maintain her home. Becoming the mother of four children, she was an important person. Much depended on her success to lighten their home with happiness.

It was just two years after her fourth child was born that her husband was killed in an automobile accident, once again leaving her alone to carry on.

Not wanting to accept charity or welfare, her education limited, she had to seek work where it was available. She attended Junior College evenings to further her education and gain more knowledge for the future. Cleaning our office one day a week we began to know her and to recognize her great personality. She was asked if she would like to work with us in the office. I was elated to have her and began training her on the telephone, then on the radio, then to the position she now holds as payroll clerk and my personal assistant. She does a great job and takes on many duties that helps our office to progress.

Her life has been a hard one, but she has always shouldered her burdens, and now takes her memories with a smile. Her activities are swimming, dancing and skiing. She is a member of the Free Methodist Church in Springdale, and a wonderful Christian.

(She makes our office a place to enjoy, where there is never a dull moment. My beautiful Joy! She's my friend, and to me, she is already Woman of the Year.

The *Logan Citizen Patriot Newspaper* published an article: "Mother Works Her Way Up to Club's Woman of the Year." She received many congratulation letters and cards.

Joy's spirit lifted. Having many Christian friends and ABWA friends helped her to feel better about herself. Thank God for a friend—Teressa—she knew the burdens Joy was carrying with Gale and how brokenhearted she was. What a friend we have in Jesus.

Gale and Bruce moved from Logan to a little town near Adrian, where some of his relatives lived near them. They didn't get in town very often to see us, but Gale called once in a while to let us know how she was, and we visited her once in a while.

Joy decided to sell the house and buy a large mobile home that would be closer to work; she didn't want to drive those fifteen miles to and from work anymore especially during the winter months. The mobile home park where she moved was Indian Village, an adult park only two miles from work. It was a nice mobile home park and very convenient for shopping and visiting family.

The new officers for the year 1977-1978 were chosen, and Joy was elected president of Apollo Chapter, American Business Women's Association. Other officers were vice president, Joy Jewett; recording secretary, Marie Robins; treasurer, Marie Engel; and corresponding secretary, Kaye Zanella.

American Business Women's Association is an organization that gives scholarships to young ladies who qualify for grants, helping with college expenses.

One of her bosses had a sign on her desk the next morning after the election reading:

"BIG CHIEF"
Good morning, "Madam President"
Congratulations, we are very proud of you.

It had a big red feather attached to it. What a pleasant surprise this was; it gave her more encouragement and also gratitude for the management of the company.

Many letters of congratulations were sent and prayers spoken for her and the new responsibility she had been elected to. Joy prayed God would help to fulfill those obligations with dignity and honor.

August was the first meeting to conduct as president. She was so nervous and felt unworthy. After the pledge of allegiance to the flag of the United States of America and the flag of ABWA had been said, everyone was seated.

Joy said, "Now we will say the benediction."

Teressa stood up and said, "Good night, this is the shortest meeting I have ever attended."

Everyone laughed, and Joy realized what she had said, so quickly she said, "Please excuse me, I meant the invocation," praying silently, *Oh God, forgive me.* A spirit took away fear and nervousness. Sometimes fears are so unfounded. God must have orchestrated the moment for her to show her not to be fearful and to trust Him to guide one through all situations. She had prayed and was humbled, thanks be to God. From then on, conducting the meetings each month became easier and more pleasant.

Having a friend like Teressa Harrison was godsent. He knew what she needed in her life to release insecurities and an inferiority complex. She was an encourager and gave support whenever and wherever needed, helping along the way of self-confidence.

The year was going by fast; Thanksgiving and Christmas had been celebrated, and the New Year was here, 1978. Gale's baby would be here soon, and Joy was worried; they lived so far from the hospital. She just had to trust in the Lord and lean not on her own understanding. He will take care of her and the baby. Keeping busy helped the time to go by faster. Making tablecloths and napkins with swedish embroidery and decorating them was a good time-consuming and enjoyable thing to do in the evenings. They make very nice gifts to give to family members and friends.

The phone rang on a cold January 22, and Bruce was on the phone and said, "We are at the hospital, and Gale is about to have the baby, she wants you to be here with her."

"Tell her I will be there as soon as possible," Joy told him.

Joy arrived at the hospital just in time to see the baby come into this world, a healthy baby boy, crying his heart out with healthy lungs. Bruce said, "Hello, Bernie Lee Crane."

Thank God Gale was all right and happy. It was all over, and Joy wanted to hold the baby in her arms. "This is the first grandson. There are three granddaughters, Debbie Marie is thirteen years old, Misty is seven years old, and Desare' is six years old," Joy said.

Gale was very upset when she found out one of her best friends had been staying with Bruce at their home and was having an affair with him. Joy had told her he was not a good man, but she would not believe her; she had to find out for herself. She and the baby were discharged from the hospital, and they went back to their home near Adrian to live, struggling along the best they could. Bruce was without employment, and the family helped them out with the expenses as much as they were able to do for them.

Bruce couldn't find work, and they moved back in town to live with his parents. Looking for work was unsuccessful, and he was growing weary of no employment, so he decided to join the army so he could provide for Gale and

Bernie. Gale moved in with one of her girlfriends until Bruce's training was completed and he could send for her to go wherever they would station him.

Bruce went to Furth, Germany, to serve his allotted time he had signed up for, and he wrote to Gale all the instructions for her to come and be there with him. As the arrangements were being made for her and Bernie to go, she got their visas, birth certificates, and shots that were required, then waited patiently for the tickets to arrive.

She was only seventeen years old, still a child, going so far away from home and family, with a child six months old. Anticipation and excitement filled her soul as she waited. She had no fear. This was a new experience. Going to Germany was all she could think about and hope for, believing all things would be beautiful between her and Bruce once more.

Arriving safely in Germany, Gale called to let them know she had arrived and had a very good trip and that Bernie was very good and traveled like an old professional. Bruce found an apartment off base, and their neighbor was a preacher and his family, in which Joy was happy to hear for Gale and Bernie's sake and welfare. Joy worried about them.

Gale liked being in Germany and was thankful for the opportunity and meeting new friends and touring around the city by the trolleys and buses. She didn't fear going places alone with Bernie and tried to understand the language as much as she could to find her way to get on the right means of transportation.

# CHAPTER FOUR

## *A DREAM COME TRUE*

This year was going by fast with working and church and ABWA involvement. Time seemed to slip away faster by keeping busy. The holidays were coming along and would occupy their thoughts of celebration and looking forward to each one. Joy's sister, Clarice, and her family usually came over for Thanksgiving, celebrating at Darwin and Annabelle's home, enjoying a wonderful meal and getting together with family.

Thankful for each and everyone God has given to her and thinking to herself, "Oh, how much Dean has missed all these years with the children and grandchildren." These are treasures of memories being formed in the minds of family and love so strong to build upon in their own lives, a foundation of love and happiness remembered throughout life as responsibilities grow to become adults.

Christmas—how much fun it is shopping for everyone, making choices for each one individually and wrapping them carefully, personalizing the present with love from the heart. With the menu planned and different dishes of food brought, a beautiful table is set for the family to share and to eat together, giving thanks to God for this day of the birth and celebration of our Lord and Savior.

When dinner was over and the presents were being opened, some tore off the wrappings so fast looking for what is inside, and others gently opened with care and consideration of the effort that was put into it. Giving to those we love as Christ gave to all and enjoying the reaction of their joy and happiness is the main theme for Christmas. Seeing the children laughing and playing together, getting to know each other a little better. Even though they are cousins, they don't get to spend much time together because of the parents working and busy schedules.

A new year, 1979, is here now, and what will it bring? Joy thought, *I live one day at a time with faith, believing and trusting because I am God's, and He will direct my path.* Clark was having a hard time finding work and was tested at the Vocational Rehabilitation Center. The test stated he qualified and his skills would be best utilized if he would work in a factory on machines.

They advised Clark to go to the Vocational Training Center in Plainwell, Michigan, for a machine shop course.

Joy took Clark to Plainwell and visited him regularly. This was a year-long course, and when he finished the course and received the certificate, he decided to take the general education degree course so he would receive his graduation certificate.

July 13, Darwin Godman II was born. Darwin and Annabelle were very proud parents of their little boy, so wanted and loved. Little Desare' was a little jealous of this new arrival because she had all the attention of everyone around, including many friends, for so long.

Before Gale had planned on going to Germany, Joy started corresponding with one of her cousins over there. She wrote by sending a letter to the clothing store her uncles inherited from her grandparents by addressing it to the Karl Wise Clothing Store, Neustadt/Weinstrasse, Germany. Two months later, she received a letter from one of the cousins, Gilda Conrad, who was able to write in English. She was so happy Joy contacted her and the family because they haven't heard from her father's family for many years. Joy's mother wrote to them periodically before she passed away in 1959.

Gilda's letter brought her up to date on the remaining family members and their families. She wrote, "I had to read the letter in German to all the others who could not read or speak English, and they were so pleased that you had written to them."

Joy's father's youngest brother was still living—Uncle Carlyle and his wife, Lydia.

Gilda's brother Warren helped Carlyle manage the Carl Wise Bus Company, another business inherited from her grandparents. Carlyle was seventy-eight years old and still going strong.

Cousin Dyson was managing the clothing store along with his wife, Heidi. Their daughter Dany was fifteen years old, and a son, Carson, was thirteen.

Gilda's husband is Eric Conrad, and they have two boys, Richard and Earl. They could speak and write English well. They chose to learn it in school as a second language. Gilda and the boys were the only ones that could speak, read, and understand English.

Joy thought, *I am so thankful to hear from her and all this information she had written to me. It gives me more information about the family as I am journaling a family tree to document the generations of our family. I want my children to have this information for further references as they get older and who may want to continue on with their generations, because many people don't even know who their grandparents are or where they came from. I grew up and meditated on so many different aspects of life. I dreamed of going to Germany and meeting my father's family. It was something that I held in my heart for many years.*

Gale wrote and asked, "Mom, do you think you could come to Germany while we are still here? You could visit your father's family while you are here too. You can write to them and let them know you would like to see them. I would sure like to have you come, and I can meet them also. It would be so much fun and a chance of a lifetime. We can take the train from Nuremberg, where we live, to Neustadt."

Joy thought, *This is such a good idea, and if at all possible, I would like to go.*

She had an income-tax refund coming, and Ethel Street, one of the ladies she was housekeeper for, told her, "Joy, you have been such a good person, and you deserve to have this opportunity, and I am going to give you three hundred dollars to help pay for the trip, so you let Gale and Bruce know you are going to come."

"What a wonderful surprise," she told Ethel. "That is a lot of money, are you sure?"

She replied, "Joy, I want you to go not only to see Gale and her family but to see your father's family as well. Now you make arrangements to go, check out which airlines and flights you have to take, and let your cousins know when you will be there."

What excitement! She was bubbling all over to think that such a good friend would do this for her. Ethel worked hard at the famous Rubber & Tire factory, and she put in many overtime hours and was a very generous person, always doing things for her two daughters and giving faithfully to the church.

Joy decided to call Gale to let her know she would be coming and to get the information about the city she would be flying into and was anxious to talk to her. Anticipation and joy filled her heart to think that this wish she had wished for so many years to be able go to Germany would be coming true. She dialed the long-distance number Gale gave her to call—it was the chaplain for the army base; he and his family lived in the apartment below her and Bruce. Paul had given them permission for her to call them at his number, knowing she needed a contact in case of emergency.

"Hello, this is Gale Crane's mother in Michigan, may I please speak to her? I have some good news for her," she said.

"Yes, you may, I will call her to the phone, please wait," the gentleman answered.

"Hello. Mom?" Gale asked.

"Yes, I wanted to let you know that I will be able to come to Germany. With Ethel's help and my income tax return, I believe I can afford the trip."

"Wow! Are you really coming? Ethel is such a good and thoughtful person," she said with such joy. "You can come here and stay at our apartment for a while, and then we will go to see your cousins in Neustadt. I am so excited, Mom, I miss you so much."

The information about the airport she would fly into and continuing the flight to Nuremberg was explained. They talked about picking her up at the airport and maybe sightseeing along the way back to their apartment. Gale knew all this information because she and Bernie had taken the trip months earlier.

This was so exciting for Joy, and she thought, *My dream may come true. I will get to meet my father's family. His youngest brother and his wife are still living, and so are my cousins and their families. Thank You, Lord, for Your continued love for me and my family.*

Much had to be done: apply for a passport, get the airline tickets, arrange for time off work, and get someone to take her to the airport and to be picked up when arriving back. The anticipation was overwhelming and so hard to believe.

Joy loved her father so much, and since she had found out what he had done for America during the first World War I. She felt so blessed finding this out and was able to share it with her mother before she passed away. She wanted to go to Germany and give them information about their family and share pictures with them, intending not to tell them about her father's spying.

All arrangements were made, and the time was nearing to leave, when Joy received a phone call from Gale.

"Mom," she said, crying, "the army is making me leave Germany because they told Bruce, 'Your wife defaced government property.' Mom, we came home one night, and some army guys were harassing us and pushing us girls around, and I punched him in the face real hard and left some cuts and bruises on his face, and they called it defacing," she said.

What a shock to hear this. "Now what am I going to do?" Joy asked her.

She said, "Mom, the chaplain that lives in the apartment below us said you could stay there for a few days until you get in contact with your family in Neustadt and make some arrangements with them."

"Gale, I don't know if I can afford all this extra expense or not, I will have to get transportation there," Joy said with disappointment.

"Mom, Bruce will pick you up at the airport and take you to the chaplain's home, and you can call and let your family know what happened and that you will be there early and stay longer than you expected. That's all you can do, Mom, I am sure they will be more than happy to see you. I am so sorry," she said sadly.

"Well, Gale, I am sorry too. I was looking forward to seeing you and Bernie and spending time with you. Maybe I will just cancel the trip and stay home," she said reluctantly.

Gale was crying and said, "Mom, please don't do that. You wanted to meet your family, and this is still an opportunity of a lifetime for you, and I know you will be so sorry if you don't come over here now."

"I will pray about it and let you know soon. When are you coming home?" Joy asked.

She answered, "As soon as the army books my ticket. I believe about the same time you will be leaving there. So we won't get to see each other."

After talking to Gale, she called Darwin and told him, "I am canceling my trip because of what happened with Gale and Bruce, and she would be coming home."

And he said, "Don't you cancel that trip, I will give you money, and I will take you to the airport to make sure you get on that plane, OK? Just let me know when you leave."

"Yes, thanks a lot," she replied. She was grateful for Darwin; he has been so good, always being there when she needed him. *Thank God for my children, He knows just what we need.*

She called Gale. "I have some good news, Darwin gave me some money and told me he would take me to the airport to make sure I would go. Let Bruce know I will be coming as I had planned and to meet me, OK?" she said.

"Oh! Mom, I am so happy for you, please tell Darwin I said thanks. I love you!"

Thanksgiving was held at Darwin and Annabelle's home, in the recreation room. The home was beautiful, so many unique features, like a hanging room from the ceiling with an elevator to reach it, a pond with flowing water coming from a mountain-shaped wall with beautiful mountains and a sky painted to the cathedral-high ceiling.

Attending were Grandpa and Grandma Godman; Gilbert, Sandra, and Steve Long; Barbara and Ned Barnes; Clarice and Richard White; their daughters, Christina and Shirley, and son, Phillip; Donald and Sherry with Lori and Brent, Debbie Marie, and Misty; Clark, Gale, and Joy. Also Desare' and little Darwin.

This is a family to be thankful for—four generations seated at this table. What wonderful fellowship and love was shared throughout the day by everyone.

They all helped carry the dishes and food to the kitchen upstairs. Joy said to Darwin, "You need to put a dumbwaiter in so we don't have to make so many trips." A week later he did. He had planned to do it before anything was said. It saved a lot of steps, taking the groceries from the garage and carrying the laundry up and down the stairs. After dinner Debbie Marie, Lori, and Shirley spent the night at Grandma's house—a slumber party. It was fun for her having the girls stay the night and play games, plus they had a giggling good time.

The next day Donald and Darwin brought a large box of venison they shared with them, and they were very thankful for that because it had been some time since they had any venison.

All arrangements for the trip to Germany were in place. It was December 1, 1979, and time to go to the Detroit Metropolitan Airport. Pictures were taken when Joy was ready to go.

Lana Beal, of Beal's Flowers, had given Joy a beautiful large pink orchid to wear. She bought a hat, something very seldom ever worn. She thought the people in Europe wore hats, so she decided to wear one because she didn't want to look out of place, like a tourist.

At the airport, Darwin and Annabelle stayed with her until it was time to board the plane to New York. Annabelle asked, "Are you afraid?"

She answered, "No, I have flown a lot going to ABWA conventions in different states, I think it is so neat to be able to fly. I am like a little kid so anxious to look out the windows and see the landscape below as we are flying.

Besides, I trust in the Lord and believe I am in His hands to protect me and give me a safe trip."

Kisses, good-byes, and thanks were said as she boarded the plane. *What a day to remember for the rest of my life, a dream about to come true,* she thought as she walked to her assigned seat on the plane. She settled in, buckled the seat belt, and heaved a big sigh.

Arriving in New York, she found the airline and flight to take, checked in, and presented her passport to the ticket agent. Still excited and looking forward to this whole new experience, she began to look back on her life and how far she had come to this point.

*In 1947 my husband bought property ten miles from where I lived, and when I went out to see it I wondered,* Where in the world is he taking me? *Now here I am going to Germany, and I feel no fear at all, only love that bids me to go. You've come a long way, baby,* Joy thought. This was a huge plane, and the seats were very comfortable, the meals were good, and the passengers who spoke English were very friendly.

It was a long way from New York to Berlin, and departing the plane going into the airport was overwhelming. Joy was not able to speak any German and had to find the next flight going to Nuremberg. Berlin was still in the Iron Curtain section of East Germany. It seemed very strange knowing this was not a free part of Germany. She was thankful to find the next leg of the journey to reach her destination to Nuremberg. She was able to make the money exchange so she would have the right currency. She walked about to stretch her legs while absorbing and being astounded at the scenery all around. Bruce was there to meet her, as planned. It was good to see a familiar face, one who spoke English and greeted her with a big hug. He helped carry the luggage to the car and further explained the situation that caused Gale to leave. She thought, *Here I am in Germany,* wow.

He asked Joy, "Would you like to see some sights on the way back to the apartment?"

"That would be very nice of you to show me. I am so excited to be here," she replied.

They visited a large church in the city of Nuremberg that had been bombed completely to the ground during the war and was rebuilt, stone by stone, board by board, to the original plans and specifications. It was amazing how it had been restored with such perfection and detail. It was just awesome to be there and to witness this restoration.

She thought, *God restores our lives piece by piece to become a new creature in Christ Jesus. If man can do this with material things, just think of what God can do with His own creation, renewing from the inside out when each individual accepts Christ, who took our place on the cross and died for us, paying for our sins. "The wages of sin is death, but the gift of God is eternal life, the gift is Jesus Christ His son," Romans 6:23. Believing this, we are now new creatures in Jesus Christ, learning to grow in "grace in the knowledge of our Lord and Savior Jesus Christ. To Him be glory both now and forever," 2 Peter 3:18. He cleanses us from all unrighteousness and fills us with the Holy Spirit.*

Meditation is good for the soul, and being here in this church reminded her that man may destroy, but only God can rebuild. These people had a lot of faith in God to do this tremendous job of rebuilding this place of worship. He lives in their hearts and minds.

Walking away from the church, she said a silent prayer, "Thank You, God, for the faith You give to those who will carry on the truth, even though trials and tribulations come, they go forward with the light to the next generation of believers. Awaken my heart."

They drove to Bruce's apartment house and talked to the chaplain about staying with them and phoning her cousins. Paul and Brenda, a friendly couple, had a two-year-old boy and they made her feel very comfortable while she was there. They helped her find the telephone number for the train schedule she would be taking to and from Neustadt/Weinstrasse.

"Hello, this is Joy, and I am in Nuremberg with my son-in-law," she said.

Gilda answered, "Hello, it is good to hear from you, we are all excited."

Replying, Joy said, "Something has come up, and I can only to stay here only for two days, and I wonder if it is all right for me to come sooner than you expected me?"

"Yes, we will be happy and will arrange for your stay, don't you worry about anything. Let us know the train schedule, and I will meet you," Gilda declared.

Joy said, "I will be wearing a fuzzy black coat and hat."

She replied, "I will know you when I see you. We have pictures your mother sent us, and when my father saw your picture, he said, 'She is a happy child.'"

"Thank you so much, I will see you soon," Joy replied with excitement in her voice.

"What a relief! Thank your Lord for your love to me."

Praying first, Joy slept like a baby that night, feeling loved and secure. Awakening, she prayed, "Thank You, Lord, for a good night's sleep and a new day to travel in a strange land, help me to have a safe journey." Thanking Paul and Brenda for their hospitality and help, she was ready to take the last lap of the journey.

Bruce went with her on the bus to the train station and said their good-byes. And Joy thanked him for all he had done to make things comfortable for her.

All signs were in German; everyone around spoke German. She was keeping calm until she spotted signs that helped find the right gate to enter. It is like being in another world and you are the only one different, but by the grace of God, she continued on to the destination, observing the scenery along the train tracks as the train wheels sounded, *creekety, creekety, crack.*

"Neustadt/Weinstrasse," the porter announced, and she did recognize that. Getting the baggage all together and ready to depart was a relief, knowing she was almost there, with excitement, tear-filled eyes, and overwhelming joy. Stepping off the train, she stood and looked around; no one came forward. The crowd dispersed, and she could see one lady at the other end of the train station.

That lady came running toward her, saying, "Joy?"

Answering, she said, "Yes! Gilda?"

They embraced, and the wonderful love of God filled both of their hearts. They were cousins born far away from one other, and yet the love that passes all understanding was felt between them.

"How happy I am to see you, did you have a good trip?" she asked.

I replied, "Yes, you said you would know me when you saw me, how?"

She explained about the picture. "You haven't lost your smile, Joy."

"We are going to see the rest of the family now. They were all working, so I came."

Joy and contentment filled her heart as she said to Gilda, "I am so happy to be here because my longing to meet my father's family has come true for me, which I have dreamed since I was a little girl. It is like fitting in all the pieces of the puzzle."

Gilda replied, "Joy, we are all so happy you decided to come to visit us, and we have prepared a place for you to stay while you are here. We wanted you to have your privacy and not be disturbed in the mornings as we rise up and get ready for work. Then midmorning we can come and pick you up, and we will go sightseeing."

She answered, "It is so thoughtful of you to do this for me, I am so thankful and did not expect you to do that for me. I don't think it would be any inconvenience in the mornings for me at your home, but if you feel better doing it this way, it is all right with me. I am so excited about being here with you and getting to know you all."

Gilda said, "I will take you to the hotel and register you now, then we will go to meet the family so we can spend this afternoon and evening together getting acquainted."

The hotel was luxurious; the room was pleasant and comfortable, with extra-soft pillows, a feather-filled comforter; it was like sleeping with a cloud covering her. Seventh-floor view of Neustadt/Weinstrasse was a panoramic view, with mountains looming in the background. A dream come true—joy filled her heart like it had never before, except when Jesus came in her heart and took away all sin and guilt. He brought joy to her soul and blessings.

Joy thought, *My father Karl was born here, the eldest of four boys, and wanted to go to America, and his father took him to the ship and saw him off. That must have taken a lot of courage going alone so far away to another country.*

Arriving in America, he learned the English language while working with other people from Germany who helped him so he could become an American citizen. A few years later, Karl studied hard, took the examination for citizenship, and later joined the army. He became a spy for the USA, the land he loved. When the war was over, he met and married Joy's mother, Betty, and they had seven children. He passed away in his sleep at fifty-four years old. He had heart trouble and had been celebrating Valentine's Day at the servicemen's canteen in Mondale, Michigan. Karl loved doing things for the servicemen who were away from home because he knew personally how it felt, after the First World War was over, to be alone and with no family to go to.

"Now here I am in Germany, visiting and getting to know his family so many years later."

44

*Citizenship*. Do you realize just what that means? Being born in this country (USA) is taken for granted by so many.

I know many have parents or grandparents who came to America from other countries and have told their stories and about the trials they had endured. There are so many nationalities from all over the world coming to America, land of the free and opportunities for a new life. They came and worked hard and studied for the examination to be able to apply for their citizenship papers as soon as they could. Now this was their home, the land of the free and the brave, and they had as much opportunity as anyone else to fulfill their dreams. They were Americans.

Joy's father proved who he was and how much he loved America. No one knew what he had done, not even her mother, until years later after Karl had passed away and Joy went to work for Mr. and Mrs. Lincoln. They told her they were looking for a painter to paint their home, and Joy suggested, "My brother is a painter, he works in a factory nights and paints during the daylight hours."

Mr. Lincoln asked, "What is your brother's name?"

She replied, "Louis Wilson."

Looking puzzled, he asked, "Was your father Karl Wilson?"

"Yes," she replied. "Did you know him?"

Explaining, he said, "Why, yes, do you know what your father did during the First World War?"

"All we were told was he was an ordinary soldier," she answered.

"Oh no—I flew the plane that dropped your father in Germany behind enemy lines to get secrets for the United States," Mr. Lincoln said.

She replied, "Oh my goodness, we never knew that, I don't think my mother knows it. I can't wait to tell her and my brothers and sister."

Joy was so astonished and proud of her father, a secret serviceman, or secret intelligence agent as they called it. When she told her mother, she was astonished and said, "No wonder he had so many different men visiting him and couldn't tell me who they were or why they were there. This explains a lot of questions I have had in my mind for many years."

The whole family was surprised and had so much more respect for him and gave him honor for his dedicated service to his country, America.

This is what *citizenship* means to Joy: "We are God's citizens in this world today, belonging to our Heavenly Father, doing his work, loving one another."

As she pondered over these thoughts, she realized she could not tell Gilda or the family about this fact she had been told about her dad.

With awe and wonder, she couldn't believe she was here. Her heart pounded realizing what the war had done to the European countries and how America was spared from it.

# CHAPTER FIVE

*FULFILLMENT*

The city was so quaint with brick streets where individual specialty shops were on both sides of the street, such as the meat shop, the bakery, the vegetable shop, the beer and wine stores, jewelry stores, clothing stores, hardware and home appliance stores. What a sight to behold, so old-fashioned and unique. The owners closed the store at noon and went home for lunch.

As they approached the bus company door, Uncle Carlyle was there ready to greet her with open arms as she walked up to him, hugged and kissed him, and said, "I am so happy to meet you." And he looked so surprised that she would be so bold and yet comfortable to embrace him with such openness of love. He could not speak any English.

Then Gilda's brother, Warren, came over and hugged her and said something in German, but she couldn't understand and answered with "Hello, I am so happy to meet you all." Then Gilda translated it for him. She and her two sons, Richard and Earl, were the only ones who could speak or understand English, so they translated from German to English and English to German so the others would know what was being said and so could she. She felt the Holy Spirit among them, even though the language was different.

They arrived at Gilda's home to meet Eric, his sister, Hilda, and their mother. They were greeted at the door with big smiles and hands held out, ready to shake Joy's, and each spoke one sentence they knew in English. Eric said, "Hello, Dolly."

And his mother said, "God save the queen."

Gilda said, "They have been practicing so they could greet you in English."

She thought it was so sweet of them and hugged them and said, "Hello to you also, I am so happy to be here and spend some time with you all." Gilda translated as she spoke.

They all gathered in the living room and Dyson, Heidi, his wife, and their two children, Dany and Carson, came over. Dyson is the son of Uncle

Carlyle and Aunt Lydia. Uncle Carlyle was seventy-seven years old, the youngest and only living brother of her father. He and his wife, Lydia, came to join them. Carlyle was short and round like her father; she could see the resemblance and the same mannerisms.

They talked and showed many pictures. Joy told them, "I brought my family with me, many photographs to look at." They were pleased and enjoyed looking at the pictures, learning about her brothers' and sister's families. She showed them her family and told about their families, the kind of work they did, and where they lived. They had a wonderful time of sharing and getting to know each other. Aunt Lydia showed Joy some of the beautiful crocheted doilies and handkerchiefs Betty had made and sent to her many years ago. She treasured them; they were like new. Cousin Warren reminded her of when he was a German prisoner of war during the Second World War and was a prisoner of war in South Dakota, and Joy's mother sent him a radio and some cookies when she found out he was there. He had written to her.

Warren said, "I didn't want to fight in the army. I had to, like so many others. I was treated very well by the Americans, and I didn't mind being there. I wrote to your mom and let her know where I was and said it would be nice to have a radio so I can keep up on what was happening in the war. So she sent me a very nice radio, and that helped pass the time away until I was sent back to Germany."

She said, "Yes, I know what you mean. My brother didn't want to fight either, but he was drafted and had to go and was in for over three years without a leave home. When he was in Germany, he came to your mother's home and knocked on the door, but no one would answer, so he left. He wrote to my mother and told her about it and said he tried."

Gilda said, "Joy, I was there and heard him knock, but my mother and I were there alone and were afraid to answer the door because we didn't know who it was, we could see it was an American, but we were scared. I was just a teenager."

"I understand, Gilda, at that time you couldn't trust just anyone because there were some, a very few, soldiers who weren't very nice to even the civilians, and that is so sad."

As they exchanged these stories and experiences, they could sense the love and understanding of each of the families and the closeness it brought to them as a family.

48

They continued to share stories and experiences. It was getting late, and they had to get up and go to work and school the next morning, so they all went to their homes. Uncle Carlyle and Aunt Lydia were the last ones to leave.

Gilda said, "Carlyle surely had a good time, he is usually the first one to leave and go home, but tonight he was the last one to leave. I am so happy he enjoyed himself."

They decided to take Joy to the hotel so she could get some rest and be ready to go sightseeing the next day. Gilda had a big day planned for her.

"Thank you so much for the wonderful evening with all of the family, it was priceless, and I will never forget this trip as long as I live," Joy told Gilda and Eric.

"It was a pleasure to be able to have you come and spend time with us." Gilda was speaking for Eric also, because she knew he felt the same way.

Joy was tired and ready to get into that comfortable bed and fall asleep. It was hard for her to imagine she was here in Germany, her father's birthplace.

Awaking in the morning, Joy looked about the room and remembered where she was. Joy filled her heart as she arose from bed, showered, and dressed to go down for breakfast, which was included in the hotel's first-class room accommodations. She felt like a queen or someone royal during breakfast, and wonderful service was given by the waitress.

Gilda arrived, as planned, at the hotel on time to go sightseeing and visit some of the little villages and castles nearby. She brought her little book that translated English words into German and German words into English because as she said, "Joy, sometimes you say words that are hard for me to remember the meaning of, so this way I won't get confused."

Gilda explained, "The epithet of Neustadt an der Weinstrasse, 'on the wine route,' that distinguishes it from twenty-six other German 'Neustadts', while suggesting optimism and zest for life, is not very helpful in locating it. In fact, it lies in the Palatinate of the Rhine, about twenty kilometers to the west of the Mannheim-Heidelberg-Speyer urban region as the crow flies. Neustadt an der Weinstrasse has, by far, the largest wine-growing area of all the German wine towns, favored by nature in its location and today as a rejuvenated town, thanks to a successful renovation of the old town center."

It was a beautiful day, and they went to a castle. Winzingen Castle, known as the Haardt Palace, is closely linked with the history of Neustadt. It is joined to a Wihelminian-period villa that is now a hotel. The Romanesque St. Nicolas Chapel, partly restored, is a valuable historical monument that still indicates the former splendor of the Winzingen Castle.

Traveling and taking in the beautiful sights, they talked about their families and what they had done in the past. She told Joy about her husband's car dealership, Conrad Autohaus. His mother and his sister, Hilda, have a separate apartment in their home. Hilda is the bookkeeper for the company and is a very gracious lady.

Traveling north to Wachenhiem, they saw some castles and observed the architecture of the buildings and the beautiful view from the sites as Gilda explained to her some of the history she knew about each one. They traveled on to Bad Durkeim and had lunch at a little unique café specializing in desserts that are beyond anyone's greatest expectation. Oh, so many to choose from—they were picture-perfect to the eye and flavor-satisfying to the taste. "I have never seen such a variety of desserts, this alone was worth the trip," Joy said.

Gilda helped her to decide which one she thought Joy would like and had never eaten before, and it was a good choice: a slice of Bavarian cream coconut cake. Plus Gilda bought a variety of goodies to take back home.

They stopped by the hot springs in Bad Durkheim and toured the facilities, observing the beautiful shrubbery landscaping the entire property. Joy said, "Oh, how beautiful!"

Gilda said, "Hilda and I come up here a couple of times a year to the hot springs and go in the water for the relaxation of our muscles and to calm us from stress. It feels so good and calms us both down after a day in the hot springs and away from work and everyday routine."

"You are lucky this is so close to your home. I don't know if there are any hot springs in Michigan. In fact, I had never heard of them before now," Joy said.

It was getting late in the afternoon, and they headed back to Nuestadt an der Weinstrasse. Gilda's family would be arriving home from work and school by the time they arrived.

"What a wonderful tour this part of Germany was, so beautiful and hard to believe what war had done to this country and others around it, yet thirty-three years of growth and healing has brought it back to the glory of God. Plus the sweat and toil of the people who dedicated their lives to rebuild the buildings and roads of their land," Joy told Gilda.

Gilda explained that this was the wine road all the way to France, and that is why it is called Nuestadt an der Weinstrasse (Wine Route). They have a wine festival every October in Nuestadt, and it is a big celebration. Many people come from all over Germany and France to take part.

Gilda said, "We will take the Wine Road south to the French border tomorrow and see a few more little towns, castles, and vineyards on the way. I hope you are enjoying the trip and the country."

She replied, "Oh my goodness, yes, I am so thankful for what you are doing for me, and I will always remember this trip over here and the joy it has given me being with you all."

They arrived back at Gilda's home, and Eric said to Gilda, "We are all going out to dinner so Joy can have some German specials we are privileged to buy at the restaurant." Gilda translated what he had said to Joy.

There were twelve seated around this big table. The waitress took their orders, then brought many empty glasses and pitchers of beer, placing one huge glass in front of Joy. She couldn't believe her eyes. Looking so surprised, she couldn't say a word.

Gilda explained, "Joy, you take a sip and pass it on, and we will all take a sip of wine. This is a tradition when we have a guest, and we all get together, breaking bread and wine."

She thought, *Oh my goodness, I haven't had a drink of any alcoholic beverage in about twenty years since my spiritual rebirth with Christ.* They all got a big kick out of her surprised look as if she had to drink all the glassful of wine, and they all laughed so hard, and so did the waitress. After dinner, they stayed and talked for a long time and enjoyed the music that was so different from American music and songs.

Eric dropped Joy off at the hotel. She was very tired and sleepy by this time and was pleased to get in that comfortable bed and get some sleep. She closed her eyes and thanked God, "What a glorious day this has been, Lord. I thank you for my life and the many opportunities you have given me, the family and friends who have made this possible for me to be here to fulfill my dream of meeting my dad's family. Bless each and every one of them, Lord, and give me a good night's rest. Amen."

The morning sun was so bright. Waking up, she thanked the Lord for a good night's rest and another day here in Germany. Gilda called and said she would pick Joy up in an hour. She dressed and went to breakfast and was seated at a table on the enclosed terrace, and enjoying the city landscape all the way to the mountains and as far as she could see was rewarding and delightful. She could see castles, empty now, built ages ago by rulers and mighty people and a history of generations that reigned during those eras.

Joy thought, *I better go to my room now and wait for Gilda.*

They headed south on the Wine Road and stopped at several tourist sites as Gilda explained about each one's history and significance as they took the time to observe each one and take photos along the way. They stopped for lunch in Bad Bergzabern, looking around for a while, taking some pictures, and they bought some postcards and souvenirs.

They reached Weintor-Schweigen at the border of Germany and France around 2:00 PM. They walked around to get some exercise and visited the gatehouse on the border. Gilda translated what the inscription said, explaining about this place on the border and why it was there. Everything seemed to be so interesting, but it was hard to remember all of them as they drove away. On their way back to Nuestadt, they took a couple of side trips to small villages with interesting buildings and landscapes different from the rest along the way.

They stopped for tea and dessert at another bakery full of so many choices to pick from, but Joy decided to get an éclair because she hadn't eaten one in many years, and she knew this one would be so much better than any one she would get back in Michigan.

*What a wonderful trip this has been so far with family and seeing Germany and walking on the streets my dad walked on so many years before, until he was eighteen years old. Am I dreaming? No, this is really true!* she was thinking to herself as they arrived back at Gilda's.

Joy thanked Gilda for the trip and lovely lunch. She would not let Joy spend any money at all, not even for postcards, and Joy thanked her for her generosity.

There had been plans made to go out to dinner again this evening with everyone to a different restaurant, out in the country a bit, with an older German-fashioned menu. The evening was pleasant with all the family together again enjoying an exquisite meal in each other's company, here around this big table, breaking bread and drinking wine together. Joy was very happy and content being here with family because since she was a child she wanted to meet her father's family, and here she was, the only one of their family ever to come to Germany (except her brother Karl Junior when he was here in the army, but he didn't get to see any of the family).

After dinner they all went to Gilda and Eric's home for dessert and coffee to talk and enjoy each other's company with stories they shared, getting to know each other in a deeper understanding. Time went by so fast; it was getting late, and they had to get up in the morning to go to work. Eric took Joy back to the hotel for another good night's sleep.

Gilda came in the morning to pick Joy up for another day of fellowship and closeness of being cousins about the same age and having such a different background and experience through their lives. Joy felt such love for them all and was so thankful for being there and spending time with them. Her heart beat with such joy, unspeakable, and her spirit was full of gratitude.

Gilda had planned a big dinner for that evening at home with all the family present. She had a special meat dish Joy never had before; it was a large ham wrapped and baked inside homemade bread, plus fresh vegetables, sweet potatoes, and so much more—a feast for a king.

What a dinner—the table was set with a lace tablecloth, beautiful china and silverware, fresh flowers, and candles in the center, such elegance and yet family oriented for a time to share each other's company.

Eric told Gilda something, and she explained it to Joy, "Joy, Eric said, 'Joy must have a lot of courage to come to Germany not even knowing how to speak the language.'" (Eric couldn't speak English.)

Joy explained, "Gilda, 'perfect love cast out all fear'" (1 John 4:18 KJV).

Gilda replied, "Joy, you say the nicest things, and I believe you really mean it with all of your heart."

"I do and I am so happy I came. I will never forget your love and hospitality," she said.

Even different languages cannot separate the love that is felt by each other, nor the miles as far away from one another. The spirit of love is everlasting, deeper and wider than any ocean and higher than one can soar. God fills our heart with His love so we can share it with others. Love is the strongest force there is. "God is love and he that knows not love, knows not God, for God is Love" (1 John 4:7 and 8 KJV).

Christmas season was here, and the decorations were up all over. There were beautiful sights, bright lights, music playing, and the hustle and bustle of people shopping and visiting families and friends with good cheer and happy faces. The Christmas Market was full of homemade gifts, baked goods, artists' paintings, blown glassware, and many other articles to give for presents. It was a sight to behold. Joy had never seen such a variety of precious handmade arts and crafts anywhere. *Christmas in Germany,* she thought.

Gilda and Joy strolled around and looked at most of the displays with awe and wonder. The wind begin to blow, and it was getting much colder, so they decided to leave and go back home where it was warm and cozy.

They had dinner around the kitchen table this night with Gilda, Eric, and their sons, Richard and Earl. The boys spoke English and were able to converse with Joy very well and would translate for their father what had been said. The meal was very good, as usual, and she enjoyed herself, eating German food like her mom cooked.

*The German language seems so hard to learn,* Joy thought. *My dad didn't teach my mom or any of our family [children] how to speak or understand it.*

The next day, Joy slept in and rested until noon. Gilda came to pick her up to go shopping and then go to cousin Dyson and his wife Heidi's home for dinner.

Dyson's family lived upstairs of the Wise Clothing Store in a lovely apartment with their son, Carson, who was about fourteen years old and their daughter, Dany, who was sixteen years old. Such well-behaved children, so polite and friendly, they wanted to know more about Joy's family, the kind of work they did, and how many grandchildren Joy had.

Heidi served a good meal, with fried red cabbage and onions, potatoes, homemade bread, and dessert. Another old-fashioned German meal that was very delicious.

There was a big picture above Dyson's desk of her father, his three brothers, mother, and father that had been taken before Joy's dad left Germany.

She was astonished and said, "I wished I had a copy of one like it."

Dyson took Joy for a tour of the store and explained, "Heidi was the one who did all of the buying for the store in Paris and other big cities." She was a very pretty and gracious woman, so cheerful and friendly to be around.

Dyson, Uncle Carlyle's son, managed the clothing store, while Uncle Carlyle and cousin Warren managed the Wilson Bus Company.

It was about time for Joy to be leaving to go back home, and it was hard to think about it because she was having a wonderful time with all of them. It had turned out to be a trip she will never forget and would always be thankful for, a once-in-a-lifetime experience, thanking God. The next day, Joy would be leaving to go back to America, and the plans were being made about the schedule and pick-up time for the train.

What a wonderful surprise, everyone in the family prepared to go to the train station with Joy to say good-bye. They took time off work to go there. It was hard to say good-bye to them. They all had tears in their eyes and gave Joy big hugs and kisses. Dyson handed Joy a package and said, "I had a copy made for you of the picture I had on my wall, you liked it so well we decided to do this for you."

"Oh, thank you, I will have copies made for my brothers and sister. This has made my trip complete and so wonderful, thank you, thank you," she said, with tears falling.

Heidi gave Joy a beautiful silk scarf for a going-away gift from them all.

"My heart is pounding with such joy and happiness you all have shown to me ever since I came here, thank you all so much," Joy assured them.

The train came to a stop, and Joy boarded it, waving good-bye with tears flowing down her cheeks. She had to be alert and make sure she doesn't miss her place to get off and change trains. Not knowing the language, she had to keep her eyes open to recognize any of the signs that looked familiar while meditating on the experiences she had.

She thought, *I have so much to tell my family about this trip, and the joy that is in my heart—unspeakable. I feel like I am on cloud nine.*

Arriving in Berlin, Joy was happy to get off the train and find a place to stay for the night until her flight left. She wanted to do some shopping for souvenirs to take home from Germany. She found a nice little shop, and the lady understood some English to help her, especially with the dollar exchange and the amount she was spending.

Here she was in Berlin, all alone and couldn't speak or read the language. Joy began to pray to God, "Please keep me safe and help me find the right gate for boarding the plane."

The flight was a long one, but the plane had many empty seats, and Joy was able to lie down and get some rest; plus the meals were very good. Some passengers were very friendly and conversed about their trips and experiences, and she shared her experience.

*It won't be long now and I will be home in my own bed,* Joy thought.

The plane landed in New York. *What a huge airport,* she thought as she looked for the concourse that would lead her to where she would board her next flight.

*This is the last leg of my journey, and it will be short compared to the one I made coming across the ocean. I love to fly and enjoy going places and seeing God's variety of beautiful lands, mountains, oceans, lakes, and rivers. The big cities didn't thrill me at all, I am too much of a suburban gal, quiet and peaceful,* she continued talking to herself.

Leaving the Detroit airport and driving on Highway I-94, she said, "There is no place like home. No matter how humble, it is my home sweet home."

*Being born in this country is taken for granted by so many, and until we have an incident happen, like a hostage crisis, we don't think too much about it. Especially the freedoms and the privileges we do have here in America,* Joy thought.

Parents and grandparents came to America from other countries and made the voyage with their families or by themselves. There were many nationalities coming and making new friends. Joy's father came to America when was eighteen years old. The eldest of four boys, he wanted to come to America to be free. He settled in a little town in Pennsylvania and studied for his citizenship and applied for it as soon as possible and received it. When the war broke out, Karl Sr. joined the army. After the war, he was sent to Percy Jones Hospital in Battle Creek, Michigan, to recover, and he met Joy's uncle Larry who invited him to Christmas dinner in Logan, Michigan, where Grandma and Hank Wilson lived, along with their children, Uncle Eugene, Aunt Mildred, and Betty, Joy's mother. They courted and married in May 1919 and had a family. There were five boys and two girls, during which Karl opened a clothing shop, meeting many influential people who guided him into politics. When the Depression came, he lost the store through bankruptcy; no one was buying new clothes.

Karl knew many people and enjoyed being in politics and was hired as the sergeant at arms in Carlson, Michigan, at the Capitol. He had his children help pass out flyers for whomever was running for office. One time it was Al Larry, and Karl paid them, not much but it was a lot to the kids.

During World War II, he opened a servicemen's canteen in Mondale, Michigan, for all the branches of servicemen to attend, with dancing, meals, and a place for the servicemen to go while away from home. Karl knew what it is like being away from home.

Being a good citizen is so important and helpful to others. The American Legion of Foreign Wars was the sponsor of the canteen.

## A LITTLE GOES A LONG WAY

I lit a candle in the dark, to me it was just a spark
Compared to the light God did give, Jesus Christ, so we could live.
His light does eternally shine all through these years so divine.
Each one of us may also see what God did for you and me.
If we will but one candle light for someone lost alone with fright
To guide them safe home at last from all the fear and guilt of the past.
A life with Christ is what one needs. He is ready. With open arms He pleads.
"Come to me, and I will give new life of happiness to live,
Everlasting through the years, and I will wipe away all the tears."
So light a candle in the dark, even though it's but a spark.
With love and understanding, still along with all that is God's own will.
The light will shine forever and ever more.
No one can put it out, God will restore.

Written by Joy

# CHAPTER SIX

## ON THE MOVE

Arriving back home, Joy was still on cloud nine, so to speak, about the trip to Germany, and meeting her dad's family was a joy unspeakable. Wherever she went, she spoke about her trip and how it fulfilled her dream.

Alas, now she has to come back down to earth and to reality once again. It will be time to go back to work in a couple of days, so she better rest and call her family and let them know she was back home. They planned a family dinner so Joy could tell all about her trip; this would give her an opportunity to give them the souvenirs she purchased for them.

January 1980, another cold winter and time to get back to the routine of work and domestic responsibilities, but now her spirit was soaring high, and life wasn't such a chore as it had been. God had answered her prayer, and how thankful she was to believe and receive His love and grace once again.

Teressa and everyone at work were happy to see her back. They said, "We sure missed you, Joy. Your smiling face and sense of humor we all enjoy every day. Eventually you can tell us all about your trip and where you went and what you saw, we are happy you are back to work now."

Joy replied, "It is good to be back and see everyone again, and I have a lot to tell you about my trip and my family."

The days were still dark. Joy learned how to do scottish embroidery from her sister, Clarice, and she decided to make some tablecloths and napkins for the families in Germany. She used checkered material, each one a different color, with eight napkins to match. There was pink, blue, green, red, purple, orange, brown, and yellow. This took many hours for each one to be completed, but they were so beautiful and unique for a fine table setting. After they were completed, she wrapped them up in a box, putting a letter explaining, "Gilda, here are some tablecloths and napkins for each of you, and you can decide among yourselves which color you want. These are my gifts of appreciation to each of you for all you did for me while I was there in Germany. I had copies of Grandpa, Grandma, and their son's portrait made and gave them to my brothers and sister.

Later Joy received a letter from Gilda, and she said, "When I opened the package, I thought it was like spring flowers, so pretty and colorful. Thank you so much. We will cherish them."

The winter months had gone by fast, and spring was here before they knew it. The tulips were blooming, and the robins were singing their lovely song, and new life was springing up once again. God is so good. This was a reminder of His power and love. How great thou art.

Life had been quiet and peaceful while going about the routine of each day, one day at a time for Joy and the family. She would go visit her brothers and their families to keep in touch and let them know she cared and loved them. She also visited Karl Junior's wife, Darla, and their daughter, Marie.

Clarice and James and their family would come and visit about once a month, and Joy would go over to Carlson to see them for a visit as often as she could, because their families have been close throughout many years, helping one another when needed.

Summer was here, and they learned that Darwin and Annabelle were expecting a baby in September. Darwin Junior would be one (1) on July 13. *My, time does fly by like a cloud in the sky. It just disappears and rains down many blessings on me. This will be the sixth grandchild for me,* Joy thought.

Darwin was working hard every day at his job and still working on the home they lived in; it was so big and beautiful and so different. A hanging room suspended from the ceiling with railings around it, and an elevator situated on the staircase landing going up to it. A complete wall painted with sky and clouds above shapes of mountains from top to bottom with a waterfall flowing into a pond below with fish in it. On the mountain ledges, he put miniature animal figurines and trees to make it look natural while enjoying card games up in the hanging room. They got tired of hauling groceries up the stairs from the four-car garage, and so Darwin put in an electric lift to do the job and save climbing the stairs so many times.

Darwin had a large circle bed made for Annabelle that she wanted for their master bedroom. It looked so nice, like one *House Beautiful* would advertise. The master bath had a black sunken tub with golden faucets and fixtures that looked like swans' heads and the same decor throughout the rest of the bathroom, black and gold.

The house was set back from the road a quarter of a mile and had outside water fountains. One, a large one, was at the main-door entrance and another on the side of the house with the water flowing into the big stream going by the property. These were fed by a natural flowing well.

Whenever the family had a holiday celebration, they would all go to Darwin and Annabelle's home; they had such a big recreation room in the basement, and they could put up a very long table for most everyone to sit very comfortably. That is when the lift came in handy sending the food and dishes up and down on it. Ingenuity is great when Darwin could build something so useful and a labor-saving device for everyone. Ideas are the beginning of something that will come to pass as a result of them.

September 1, it is Darwin's thirty-third birthday and about time for the new baby to come into this world, one we try so hard to make better for our children to grow up in. A little girl, Rose Ann, was born on September 12, 1980, a joy to her parents.

Gale and Bruce moved to California at his base, Fort Bragg. Bernie was two years old now and was a handful for Gale. He was a very busy little guy, as all two-year-olds are.

Joy kept busy with work, the American Business Women's Association, and visiting with family and enjoying her life as all was going good and she was contented and happy.

Darwin had decided to move to Alaska and was preparing a trailer to haul his furniture and some building materials for the trip. In the spring of 1981, he took a trip to Alaska to buy a piece of property to build a home on and was able to find an acre of land out in the country, by the town of Wasilla. With everything ready to be moved, they packed their personal things, plenty of water, food, and essential items. This was a brave move with a wife and three children: Desare', ten; Darwin Junior, two; and Rose Ann, almost one year old.

The day they left was sad for Joy, with another family gone so far away to live. Darwin had put Annabelle's rocking chair on the top of the trailer (it looked like the *Beverly Hillbillies* truck.) They were on their way—a long, hard trip for them all. Joy prayed.

A pleasant surprise came when Gale called and told Joy she was pregnant and was expecting a baby late in October 1981 and how happy she was, and she wanted a little girl.

The summer went by, and Joy was planning to go to California to see Gale and the new baby in November after Thanksgiving. She booked her flight. She liked flying because it took so little time compared to driving in a car, and besides, she would have more time to spend with the family and go sightseeing. This would be another new place she had never seen or been to before and a warm place to get out of the cold for a while.

It was a pleasant flight. Gale and the children were at the airport to pick her up, they were all smiling from ear to ear and so happy to see Joy.

Bernie couldn't stop talking and wanted attention from Grandma. He was almost three years old now and so active and rambunctious, a typical boy, so to speak. In the meantime, Joy was anxious to see the new baby girl, Angel Marie.

"What a pretty little gal she is," Joy told Gale. "Is she a good baby?"

"Why, of course, she is, Mom, she sleeps well and is such a happy baby. We are so happy she is a good baby and doesn't keep us up all night, only when she gets hungry."

Joy asked, "How are you doing? Fine, I hope, getting your strength back to normal. Are you nursing her?"

Gale said, "I tried, but I don't have enough milk to nurse."

"That's too bad, they are much healthier when you nurse them, and you don't have to bother with washing and sterilizing bottles all the time," Joy said.

They finally arrived at the house. They cooked dinner, then they decided to stay in for the evening because Joy was very tired from the long flight.

Awaking early in the morning, after breakfast, they decided to go for a drive down the coast of California to see Monterey Bay and the city of Carmel, a very quaint little town with old-fashioned individual stores so interesting and unique. The day was going by fast. The children were tired, and so they decided to go back home and get some rest.

Gale said, "We are planning to take the beautiful drive up to Big Sur, a tourist favorite, along the coast in a day or so, if you want to."

"Yes I do, it sounds really exciting and a panoramic view as you explain it," Joy replied. It was as beautiful as Gale said it was and so peaceful watching the ocean.

"This has been so much fun to be with you and your family. I don't want to go back to Michigan, but I know I have to because I have a job," Joy told Gale.

Little Angel Marie was so sweet and cuddly, a happy baby, and Joy would surely miss her very much along with the family.

The time for Joy to leave for home seemed to come so fast and was here now, and Gale called and asked a friend, "Could I borrow your car to take my mom to the airport in San Francisco?"

He said, "I just had it worked on, and it should be in good condition for you to drive, but you be very careful with it."

Gale agreed with him, and they were on their way to the airport on a beautiful sunny day, driving into San Francisco safely until Gale turned left, and a drunken man ran the red light and hit them, smashing the front end. Joy had Angel Marie on her lap, holding on to her very tight. Thank God she was safe, and so was everyone else.

Here they were in the middle of San Francisco, and Joy had to get to the airport so she wouldn't miss her flight. The manager of the hotel came out to help them and told them, "Go into the hotel and find a seat, and if you need to, we will put you all up free for the night because you are frightened and have to wait for the police to come."

Joy explained, "I have to get to the airport to catch my flight before it is too late."

He replied, "We have a shuttle that takes our customers to the airport, and we would be happy to get you there on time."

Joy thanked him and told Gale and the children, "Good-bye, I love you so much, and you will be all right and will have a safe place now and a way home also."

This was another blessing from God. He takes care of us and keeps us safe throughout our lives and also our children's lives. Only by the grace of God and His mercy and love for us are we safe no matter where we are. He answers our prayers and is always faithful, providing just what we need when we need it. Joy thought about this all the way back home to Logan, thanking God continually.

Darwin and family arrived in Alaska after some trials: the children threw things out the back window of the truck and someone flagged them down and told them. The kids were having fun until they got caught. Then a half a mile from their property, Darwin thought he had missed the road to turn on and tried to back up and ended up in the ditch. He finally got the truck and trailer out and were on their way to the property.

He had a big job ahead getting the lot ready to build a basement and find work. He got there with only seventy-five dollars in his pocket and a lot of hope and many prayers. They used the trailer for their living quarters along with a tent to keep supplies dry. Darwin finished the basement, framed in the house, put in some windows he had brought there from Michigan, and insulated it all extra well because the winters would be cold. He had already built an outside toilet. What a change from the big fancy home they had, but they were happy.

A new year was here, 1982. Vacation was over, and it was back to work again getting down to business, ABWA meetings, normal daily duties and chores. Joy had to write letters to Darwin, his family, and Gale and her family, keeping them up on the news in Michigan. She had to send packages of food, like cake mixes, pancake flour, sugar, and whatever Joy thought they might need, and she knew what it is like starting out new. Annabelle, Darwin's wife, wrote back and thanked Joy for all of it and asked, "How in the world did you know I needed those things? We have been building, so we will have shelter this winter before it gets too cold, and we don't get to have many extra goodies to eat. The neighbors bring us baked dishes sometimes, and we all enjoy that."

Writing back, Joy told Annabelle that she knew what she was going through because she had gone through the same thing years ago when they built their home.

Donald and his friend decided to go to Alaska for moose hunting and to look for work also. It was hard to find carpenter jobs at this time in Michigan. Joy asked Donald, "Will you take Clark with you too? Clark had been laid off and couldn't find work. I will give you the money I received, refunded from income tax, to help pay Clark's share of traveling."

Donald answered, "I was going to ask him if he wanted to go anyway. I am glad you are willing to let him go that far, I know you worry about him since his accidents."

"Lord, have mercy, all of my children will be gone now—Donald, Darwin, and Clark in Alaska and Gale in California. It will surely be lonesome now."

Joy received a phone call from a friend whom she hadn't heard from in a long time; it was Jessie. She had gone to Alaska in 1956 with her husband, John Linds, and their son, Clark, because the government was giving away land in Alaska, and John wanted to go for the free land and to find work. They joined a caravan of many other people—single men and families from the Michigan area that signed up to go at the same time and organized by the people promoting the project.

"Hello," Jessie said. "Joy, this is Jessie, I was married to John Linds, remember me?"

"Oh my goodness, I sure do. How are you? It has been a long time, are you and John divorced?" Joy asked.

Jessie answered, "Yes, I remarried, a man in Alaska, and we moved back to Logan after my mother passed away. We bought her house from my sisters, and we live over on Bates Street now. I looked you up in the phone book to see if you were still in the area or not, I am so happy I found you."

"Let's get together so we can catch up after all these years, I would love to see you. Why don't you come over? We have a pool here in the mobile home park, and we can go swimming and enjoy the sunshine," Joy suggested.

Jessie replied, "That would be great. I am about to burn up, we are used to the Alaskan weather, it is not this hot. I will be right over. I believe I can find your mobile home."

*It is great hearing from her, what a surprise after all these years,* Joy thought.

When Jessie arrived, they greeted with hellos and hugged one another happily. Joy made some lemonade, and they went to the pool for a swim, renewing their friendship and catching up on current events.

It was good to see Jessie and learn about the past years in Fairbanks, Alaska.

Joy told her about her sons going to Alaska and her daughter in California, and it was going to be nice having her back.

They had been friends for many years. Her ex-husband, John, and Joy's husband, Dean, both worked at Lorring Factory and were hunting buddies. They went rabbit, pheasant, and duck hunting together. Then planned to go deer hunting in Northern Michigan, taking their wives with them also. This was the fall season of 1953.

John and Jessie had a son, Clark, a few months before Joy's son Clark was born on November 7, 1954. And they all continued getting together until John and Jessie decided to move to Alaska. Joy recalled in her memory.

Jessie said, "John was drinking so much he wouldn't work, and after a while, I got fed up with it and divorced him. Later I met Douglas, and we courted awhile, and I grew to love him. He was kind and loving, then he asked me to marry him, and I did."

"I am happy you found a good man and he makes you happy and content. Agreeing to move back to Michigan, that was a big decision," Joy said.

"How are you doing?" Jessie asked.

"A lot of water has gone over the dam in these past years, and I will eventually fill you in on some of it. Dean got worse with his drinking and was abusing me. I was pregnant, and then he started beating the children, and I got very upset and picked up a baseball bat and hit him over the head with it and knocked him out cold, and I put the bat on my shoulders, and all I could think of was 'Kill him, kill him.' Darwin yelled, 'Mom, stop! You will kill him.' Thank God! My mind snapped, and I said, 'Oh my god, what have I done?' After that, it got worse, and I pleaded for him to go see a doctor or physiatrist, and he promised he would, but he backed down. I asked him to please stop drinking, but he wouldn't."

Jessie said, "My word, Joy, why in the world did you put up with it?"

"I wanted to make a go of our marriage, and I loved him," Joy replied.

"I left with Clark, I believe it was the coldest day in January 1961, and I decided to go to Florida to find work. Eventually I returned and talked to my father-in-law, and he told me, if Dean got abusive, to call him, and he would come and get me. Well, Dean threatened me with his shotgun, the boys took it away from him. I called Dad Godman. He came and took me and the boys home with him. We decided to have Dean committed for his drinking problem and abuse," Joy explained.

Jessie asked, "Did it help him?

"He was there for six months, and when he was discharged, he started drinking again, and he said, 'Nobody is going to stop me from drinking.' We sold the house, two cars, a boat and motor, and a camping trailer because he wouldn't work, and we moved to a little town, Springdale. Gale was born June 5, 1961. Donald's birthday was June 6. He was fifteen, Darwin was thirteen, and Clark was eight years old. Two years later, Jack was hit by a drunk driver and died two days later. So you see, that is a brief synopsis up to then," Joy said.

"My goodness, I thought I had it bad, but you endured much more than I did. It is getting near dinnertime, and I need to go home and get it ready for my husband," Jessie said.

Joy said, "We will have to get together again, and I will finish the rest of the story."

Gale called and said, "Bruce and the children and I are going to move to Florida where his mother and brother live. Bruce was discharged from the army and doesn't want to live in California. I will let you know when we get there. I will call and give you our address."

Joy replied, "I'll keep you all in my prayers for a safe trip and good health."

"Mom, I really miss you, and I hope to see you, maybe you can come to Florida on your next vacation."

"I miss you too and the children, I will have to think about Florida when the time comes. Just keep in touch with me and let me know where you are," Joy said.

The leaves on the trees were changing colors—red and different shades of orange and yellow—just a beautiful picture to look at, one only God could create in the fall. Joy went on with her everyday chores and her job as secretary and bookkeeper. As time passed, she went to visit her brothers and her sister as much as she could, keeping them informed about her children and their families.

Gale called, "Mom, I am coming home. I can't stand it down here with Bruce and his mother anymore. He is getting into drugs, and I won't take it. My children don't need this kind of life, and neither do I. Can you get tickets for the kids and me?"

"If you are sure that's what you want and are done with him, I will call and get the tickets, and they will have them ready for you at the airport, and I will let you know the airline, flight time, and number," Joy happily replied, thinking, *Thank God, she has awakened to reality about Bruce and his family.*

Hanging up, she spoke out, "Hallelujah! Hallelujah! Praise the Lord for He is good."

She wouldn't have to take a vacation; now Gale and the children would be there soon.

Donald had returned from Alaska. He didn't want to live there, only to hunt and visit Darwin and his family. Clark stayed in Alaska and found work at a gas station close by Darwin's home. He enjoyed the beauty, clean air, and lots of fishing, which was good for Clark; he needed that. Although Joy missed him, she realized how much Clark needed his independence. He was twenty-eight years old now had been through some tragic accidents and recovery.

Arriving home, Gale and the children were happy to be there and to have a peaceful, clean place to live. Although she knew she couldn't stay too long because the mobile home park didn't allow children, she could stay for a month, and then she would look for a place to live. In the meantime, they enjoyed every minute together, just hanging out, catching up on everything, and visiting with family.

Angel was such a sweet baby. Bernie had grown and was very active and demanding of attention, of course, a little jealous of the baby getting so much attention he used to get.

Gale filed for a divorce and was granted one, and Bruce was ordered to pay child support, but he didn't. So she went to the welfare for help to get a place to live. They granted her help as soon as she found a place and reported back to them the particulars. She found an apartment in the city of Logan and moved from her mom's home. Joy helped with the groceries until the food stamps were available for them and provided the transportation to wherever she needed to go.

Her friends would visit them and take them places to get out of the house for a drive to the park for Bernie to play on the swings and just run around for exercise.

# CHAPTER SEVEN

## ONE GIANT STEP

Lo and behold! Darwin, Annabelle, and the children came to Logan from Alaska to visit. What a wonderful surprise. It was Thanksgiving time, and Joy reserved the clubhouse at the mobile home park for their dinner. What a wonderful celebration. Even Grandpa and Pearl Godman were there, the whole family, but Clark, he stayed in Alaska.

Darwin had sold his truck so they could afford tickets to come and see everyone. Annabelle wanted to come back to visit her family. She was the eldest of ten children and missed them very much. Donald, Sherry, and their family came also. He told about his trip to Alaska and that he was thinking about moving out west somewhere. He liked it in Colorado, so they would go and look the land over and decide.

Everyone had such a good time; the children played and got reacquainted with each other as the adults caught up on what had happened throughout their lives since their last meeting. The food was delicious, and there was plenty of it. The women were all good cooks. There was such a variety to choose from; it was hard to decide. No one left hungry, but full.

Time passed, and Christmas Day was spent at Donald's home. The family gathered there for the festivities, eating, exchanging presents, and enjoying the whole day of celebration of our Lord's birth with each other.

Darwin and his family would be going back to Alaska soon and would be missed by all. It had been so good to see them all. The children had grown up, and it was fun being with them.

*Another year almost gone by, where does the time go?* Joy thought.

A new year was here; what would it bring? Joy's faith has grown as she thinks of the passage from Isaiah 40:31, "They that wait upon the Lord, shall renew their strength, they shall mount up with wings as eagles; they shall run and not be weary; they shall walk, and not be faint."—a promise from God given to strengthen her faith in Jesus Christ.

Michigan was experiencing layoffs, poor economy, less building and construction being planned, and companies going out of business. The company Joy was working for was thinking about moving to Texas because they wanted to get away from the union scale for operating engineers, truckers, and laborers. Carpenters were affected also.

Donald and Sherry sold their home and prepared to move to Colorado. A picnic was planned to say their farewells and let them know they would be missed by all. Joy was sad but thought they needed to go where there was work and didn't blame them for the decision they had made. Everyone has to do what is best for their family.

All three boys had left Michigan now, making their homes in some other state. Joy prayed for them all continually, knowing God would keep them safe wherever they go.

Joy visited Gale as much as possible and spent time with her. One day Gale went to the office where Joy worked and brought the children. The company had a dog to guard the premises at night. Bernie went over to pet the dog, and the dog bit him in the face, leaving torn gashes on his face, bleeding badly. Joy took Bernie to the emergency room and had stitches put in. They waited to see if the dog had rabies or not; he didn't.

Another exciting moment in Joy's life—it was scary for a while for Bernie and Gale. Bernie's wounds healed, and a small scar remained where the dog had bitten him.

The holidays were coming. Shopping for presents and getting them ready to send to the families in Alaska and Colorado was fun, deciding what to send to each one, not knowing what they wanted or needed. As she shopped and looked around, ideas would come to her, and she bought something personal for each one, mailing early to get there on time.

Opening gifts from far away must have been fun for them all, Joy thought.

In the meantime, Thanksgiving had come and gone, and she started shopping for the rest of the family. Donald's daughters, Debbie Marie and Misty, were in Michigan with their mother and James. Bernie and Angel were fun to buy for; they loved toys, no matter what kind. They came to stay overnight with Joy many times. It was fun and good to have them there. She loved her family so much and thanked God for each one.

The year of 1983 was here now, and the winter was cold and windy, and there was lots of snow again. To keep herself busy, she searched for records of both sides of the family to start a family-tree picture of limbs showing the family names on Dean's side of his family and names on Joy's side of the family back a few generations. She wanted her children to know their heritage, the families' birth and time of death (those who died), and the generations.

This was very time-consuming but very rewarding to her. It gave her a lot of answers to many questions she had thought about, keeping her mind on this instead of her job.

"What will I do if the company I work for moves?"

Writing to Darwin and Annabelle, she told them, "I don't know about my job, they are talking about moving to Texas, and I know I don't want to live there. So I will be looking for work elsewhere or go unemployed. I have been working for this company for over sixteen years."

Darwin wrote back and said, "Why don't you come up to Alaska and look for work? They have plenty of jobs up here, and I am sure you could find something with all of your office experience. I will send you money for a ticket. You pick the date you want to come, and we will pick you up at the airport in Anchorage. We all would love to see you, Mom."

Answering Darwin's letter, she wrote, "I will let them know I want to take my vacation time the first of August, for two weeks, so they can plan on me going."

It was all planned. Joy looked forward to the trip. She loved to fly because you can go a long distance in a short time. It was so thrilling for her; she was like a little child.

Gale and her children were all settled in, and so far everything was going all right, and Joy didn't have to worry about her and the children while she was gone.

The flight was a long one, and Joy was tired. She couldn't sleep because she was so anxious to see them all. Landing at the Anchorage airport, which was a very small one compared to some of the other airports she had been to, she gathered her luggage, ready to depart the plane. Darwin, Annabelle, Darwin Junior, and Rose Ann were there to greet her at the airport entrance. They all ran and hugged and kissed her saying, "Grandma!"

Joy was delighted with the greeting and said, "It is good to be here and see you all."

Joy asked, "Where is Desare?"

Annabelle explained, "She went to church camp and will be here soon on a plane. She doesn't know you are here, and when she sees you, she will be surprised. It won't be long." Joy hid so Desare' wouldn't see her until she walked closer toward the family.

There she was, Desare', coming toward the gate where her parents were (it was a small plane, and the passengers got off outside and walked to the exit gate). She ran to hug her mom, dad, brother, and sister. And she said, "I don't ever want to go there again."

Then Joy stepped out and said, "Hello, Desare."

When she saw Joy, she looked puzzled and asked, "Am I in Michigan?"

Her mother said, "No, Grandma came here to visit us, and she just got here too."

"You didn't tell me she was coming, why?"

"We wanted to surprise you, so we thought this would be a good way to do it."

"Oh, Grandma, it is so good to see you again, did Mom tell you I won a new bike for picking up the most trash on Cleanup Day?" Desare' asked.

The ride to Wasilla, the little town they passed by, seemed long, but it was beautiful all the way there. It was almost fifty miles to their home, which was near Houston.

After a good night's sleep, they went sightseeing in the area, so remote in wilderness beyond comprehension. Awestruck with the vast miles of country, trees, and more trees everywhere, greenery as far as the eyes could see and the mountains imposing up to the sky majestically. What a grand view to see. Joy was impressed with Alaska.

Darwin had planned a trip to Denali Park, to take a bus ride up to see Mount Denali close.

They had to be there early to catch the bus, which was free, so they stayed in their tent that night. Clark came along also, which was nice to be with him again. The children were good campers because Darwin took them camping and fishing a lot.

They were the first ones on the bus. They took sandwiches, sodas, chips, and cookies with them. It was going to be a long ride all the way up there, stopping at the halfway point.

They got to see moose, elks, bears, a fox, and many little creatures along the way. It was a bumpy ride, but so beautiful. Whenever someone spotted an animal, the driver would stop so everyone could see it. Cameras were plenty on the bus; tourists from all over came to see Denali mountain and the wild animals. Most everyone on the bus was very friendly. Clark sat beside a lady and talked to her about his family.

He told her, "My mother is up here looking for work but hasn't been able to find anything yet in her line of work."

She said, "She ought to take my job. I am giving them two weeks' notice that I will be leaving Alaska, and I hate leaving them because they are good people to work for."

Clark turned around and said, "Mom, maybe you could take this lady's job, she can tell you about it. Mom, this is Mary, Mary, this is my mother, Joy."

"Hi, Mary," Joy said. "What kind of work do you do?"

"I am a live-in housekeeper," she replied.

"Oh, I don't want to do that, I have done that for years. I work in an office, and I have sixteen years' experience with payroll," Joy explained.

"This is a Jewish family with a five-year-old boy and a one-year-old little girl, but you won't have to do any babysitting, Arnold goes to preschool, and Sharon goes to a babysitter. Michael and Barbara Gooding are their names. If you would like to call them, I will give you their phone number. You'll have nice living quarters, and you can use their car on the weekends and have a couple of hours by yourself. Please think about it," Mary said.

Clark gave Mary Darwin's phone number to call and see if Joy found a job or not.

They slept in the tent, packed, and left early in the morning to go back home. Arriving home after the long journey, everyone was worn to a frazzle, so to speak.

*It has been so much fun being with my sons. I am thankful to be able to enjoy this trip to Alaska. My! What Dean has missed not seeing his family grow up and seeing all the grandchildren,* Joy thought.

Darwin took Joy into Anchorage to look for a job. Answering the want ads, she had no luck finding one. They wanted someone younger and who lived in Alaska, and they didn't want to hire outsiders. Joy was fifty-five years old and still needed a job. She was getting discouraged and was thinking about the job Mary told her about. She loved it in Alaska.

She thought, *If I take that job, I could go to school and learn more bookkeeping on my time off in the afternoons.*

Mary kept calling Joy, asking her, "Will you please at least go and talk to Barbara and find out about the job and what is required of you to do?"

It was getting close to the time for Joy to go back home to Michigan, and she asked Darwin to take her to see Barbara about the job.

Darwin said, "Mom, are you sure you want to move up here?"

"I'll talk to Barbara first and find out if I want the job or not."

Darwin dropped Joy off at Barbara's and said, "I will be back in an hour to pick you up."

Joy rang the doorbell and introduced herself when Barbara appeared.

Barbara said, "I will show you around the house and explain the duties you will be performing and your wages. You will not have to babysit the children, I believe Mary told you that. You can take the car on the weekends, we will insure you as a driver. You will have private quarters and bath."

Barbara was a very gracious lady and explained well the details of the job. As Joy looked around the house, she thought to herself, *This house isn't too big, and I believe I would be able to do the work required. Cooking the meals, doing the laundry, mopping floors and sweeping the carpets, grocery shopping, taking clothes to the cleaners and picking them up—fundamentally doing daily household chores.*

Joy told Barbara, "After looking around and thinking about it, I believe I would like the job and would be able to handle it, but first I need to go back home to Michigan and give my employers a two-week notice and decide what I will do with my car and home."

Barbara asked her, "Are you sure? Why don't you go home, think about it for a few days, and then call me and let me know. You don't want to make a decision and be sorry for it."

"That sounds like a good idea, thanks," Joy replied.

Darwin came back to pick her up just about the time Barbara was through interviewing.

Joy said, "That was good timing, we just finished the interview and had a good talk, getting to know each other. I believe I will take the job, because with time off in the afternoons, I could go to school and get more education in bookkeeping."

"I thought you wanted an office job and didn't want to do housekeeping anymore!" Darwin said.

"Darwin, I need a job unless I move to Texas, and I certainly don't want to do that. If I take classes and get a certificate in bookkeeping, it will be easier for me to get an office job. I am going home and thinking it over and then I'll let Barbara know," Joy explained.

"I guess you are right. If you want to move up here, it is a big step," Darwin said.

Joy called Gale. "Hello, I am back home, I would like to see you and the children. Whenever you can, come over, OK?"

"I will be right over, Mom, it will be good to see you too," Gale replied.

It was so good to see them all. Hugs and kisses were shared among them all, and questions about the trip were answered. These were happy moments to remember.

Gale said, "I have been dating a man who is part Indian, and he wants me and the kids to move to Arizona with him, and I am going to."

Joy told her, "Gale, you don't know anyone in Arizona, and if you need someone, you will be alone with the children. You don't know what kind of man he is, don't do it!"

Gale, with her hands on her hips, boldly replied, "Mother, let me live my own life."

Joy was burning inside with the thought. *How can she do this?*

"OK, you go, I am going to Alaska to live. I will be leaving in two weeks," she said.

She called Barbara and said, "I want the job, and I will be there the day after Labor Day."

"I am so happy to hear that, we will pick you up at the airport," replied Barbara.

There was a lot to do: selling the mobile home and her car and packing her belongings to store in Louis's (her brother) warehouse until other arrangements could be made.

Monday morning, time to go back to work—entering in the door, Joy said cheerfully, "Good morning, everyone."

"Good morning, it's good to have you back, we missed you. How did you like Alaska?"

They all had many questions.

"I loved it! I am moving to Alaska. I have a job, and I am giving my two weeks' notice this morning," Joy said enthusiastically.

"You're not! You always wanted to move to Florida," Teressa said, astonished.

She replied, "Yes, I am, I can't move to Texas when the company moves, so I took a job in Alaska. Believe me, it was hard, but I have two sons in Alaska, one in Colorado, and Gale is going to move to Arizona with some guy she has been going with, and I don't want to be here by myself. I guess Gale is a glutton for punishment. I can't talk her out of going. It breaks my heart. She gets out of one bad marriage and plunges into this situation not knowing what is ahead of her. She said his brother lives in Arizona."

Sitting at her desk, she continued, "Well, I guess I had better get to work on the payroll. Stella, did you have any problems with it while I was gone?"

"No, between Teressa and me, we were able to get the work done, I am glad you are back and you had a nice time. I missed your laughter and little jokes," Stella stated.

Making arrangements with her brother Louis, Joy moved what she hadn't sold to his warehouse and stored it. She was thankful for him letting her use the space for nothing. She also made arrangements for him to sell the mobile home. Her boss, Robert Gibson's daughter, bought her Mercury car, so about everything she had planned to do worked out.

It was the last week in August 1983. The American Business Women's Association's monthly meeting was held, and the members all wished Joy good luck with her new job and a safe flight to Alaska. The ladies had taken a collection and bought Joy a beautiful gold necklace for her going-away present.

"Thank you all so much, this is beautiful. I have never had anything real gold before. It has been a pleasure being part of the Apollo Chapter of ABWA, I love you all," she said with tear-filled eyes.

Arriving at the Gooding's home, Joy met Michael, Barbara's husband; Arnold, the son; and little Sharon, their daughter. Later, she was shown to her living quarters at the end of the recreation room on the lower level; it was a large bedroom, very comfortable, with a large bathroom. *This is a beautiful home. I am very pleased with the decision I made,* Joy thought to herself as she unpacked her luggage.

Later, Barbara came down to talk to Joy about the work schedule, the meals, cleaning, and what was expected of her, and gave her a map of the city to use when she went grocery shopping and to the cleaners. Joy could make some of her recipes for the meals, and they would have some for her to make also. The first meal she fixed, she sat in the kitchen to eat, and Michael said, "No, Joy, you are family, you eat with us."

The days went by fast, and Christmas soon would be here. This family was Jewish, and Joy had never been around a Jewish family before, but she knew they didn't worship Jesus the Christ but watched how they celebrated their holidays and their customs. It was very interesting to her. Michael would explain what they meant and why they celebrated, keeping the memory of special events of the Torah (the first five books of the Bible) alive.

Barbara was a certified public accountant, and Michael owned a souvenir warehouse business; he sold to local souvenir shops and big-box stores. He let Joy buy some at a discount price. She sent T-shirts, stuffed animals, hats, gloves, and many other items home to her family in Michigan and for those in Alaska also.

Joy was able to go visit Clark, Darwin, and his family on the weekends. They let her use one of their cars. Barbara paid her well, much more than she earned back in Michigan. Plus she didn't have rent to pay, car insurance, or utilities.

Joy had gone to the doctor, and he gave her diet pills, and she lost a lot of weight. She went from 200 pounds, size 20, to 134 pounds, size 10. She was full of energy.

Michael decided to buy another home, a much larger one only two blocks away. Packing, lifting, and moving boxes to a new house with three floors and lots of steps helped contribute to the cause of Joy's bladder dropping. The muscles holding it up gave out, and she had to have an operation to make an adjustment.

Darwin was in the hospital room when they were giving her a blood transfusion, and he asked, "Has that blood been tested for HIV? If not, you are not going to give it in my mother."

"Why, yes, it has, sir, we test all the blood for HIV, look here on the label," she said.

A couple of days later, Joy noticed, on her left arm where the IV was inserted, a red streak going up her arm as far as her elbow. She turned the nurse's light on for help, and when she came in, Joy asked her, "Is this supposed to be like this?" She knew it wasn't.

The nurse ran out the door, and soon two other nurses were in there removing the IV from Joy's arm, and they gave her a shot and said, "There, that should take care of it."

After convalescing and getting her strength back, she was able to continue her work.

The Sunday school class went to the roller rink to skate and of course, Joy wanted to go too. She used to do many dances on skates. Clark was there also. And while she was skating, she turned around to skate backward. Someone had dropped a small rubber snake on the rink floor, and Joy tripped on it with her skates, and down she went, hitting the back of her head on the floor. That ruined the night for her.

One afternoon Joy was taking the garbage out to the garbage shed. The driveway sloping downhill was very slippery. Oops! Joy's feet went out from under her as she went down and hit the back of her head on the ice. "Oh my goodness, not again, I had better slow down," she mumbled. Going back in the house, she lay down for a while and began to feel much better.

Joy liked her job very much, and she loved the children. Sharon would go into her room and want Joy to rock her and sing to her.

Joy decided she wanted to take ice-skating lessons because she loved to ice-skate. On some afternoons, she went to the ice arena close by the house. Then she heard about lessons at the University of Alaska Ice Arena for all ages. She signed up for them and went in the evenings. It was so fun learning the basic steps and doing it the right way. She had to overcome all her old ways she had learned years ago. The teacher was giving her lessons on a waltz jump; Joy tried it and fell down backward on her head again. She saw stars. It almost knocked her out.

Joy looked up at the ceiling and said, "Lord, are you trying to tell me something?"

The teacher asked, "Are you all right? Can I help you up?"

"Just let me sit here for a minute, and I will be OK, thanks anyway," Joy replied.

That was the last of the ice-skating and the roller-skating. She decided to act her age.

Joy had promised Debbie, her eldest granddaughter, she would go back to Michigan for her wedding to Mitchell Schultz, on August 4, 1984. Christina, her niece, was going to marry on August 11. Also, Joy's family reunion was held that month as usual. Desare', Darwin's daughter, went with Joy to Michigan and enjoyed seeing the relatives.

The year was passing by. Thanksgiving and Christmas had come and gone, and a new year had begun. With a song in her heart, Joy looked forward to another year in Alaska.

She liked her job so well she had forgotten about going back to school for bookkeeping.

Meeting new friends at church and fellowshipping with them on her weekends, when she didn't go to Darwin's and visit, kept her contented.

Annabelle, Darwin's wife, was pregnant, expecting in May. They hadn't told anyone yet because they wanted everyone to be surprised. A midwife came to the home for the birth of a son, Donald. Annabelle had a natural birth, without any sedative. Joy stayed at the house for a few days to make sure everything would be all right with mother and child.

"This is the eighth grandchild now. What joy this brings to my heart, the many blessings God gives in life as we continue to trust in Him," Joy told Annabelle.

June 1985, Joy traveled to Colorado to see Donald and Sherry. They took her up to Pikes Peak. The summit is 14,110 feet. This was a beautiful drive, and experiencing the height was different from anything she had ever done. They could see Pikes Peak from their home near Florissant, a small little town where fossil beds are located. They visited Cripple Creek, an old-fashioned Western town, where donkeys roaming the streets were a normal day's occurrence.

Driving over the expansion bridge at the Colorado River Gorge was thrilling; the view was spectacular. There were many natural arches. Landscape Arch, believed to be the longest natural arch in the world, and Delicate Arch, a structure surpassing grace, poised at the edge of a great amphitheater in a setting of bare red sandstone, are some other attractions they saw.

It was good to be with and go places with Donald and Sherry. Joy was going to Phoenix to visit Gale and the children before she went back home.

Gale picked Joy up at the airport and told her about John, the man she came to Arizona with. "He got into some trouble and was sent to jail. I am all through with him, he drinks and is mean, that Indian part of him comes out," she explained.

Joy said, "Gale, I told you not to come with him, now what are you going to do?"

"I know, Mother, another bad choice I made. I am getting help from the social services, and his brother and his wife have been very kind to me and the kids," she stated.

"I am happy I came here to see how you are all doing. I worry about you all the time. I hope you don't go back to him when he gets out," Joy said.

Gale's home had a swimming pool. They were able go in and to cool off. It was hot, and they spent most of the days at the pool. Joy loved being with them; she missed them.

She only had a week to spend with them before it was time to go home and back to work.

Waiting at the airport, the children wouldn't let go of Joy. They kept saying, "Don't go, Grandma, we want you to stay with us."

"Grandma knows and would like to stay here, but I have to go back," Joy explained.

Teary-eyed, she boarded the plane, thinking, *It is so hard leaving Gale and the children.*

Arriving back in Anchorage was a relief from the heat and was very comfortable. She appreciated the weather after being so warm.

Vacation was over now, and getting back to the routine, Joy was so thankful for her job and employers. They were very kind and understanding about giving her the time off she needed to travel.

Misty, Donald's youngest daughter, came to Alaska to visit. Joy and Clark took her to visit Darwin's family and see the mountain scenery along the way. Misty and Desare' were less than a year apart and were enjoying each other's company, while Joy held Donald and paid attention to Darwin Junior and Rose Ann, who were happy to see Grandma.

*The next day they took Misty on some trips to see to see the beauty of Alaska and how big it is. They decided to go to Whittier, a small seaport town southwest of Anchorage, driving on the Seward Highway, rated one of the most picturesque highways* in the USA with many curves close to the mountains, and when you look across the inlet, you can see the mountains and their reflections on the water along the inlet.

"What a beautiful drive that was," Misty said as Clark parked the car.

They waited a short time for the train, and after it arrived, they got aboard. The train went through two tunnels, a short one and a long one. This was the only way to get there besides a boat. It rained all day and wasn't as pretty as usual, but they made the most of it, walking around when it stopped for a while. They were all disappointed and made a short day of it.

"Here it is, about the end of July and so much rain, Whittier is known for a lot of rain," Joy told them.

On the way back, they stopped at Girdwood, a little town where skiing is popular. Many people from Alaska go there to ski, as well as those from the lower forty-eight states.

"The hotel has a nice little restaurant that serves real good soup and sandwiches, with homemade bread, we will go in and eat something warm," Joy said.

Misty and Clark agreed with her and said, "Let's go."

*Nineteen eighty-five has been a busy year for me,* Joy thought.

Gale was working at a bar. One evening she dated a cowboy; they went to a dance, and he danced with all the women except Gale. Vern noticed it and asked her to dance with him. They danced and liked each other, and he took her home with him, and she never left.

She decided to move in with him permanently with the children. They moved her from Phoenix to his place in early fall of 1985. His mobile home was located on his parents', the Garcias, ten acres, along with his two sisters and their families in mobile homes also. Vern had been married twice before. Gale got acquainted with Vern's family and adjusted to the country atmosphere.

She was pregnant and expecting a baby. This would be Vern's first child, and he was delighted, and so was his family. He had twin stepsons by a previous marriage.

Vern had a job at Holland Plant, making good wages, and was able to take care of them. Bernie and Angel enjoyed the outdoors and had other children to play with, and Vern's family was good to them.

Gale phoned her mother and told her about the baby, and Joy told her she and Vern should get married soon to give the baby the father's name and his insurance company would pay the bills.

They talked about it several times, and then they would get in a fight and postpone it again. This went on until they finally decided to go to the courthouse and get the license and make arrangements to be married. This was in March 1986. Elisabeth was born June 1986, a bundle of joy. Joy and the Garcia family were delighted.

Laurie, Joy's niece, came to Alaska in August to visit and to tour the state. They drove up to the Denali Park, stayed in a hotel, then made arrangements to take the bus up to see Mount Denali. Some people call it the McKinley Mountain, named after President McKinley. Alaska residents call it the Denali mountain, which is an Alaskan name.

This was a beautiful drive. They saw moose, caribou, bears and their young, foxes, rabbits, eagles, and many other little critters. Whenever someone would spot an animal, the bus driver stopped so the passengers could take photographs of it. This was very exciting for Laurie to see. Joy had been on the bus tour before and was aware of the sittings of the animals and scenery along the way.

The drive back down the Parks Highway was interesting. They stopped at some of the little towns, Cantwell and Talkeetna, to pick up some souvenirs for Laurie and talk to some of the people traveling. One couple they talked to were from Michigan, and they were acquainted with a family that Laurie knew—what a small world.

Laurie went out to Darwin's to go salmon fishing with a friend. They went way back in wooded areas, came to a swamp, and had to take the three-wheeler through the swamp. It was a muddy, bumpy ride, but Laurie had a good time. She loved it. Finally arriving at the fishing hole, they started to fish. The fish were biting, and they caught their limit, such big ones too. Laurie said, "I have never had so much fun in my life."

Another beautiful place they went to see was Portage Glacier south of Anchorage on the Seward Highway (one year voted as one of the most beautiful highways in the United States). Along the way is a small town, Alyeska, a well-known skiing resort. A large hotel there has a German restaurant that serves delicious homemade bread and soups. They stopped on their way back home and enjoyed the soup, sandwich, and a cinnamon roll.

Laurie said, "I will probably be back to Alaska again, it has been so much fun."

# CHAPTER EIGHT

## *ADVANCING*

Clark was working at Redmond Vista Apartment, cleaning, and doing part-time for Martin's Maintenance in Anchorage. He attended church regularly, accepted the Lord as his Savior, and was baptized. He met Martin; they became friends, and Martin hired him.

Clark let a man he met at church live with him because he needed a place to live for a short time. Clark said, "You can stay until you find another place, but I will set some rules—no smoking or drinking inside."

Clark went to a prayer meeting one evening, and when he arrived back home, his mobile home was burning. It was totally ruined. The man had been smoking and fell asleep. Clark had the mobile home all paid for but one payment and didn't have it insured. This was quit a blow to Clark. He worked hard trying to be independent and to better himself. He forgave the man and decided next time to have his home insured.

His friend Martin asked Clark to stay with him because Clark didn't have a place to live, and he was very thankful for a good friend and employer, but he eventually got tired of janitorial work and signed up to go to truck driver's school in Tucson, Arizona, in the later part of March 1986. His possessions were all destroyed except what clothes he bought. This made it easy for him to relocate somewhere else and better himself.

The Sunday school class he attended had a going-away party for Clark and gave him some farewell gifts: summer clothes, shorts, sleeveless shirts, a bathing suit and sunglasses, and a traveling bag. They had all been friends and hated to see Clark leave Alaska.

He arrived in Tucson at the school and filled out all the paperwork. He took the physical examination, and the doctor inquired about the tracheotomy scar on Clark's neck, and he explained about his severe head injury he had when he was seventeen years old. The doctor then denied him entrance in the school. He told Clark it would be a risk, that with a serious head injury like he had, he may have a seizure and cause an accident, and they couldn't risk training him for truck driving. Clark was very disappointed but understood their reason for not letting him and thanked them for giving him the opportunity to at least try.

Clark called Gale and let her know what happened, and she suggested, "Why don't you come over here and stay? We have a little camper you can sleep in, and you can eat with us."

"Thanks, Gale, will it be all right with Vern?" Clark asked.

"I am sure it will. This way, you can look for work and not worry about a place to live. I will give you the directions on how to get here. It will be so good to see you, Clark."

Trying to find work wasn't easy. It was summer now and very hot. He wasn't used to hot weather but enjoyed his new shirts and shorts he received.

Elisabeth was born June 19. Vern's family was happy for him because he didn't have any biological children, but he had his twin stepsons from his previous marriage.

Finally Clark found work at an office-furniture company, cleaning offices and picking up and delivering machines, and he worked there for about five months and then decided to move to Phoenix. After Christmas, he packed his belongings and moved there in January 1987. He was hired at a circuit print company and worked there for two and a half years and then decided to move back to Tucson.

August was here, and Joy had planned her vacation to go to Michigan to see her family and grandchildren. Debbie Marie was expecting her first baby, and he would be Joy's first great-grandchild, and she wanted to be there. He was born on August 12.

Joy thought, *Dean has surely missed the years of his children growing up and now the great-grandchildren also. What a blessing it has been enjoying these newborns in the family and spending time with them as much as I can. Just think, little baby Alan.*

She visited her brothers and sister and her family, and they all went to the family reunion at the lake. It had been some time since Joy had been at a reunion. Everyone was happy to see her, and they asked her a lot of questions about Alaska, like "Do you live in an igloo?" "Is it really dark all the time?" "Is it really cold there?"

She answered, "No, we have about four to five hours of daylight in the midwinter, and in the summer, the sun shines until after midnight. It is so beautiful there with the mountains, they are so big and the Cook Inlet is close, and the weather isn't much different than it is here in Michigan. Alaska is a very large state, and Anchorage, where I live, is a city that is medium in size, but very modern with large high-rise buildings and very friendly people."

They were all so interested and listened to Joy tell some interesting things they had never realized before. And neither did she until she experienced it.

It was time for her to return to Alaska and get back to work. She liked her job very much because she didn't have to pay rent, buy groceries, or own a car, and she had many privileges living with the Goodings. They were very good people to work for. She felt secure there.

At Christmastime, Joy was able to put up a Christmas tree with lights. They were a Jewish family and celebrated Hanukkah (Festival of Lights).

After Christmas, the Goodings informed Joy they were going to move to California and were going to sell their home. This was a shock to her. She thought, *What am I going to do now? I will see about furthering my bookkeeping and secretary skills by going back to school. I had thought about it when I first came here to work.*

She asked Barbara, "Can I take two or three hours off in the afternoons to go to school? I need to refresh my office skills, it has been some time since I have done office work."

Barbara answered, "Yes, if you can keep up with your work here at the house."

Joy replied, "I did it back in Springdale when I went back to college and worked too, I believe I can do it."

She said, "All right then, I wish you all the luck in the world."

Joy applied for a student loan and received one, then enrolled in the Clerical Skills Training Inc. She did most of her work in the morning and went to school in the afternoon, came home and got the evening meal ready, and cleaned up the kitchen. Then she went to her room and studied, sometimes until two o'clock in the morning. She enjoyed learning and getting to know other students.

On April 24, 1987, Joy received her certificate saying, "This is to certify that Joy E. Godman has completed the course of study prescribed and is therefore awarded the SECRETARIAL SCIENCES DIPLOMA."

Also, the other students created an award stating, "This Honors Award is Being Given To Joy E. Godman for Breaking the sound Barrier in the

Ten-Key Calculator, At 220 Plus. This has earned you the Title of THE TEN-KEY WHIZ KID."

At graduation Darwin, Annabelle, and their family came from Wasilla, and the Goodings (Arnold and Sharon their children) attended and congratulated Joy for completing the course and keeping her word to do the housework as she promised. It was so good to have another hurdle accomplished. Now she would need to look for a job.

The next day, Michael informed Joy she would have to purchase an automobile because they would be needing theirs, and she would need one when they moved. Joy went to the used-car dealership and found a small car and purchased it and the insurance. It did seem good to have her own car now to come and go when she wanted to in the evenings.

There was a lot of packing to be done because the Goodings sold the house and were going to move to one close by until they went to California to purchase a new home.

Darwin and Annabelle had another baby boy on May 24, 1987. A midwife delivered the baby at home; only this time, she had a very hard time birthing. Annabelle bled more than she should have, and the midwife called the doctor, and he advised her on what to do. The baby was fine. They named him Larry after Grandpa Larry J. Godman.

A neighbor lady came over to see Annabelle and the baby. While Annabelle was holding little Larry, they were both smoking cigarettes, and the smoke was making the baby cough. Joy said, "Give me the baby. What are you doing? He was just born, he doesn't need smoke blown in his face." Joy disliked smoking anyway. She took the baby into the living room away from the smoke.

Joy stayed with Annabelle and the family for a few days to help with the baby, the other children, and the household chores. Darwin was up north, working, and wouldn't be home for a while. He called regularly to see how Annabelle and the children were doing.

The Kendalls, Jordan and Sally, were the new owners of the Goodings' home. They had a son, Larry, and two daughters, Karey and Molly. Sally asked Barbara, "Does Joy come with the house? I would like to keep her for my housekeeper."

Barbara answered, "No, Joy is going to work in an office. She's been going to school."

Sally called Joy and asked her, "Would you like to babysit for me on Wednesday nights? I go to ceramics, and Jordan would like you to come over and cook dinner for them, and we would like for you to babysit on Saturday nights sometimes also."

Joy replied, "Yes, I could do that. I will be there Wednesday evening."

Jordan was happy with Joy's cooking and thanked her for helping him out; he said he didn't like to cook. They got acquainted with each other, talking over dinner about their families, and Joy told him about her sons and daughter.

Jordan told her, "Sally is the daughter of David Delany, owner of Covel Industries, one of the largest companies in Anchorage, and I am the lawyer for the company."

Joy looked forward to going over there every week. She enjoyed the family. Some Saturday nights she would babysit so Sally and Jordan could go out dancing.

The children were easy to attend to. The baby was fine until it was time to go to bed, then she just cried (she missed her mother), so Joy carried her all around the house until she fell asleep. As she got more used to Joy being there at nighttime, she settled down.

Sally made some beautiful pottery figurines and gave them to Joy, a set of Praying Hands because she knew Joy was a woman of faith.

Joy told her, "I am so thankful, and I know you put a lot of work into this."

The move to the new residence went smooth, and unpacking and setting up housekeeping again wasn't too strenuous because they didn't unpack everything because of the next move to California, so they didn't plan on staying in this house very long.

A trip to Arizona was planned, and Joy went to Arizona to see Clark and Gale and family. After she arrived, they all decided to take a trip to Colorado to see Donald and Sherry. They rented a van so there would be room for them all and drove to Florissant, Colorado.

Gale was pregnant with Renee, and Elisabeth was almost one. This was so much fun being with her family. Cousins got to meet one another. Sherry's children, Lori and Brandon, were there. This was the summer of 1987. Joy was in her height of glory to be there.

Donald's daughters were there also: Misty and Debbie Marie and her little son Ricky (he was almost one also). Joy thought, *Just think of what my husband, Dean, was missing, a family so loving and with lots of girls too. He wanted a little girl so bad. I can't dwell on that. It is the past, and this is the present.*

Donald and Sherry took them sightseeing to many beautiful places. They all enjoyed just visiting and catching up on all the family activities. His horses were an attention-getter. He and Sherry loved to go trail riding on the weekends when he wasn't busy working on their home he built. The time had come for them to go back to Arizona, and Joy had to get ready to go back to Alaska. She had to look for a new job, and Clark had to go back to Phoenix to his work also. Departing was sad for them all. They lived so far apart and had busy lives, but one thing good about it—Joy got to travel and see many new places she had never seen before. Soon she would be going back home to find work.

Joy answered many want ads about a job, and they all told her, "We are looking for someone younger, we're sorry." No matter where she went, they told her the same thing. She finally decided to go to an employment agency to get help. She had to pay a fee, and when she got a job, she had to pay them a percentage of her wages for three weeks until her bill was paid. Her agent called her and let her know whenever there was a job available. Joy would change clothes and put on a suit, hose, and high heels to look professional. After many times being told she was too old, she told the agent, "Please don't call me unless they want a mature woman." After two weeks, the agent called Joy and told her, "I have a gentleman who asked for a mature woman, and I have four or five others looking for work also. I am going to send you there first because you have been so patient." Joy took the man's name and address and thanked her agent.

Joy wondered whether this would be another dry run, but she asked the Lord, "Please, I need Your help very much. You know, Lord, my situation, and I trust You will be there for me as You always have been throughout my life."

Joy went in and asked the receptionist, "I am here to apply for the job the employment agency said was available, am I in the right place? May I see the person who will interview me?"

The receptionist said, "I will be the one to interview you. Mr. Slaydon asked me to do it, and I don't even know what to ask you."

Joy said, "Just ask me if I can do what you do."

Delores proceeded to ask Joy, "How much experience do you have working in an office? What kind of work did you do and for how long?"

Joy told her about it. "I worked sixteen years with a large construction company in Michigan. They had three different companies—a large equipment company, a trucking company, and an asphalt company—and I did the payroll for all three of them. There were unions wages of all categories involved. I had to make all the reports to each one. I added their hours from time cards, applied the proper wage for the job they did, deducted the Social Security, all the taxes, etc. Typed the paychecks and kept the journals separate for each company. Anything to do with payroll I did."

Delores asked, "Did you work in the general journals?"

"I just finished school for a bookkeeping and secretarial certificate. I learned all about that, debits and credits, etc.," Joy replied.

"We have a few other women to interview, and Mr. Slaydon will make a choice whom he wants to interview, then he will make a decision, and we will let you know," Delores explained. "I will call you by Wednesday afternoon."

Joy thanked her and left the office and waited for an answer.

The phone rang, and it was Delores. "Joy, we want you to come in the office, and Mr. Slaydon wants to interview you, can you make it about 2:00 PM tomorrow?"

"Yes, I can, I will be there," Joy replied happily. "Oh Lord, please let me be hired."

Mr. Slaydon seemed to be a very nice gentleman. He asked Joy to sit down. He wanted to know more about her. He said, "I see you have been working for Barbara and Michael Gooding for four years, why are you leaving?"

She answered, "They are moving to California, and I didn't have any other choice but to find the kind of work I had done in Michigan."

He replied, "I talked to them, and they highly recommended you and said you were an excellent worker, trustworthy and faithful. Are you a Christian?"

"Yes, I am," Joy answered.

"I am going to talk to one another lady, and then I will let you know what I have decided tomorrow," he stated.

The next day Joy received a phone call from Delores who said, "Mr. Slaydon chose you for the job. Come in so we can make arrangements for you to start work."

"Thank you so much, I will come in the morning at 10:00 AM," Joy stated.

Joy told Barbara, "I have another job and would be leaving soon. I will find an apartment as soon as I can. I want to thank you and Michael for being good employers as well as friends to me."

"We are happy you found a job, who will you be working for?" Barbara asked.

"P&L General Contractors, Mr. Slaydon is the owner," Joy replied.

"He called us about a reference, I am happy he hired you," Barbara said.

Looking for an apartment was time-consuming, but finally Joy found one. It was an efficiency apartment—she didn't need anything bigger—and she put a deposit on it.

Joy's son Donald was planning on coming to Alaska, and she called him and asked him if he would go over to her brother Louis's and get all the things she had packed and left in his warehouse before she came to Alaska.

"Yes, I will, Mom, I am bringing an empty trailer with us to bring back the moose. So I will go and get your things. You called just in time, we are about to leave in a couple of days. Stan Hulet, Bob Vaughn, David Ryan are coming with me," Donald said.

"Thanks, that will be about the right time. I have an apartment to move into. This is another big change in my life, a different place to live and a new job all at once," Joy said. After hanging up, she bowed her head and thanked God for His eternal, loving care.

Monday morning Joy reported to work and was very excited going back doing bookwork instead of housecleaning.

Delores greeted her and told her, "I will be training you in the procedures I do and let you get acquainted with the files and my daily routine for two weeks. I will be leaving then, I gave Mr. Slaydon my two weeks' notice. Are you going to be OK with this?"

"Yes, I will. I believe I will catch on fairly quick with your help guiding me through," Joy answered and was ready to start anytime Delores was ready.

Donald had arrived with his trailer and loaded her things from Barbara's house and took them along with the things he brought with him to Joy's apartment. "Boy, it is like Christmas, opening all my things I've had in storage for four years," Joy remarked.

Donald and his friend left and went out to Darwin's to go moose hunting with him. October and November flew by, and it was getting close to Christmas and shopping for all the family. Some presents had to be mailed to her children and their families in Arizona, Michigan, and Colorado. It was fun shopping for items with Alaska on them. The children liked to take their gifts to school and show the other students.

Clark called Joy and told her, "I am seeing a young lady I met at the apartment building I live in, and I believe it is serious, Mom. I think I love her and want to marry her."

Joy replied, "Clark, you should date her for a while and get to know her to make sure you really do love her and she loves you."

Clark replied, "Mom, I am sure, we are in love, she understands me. I told her about my accident and that I have short-term memory loss, I forget things sometimes, and I have to write notes to myself, and she said she understands."

Joy said, "When do you plan on asking her to marry you?"

"Soon, as soon as I can get a ring for her, and she can plan the wedding, sometime in December I believe."

They were married December 24, 1987. Gale, Vern, and their family attended the wedding in Phoenix. She was a beautiful bride, and Clark was a handsome groom. Joy sent a wedding present and congratulations because she couldn't attend.

In extreme cold weather, Joy had to plug her car in an electrical outlet at night so the motor would start in the mornings. It was cold; frost and snow accumulated on the windshield and had to be scraped off. At Barbara's house, she didn't have to get outside to go to work. This was like it is in Michigan. She was happy and content with everything and enjoyed her life as each new day came and went by. The job was going well, and in the winter months when the Slaydons went to Hawaii for three months, Joy would house-sit for them to make sure the pipes didn't freeze and no other disasters happened.

Summertime was here now, and the flowers were blooming; they were so big and beautiful, many flower baskets hanging full of flowers. What a sight to see all over the city streets downtown. The city didn't do things like that where she came from. She had never seen such beautiful flowers like these before.

Angel Marie wanted to come to Alaska to see Grandma. Gale checked with the airlines to see if a child her age (seven years old) could fly alone and come up to Alaska. They informed Gale that she would have to stay with Angel Marie until she boarded the plane, and her grandmother would have to have a signed permission slip and identification before they would release Angel in her custody. Angel Marie was a very brave little girl. She boarded the plane in Tucson, and the stewardess kept track of her while she was aboard. She was a very talkative little girl, and the gentleman that sat next to her carried on a conversation with her. She talked a lot about her grandma. This was in the summer of 1988.

When she departed from the plane and Joy was identified to take her, the gentleman came up to Joy and said, "So you're the grandmother I have heard so much about. Your little granddaughter is so smart, she even speaks Spanish."

Joy replied, "Yes, I know it, how many seven-year-olds you know would go by themselves on an airplane?"

"Not any that I know," he answered. "She is a jewel of a child."

Darwin bought an old school bus and tore out most of the interior and made a camper bus with a kitchen, bathroom, tables, and seats. Then he built a top structure, with three separate rooms with beds, electric outlets, and small windows. When it was set up, it had a set of stairs and a walkway along the side to enter in each room. When they were going to travel, the building folded down flat and was secured by straps. He was going to start a tour business taking tourists sightseeing around Alaska for a week at a time. With a lot of hard work, he completed the bus, and it was ready to go.

Desare', Darwin's eldest daughter, came into town and stayed with Angel Marie while Joy worked. On weekends, they all went sightseeing to Mount Denali State Park and also went south to Seward to take a tour boat to see the fjords and whales, otters, and many bird species. Angel was so thrilled; she had never been on a big boat or seen so much water.

This had been a special time for all of them, and it was hard to see Angel go back home. Good-byes were said, formalities getting her on the plane were handled, and she boarded the plane and was on her way home. She would surely miss Angel Marie.

Joy looked forward to going to church on Sundays and Wednesday evenings. She had met a few ladies who were either divorced, widowed, or single. They all became friends. They met after church on Sunday and would all go to lunch, sometimes at the same place. After lunch, many times they went to one another's home for Bible study and fellowship, getting to know one another, telling their experiences through life and about their families.

One of the ladies, Darla Stark, asked, "Joy, I have a room I want to rent, would you be interested in renting it? You would have kitchen privileges and the whole house, it is a big home, and I would love to share it with you. Besides, there is a garage too."

Joy answered, "Yes, I have been at your home and would love to accept your offer."

With help from some of the ladies, Joy moved to Darla's home. It was farther from work but was such a nice place to live, and she wouldn't be all alone.

Darla had card parties on Friday evenings, and many from the church came and played cards. Later in the evening, they had a snack and discussions about current events, family, or other subjects. It was good for Joy to get acquainted with other church members and for them to get to know her better.

Billy Graham's Evangelic Association came to Anchorage, and Joy helped with counseling those who would go forward to accept the Lord. One of the young ladies she had counseled, Rose Caseman, kept in contact with her, and they became good friends.

# CHAPTER NINE

## ERUPTION AND SPILL

Joy decided to go to Phoenix to meet Clark's wife. She stayed a couple of days, and then they took her to Gale's in Tucson. It was a nice visit, and it was good spending the holidays with all of them. Clark and Samantha didn't stay long; she had to go to work.

A few days later, Clark called and asked, "Mom, can you rent a car and come and get me? Samantha and I had a fight, and the police officer told me, 'You should move out so there won't be any more trouble.'" Clark continued. "I packed my things and went to my car, and it won't start, and I don't have much money. I will tell you about it when I see you."

Joy answered, "Yes, I will. Vern can take Gale and me to get a rental car, and we will be there as soon as possible, you go someplace, like a gas station, where you can keep warm. Gale knows where you live and said there is a gas station on the corner of your street."

Gale told Joy, "I thought they weren't getting along very well, she gets upset with Clark because he doesn't remember things."

Joy said, "Yes, I know. Samantha called me and told me she was going to take Clark to a psychiatrist to see if he can help Clark. I told her the neurologist at the hospital told us he had permanent damage to his short-term memory and he would always have it and he was lucky that it isn't worse. He would have to keep notes to remind himself."

"Yes, I know. She didn't have any patience with him, but he always was very kind to her."

It was very late when they arrived at the gas station, and Clark was ready to go with them, and he said, "Thank you, Mom, for coming, I didn't know what to do or who to call."

She answered, "Clark, you know I would come and help, you are my son and I love you."

"Mom, Samantha wanted to go out dancing, and I didn't want to go, and she got mad and kept hitting me with a broom, and I pushed her down into the couch," he said.

He continued, "Then she called the police, and I explained to him, 'She hit me several times with the broom. I asked her to stop, and she wouldn't, then I just pushed her, and she fell on the couch,' and he told me I should leave to prevent any more confrontations."

"You did the right thing, Clark, how long has this been going on?" Joy asked.

"She filed for a Decree of Dissolution of Marriage on August 5, and I signed it on October 28, 1988. It hasn't been finalized in court yet," Clark said.

"Why in the world didn't you tell me?" Joy asked.

"Because I thought we could work it out, so I tried. She liked to go to dances and drink. I told her I don't drink. That's what she wanted me to do tonight, and I refused," Clark said.

"This is some way to spend New Year's Eve. It is supposed to be 'Happy New Year!'" Gale sarcastically remarked as they arrived back home early in the morning, exhausted.

*New Year's Day 1989, another year to be thankful for, even through trials and tribulations, what will this year be like?* Joy wondered.

After a few more days, it was time now for her to go back home to Alaska. Clark would be staying at Gale's until he decided whether he would stay in Tucson or move back to Alaska. He couldn't find work, so he called Martin, his friend in Alaska, and asked, "Would you hire me if I come back there?"

Martin told him, "Yes, I will be glad to. I need help, and I will pay your way up here."

"Thank you very much, you are a good friend, I will be there soon."

Joy was happy that Clark was coming back to Alaska. She wouldn't worry now.

Work was going well. Joy was happy; living at Darla's home helped renew her spirits and brought her hope for the months to come. Daily routine continued through the winter and springtime. She enjoyed the ride back and forth to work; it was a beautiful drive.

Clark was working and staying with Martin again. They are good Christian friends and enjoy each other's company. Martin understood Clark's memory problem and was very compassionate with him, yet he kept Clark on his toes, doing the work sufficiently.

Clark received word that the divorce was final on February 22, 1989. He had never told anyone except the family that he had been married, so Martin didn't know it.

Joy decided to attend another church. She wasn't happy where she was attending. The doctrine was different than what she believed, so she went one Wednesday evening to the prayer meeting at a church of the same denomination she had attended for years when she was in Springdale, Michigan. She was greeted with a smile and a cheerful "Hello." The adult class was having a Bible study. She enjoyed the class and the people she met. The next Sunday she met the pastor and explained why she left the other church, and he said he understood. She felt more at home here among the congregation, and they were all very friendly. From then on, this was the church she attended and worshipped at.

Darla decided to sell her home, and Joy had to think about finding an apartment to move into. She helped Darla with a garage sale and decided to buy some of her furniture so when Joy moved, she would have some. Darla let her pay it off installments.

Joy called Clark and asked him, "Do you want to move into a two-bedroom apartment and share the rent with me?"

Clark said, "Yes, I am tired of sleeping on the couch and having no place for my clothes."

Darwin and Clark helped Joy move all the furniture and other items. She had bought some nice furniture for the living room, bedroom, and kitchen from Darla and a complete bedroom set, from another friend, for her bedroom. It was a split-level apartment house; their apartment was on the bottom level, with the windows looking out at ground level.

It was good to have Clark with her. She loved her family and liked being with them.

Joy had planned to go to Tucson because her sister, Clarice, and Richard, her husband, were going to be there at Gale's in April, and they were looking forward to seeing Joy.

Larry Godman passed away. Darwin decided he would go to the funeral in Michigan.

"One of our family should go and pay our respects. I can't leave. I am house-sitting for my boss and his wife, they have gone on their yearly trip to Hawaii," Joy said.

Grandma (Pearl) had been in an elders' home for a long time with Alzheimer's disease. It was getting hard for Larry Godman to cope with it, and he just gave up wanting to live. He was seventy-nine years old and didn't like living alone, and he missed Pearl too much.

April was here, and Joy went to Tucson. Clarice and Richard had their fifth wheeler parked in Gale and Vern's yard. Clarice's son, Phillip, and his wife, Jan, and their family came out from Michigan, and Donald and Sherry came down from Colorado. It was so good to see them all, and they all had fun reminiscing about the years gone by and what is happening now with them.

Bernie had come back from Bruce's and hadn't changed his attitude toward Vern at all; in fact, he was worse. He climbed up on Clarice and Richard's fifth wheeler, running and jumping on the roof. Richard was very upset with him, and when Vern came home from work, he paddled Bernie, which he needed. From then on, it was hell to pay for Bernie.

Gale had been working at Old Tucson, a tourist attraction, and she had tickets for us all to go and see where some of the Western movies were made. It was fun. The actors fell off the roof while they would act out a make-believe bank robbery. They had dinner at one of the diners; the waitresses dressed in an old-time costume. Things were like it was in the old wild west era. There were fourteen of us, including three babies in strollers.

Clarice and Richard traveled all over the United States with their fifth wheeler, and they stayed at Gale's for about a month after Joy left to go back home. Gale enjoyed having them stay. Clarice helped with the little girls and cooking meals when Gale went to work.

She was very grateful for the help, and she loved Aunt Clarice and Uncle Richard. Vern worked at Hugins Aircraft Plant for fifteen years and had many promotions. Vern's mother and father live close by and visited with Clarice and Richard while they were parked in Gale and Vern's yard. Mrs. Garcia worked for the college, and Mr. Garcia repaired small machinery. They have ten acres they live on with their families. Vern and Gale live in big mobile homes and all get together and have cookouts.

It was time for Joy to go back to Alaska now. It was hard leaving the family here, but she had family in Alaska also. It's good she can travel to different parts of America, and she likes to fly. As she boarded the plane, she thought, *It is amazing how little time it takes to get so far away when you fly, and it takes so long when you drive that far by automobile. I guess that is why I like to fly, it saves time and gives me more time with family.*

Clark was happy to see Joy come home. He said, "It is good to see you, Mom, I missed you. I don't like cooking for myself, it is not as good as your cooking."

Hugging him, she said, "That is a mother's job, and I like to cook anyway. I guess it is because I like to eat. It is nice seeing you again too, Clark, how are things at work?"

"About the same, we got a couple of new places to clean, so I am getting plenty of hours to work. That makes Martin happy too. He is working for the school too," Clark replied.

Angel Marie wanted to come to Alaska again, and Joy made the arrangements for her to come and stay for a while. She went through the same process as before and wasn't afraid to come by herself. She was almost nine years old now and more mature for her age.

Mount Redoubt had a volcanic eruption and spewed ash all over the city. Planes couldn't fly, and traffic was almost at a standstill. It left ash all over everything and was a mess to clean up. Darwin was working up at Lake Katie and had to stay an extra two days because the planes couldn't fly them out; they were grounded.

Joy told Angel Marie to collect some of the ash, put it in a jar, and make a poster depicting a mountain erupting to take back to her school to show the teacher and her class. It was an interesting event. Joy never witnessed anything like it before.

Our neighbor Esther lived in the upper apartment, and she took care of Lisa, her granddaughter who was younger than Angel Marie, and they became friends. Esther was a seamstress and taught the girls to sew; they spent many hours learning and making items they wanted. There were other children in the neighborhood to play with and go bike riding with after most of the ashes were cleaned up.

Clark took Angel go-kart riding and miniature golfing whenever she talked him into it; they lived close by. He worked evenings and was able to go during the daytime. On the weekends they went to Darwin's. Desare' took Angel riding on the three-wheeler around the neighborhood. She enjoyed that and wanted to drive it; Desare showed her how and rode with her, but they went just a little ways in front of the house. Angel received plenty of attention, because back home, Gale's in-laws ignored her and Bernie, her brother. Ever since Elisabeth and Renee were born, their grandchildren, they didn't spend much time with Gale's children anymore. Angel Marie felt neglected, and sometimes she was blamed for some things that went wrong when the children were playing.

Joy could see the way she and Bernie had been treated by the family the last time she was there and didn't like it at all. Vern didn't get along with Bernie; he always hollered at him and said he was ignorant. Bernie asked his mother, Gale, if he could go and live with his dad in Florida because he couldn't take it any longer the way Vern was treating him. Bernie was almost twelve years old now and was getting very rebellious with Vern. Gale contacted Bruce and asked him if Bernie could go there and live with him because of the situation that was going on with Vern and Bernie.

Bruce told her, "Yes, he can come, it will be nice to see him again. Let me know the flight number and the time I can pick him up at the airport."

Gale said, "Thanks, I will let you know all the particulars when I find out."

Joy telephoned Gale to let her know when Angel Marie was coming home. She found out that Bernie was going to be staying with his dad for a while and why. Joy was a little apprehensive about it, but at least he would be getting one-on-one attention with his dad.

While waiting for the plane with Angel Marie, they saw a young boy about her age acting very frightened to go on the plane by himself, telling his folks he was afraid. Joy told Angel, "Go over and tell him you flew up to Alaska all by yourself when you were only seven and you are going to do it again now, there is nothing to be afraid of." So she did, and he looked at her wide-eyed and said, "Really!" And then he turned to his folks and said, "I am not afraid anymore." Angel Marie sat down beside him and stayed with him, then they boarded the plane together waving good-bye to us all. His parents walked over and thanked Joy for sending Angel Marie over to give him the courage so he would get on the plane. He had never flown alone before.

Gale called Joy and was crying. "Mom, our mobile home burned down, it is completely destroyed. Thank God, Vern's aunt, Betty Ann, was there taking care of the children and got them outside. I took Vern to a union meeting and then had to take Renee to the hospital because she wasn't feeling good, and when I was coming home, I turned the corner and saw the trailer burning and screamed, 'Oh my god, that is my house, my kids are in there.'"

Joy said, "Oh no, Gale, did anyone get burned? What are you going to do now?"

Gale replied, "The kids are all right, Betty Ann got them out in time. She saw smoke coming from the bottom of Angel's bedroom door and opened it, and Angel Marie and her girlfriend were trying to get the fire out on the bed. They had a lamp on the bed, and it caught the bedcovers on fire, and it was blazing by that time, so Betty Ann told them to get outside while she went and got Elisabeth from the living room. Thank God, Mom."

Joy replied, "You can replace trailers, but you can't replace those children."

"We will have to rent a place for a while until the insurance company pays us, then we will buy something else," Gale said.

Joy was still working for the Kendalls, getting their dinners, when the Valdez oil spill occurred and Jordan was appointed to manage getting crews together for cleanup.

She overheard Jordan calling many people, trying to get workers for the jobs. When she had a chance, she asked him, "Jordan, my son in Colorado isn't working right now, I am sure he would come to Alaska to help out if you need him, do you want me to call him to see if he would come?"

Jordan answered, "Yes, we need all the help we can get. Call and see if he can come here."

Joy phoned Donald and asked him, "Jordan Kendall needs helpers for that oil spill in Valdez, and I told him you might be interested in coming up here to work, will you?"

Donald replied, "I sure will. I need work, and that will be very messy but interesting. I will get a flight out of here as soon as I can, let him know I am coming. Thanks, Mom."

Donald arrived in two days, and Joy took him over to meet Jordan to get signed up to go to work. He was used to carpenter work, and this will be completely different for him.

What a mess that oil made: seabirds, otters, fish, and many sea critters were drowning in oil, and oil deeply soaked in the shore and rocks because of one man's big mistake coming into the inlet. It took day after day and hour by hour to try to clean it up. Many fishermen couldn't take their boats out to fish and lost their livelihood; many went bankrupt.

Alaska's big oil spill was in the news for some time, saying the oil companies were not prepared for such a disaster, and this was a good example that it does happen.

The summer had been an interesting one for Alaskan residents—Mount Redoubt volcano erupting and the oil spill disaster was overwhelming for everyone.

Back to work and the routine of things again, but Joy liked to have things orderly with not too many surprises. She has had enough of them in her life so far.

Thanksgiving and Christmas were spent at Darwin and Annabelle's home. It was fun to go there; the children like to play games. Desare' was eighteen now and had the same boyfriend for two years. Darwin Junior was ten, Rose Ann was nine, Donald was four and a half, and Larry was two and a half years old. They were all growing up so fast.

Sometimes Darwin Junior and Rose Ann came in to stay with Joy and Clark for the night. They liked to go with Clark on the go-karts in the summer and play miniature golf indoors in the winter. Eventually little Donald was old enough to come and stay too.

Another year went by; it was 1990. Debbie Marie, Donald's youngest daughter, and Mitchell had another baby boy, Cody. He was born on January 6. Thank the Lord he was a healthy baby and the second great-grandchild for Joy. *The Lord has blessed me abundantly with children and grandchildren. Blessed be the name of the Lord,* Joy thought.

The daylight hours were growing shorter, and the nights were growing longer. Joy went to work mornings in the dark, and it was dark when she went home, although she didn't mind. She was happy and contented with her life; it was peaceful.

Clark continued to work for Martin, and they decided to go on vacation together in Hawaii to get some sunshine and a tan; they did. They were happy and well rested and ready to go back to work, with a brighter outlook when they came back home. Clark invited Martin over for dinner sometimes and to play card games when he wasn't busy that evening. Martin was dating a lady; it wasn't a serious relationship. She had a young daughter, a very well-behaved young lady, and it was a pleasure to have her visit also.

Joy's boss and his wife, Lawrence and Pearl Slaydon, left to go to their condo in Hawaii again for their yearly vacation; they stayed at least three months each time. Joy went to their home to house-sit all the time they were gone. It was nice to have a heated garage to drive her car into every day. This was a large home with a beautiful landscaped yard. Sometimes moose would lie there all night and sleep. What a sight to see.

Separating the mail and sending the important mail and the daily newspapers to them once a week was one of the chores and just being there so it looked like someone was occupying the home.

After church services, Clark came over for dinner with Joy, then they spent Sunday afternoon watching television, and they usually went to a prayer meeting in the evening.

Routine day after day helped the hours pass by, but Joy liked routine in her life. It was easier to plan other things ahead of time knowing when to fit them in her schedule. Going to the office every day was easy. There wasn't much to do: answer the phone and record who had called, open the mail and separate it—the usual things to do.

When Joy got all the business taken care of, she wrote in a journal she kept for her memoirs. Maybe she would write them into a book for her children and family one day.

Time was flying by, and Lawrence and Pearl would be back home soon, and Joy would go back to her little apartment.

Joy thought, *It is my home sweet home, no matter how humble. I am thankful for a job so I can afford a place to live and have food to eat. Thank You, Lord, You have provided for me and my family for many years.*

The Slaydons decided to sell their condo in Hawaii. Most businesses were not doing very good, and he didn't want to keep paying the expenses a condo requires. The economy has been bad for some time now, and there is no work for construction companies. Home building came to a standstill, and many people were out of jobs.

Joy asked Lawrence, "Is it all right if I take my vacation after the taxes are all done? I want to go to Colorado to see my son, Donald, and his wife, Sherry."

He answered, "Yes, when you finish your books, then Harold will take it from there, he needs to make sure, in case there are questions, and if everything is all right, you can go."

"Thank you. I want to go see them and spend time with them. I usually go to Gale's or back to Michigan, but this time, I want go to Donald's."

The accountant checked all Joy's information to see if everything was ready for him to complete the income tax report for the year, and he said, "It all looks OK, if there are any questions, I will call."

Joy asked, "Harold, I am getting better, and it doesn't take me as long to do the year-end trial balance. Thanks for all your help and being patient with me."

He replied, "Joy, you are doing fine, I know it isn't easy on your first job like this. Practice makes perfect. Soon you will be doing it like an old pro."

"I sure do hope so, and Lawrence keeps me working."

Plans were made to go see Donald and Sherry for two weeks. Time passed, and Joy was on the plane heading for Colorado. They picked her up at the Denver airport and went to dinner at a really nice restaurant where the decor was like the outdoors—a lot of large plants, trees, beautiful flowers, and waterfalls flowing into ponds, what an experience.

The drive from Denver to Donald's was different. They showed her some sights along the way, and Donald told her, "We will be going sightseeing during your stay. There are many places to visit and see, so we will go back home now so you can rest up."

Joy agreed with him, "I am rather tired because I took the midnight flight from Anchorage, it is a long time on the plane and didn't get much sleep on the plane."

Arising early, they had a good breakfast and prepared to go see the Florissant Fossil Beds National Monument on the road they live going to the small town of Florissant, just a dot on the map and a few miles to Woodland Park where they had lived when they first came from Michigan. It was a nice little town, and they went shopping for some souvenirs. The rest of the day was spent just relaxing and talking, catching up on all that was going on in the family. It was what Joy needed. It was so good to be with them and spend time just hanging out, enjoying the beautiful scenery. They could see Pikes Peak Mountain from their front door; it wasn't very far away. It rained, and Donald said, "It rains every day about this time for about an hour and then stops, and the sun shines the rest of the day."

In the evening, a herd of caribou went through his property, at least forty or fifty of them.

Joy was so surprised and asked, "How often do they come through here like that?"

Donald said, "Every day about this time. When we first moved here, there were many more. We are used to them now, they don't stop but move on. This is probably their route to their grazing grounds nearby, I figured."

"Boy, that is some sight right out in your yard, and so many of them," Joy replied.

"We don't pay much attention to them anymore, they come and go through here so fast," Donald laughingly said. "I am glad they don't stop and leave their poop in our yard."

The next morning after the horses were fed and watered and the chores were taken care of, Donald said, "Don't fix breakfast, Sherry, we're going to Cripple Creek for breakfast." Then he continued telling Joy, "They have changed the town over to a gambling town, and one hotel gives away free breakfast on the weekends to bring the tourists in there to gamble. So we go every once in a while to have breakfast, they don't care if you are staying in the hotel or not. People tell others, and it is a good advertisement for them."

Joy said, "You mean to tell me they took those little old-fashioned stores out—they were so much fun to shop in, I found things there I haven't seen in years—and they have changed them into casinos for gambling?"

"Yes, they did. We liked the old western atmosphere and the unique stores selling things folks like to buy that were from years ago," Sherry said

They arrived at Cripple Creek, and on the outskirts of town, the donkeys were freely roaming around. They used to roam in the streets nearer to downtown, but evidently they were chased out of town to prevent tourists stepping in their droppings. It is a sight to see this old western town alive and doing business, but they all liked it the way it was.

Breakfast was very good—all you could eat. It was cafeteria style with many selections to choose from, coffee and beverage also free. Everything tasted fine, and they all had plenty.

They spent most of the day looking around the little shops that were still open and didn't have gambling on the premises. It's like going back in time to see these gadgets.

"It is amazing how far we have come in society and the change of the items we use for everyday chores that have been made. I wonder what it will be thirty or forty years from now?" Joy asked Donald and Sherry.

Joy thought, *This is a beautiful state. If I had a second choice of where I wanted to live, I would pick Colorado, it is unique and different. I can see why*

*Donald and Sherry decided to live here, but I still like Alaska, and the beauty there is my first choice.*

Another day was almost gone, and they were all ready for a rest before dinner, especially Joy. This high altitude made it hard for her to breathe normally, and she tired out quickly.

*It was good to spend time with them. We enjoyed each other's company and talked about old times and which sights we would be going to during this week. They had visited most of them since they built their home and taken others to the same attractions I have been seeing, plus they go trail riding with the horses often seeing the backcountry.*

After breakfast the next morning, Donald decided they would go to the Royal Gorge, a deep rock gorge of red granite with an incline railway and a high suspension bridge. "My, how beautiful yet scary looking down from the middle of the bridge." Joy added, "Can you imagine working on that bridge? Those men must have been very brave and happy when it was finished."

Donald replied, "I don't like working on a high roof, let alone a bridge like that. Some of the workers must have some interesting stories to tell about different things happening."

"Shall we will drive over to Pueblo for a tour of the town? It is an interesting place to visit and check out the western shops. We like to look at their horse-riding gear and see what is new on the market," Sherry suggested.

"Sure, I like to go to places and see things I haven't seen before, even horse-riding gear," Joy replied, laughing.

It was getting late, so they decided to head back toward home, and if they weren't too tired, they would stop and take a tour around the Garden of the Gods, just a little ways outside of Colorado Springs. "It was relaxing and peaceful riding along and observing the lovely scenery, especially with someone else driving the car. The driver has to concentrate and can't be looking around at everything," Joy noted.

Donald said, "I've seen this many times before. I don't mind driving, I do a lot of it when I go to work down here in the Springs."

They decided to go out for dinner in Colorado Springs to a Green Garden Restaurant. Joy had never eaten there or heard of them, so this was all new to her. It was different, and she didn't know what to order, so Sherry suggested a few which she had eaten before and liked, so Joy chose something she had never eaten before, and she did enjoy the meal.

It is a beautiful ride from the Colorado Springs up the mountains forty-five miles to Donald and Sherry's home, so colorful with wildflowers of all colors growing.

Another day and Donald said, "We haven't driven up to Pikes Peak yet, so we will do it today. It is such a nice sunny day, and the view from up there will be fantastic."

A unanimous response from Sherry and Joy was "Yes, let's do it today!"

The ride was climbing and winding roads, getting colder the higher they got to the Peak. The side of the mountain had snow, and Donald stopped and etched ALASKA in big letters so it could be seen from the cars as they drove by, and he said, "We let them know visitors came all the way from Alaska to see Pikes Peak." Christmas Village was a special place to see, Christmas all the time, Santa Claus and his elves waiting on customers.

After all the sightseeing and traveling, it was time for Joy to leave and go home.

# CHAPTER TEN

## *ACCOMPLISHMENTS*

Getting back to the routine was easy. Joy had been with her oldest son, Donald, and his wife for two weeks and enjoyed her trip, and she had many good memories to sustain her for quite a while. Her family has always been one of the highest priorities in life along with her Lord Jesus. Being a mother has many responsibilities, and once a mother always a mother. The children grow up but not away from her heart.

Summer this year turned out to be nice, and there was not as much rain. There were many tourists that came; it seemed like there were many more than usual this year. Some flew, some by cruise ships, and many motor homes and pulling trailers. This was a good time for Darwin to get his bus finished for the tour to start. He had to advertise about the different trips and times to choose from. The brochure read,

EXPERIENCE ALASKA-PERSONALIZED TOURS. Yukon Float and Denali Park Tour, King Salmon Float Trip & Denali Park, Silver Salmon Fishing and South Central Alaska Sightseeing and many other options.

A camera club came to Alaska from California to take the tour and take wildlife photographs. When they came back from their tour, they had nothing but praises; they even booked another tour for the next year. They enjoyed majestic scenery, peace and tranquility, wildlife sightings, comfortable camping at overnight campsites, a tour route that passes several glaciers, taking close-up photos of the blue ice glaciers, deep crevices, and numerous variety of wildflowers. There was a camper bus with a pop-up top that converts into individual eight-by-eight rooms for privacy. Each carpeted room has lights, heat, a six-inch-thick mattress, outlets for twelve-volt hair dryers and curling irons (provided by us), a mirror, and a folding chair.

This bus was equipped with a full-shower bath, a kitchen, a two-hundred-gallon water-carrying capacity, and instant hot water for nightly showering with furnished towels and washing clothes. They toured in a passenger van with the Mobile Hotel providing support for home-cooked meals, lodging, showers, restroom facilities, and more. This is just a sample of Darwin's hard work he put into the tour bus, Mobile Hotel.

Darwin drove the bus, and Annabelle drove the van, when they stopped for the night. Darwin took the tourists on hikes, etc. Annabelle did all the cooking and cleaning up.

Business slacked off, and there was not much response for the tours. People like more modern facilities rather than the rugged outdoor types. The business lasted about three years, and finally Darwin parked the bus and didn't advertise anymore. He said, "It was fun while it lasted." The photographers wrote and said they enjoyed the trip and he was a good guide.

Living in Alaska has been rewarding in many ways—good jobs, many friends, such beauty all around, and the midnight sun is so unique. It gets late at night, and you don't realize how late it is and the children don't want to go in the house and get ready for bed; they think they have plenty of time to play. Many people put dark curtains up to the windows so they can get to sleep, but Joy is usually so tired she just closes her eyes and drops off in a deep sleep and is rested for another day at the office.

Clark met a lady at a friend's house, and they talked for a while, and she asked Clark if she could borrow his car to go get something. Clark, trusting her, gave her his keys, telling her, "Come right back. I have to leave soon."

Clark waited and waited, and she never showed up with his car, so he called Joy and asked her, "Will you come and get me? I will explain when you get here."

Joy asked, "Where are you? I will be there as soon as I can."

Getting into the car, Clark said, "I will never trust another woman with my car keys again. I have been waiting for hours for her to come back, and nobody there knew where she went."

Joy suggested, "You better call the police and report your car missing and give the description and license plate number."

Returning home, Clark called the police and reported it to them, and they asked, "Did you give her the keys, or did she just take them?"

Clark replied, "She asked me if she could borrow my car, and I gave her the keys hours ago, and she never returned with it."

The police took the description and the license plate number of the car and said they would issue a stolen-car report. Two days later, the police called

Clark and told him someone reported a car parked in a mobile home park that didn't belong there, and the police investigated it, and it was Clark's car, and he should go and check it out because they would have it towed away if it wasn't his.

The mobile home park wasn't very far away from their apartment, so Joy took Clark there, and sure enough, it was his car, all banged up from an accident. He was able to drive it back to the house. He had another key for it but was very upset with himself for being so gullible and trusting, but that was Clark's nature—kind and compassionate. He never did see that lady again nor the so-called friends he had been with.

Sometimes it takes a jolt like that to help us understand that all people are not honest, law-abiding citizens and don't care about anyone except themselves. Joy knows she has been in situations similar to that one, yet we must go on and keep our faith in God, and He will take care of us, and we can have peace doing the right thing.

Fall season was about over now, and the cold weather was slowly coming. Here in Anchorage they look up and see the mountaintops and the new snowfall—they call that "dusting." It won't be long now before the snow will be down here in the "bowl"—that is referring to Anchorage. It is fun watching after each snowfall how far it has come down.

*Thanksgiving and Christmas seem to go by so fast, now what will the new year bring?* Joy thought. *Nineteen ninety-one—I have been here for eight years, and I don't know where they went. It seems like keeping busy makes the time go by faster, and the grandchildren and great-grandchildren grow up so fast, especially when I don't get to see them very often. I sometimes think of what my husband is missing not being here and seeing all the blessings God has given me.*

Joy received a letter from her cousin Arlene writing, "I want to let you know there will be a family reunion, and I want to know if you will be coming to Michigan this summer and if you can make it by the first weekend in July. It has been a while since we had a reunion, and we are all getting older, and it would be nice to see everyone again."

Joy wrote back. "That sounds like a good idea. I will get in touch with my children and see if they can plan on attending also. I know Darwin's family won't be able to come. Just let me know the time and place, and I will make my plans and ask for the time off."

Clark was still working for Martin Maintenance afternoons until late at night, so he slept late in the mornings, and Joy had to be at work at 8:00 AM. They didn't see much of each other during the week but went to church together and out to dinner usually on Sunday afternoon. This was a routine for them. Sometimes they would invite friends over for dinner on Sunday and to play games; this broke the monotonous routine.

Martin was seeing a lady friend named Sue. She had a daughter, Nicky. They came with Martin to have dinner with us once in a while. They enjoyed their company.

Joy called Gale and asked, "Can you go to Michigan for the reunion the first week of July? They want to get as many family members as they can to go."

Gale replied, "We will try to save the money so we can go. I would love to go, but our car isn't in very good shape to drive from Arizona to Michigan, Mom."

Joy said, "I will help pay for a rental car that will be safe driving that far, so let me know whether you will be able to go or not."

Reunion plans were made for those who would be attending, where it would be held, and the weekend when it would be held. Several families took their motor homes, campers, and tents to stay overnight and fellowship, because they hadn't seen each other for a year or more. Many were from out of town or out of state. This year they would meet at Swan's Lake in Concord. This was a good place to swim and boat, and there was plenty of playground equipment for the children to play on.

Most of the older generation had passed away or were too ill to attend. Joy's generation was now the elders. Her three brothers, Franklin, Louis, Carlyle, and sister, Clarice, and her family and many of her cousins and their families came this year.

Her oldest brother Karl Junior's wife, Darla, and their daughter, Laurie, were in attendance. Also Louis's daughter Deborah, her husband, and their children came and were going to stay in their tent for the weekend.

Gale, Vern, Bernie, Angel, Elisabeth, and Renee were able to come. It was a long drive with the family, yet they were so happy to be able to come and join the rest of us. The children got to meet their cousins and second cousins they had never met before, and they all had a wonderful time playing and swimming together the whole weekend.

Early one morning, Joy had a flashback. "I remember the time Dean, the kids, and I were camped at this lake, and he was so abusive with me and the boys. That was a long time ago, and I need to forget it and enjoy this weekend. He is not here anymore to ruin my life." She drank her coffee and enjoyed the quiet morning and thanked God for family. Since moving to Alaska, Joy hadn't been able to see most of her cousins and family. Joy's mother's sister Aunt Lucille's children, Arlene, Brandon, Andrea, Jason, Warren, Carol, and Chet, were all there with their children also.

The meals were a variety of meats, casseroles, salads, and desserts— so much to eat and very good (many good cooks among the family). God provides in every way for each one of His family. We are the children of our Father and Lord; one day we will have a great big reunion in heaven with Him and His Son, the Lord, Jesus Christ.

Before leaving the campground, there were plans made for next year's reunion, and many good-bye hugs were given and promises to write letters and keep in touch.

Joy continued her vacation visiting friends and relatives at their homes and going out to eat. She always wanted to go have Coney hot dogs. They were her favorite meal out.

The American Business Women's Association's monthly meeting was held while Joy was in Logan seeing all the members, and she gave a little speech about Alaska, how well she liked it in Anchorage, and her job she has had since 1987. Some of the ladies said they might take one of the cruise ship tours to Alaska and would let her know and maybe meet her someplace in Anchorage when the boat docks. Also Lesley and Chuck, her husband, planned on driving their motor home up there, and they too would let Joy know so they could get together. They were all very interested in what kind of work she was doing and how long she planned to stay in Alaska.

Joy told them, "Alaska is my home now. I like living there. I have met many new friends and have a church I attend regularly. Clark and I live together and share the expenses, so it is easy for both of us. He is easy to get along with."

Joy had been staying with Teressa, her good friend from James Thompson & Sons who was going to take Joy to the Detroit airport in a couple of days.

Looking forward to going back, Joy thought, *We will be moving into a new office building as soon after I arrive, that will be a job getting all the files boxed and marked. We will be sharing an office with Patrick Gordon, a longtime friend of Lawrence's.*

It was farther to drive to work, but it was a very nice office with plenty of space to share with Patrick. It was good to get everything settled and the files back in the cabinets where they belong. It was almost like starting over again. Patrick had the coffee made to start the day with. He was a very kind and thoughtful man, and his brother was also.

Joy was missionary coordinator for the church and kept up to date with the news of the missionaries and their prayer requests to report each Sunday to the congregation by typing and handing them out to each class so they could pray for them. This was done after her office work was done, after-hours. This was so interesting for Joy. She realized how many missionaries dedicated their lives to Christ that the church supported in many other nations, teaching about the salvation of the Lord, Jesus Christ.

The days were going by quickly, and the holidays would be here soon. Thanksgiving and Christmas were celebrated out at Darwin and Annabelle's with the family. It was heartwarming to be with them. Desare' was twenty years old and was still dating Aaron; they have a very serious relationship. Desare' was working at the pizza shop in Wasilla and wasn't too fond of that kind of work, but it is hard for teenagers to find any kind of work.

Martin informed Clark, "The school district is hiring people for custodian work, the same thing I am doing, and you should go and put in an application because it would pay more than what I am paying, and you will get more hours. You will start as a substitute custodian first on trial, then you will get a permanent position."

Clark answered, "Yes, I will do that. I'll go and put my application in. I want a job there."

Joy said, "Clark, I am happy Martin had told you about the job at the school district. They have very good benefits for their employees and will give raises from time to time."

It was about a week later the school district employment office called Clark to come in for an interview the next day, and Clark by then had decided not to take the job.

Joy and Darwin told him, "You are crazy not to take the job while it is available. There might not be another chance for a job like that."

So Clark called them back right away and said, "I am sorry. I do want to come in for an interview, I want the job after all."

Thank God they accepted his second reply. This was in 1992, a new beginning for Clark with a new job. He worked at several schools as a substitute until December when he took a permanent position and still worked for Martin part-time.

It was a cold winter, with lots of snow that covered their windows because they were in the lower level of the apartment house. Joy thought, *I am thankful to have a garage to put my car in so I don't have to shovel it off. Life is better, and I am content with everything and at peace with myself.*

The Slaydons went on their usual winter three months' break down in the lower forty-eight, and Joy had to house-sit once again. During this time, another big snowfall came, so no one could go anywhere. The snow was so deep, and the plows couldn't keep the roads clear enough to drive on. So she didn't go to work either; it was a day off for her.

Looking out the living-room windows—which were the full length of the room, about twenty feet—at night she could see the view of the city lights shining so bright. What a sight, like sparkling diamonds. In the morning quite often, the moose would be just waking up from their sleep under the pine trees in the yard and trying to reach something to eat off the tree branches.

Joy thought, *Only in Alaska could one see such sights with the mountains on the other side of the house that were also visible, what beauty to behold.*

Spring was here, and the Slaydons had returned home, and Joy was back in her own place. Clark was enjoying his job with the school district, going to different schools wherever they needed him. He met many other employees, and they became friends.

Joy and her neighbor Esther became good friends. As they got to know each other, they found out that both of them had husbands that drank a lot and were abusive—only difference, Esther divorced her husband, but later on when he got very ill, she went to help him before he passed away. She had worked hard raising her children alone: two sons and a daughter that had one daughter; the boys never married. It was good to have someone to talk to that understood about the life Joy had lived. Esther had been there and done that, so to speak, also. They were both thankful they have a peaceful and quiet life now and didn't have to worry anymore.

Summer was here, and the beautiful flowers were in bloom now. Everywhere Joy went she saw where people in Anchorage planted flower gardens. It brightened up the scenery, and they were so big. The sun shines until midnight and helps them grow faster and bigger.

Desare' called Joy and asked, "Can I come over and talk to you, Grandma?"

Joy answered, "Why, yes you can, I will be here, it will be good to see you. I will put the coffeepot on."

A short time later, Desare knocked on the door, and Joy let her in and gave her a big hug and kiss, saying, "It is good to see you, what's up?"

Joy poured the coffee, set out some cookies, and they sat down at the table, and Desare told Joy, "Grandma, I am pregnant, and Aaron doesn't want to marry me yet."

"*For goodness' sake,* Desare, how far along are you?"

"About three, almost four months. I don't know why Aaron is acting like this. We have been together for a long time, since we were in school," Desare said, sobbing.

"So what does he plan on doing? He has a responsibility, helping you and the baby," Joy said, quite frustrated.

"Things never change in this world. Men beg and beg to have what they want and make big promises until the girl gives in, he gets what he wants, and just goes on his merry way, taking no responsibility for his actions. Promises, promises, that is all she gets," Joy said. The she stood up and put her arms around Desare' and consoled her. She then added, "I guess you will have to give him time, maybe he will come around sooner or later. Time will tell, Desare'. Some guys don't like to be pushed into marriage until they are ready."

"Grandma, I love him, and I thought he loved me as much as I love him. Now I wonder," Desare' sobbed and then added, "I am almost twenty-one years old, so I am responsible for this as much as he is, and I will have to accept it and have the baby."

Joy added, "Desare', God is a forgiving God. He knows us and knows we are all weak and realizes we are human beings, because He made us, and we have that sinful nature in us, the same as the first man, Adam, had. So you

113

see, it is born in us until we are 'born again' and Christ dwells in us to give us strength to want to obey, the old nature is gone, we have been transformed into a new life with Christ."

Desare' responded, "Thanks, Grandma, I knew you would understand, but it is hard to think that Aaron won't even talk about marriage."

Joy said, "Desare', most men don't like to be pushed, they have a mind of their own."

"What am I going to do, Grandma?" Desare' asked, concerned.

"Continue working as long as you can, and just start preparing for the baby to come. You have a few more months to go yet, and maybe before long, Aaron will change his mind. Sometimes it is a shock to them, and it hasn't sunk in just yet," Joy suggested.

"I feel better now since I talked to you, Grandma. I have been afraid and didn't know what I was going to do. I couldn't go and talk to my mom because she doesn't care for Aaron. I've loved him for a long time, and I didn't want to go with any other boys," Desare' said.

"Yes, I know, that is the way I felt about my husband too. I was only sixteen when I got pregnant with Donald, my first son. and I was seventeen in October and got married in November. So you see, Desare', I have been there and done that, and I can understand what you are going through. My mother didn't like my husband, Dean, either," Joy admitted.

Desare' said, "You have helped me a lot, Grandma. I am glad I called you. Now I can look forward to having the baby and loving it with all of my heart."

"Desare', we have all sinned and come short of the glory of God, and we can't judge anyone, so we can't throw the first stone or talk about other's sins. God is the one who judges in His own time for judgment," Joy comforted her.

The day had slipped by, and it was getting late, so Desare' said, "I better go home and get some rest, I have to work tomorrow a full day. Thanks so much, Grandma. I love you."

"You are welcome. I know you love me, Desare', because you came to me knowing I love you and would understand," Joy answered.

Good-byes and hugs were given, and both were happy with the counseling and the peace Desare' felt in her heart.

Joy prayed, "Lord, thank You for the wisdom to talk to Desare' in a way that will help her to make the right decisions from here on with her life choices. Fill Aaron's heart with love for Desare' and the baby so this can be a family."

Harold and Katie Ellington (Lawrence's CPA), asked Joy if she would like to stay at their home with their children while they went on a vacation for two weeks, and Joy said she would. The son, Clark, had a paper route, and Joy helped him place the papers into the sleeves before he delivered them really early in the mornings. Joy went to work every day and then went back to get the dinner for them, and after, they played games whenever they didn't have homework to do. Sarah was a very intelligent young lady, pleasant to be around and helpful with the kitchen work. They were fun to be with.

Joy's extracurricular activity seemed to be either house-sitting or babysitting since she came to Alaska, but she enjoyed doing this because the time passed by faster with having other things to do besides just working. She was trusted with their children and their homes and appreciated that Joy was willing to do it for them.

The fall colors were prominently bright and beautiful throughout the state, and it won't be long before the leaves fall and have to be raked. A sign that Halloween was on its way, pumpkins and different kinds of decorations will appear on the porches and lawns. Most children love Halloween, because they can go trick-or-treating in their costumes and collect lots of candy and other goodies when they ring the doorbells. Many of the schools have parties for the children so they will be safe and stay off the streets, which is good also. Some of the families take their children round in their cars to be safe, especially when it is cold or raining.

# CHAPTER ELEVEN

## *READY TO GO*

The holidays and the celebrations with families getting together had come and gone once again, and another year was already here, 1993. Joy thought, *I have been in Alaska for ten years now, and they have gone by so fast, and I am very content with my life now.* The winters were very cold and snowy, but Joy was used to it. She came here from Michigan; she lived there for fifty-five years until she came here. She was very happy with the choice she made to come here for work and find new friendships.

On January 29, Aaron called Joy and said, "Grandma, Desare' had a baby girl today, and they are both doing fine."

Joy said, "I will go up to see her in the hospital, what room is she in?"

"She probably won't be here very long, she gets to go home in a couple of days. They don't keep them here very long anymore, but I will let you know, Grandma," Aaron said.

Joy said, "I will be up there to see her before she goes home, I want to see the baby."

Aaron and Desare' lived in Eagle River, a little town ten miles north from Anchorage, and Joy could go and help her when she needed help with the baby.

Desare' did fine and said, "I don't need any help, Grandma. I helped Mom with Donald and Larry, thanks anyway for asking." Joy found out later that Aaron was smoking pot and didn't want her to be around because she wouldn't like it at all, which is right.

Desare' got angry with Aaron because he kept smoking around the baby, and she asked him to stop but he wouldn't. She left him and found another apartment for her and the baby, Amy. She wasn't going to have Amy breathing in the fumes.

Desare' moved into an apartment close to work so she could walk to work because she didn't have a car. She asked Joy if she would babysit Amy in the evenings, and Joy agreed to. After work she would go to Desare's to sit with the baby. On Sundays Joy would take Amy to church with her. She wasn't the only grandmother with a baby there; one of the other ladies had her grandchild also. Only difference was it was Joy's great-granddaughter and Rose's granddaughter, another generation.

After a few months later, Aaron came to visit Desare'. "She is at work," Joy said.

Aaron told Joy, "I want Desare to come back to me."

Joy told him, "Aaron, you don't have a job, and you need to show some responsibility toward Desare' and Amy. She is doing fine with her job and my help with the baby, plus if you do get back together, you need to get married."

"I agree with you, Grandma, I am looking for work and haven't been able to find any," Aaron replied and added, "I better leave now, tell Desare' I was here and would like to see her as soon as she has the time. Good-bye, Grandma."

"Good-bye, Aaron, I do hope you get your life straightened out for your own good. I will tell her you were here," Joy said.

Desare' was surprised to hear that Aaron had been there and said, "I am glad I wasn't here, Grandma, I don't want to see him."

Joy said, "He wants you to go back with him. I told him he needed to go to work and be responsible enough to support a family and do what is right by you and Amy."

"Thanks, Grandma, I couldn't have said it any better," Desare' replied.

Joy continued to babysit Amy and help Desare' whenever she needed her. In the meantime, Aaron had found work and was trying to get enough money ahead to afford an apartment for them in Wasilla, where he was employed. He came to Desare's to visit her and Amy. He convinced Desare' to move out to Wasilla with him, and they would be married soon. She gave two weeks' notice to her employer that she was moving and wouldn't be working there anymore, and she started packing for the move.

Later on they made arrangements for their wedding at a small church in the vicinity of their neighborhood. Little Amy was sort of the flower girl, even though she wasn't walking. She was so cute. Desare's mother wouldn't come to the wedding because she said, "I have made another engagement with a friend of mine at the same time, and I can't break it." Desare' was very disappointed and upset with her mother.

Joy, Clark, and Darwin attended, and they were happy for Aaron and Desare' doing the right thing and getting a fresh start. They congratulated the newly wedded couple and gave them a wedding gift and told them, "Good-bye, we're going home now. Have a nice honeymoon."

Desare' gave them all big hugs and kisses and said, "Thank you all for everything."

Joy received word from Alane, Dean's sister, that their mother, Nellie, passed away. It is ironic—a new life of marriage and family occurred one day, and the next thing you know, another death. That is life, a continuous reproduction, a forever plan of God, and only He knows who, what, where, why, and when God's will be done.

Everyone kept busy with work and their regular chores throughout the rest of the year. Darwin was building another house by the Wasilla Palmer Highway and spent most of his time out there doing most of the work by himself. It was a large home, and he did all the excavating of the land to level it up; put in all the cement walls for the foundation; all the carpenter work, framing, roofing, plumbing, electrical wiring; putting in the furnace and hot-water heater, flooring, and windows—in other words, the complete house. It wasn't long before he had a buyer for the house. They were very pleased with the custom building that Darwin designs for the homes he builds, all different kinds of extras included.

Joy had to take Darwin back and forth each week because he couldn't drive. His license was taken from him for too many driving-under-the-influence tickets. It is too bad, but he just wouldn't stop drinking. He has the same attitude his father had, and no one could get it through his head that it is his habit and he is the one that has to change it—no one else can.

Another winter and spring had come and gone. Desare' was pregnant and was expecting another baby in July, and she was preparing for that happy occasion. She had potty trained Amy so she wouldn't have two children wearing diapers. There would be one and a half years between Amy and the new baby, so this would keep Desare' very busy with the two.

Clark was working at the school, and he slipped on the bleachers in the gymnastics room and injured his hip that had been injured when he was nineteen years old, and the doctor said he would have to have a hip replacement because it was a very major injury. The time was set for the operation and the time he would spend in the hospital. There was a program on the television that showed an operation just like Clark was going to have that they watched, and he said, "Are they going to do that to me?"

Joy answered, "Yes, the papers you brought home describes the same thing. Didn't your doctor advise you on the procedures?"

"He probably did, but you know my memory. I forgot most of what he said, and he gave me some papers to read over so I would know what he was going to do," Clark replied.

The next thing they had to do was check with the school insurance company to see if they were going to cover all the cost of the operation and recovery. Clark filled out the forms, and one question asked if this was "a previous injury." Clark answered it by stating he had the accident when he was nineteen, and the doctor felt he was too young to replace the ball and socket with a steel one, and he spent nine weeks in traction with it. The school insurance company said they would pay for the operation and recovery.

"What a relief, thank God. God only knows we didn't have that kind of money to pay for a major operation such as this," Joy said.

The morning came for Joy to take Clark to the hospital for the operation. It was early, and as they were walking into the hospital, there were some construction workers with a jackhammer, breaking up some cement on the sidewalk, and Joy pointed to them and, being a smart aleck, said, "Look, Clark, they are practicing before they operate on you!"

Clark replied, "Mother, I am worried enough without you trying to be funny."

"I am sorry, I was just trying to make a joke and make you relax for a while," Joy said.

He was in the operating room for a long time, and she prayed everything would go right according to the doctor's calculations. They had to replace the ball and socket of Clark's hip joint, and he would be convalescing for some time in the hospital as well as on crutches when he was able to go home.

When he arrived home, the home health care nurse came in with different articles he needed, like a chair that was electric for him to get in and out of, a high seat for the toilet, a stool for the bathtub for him to sit on, and crutches. She came three times a week to check his vitals and to see the progress he was making. She said he was a good patient and was doing fine. She eventually came only once a week for a while and then stopped because he was healing very well. Then he was able to get out and go places with his crutches without the fear of falling and injuring his hip again. He wasn't ready to drive yet, so Joy took him whenever he wanted to go anyplace.

Clark started to get restless; he had always been very active and wasn't used to just sitting around doing nothing. Even television was getting boring. One day he saw on television an advertisement that the government was lowering the interest rate for first-time home buyers, and Clark got very interested and said, "Mom, let's check into it. I have some money saved for a down payment, I should qualify for a home loan."

We got the papers to fill out to see if Clark qualified and took them to the bank. They examined them and told Clark he qualified for a loan up to $100,000 and he could start looking for a home. Clark was happy. It lifted his spirits, and he was eager to start right now.

Darwin was living with them in the apartment, and he went with them when they looked at some of the houses for sale. Because he had built so many homes, he could tell if the price was a good one or not. They looked at condos, two-floor homes, and all kinds in the price range Clark could afford. Finally the real estate man showed them this nice three-bedroom bungalow, newly painted inside and newly carpeted. It was just what he wanted. The snow was knee-deep all around the house. It was in January 1995.

Darwin went down in the crawl space to check it out to make sure it wasn't wet and to check the structural part underneath. He said, "It is dry, and it is a well-built home as far as I can see, it is worth the money they are asking for it. It is the best one we have looked at yet."

Clark said, "Yes, I want to buy it. I really like it, there are no stairs to climb, and it is so nice and clean."

The real estate man said, "It just came on the market and hadn't even been advertised yet. I knew you were looking for something like this, so I wanted to get you over here as soon as possible. We can sign the papers now if you want to."

Clark said, "I sure do, I don't want to look any longer, this is it. Thanks for calling us first. I really appreciate it." This was good timing because Joy was going on a trip soon, and she could help with packing and setting up the utilities before she left.

Joy had made plans to go down in the lower forty-eight because she retired from her job and wanted to take a sabbatical, to just go and travel. She had to pack her things separate for her trip and pack everything in the apartment for when Clark and Darwin moved into the new place. She thought, *I will be coming back to a new home, that's so nice.*

Joy wanted to drive back to Alaska on the Alcan Highway because people asked her if she had ever driven on that highway. They mentioned how beautiful the trip was.

Thinking about it, she made up her mind to drive back that way even if she had to do it by herself. She told everyone who asked, "I am counting on God. I am sure God will provide someone to drive back with me."

Joy had made arrangements to ship her car down on the ferry to Seattle ten days before she left. The car would be there when she arrived, and she could pick it up at the dock. Her boss, Lawrence, knew the owner, and he gave Joy a discount on the price.

Gale arranged to come to Seattle and drive with Joy through Washington, Oregon, and California. She planned to meet her at the airport and book a hotel room close by before they went to the dock and picked up the car. They needed a good meal and a good night's rest before they started on their long journey south.

Joy said, "It is so good to see you and to be able to spend some time with you alone, it has been a long time. I am so happy Vern let you come to meet me and drive with me to your home in Arizona."

Gale replied, "I had to beg him, he doesn't like me to go any place by myself. And I told him I wanted to come and help you drive through the California mountains, they are bad in the wintertime."

"We are going to enjoy it, sightseeing all the way, stopping whenever we want to," Joy stated.

The scenery through Washington and Oregon was so beautiful, trees and wildflowers like a picture painted. It was painted by God; only He could create such beauty. Going into California when they came to the mountains, it was so foggy. Joy told Gale, "I can't see anything, not even the lines on the edge of the road. I am afraid to drive. I will pull over and pray we aren't too close to the mountain edge."

"I will drive, Mom, I can see pretty good. If I can't, I will pull over and wait for the fog to lift. You pray to God to keep us safe and to lift the fog soon," Gale reassured Joy.

Finally the fog lifted, and they were well on their way now heading for the redwood forest in California. They saw the large ancient trees and their surroundings. This was so different than anything Joy or Gale had ever seen.

It was a beautiful day for the trip, and they decided to get a place to stay for the night because they were both very tired.

The next morning, they ate breakfast and then started on their journey through California down the highway and crossing the San Francisco bridge following Highway 5 for miles. Taking turns driving made it easier on both of them. Gale had been in California when Bruce was stationed there, but she didn't get to see much of the state except around Monterey and Salinas, which was near his base. So this was a treat for her to see more of the state. It was so much fun spending time together and relaxing along the trip, just going where they wanted to go and seeing sights neither of them had ever seen. They had an ice cooler in the car and made sandwiches for their lunches and snacks, but they would find a motel to sleep at, and then they would go out for dinner. That would get them to bed early so they could rise early and be on their way before traffic got too heavy.

Once, the car wasn't sounding right, so they stopped to have it checked, and sure enough, it had to be fixed, so they waited until it was ready to go.

Joy said, "Thank God it was in town where we could get to a station, we could have been out in the countryside, and no one around to help us."

"You better believe it, Mom, people out here aren't as friendly as they are where we come from, besides, I would be a little afraid, wouldn't you?"

"Yes, I would," Joy answered.

Mile after mile they traveled, enjoying the scenery and each other's company until they would decide to stop and get a motel room and have a good hot meal.

They decided to go see the Grand Canyon because neither of them had ever seen it. Gale had been in Arizona for years and never had a chance to go see it. Amazing is what it is. Words can't describe it. A person has to see it in order to appreciate the beauty of it. Their journey was about to come to an end. They would leave here and go to Tucson to Gale's house. She was getting lonesome for her children and to be home in her own bed. She had been gone almost a week; that is the most time she had ever been away from them.

"It is good to see you all. You have grown so big and are good little helpers for your mom," Joy said and hugged them all. Her heart was feeling so loving.

Joy knew a missionary couple living in Nogales on the Arizona border, and she wanted to go see them before she left Arizona. She called them to see if they would be home and asked for their address. They were happy to hear from her and said it would be nice to see Joy again. Their family lived on the same block as Joy and her family. In fact, her boys went to school with Joy's sons. Martin's eldest son, Reed, was the missionary she was going to see. Angel Marie wanted to go with Joy, and she thought that would be good to have her go along with her.

It was good to see the Blakes once again. They took Joy and Angel Marie across the border to Nogales on the Mexican side. It was interesting to see how the unfortunate people lived in large boxes and shacks. Joy never realized people had to live like that.

And Angel Marie said, "Grandma, I will never complain about the house we live in or the food we have to eat. Those people are really poor."

Reed remarked, "Yes, they are, and that is why we are here to preach the gospel and help them as much as we can with food and clothing."

Returning from the trip, they had coffee and renewed old acquaintances, and Joy told them about living in Alaska and her job.

She asked, "Martin, Do you know where Grace and Sean Atkins are? I haven't heard from them in years and have wondered whatever happened to them."

Martin said, "Yes, they are in Tucson and have been there for over ten years."

"Oh my word, I have been coming to Tucson for a long time, and I didn't know it. If you have their telephone number, I will call them as soon as I get back. Thank you so much for your hospitality, it has been so good to see you all again to see the mission work you are doing," Joy said.

"What a blessing to see them and to get Grace and Sean's phone number. I am so thankful for God's love and guidance. 'Trust in the Lord with all your heart; and lean not on your own understanding. In all your ways acknowledge Him, and He will direct your path'" (Proverbs 3:5 and 6), Joy told Angel Marie.

As soon as they returned to Gale's, Joy phoned the Atkins. "Hello, this is Joy, do you remember me?"

"Why, yes, I do, this is sure a surprise. Where are you?" Sean answered.

"I am here in Tucson with my daughter, and I got your number from the Blakes when we went down to Nogales to visit them today. Is Grace there?" Joy asked.

"No, she is at work, and boy, she will be surprised too. I am not going to tell her you called. I will give her your phone number and tell her to call. She will be surprised when you answer," Sean said.

Joy said, "It will be so good to see you once again."

The phone rang and Joy answered it. "Hello, who is this?" Grace asked.

"This is Joy Godman, Martin Blake gave me your phone number, and I just had to call."

They talked for a while, and then Grace asked, "Can you and Gale come over here for lunch?"

"Yes, we can, where do you live and what time do you want us to come?" Joy asked.

Gale knew where to find the street and arrived on time, with great anticipation to see Grace and Sean. What a reunion it was; hugs and kisses were given, and questions galore were asked.

Joy told them, "I am living in Alaska, and after retiring, I needed to take a sabbatical, and I put my car on the ferry, and Gale met me in Seattle, and we drove down here. And I am going to drive the Alcan Highway back to Alaska alone, unless God provides for someone to go along with me."

"We want to go with you! We were going last year with Sean's brother and his wife, but he passed away, and we didn't go, but we really wanted to," Grace exclaimed.

"Really? That would be great. I am going to Donald's in Colorado and then to Michigan, then back home. I had planned on meeting Angel at the Seattle airport to come too."

"We could make arrangements to meet you in Seattle, and we will bring Angel with us and pay for her airfare," Grace said.

"PRAISE GOD! He is so good and provides for me always. I didn't worry about who He would provide, I just knew in my heart He would."

Grace said, "God knows ahead of time what we need, and He works everything out for all those who trust and obey His word. We are God's children, and He loves us eternally."

"I am so happy I went down to see Frank and Lacy, God led me," Joy told her.

Joy stayed at Gale's for two weeks and planned on driving to Colorado to see Donald and Sherry and spend time with them. She would be driving by herself from here on.

She said her good-byes and headed for New Mexico on Highway 10 and continued until she hit Highway 25, in Las Cruces. She had brought many Christian tapes with her to listen to as she drove along and listened to the Christian radio programs. It was peaceful and relaxing to be away from responsibilities. She had so many for so long and now was relieved and on her way just driving along, enjoying the scenery and the solitude.

She had an ice chest with groceries for snacks, milk, sandwiches, etc. At lunchtime she stopped by a fast-food place and used the restroom, then parked in the back and ate her lunch. When it was getting to dinnertime, she found a motel and got a room for the night.

Sometimes she found a restaurant to eat dinner, and other times she fixed something and ate in her room. She left really early in the mornings. Her car had Alaska license plates on, and she was careful because anyone seeing a single woman from that far away might be tempted to be harmful, and she didn't want to take any chances.

Stopping at rest areas, she made sure someone else was in the bathroom because she had heard some weird stories about women being attacked in them or their purse stolen by a thief reaching over the door and taking the purse from the hook on the door.

The miles flew by, and she was passing through Albuquerque, still on Highway 25 and a lot of traffic. Joy decided to find a motel and get a good night's sleep before she drove any farther. She remembered Albuquerque because that was where they had wait to pay the ticket Dean got for speeding. At least they went to a campground, and the boys got to go fishing at Whitewaters Lake off the cliffs; it was fun for the boys. That was the past.

*Oh! I thank God for my freedom to go where I want to when I want to. What a privilege, just to name one, we here in the United States have,* Joy thought as she drove on.

She continued on Highway 25 up past the border into Colorado and looked for a motel because she was getting tired and hungry. This should be her last stop before reaching Colorado Springs, where Donald and Sherry were going to meet her. She phoned them to let them know where she was, and they told her about how long it would take her to get there.

She found the place to meet them and was happy to see them. Hugs, kisses, and hellos were said and done. They ate dinner and then was on their way to their home up in the mountains, forty-five miles from Colorado Springs and close to eight thousand feet above sea level. Talk about beautiful scenery—this was it.

This was a great two weeks spent with them going sightseeing and just staying home and enjoying each other's company. Time really passed by fast, it seemed, as it always does whenever you are enjoying yourselves as they had been doing.

Joy had a special day she wanted to get to Michigan for and didn't know how long it would take her to get there. Donald knew how long because he had driven it many times before and gave her an estimated time. She told Donald and Sherry, "I am going to a fifty-year wedding anniversary party for George and Pamela Jenkins, and I don't want to miss it. They don't know I am coming, so it will be a big surprise for them."

Donald and Sherry said, "Give them our blessings, tell all their children we said hello."

"The Jenkinses were our closest friends and were always there when we needed them, no matter what time of day or night, they would give their shirt off their back," Donald said.

Another long journey was ahead for Joy, but she was anxious and ready to get started. Driving from Florissant, the town where Donald lives, to Denver, then taking Highway 76 to Highway 80 across Nebraska, Iowa, into Illinois and on to Bruce, Indiana, then to South Bend, then taking I-94 into Michigan, getting closer to Logan, her hometown.

She got there the day before the party and was able to have a good rest and be ready to see all the Jenkins family. George and Pamela's seven children and all their grandchildren will be in attendance. They couldn't believe their eyes when Joy walked in. She hadn't told anyone she was coming; it was a complete surprise.

This was a gala affair with so many people Joy hadn't seen for years. She has been in Alaska for twelve years now. They all asked many questions about many different things. The little children asked her if she lived in an igloo and if it was dark all day. Joy explained that Anchorage was a modern city, and in the winter the daylight hours were only about four to four and a half hours, then they get longer the closer it gets to summer, on Summer solstice,

June 21, when the sun reaches its northernmost point on the celestial sphere. The sun shines until midnight. From then on, the daylight hours begin to get shorter until winter solstice, December 22. When it reaches its southernmost point, it's dark until about 10:30 AM, then it is light until about 3:00 PM.

Joy pointed out that she never knew about the solstice until she came to Alaska. The first snowfall on the mountains is called termination dust; that was something she hadn't known. She told about the moose and bears roaming the neighborhoods and streets in Anchorage, just walking along minding their own business, finding something to eat.

# CHAPTER TWELVE

## *FAMILY AFFAIR*

Joy had many friends and relatives to stay with for the month she would be here, and she had contacted them in advance and set the dates according to their time available.

Teressa Smart, her friend from her former employer, wanted her to stay with her, and then she could come and go whenever and wherever she wanted to, a base, so to speak. Teressa wanted to take Joy out to dinner and asked her where she wanted to go.

Joy said, "You know my favorite place to eat is at the hot dog place. I get hungry for those hot dogs, no one in Alaska can make them like they do here."

Teressa answered, "Joy, I will take you to a real nice place to eat, but you want hot dogs. OK, that is where we will go. I like them too."

There was an American Business Women's meeting that week. All the ladies were happy to see Joy again. It had been a while since she was at one of their meetings. They asked Joy to give a little speech about her life in Alaska, to tell about her job and family.

Visiting family was great. Clarice, her sister, arranged a family reunion at her daughter's new home. Many attended, and all had a wonderful time catching up on the news.

"Our family is scattered all over now, and I am so thankful that Clarice and Christina planned this reunion, so I didn't have to drive many miles to each one's home. I have driven a long ways to get here, but it has been a wonderful trip so far," Joy stated.

Clarice said, "Joy, this is the least we could all do, you thought of us and came all the way back here to visit us when you could have gone anywhere on your trip."

Debbie Marie and her fiancé, Kirk Velmer, were married. Joy attended the wedding and was happy to see her and her sons Alan and Cody and also Misty, Lacy, her mother, and James, their stepfather, and their grandmothers. It had been some time since Joy had seen them all on Lacy's side of the family. It was a very pleasant time.

Louis, one of Joy's brothers, and his lady friend, Joan, didn't come to the reunion, so Joy decided to go over to Battle Creek and visit them while she was in Michigan. She stayed with them for three days. Louis wasn't well; he had to have oxygen for twenty-four hours every day, and he couldn't walk very far without getting out of breath.

Louis and Joy had always been very close and helped each other whenever they needed it, one way or the other. He had been married to Joan once. They divorced and he married Virginia, a lady somewhat older then he was. They were married until she passed away, and Louis was single for a while until he decided to look up Joan again. She wouldn't marry him, but they lived together. She was a big help to him; he really needed her because of his bad health, and he didn't like living alone.

After leaving Louis's, she went over to see Laurie, her niece living in Battle Creek also. They had a great time visiting and going sightseeing at different memorial places and parks. Laurie never married and was a retired schoolteacher. She was a special-education teacher with a master's degree, devoting her life to her work.

Joy's friend Esther Street lives in St. Joseph, and whenever Joy is in Michigan, she notifies her friends in LaGrange, Indiana, and they make arrangements to meet in Battle Creek for dinner—Jerry Hougton, Rose Storm, and Ester. Laurie went with Joy because she knew them and liked seeing them also. They too are schoolteachers.

Years ago Ester was in college and met Jerry and Rose, and they have been friends ever since. Joy used to go to Adrian College and pick Ester up to go home, and the other girls would ride along. Louise, Ester's mother, had to work and couldn't go. Joy got to know them well. They all wanted her to be their dorm mother. They all graduated and became teachers and eventually married and had families. This was always a happy reunion between them all, getting together whenever Joy was in Michigan. That was a long drive for them to come, but they wanted to see her.

The next day after breakfast, she told Laurie, "Time is passing, and I have decided to go back to Logan to visit with some of the friends I haven't seen yet. I hate to leave. It has been so peaceful and restful with you."

Laurie replied, "Joy, I understand, it seems like time just gets away faster than we want it to. I am so happy you got to stay this long with me."

*Some more memories stored in my mind to remind me while I drive all those miles I have ahead of me going to Seattle,* Joy thought while driving back to Logan.

After arriving back at Teressa's, Joy needed to check her list to see who she had planned to visit next. She had a timetable to follow, one she had written to her friends, and they would be expecting her.

Jessie Porter was her next person to visit. She and her husband Douglas had lived in Alaska for many years and moved back to Logan after Jessie's mother passed away. It was always good to get together with them. They liked to play cards in the evenings. During the day, they relaxed and just talked about old times and what was happening in their lives now. Joy stayed for three days with them.

Jessie lived on the same street Joy did before she was married. The neighbors beside her mother's house were the Andrews. Joy babysat them when they were small, and now so many years later, they are still friends. Their mother, Lois, passed away, and Mary, the eldest, has the house now, and she always invited Joy to stay with her a few days. This was on Joy's schedule also, and it was the right time for her to go over there. It was good to see everyone and just visit with them, remembering their younger days in the old neighborhood. Mary has a brother, Randy, and two sisters, Martha and Darlene. Darlene married and moved to Canada; she has a family too now. Randy married a girl named Martha; they have a son. Mary and Martha stayed single. Martha adopted two little boys. Their mother, Lois, was responsible for Joy going to church and leading her to Christ. The Andrews family are all Christians, attend church regularly, and love the Lord.

"It is always uplifting whenever I visit your family, Mary, you all love the Lord with all your heart and soul and your neighbors as yourselves. A wonderful example and witness of Christ in your life to everyone you come in contact with," Joy told Mary.

They also liked to play cards and other games in the evening while enjoying each other's company, talking and laughing at some of their mistakes they all made years ago.

Joy went over to the George Johnston Home and got her brother Carlyle to come over to Mary's and visit. He liked the Andrews. Randy was always good to him whenever he saw Carlyle at the grocery store where he hung out. Joy tried to include Carlyle in her visits with people he knew. He usually got restless and didn't want to stay long. The home where Carlyle lived was a place for older men who were unable to care for themselves. All the help there were nice and very kind to him, understanding his condition.

*The time spent here in Michigan was pleasant and relaxing being with family and friends,* Joy thought as she was preparing to leave to go to Seattle and meet Grace, Sean, and Angel Marie.

She said all her good-byes and was on her way for the long trip ahead of her. She was prepared for it knowing the weather in Alaska would still be cold when they arrived. The car had been serviced, her ice chest filled, and maps placed on the front seat for directions. It had been three months since she left Alaska, and she was anxious to get back. She loved it there; it was home to her now.

The miles seemed to go by fast as she drove on Highway I-94 to Chicago, Illinois, then to Highway 90 across Wisconsin, Minnesota, Iowa, South Dakota, Wyoming, Montana, and on to Seattle, Washington. Arriving a day ahead, she stayed in a motel to rest up before she would meet Grace, Sean, and Angel Marie at the Sea-Tac airport.

What a happy reunion—hugs and kisses were plenty, and everyone wanted to talk at once, telling about their flight. When Joy saw all their luggage, she thought, *Oh my goodness, where am I going to put all of that?* Taking it to the car, Sean said, "I don't think we will have any problem getting it all in with rearranging it all."

They did get it all in, putting the ice chest on the floor in the back. Angel Marie could sit in the seat and put her feet on the ice chest and the soft bags would be placed beside her.

"We are ready to get started, shall we go outside of Seattle and find a room? It will be easier to start out going through Canada after a good night's sleep," Sean suggested.

Yes was the unanimous answer. Everyone was looking forward to driving through Canada. Joy had a letter stating permission for Angel Marie to be traveling with her.

What a glorious time they all had talking, laughing, and singing Christian songs, driving up the Alcan Highway, so beautiful and breathtaking all the way. They took turns driving.

*What an answer to prayer. I could have never fathomed God would provide for Grace and Sean to travel with me, I didn't even know they were in Tucson,* Joy pondered.

The tourist season hadn't officially opened yet, and motel managers didn't charge the full price, and they were very gracious to them all. The road wasn't as bad as some people told them it would be—rough and bumpy. The road crew kept it pretty smooth. Finally, they were in Alaska and well on their way to Anchorage, going to the house Clark had bought in March and anxiously wanting to get there to shower and rest. Grace and Sean's sister-in-law, Loretta, would be coming in a few days to spend some time here also. She had planned to come the year before with Grace and Sean, but her husband passed away. They invited her to come and see Alaska even if she had to take an airplane. They all had planned to go to Homer, fishing with a relative, and Joy told them to take her car rather than rent one. Sean said, "I am not going to fish, I don't like to fish."

Well, after they got there, Sean got a license and went on the big fishing boat, had a great time, and caught the most fish. He was a happy camper and decided fishing was really great. Grace and Loretta teased him about being so sure he wasn't going to fish. They had a great time taking them all sightseeing and playing games in the evenings.

They were all so grateful for being able to come to Alaska after the disappointment of Sean's brother passing away. They took them to the airport and said their good-byes. On the way back from the airport, Joy thought, *I thank God for friends like that.*

Angel and Lisa, Ester's granddaughter, became friends and spent time with Ester in their upper apartment, showing them how to sew and make different things when they weren't playing outside with some of the other neighborhood children.

Joy got word from Bernie, Gale's eldest son, telling her his girlfriend, Hilda, was pregnant with his child. She already had a two-year-old boy named Bernie. They also lived in Florida, and Bernie worked for his dad, doing flooring installments, carpets, and tiling.

Gale left Vern and came to Alaska with the other two girls, Elisabeth and Renee. They were having marital problems, and Gale couldn't take it any longer. Joy was happy they came because she didn't want Gale to go through what she had been through. Gale eventually found a job and an apartment not too far from Joy's. She filed for a divorce and was able to get help from the social services for her expenses.

Joy was notified the baby was born on August 25, 1995, and her name is Whisper Marie and was a good and healthy baby. Joy sent some girl baby clothes to Hilda for Whisper and a baby book to keep a record of her growth and pictures. This would be Gale's first grandchild, and Joy's fifth great-grandchild.

Holidays were so much fun: getting together with Darwin's family for the celebrations and his children meeting Gale's girls, getting to know them. Rose Ann and Angel became good friends, having much in common. Rose Ann was only one year older than Angel. Elisabeth and Renee went to the Creek Side School not far from Joy's. Sometimes she would go pick them up and have them come over for dinner and play games. They didn't like the cold and snow; they were used to the Arizona sunshine. Gale didn't like it either. She had met a man and was dating him. The girls didn't like him.

A new year was here 1996, and Gale was notified she had to appear in divorce court in February to finalize the divorce from Vern. Arrangements were made for her to go to Arizona. She would meet Grace Atkins to go with her for spiritual support and comfort. The girls came and stayed with Joy while Gale was gone, and she took them to school. Angel Marie went to Clark Middle School, and she took the bus.

The judge gave Gale the divorce and granted Vern permission to have the girls for all the holidays, and they would divide the cost of transportation between each of them. Gale was very distraught; she cried after the case was dismissed from the courtroom. She had loved Vern more than she had ever loved any other man, but they had so many fights and arguments, and if one didn't land in jail, the other one did. She arrived back in Anchorage and was happy to see the girls and explained what happened and how they would be able to go see their dad on holidays.

Easter was coming, and Gale made arrangements for the girls, Elisabeth and Renee, to go see their dad. They were kind of happy to go see him and their grandma, aunts, and uncles on Vern's side of the family. Angel went along so the girls wouldn't be afraid. At the airport, they got on the plane, and Renee kept crying and didn't want to go without her mother. Angel got off the plane and said, "Renee wouldn't go without Mom."

Joy said, "Gale, I will buy your ticket so you can go with them."

"I have some of my clothes still down there that I can wear, so I should be OK, thanks, Mom, you are always there whenever I need you." She boarded the plane, and they were thankful they had a seat for her. Joy thought, *Thank You, God, You are the one who is always there when I need You.*

When Gale came back to Anchorage, Joy knew the minute she saw her she had gone back to Vern. Joy could see it in her eyes, but she didn't say anything to Gale. It wasn't long before Gale confessed to Joy and told her she was going to move back to Arizona as soon as she could afford it.

"I knew you were going to the day you got off of the plane. I could see it in your eyes, and you've acted different since you got back," Joy remarked.

"Mom, I love Vern, and he said, 'We will move somewhere away from my family so we will have more privacy and won't interfere with our marriage,'" Gale told Joy.

After moving back to Arizona, Gale and the family drove to several different places to check out whether they wanted to live there or not until they reached a little town called Show Low, Arizona. They rented a place and settled in so the children could register for school. Vern had retired from work on account of his back problems. They started to attend church regularly and changed their lives around from their former lifestyle. They liked it in this area because it was so much cooler in the summertime and not too cold in the winter.

Debbie Marie divorced Mitchell. She met Kent; they lived together for a while. He liked to do things with her boys like motorbike riding. They went to the races and things males like do. Debbie Marie married Kent, and they had a little boy born on Christmas; they named him Rodney. This was her third son, and she thinks she is ready to quit having children now. They live in a small town called Preman, about twenty-five miles from Logan, close to her mother's home in Springdale.

Joy received word that her brother Franklin had passed away, from his ex-wife, Grace.

She said, "He didn't want a funeral and to just have him cremated. He died on the twenty-ninth. So I had it done, he had left a will a while ago naming me as the heir."

Joy said, "Grace, how did it happen?"

She said, "He was in his car and had a heart attack, and they couldn't revive him."

Joy thanked her for calling and letting her know. She thought about a letter Franklin had sent to her in October, around her birthday on the eighth. He wrote, "I have made a will and had it notarized, naming you heir of everything I have."

*Maybe he changed his mind and left it all to Grace. It is too late to go to Michigan now if she has already handled everything,* Joy continued thinking.

New Year's Day 1997, Joy received a phone call. "I am Janice Van Dorn, a friend of your brother Franklin. Did you know you were the sole heir of Franklin's estate? He came to me to notarize the will and have it recorded, so I know you should be the one to have everything. I went to the mobile home to put a lock on it, and Grace was there going through everything and taking things. I told her to get out, she had no business taking things that don't belong to her. I work for a lawyer friend of Franklin."

"Jan, Grace called me and told me Franklin died and she had him cremated and there would be no funeral for him and there would be no need for me to come. So I decided there would be no use for me to go to Michigan," Joy explained.

Janice said, "You better get down here as fast as you can, Joy, before she tries to get in the trailer again. When can you come?"

"I will be there as soon as I can, I will call you and let you know," she said.

Joy called and got a seat on the midnight flight because she had an emergency. They told her to have the funeral director write a letter stating about her brother's death and she needed to be there for legal purposes. Joy had never moved as fast as she did that day. Thank goodness Clark was home to take her to the airport. She told him, "I really don't know how long I will be there, but I will call you and let you know what is going on and will keep in touch. Thanks for being home to take me."

Joy's friend Mary and her sister Martha met her at the Detroit Metro Airport, and they were happy to see her, although her being in Michigan wasn't under good circumstances.

Joy explained, "I got a call from Franklin's friend, and she gave me information that I need to be here, so here I am. I will explain more of it later. I am pretty tired, I haven't had any sleep since the night before last."

After a little rest, Joy called Janice Van Dorn and set up a time when they could get together and go over everything she had to do. Then Joy proceeded to explain to Mary and Martha what was going on and what she had to do.

She met Janice, and she explained, "Joy, we will go out to the trailer and let you look at the remaining articles left after Grace removed some things. Then you will need to go to the Social Security office and check out about Franklin's death benefits."

They looked everything over in the trailer, and Joy said, "It looks like I am going to have a lot of stuff to get rid of. I can't take it back to Alaska with me. I will see if Louis wants to come over here and get what he wants."

Janice said, "There is some jewelry missing. Franklin had a large diamond ring and other expensive things that are not here. You better go over to Grace's and ask her about it."

Joy called Louis and asked, "Do you want any of Franklin's things in the trailer? If you do, I will go out there with you because Janice gave me the keys and said it is all mine, also she said Franklin had a big diamond ring and some other things including cash, he always has a wad of cash in his pocket. Will you go over to Grace's with me?"

Louis said, "I will go with you. I will pick you up, and we will go see Grace. Call her and let her know you are coming." Joy called her and set a time to see her.

Grace wasn't very happy when she saw Louis, she didn't like him, and you could tell it by her attitude toward him. She invited them in and offered them something to drink.

Joy told her, "I didn't know about the will until Janice called and told me, it surprised me, Grace. He had sent me a letter last year around my birthday, telling me what he did, but I never heard anymore from him, so I thought he changed it and gave it all to you."

Louis asked, "What about his wallet and rings he was wearing, do you have them?"

She got up and got his wallet and some other jewelry, but not the diamond rings.

Grace said, "He had been coming here for some time and told me he wanted to be cremated, so that is what I had done, and the funeral director gave me these things, but no rings." She was tearful talking about Franklin; they seemed to be closer than they had been. He divorced her several years before and married a much younger woman, and she divorced him also, and he had been alone for some time.

136

Joy and Louis decided to leave and go to his house to talk things over about selling the car, trailer, and contents. They found out it was hard to get rid of an older trailer, but Louis knew someone who wanted it. It had to be removed from the trailer park lot because they wouldn't let anyone rent it. It needed a lot of repair work done.

Going to the Social Security office, which was located downtown on Michigan Avenue, the next day, it was so cold and windy. Joy thought, *It isn't this cold in Alaska.* Then she had to go to see the funeral director about a letter verifying Franklin's death so she could present it to the airlines for her discount.

After visiting relatives and friends, she needed to get back home to work. This was a busy time of the year, getting the books balanced and ready for the CPA to figure Lawrence's tax return. And besides, Clark and Darwin were happy to have Joy back home; they missed her presence and her cooking.

Joy decided to buy a different car. Lawrence's friend was going to buy a new Mercury and was selling his 1988 Mercury. He asked Lawrence if he wanted it, and he said no.

Lawrence asked, "Joy, do you want to buy it? It has only 28,000 miles on it."

She looked at it and drove it around the block, and she was pleased with it and decided to buy it. She thought, *I can sell my car, and with the money from Franklin, I can pay cash for it. This car will last me a long time.* The car was in mint condition, just like new.

Janet, a friend from Springdale now living in Alaska, was getting married to a man named Edward Darling. Joy and the family were invited to go and celebrate with them. It was a May wedding. Darwin's children went also: Rose Ann, Donald, and Larry. They had never been to a big wedding like that and were absorbing most of what went on.

"It is good to take children places to learn there is more to life than just their own little world and how to act around other people," Joy told the children.

They agreed and said unanimously, "That is right, Grandma, we had lots of fun."

Anchorage has a "Most Eligible Bachelor" contest every year in the fall, and Clark read about it and decided he would like to attend and try and see if he had a chance or not. He filled the form out, sent it in, and waited to see if he qualified to enter. He received a letter saying he would be able to enter. He rented a tuxedo, dressed all up, and went to the contest, not knowing what was ahead. He did know the men were auctioned off to the highest-bidding woman as they took their turn on the podium.

Joy thought, *Clark has come a long ways from being quiet and not very brave doing things like this. He does look handsome in the tuxedo though.*

He returned home later and said, "I had a good time, but there were a lot of other men there. Some were getting high bids and the rest of us of as high. The money goes to some charitable cause, but I don't know which one, oh well, it was fun while it lasted."

In November, Joy received word that Grandma Pearl Godman passed away. She had been in a nursing home for several years with Alzheimer's disease and didn't recognize anyone whenever they visited her. She was a very gracious lady, doing things for others, and so friendly toward everyone.

Sometime after Dad Godman had her admitted, he was discouraged and despondent and didn't want to live any longer without her, so he quit taking care of himself and gave up wanting to live. He passed away March of 1989, quite a while before Pearl did.

"This year had been another full year of events taking place in the family, never a dull moment, some good memories and some somber moments. Life is full of the unexpected that comes with it, if we like it or not, we have to accept it and go on with life. Count many of God's blessings that life brings and they outweigh any others that come along.

# CHAPTER THIRTEEN

## AN ANGEL DEPARTS

The holidays had passed, and now a new year begins in our lives. As they add up and we have faith believing only God knows what is ahead for any of us, Joy thought as she meditated and prayed a silent prayer to God, as she frequently does, keeping the personal relationship with Jesus Christ. She believes, like the song says, "As I walk through the garden alone, He walks with me and He talks with me and He tells me I am His own." It is the commitment with contentment that she feels in her heart, knowing her faith in God sustains her through the trials and tribulations that come along.

Joy had a friend named Madeline she visited frequently, and they had some long talks about each of their past experiences and enjoyed each other's company. When Madeline was ill and failing, Joy spent many hours with her; sometimes all night because she was afraid to stay alone. When Joy couldn't stay, Clark would stay with her.

A man named Royce asked Madeline if he could park his camper in her driveway for a while, and she told him just for a while because the city ordinance wouldn't allow it for long. He tried to con her into letting him take care of her finances, and she wouldn't have any part of that. He owed her some money he had borrowed to buy a truck and was asking her for more. Besides, he wasn't paying for the electricity he was using in his camper.

Madeline told Joy about it and said she wanted him to move his motor home out of there, and he just ignored her. He told her he has no place to move it.

Madeline made an appointment with the doctor and asked Joy if she would take her. Joy agreed and planned on the date that Madeline was supposed to go.

Madeline asked, "Joy, will you stay here all night because I don't feel well, and I want you to do something for me tomorrow morning."

After breakfast Madeline asked, "Joy, will you to go to the office supply house and get some forms to write out my will? I trust you, Joy, and I need to get this done. My son lives in Washington, DC, but he is so busy with work and family he can't seem to find time to come up here."

After purchasing the forms, Joy sat down and followed Madeline's instructions. She named her son and grandchildren and told Joy to put her name on there with $50,000 beneficiary. Joy was stunned and told Madeline, "Madeline, you don't need to do that, I am your friend, and I have been here for you because I love you as a friend."

After discussing this matter for some time, Madeline insisted to at least put in $25,000. After filling out the form, she got Madeline's approval and signature and said, "Madeline, I will take this to Lawrence's lawyer, Mr. Neilson, and make sure everything is all right, then we'll have it recorded. He may not charge me anything, if he does, it won't be much."

Joy humbly said, "Thank you, Madeline, you have been my friend for years, and I do appreciate what you are doing for me. It is a most generous thing for you to do."

Mr. Neilson looked the will over and said, "I believe everything is in order. I will have my secretary notarize it and make copies for Madeline. Joy, she must really like you to give you that much money."

Joy replied, "She wanted to give me twice that much, and I told her no! She insisted that I at least take that amount."

The time had come to take Madeline to the doctor for a checkup; therefore, Joy stayed with her all night so she could help her get ready. She was having trouble keeping her balance. She was such a gracious lady, so prim and proper for many years, and now it was hard for her to dress herself properly. Joy hadn't realized this until she started staying with her nights. Clark always mowed her lawn and did errands for her all summer.

Joy went into the doctor's office with her and explained to him how she hadn't been feeling very good lately, forgetting things like taking her pills when she should, etc. The doctor examined her and talked to her about different things. He had been her doctor for many years and knew her very well. Afterward he wanted to talk to Joy.

He said, "I believe Madeline has dementia and also starting to get some Alzheimer's disease and will need twenty-four-hour care, do you have her son's number to call him and let him know? And if he has any questions, please have him call me."

"Yes, she has it by her telephone stand. I will call him as soon as we get back to her house, Doctor," Joy answered.

Clancy, Madeline's son, said, "Thank you for letting me know. I will be there as soon as I can, I have to make arrangements at work. Will you be able to stay with Mother until I get there?"

"Yes I will, she needs someone to be with her all the time the doctor said," Joy replied.

It was over a week before Clancy got to Anchorage. The job he was doing had to be completed before he could leave. He apologized to Joy and thanked her and Clark for helping his mother. He said, "I know you and Clark have helped Mom for some time now, and I am so glad you called me and let me know, especially about Royce being here too."

Joy and Clark helped Clancy pack everything, and Clark did a lot of yard work as well. He took things Clancy didn't want to the dump and helped Clancy take boxes to be mailed, things he wanted to keep. He asked them if there was anything they would like, they could have it. Clancy sold her furniture and put the house up for sale.

It was hard to say good-bye to Madeline, knowing they would never see her again.

Clancy said, "We have an excellent elderly care home for Mother in Ponca City, Oklahoma. I reserved a place for her before I came so she will have a place to stay."

Joy made plans to go to Michigan to see family and friends. She hasn't been there since she had to take care of Franklin's business after his death. Laurie picked Joy up at the Chicago airport and drove to Battle Creek. The traffic on the way was congested, and it was raining, and it took a long time to get there. Laurie was exhausted by the time they reached her home as well as Sue, her friend, and Joy.

"Thank You, Lord, for keeping us safe and getting us here in one piece."

Darla, Laurie's mother, came over to Battle Creek, and they all went to the Cereal City for a look at all the buildings. Cereal's national headquarters is a huge one surrounded by beautiful flower gardens with paths leading to the different interesting places. Inside the factory, they saw how the cereal goes on a conveyer belt to each operation to complete the packaging process. It was amazing to watch, especially the different kinds of cereal, starting from beginning to the end.

They visited the large statues commemorating the people who escaped the South from slavery and the statues of people entering in a part of the

Underground Railroad. This was an eye-opener of just what these people had to go through for their freedom from slavery. They spent the whole day there because it was many acres of land all around to walk if they wanted to see everything, and they did. Joy had lived in Michigan for fifty-five years and had never seen this before. It was amazing to see. Thanks to Laurie, she has seen it.

Louis, her brother, lived in Battle Creek also, and Joy called to let him know she was coming over. She had written to him that she would be there at this time, and he would be expecting her. They had planned on taking Joy to the air balloon show there in Battle Creek, and they went the next day. They saw hundreds of balloons in the air, many colors, patterns, shapes, and sizes—what a sight! Something else Joy had never seen before—she was getting to see so many different sights and enjoyed them all very much.

Louis and Joan weren't planning to go to the reunion at Christina's because it was hard for Louis to travel that far from home. He was on oxygen and tired out too easy. It had been nice staying with them a couple of days, talking about old times and memories. Laurie came over to Louis's and picked Joy up to go to Christina's to stay for a while.

Plans had been made to go to Carlson for a reunion with family members, those that were still alive and available. It is always good to be with family, catching up on all the news, the newly born since the last time together, and to fellowship with each other.

Christina, Clarice's daughter, had a new home, and there was plenty of room in her garage to set up tables for the meals and a big yard for the children to run and play in.

There were many hellos, hugs, and kisses from everyone. It was good to see them all. Elizabeth and Jason Winters, Joy's cousins; Phillip and Shirley, Clarice's son and his wife; Laurie, Clarice's daughter, and her family; Christina and her son Arnie and his girl; Carlyle, Joy's brother who lives in Logan; Clarice and Richard; Laurie; and Joy—from the young to the elderly attending and enjoying the beautiful, warm sunny day.

Clarice asked, "Joy, are you going to stay here with us for a few days?"

"Yes, I had planned on it. Laurie will take Ernie with her when she takes Darla home."

"That will work out fine, then you can drive Christina's car. She said you could use it while you were here to save you from renting a car when you go to Logan for your visits with your friends there," Clarice replied.

"It is good to be with the family, those who usually attend because some are getting older, and we never know how long any of us will be here on earth, God only knows. We can at least spend some time together even if it is only once a year or so," Joy said.

Christina's home is beautiful. She personally planned and decorated it the way she wanted it. She had a guest room for Joy; it was homey and comfortable next to the bathroom that was decorated with windmills. Joy stayed there for four days and nights.

The drive to Logan was pleasant. Joy meditated and thought about the coming days she would be spending with her friends. *It is nice to have so many friends to visit and stay with. I guess I will go see Teressa first because her home is on the lake, Michigan Center Lake, and it was so peaceful sitting by the window, watching the ducks and their little ones swim by,* Joy thought.

Teressa came running out to the car when she saw Joy drive up. They hugged and embraced as they said in unison, "Hello, it is so good to see you."

"Teressa, it is so good to see you, I have had a busy week since I arrived. I will tell you all about it after I settle down in a chair."

"I have dinner almost ready, so you can relax before we eat and catch up on everything." It is so good to see you, and I am happy you take time to come and stay with me for a while," Teressa said.

After dinner they sat by the windows and talked and talked until eleven o'clock, and Joy was so tired she almost fell asleep sitting in the chair. Teressa opened the hide-a-bed for her. That was where Joy always slept when she was at Teressa's.

"Good morning! Did you sleep well? I could hear you snore," Teressa asked Joy.

"Good morning! I sure did, did I keep you awake? I am sorry if I did," she replied.

"We will have some breakfast and relax for a while until you decide what you want to do today. You can tell what you have been doing since you got to Michigan. I want to take you to dinner tonight, where do you want to go? If I know you, it will be at the Coney Island for hot dogs, is that right?"

"You know it is, Teressa," Joy replied, laughing.

Visiting Jessie and Duane was as much fun as usual. They were both retired, laid-back, and were enjoying their lives to the limit, resting and doing what they want to do when they want to do it. Jessie visits her twin sister, Valary, and her husband, Ted, quite often, and they do sewing projects and crafts together to give for birthday and wedding gifts. At Christmastime they make different Christmas decorations, usually any new type that they have seen.

Jessie lives on the same street Joy lived on before she was married, along with her five brothers and one sister. Whenever Joy went by the home she had lived in, she remembered her childhood and all the friendly neighbors living around them.

Mary Andrews lived next to that home. She invited Joy to stay with her for a few days to visit and just hang out. She was retired also and had plenty of time to spend with her. They sat on the screened-in porch and talked about old memories, good and bad ones.

Friendships are so precious to Joy, which came easy for her because she was one of seven children and they were taught to be kind to each other. Besides, Joy babysat the Andrews children when she was a teenager. Their mother, Lois, had to work in a factory close by their home after her husband, George, passed away.

In between these talks, Joy visited her brother Carlyle and took him to lunch, then they would go shopping to buy him anything he needed or wanted. He loved to work puzzles at the care home because he wasn't much of one to visit with the other patients. She also went to church with him on Sundays while she was in town. The congregation was always surprised and happy to see her; Carlyle always kept it a secret whenever she was in town.

The pastor picked Carlyle up every Sunday to go to church and took him home. He knew Carlyle loved to worship. He needed people around who cared for him and loved the Lord. This had been a good trip, and it was time to pack up and go back to Alaska. Although Joy would like to stay longer with her family and friends, but the ticket said otherwise. She had already extended the date to stay five more days, and she needed to get back because she promised Lawrence she would do some work for him because he was moving the office to another location, and he wanted her to help arrange the desks and furniture where she wanted them and to make sure the files stayed in order. He liked her to be happy with the arrangement, but it really didn't matter much to Joy as long as her desk was in a convenient place with a lot of room around it.

Fall was here, and it was close to Joy's birthday; she would be seventy this year. The day was October 8, 1998, and Angel Marie, Joy's granddaughter, called her to wish her a happy birthday.

"And, Grandma, I got a job at Chrispy Fried Chicken, and I bought a little truck to go back and forth to work. I am going to graduate in the spring, so don't worry about that, I want to graduate. I have a real nice boyfriend, his name is Cal."

Joy was so happy to hear from her and to know how well she was doing because she had been getting a little wild before she changed her ways.

"Angel, I am so happy for you, you were always such a good girl and was trustworthy, until you started hanging out with those wild and disobedient kids and you were starting to act the same. I am happy you are going with a nice guy now," Joy told her.

"Grandma, I really like school and the kids that go there. They are neat kids, and the teachers are so understanding and helpful, and I like my job too. It is fun to work there," she said enthusiastically.

"You have a birthday coming up, the twenty-sixth, that isn't far away, you will be seventeen, and I am seventy today," Joy said.

"Yes, I know, Grandma. I love you and miss you. Are you coming down to Show Low for Christmas this year?" she asked.

"I don't know yet, honey. I haven't made up my mind yet. I went to Michigan for over three weeks, and I will have to think about it, then I will let you know," Joy answered.

"OK, Grandma, it is so good to talk to you. I love you. Have a happy birthday," she said.

"Thank you, and thanks for calling, it was good talking to you. I love you too 'a whole bunch,' like Bernie used to say," Joy remarked.

"Seventy years, where in the world have they gone?" Joy asked herself.

The phone rang early in the morning, about 3:00 AM. Joy answered it. "Hello."

In a panic and crying, Gale said, "Mom, Angel is in the hospital, in a coma, she was in a car accident last night and was thrown out through the windshield and hit her head on a huge rock. They have her on life-support systems, and they want to disconnect them because they say she is brain-dead and there is no hope. I told them, 'No, my brother was in a coma for fourteen weeks and lived, give her more time.'"

She asked, "Mom, can you come down here? I need you to be with me and to pray."

"Yes, I will call the airport and get an emergency ticket, then I will call to let you know the time I will be there. Try to stay calm, and you pray. God is able to do abundantly above all we may ask or think, His will be done," Joy said passionately.

"Oh my God, why? She changed her life around and was headed in the right direction," Joy cried out in heartfelt pain.

Vern and his neighbor drove to Tucson to pick Joy up and explained what and how the accident happened. He said, "Angel Marie and Cal went to Phoenix to a concert, and on the way back home, she was sitting in the front seat next to him, with no seat belt on, and fell asleep at his side. Cal dozed off, and the car swerved too far right and hit a road crossing a culvert hard, and she went through the window, and the truck rolled over. Cal wasn't hurt very bad, only his knee was badly bruised. He really feels bad about going to sleep." Vern added, "I feel bad for letting her go with him, I didn't like them going so far and coming back the same night. But you know Angel, she begged me until I said yes."

"I just talked to her on my birthday, on the eighth, and now three days later, I can't believe this happened to her, Vern, I have been praying all the way here that God will spare her life. How is Gale holding up?" Joy inquired.

"When we left, not too well. She believes Angel will come out of the coma and won't let them unplug the life support. They keep telling her there is no hope," Vern answered.

As they got closer to Show Low, Vern showed Joy where the accident happened, only ten miles from their home.

*So close yet so far,* Joy thought as tears were running down her cheeks.

Vern stopped to call the hospital to talk to Gale. They said she had gone home because Angel Marie had passed away.

"Oh no!" Vern said. "And I wasn't there with her, she will be falling apart and mad because they took off the supports before you got here, Mom."

"Mom, they wouldn't wait, they said there was no hope, she was brain-dead, and the longer they kept the machines going, the more the hospital bill will be. I can't believe it, look how long Clark was on life support." Gale said, weeping.

Their pastor, John Alan, was at the house, consoling Gale when Joy arrived. He told her, "Gale, as soon as you are up to it, tomorrow we will set up a time for services at the White Mountain Church, please let me know when you want to come there."

Gale replied, "Thanks for coming over and talking to me. I needed that after my ordeal with the hospital staff, they just wouldn't listen to me. They probably know more about being brain-dead than I do, but I had faith God would bring her back to us, and I feel it is my fault for letting her go to that concert with Cal. I should have insisted and said no."

Joy called Grace and let her know. "Grace, Angel Marie was in a car accident, and she passed away, and I thought maybe you and Sean would come to the funeral."

Grace replied, "Joy, we just buried our daughter, Doris. She had a sugar seizure, her car swerved off the road and hit a tree and killed her instantly. I don't think we are up to another funeral this soon. It has only been a little over a week. I am so sorry for Gale's loss. I know what she is going through. Keep in touch, and we will get together later."

Plans were made to have Angel cremated and have a closed casket at the church. The funeral was to be held in October, the seventeenth, at 2:00 PM with Pastor John Alan officiating the services. The church was crowded, people standing all around, and they put up amplifiers so all the people on the outside could hear the service. Over a hundred young people attended. It was a solemn ceremony, weeping, teary eyed, and sad. This was a very serious occasion for teenagers to observe and realize no one knows how long they have on earth, only God knows. Angel Marie loved the Lord. Her favorite Bible verse is the following:

## Psalm 42

As the deer pants for streams of water
So my soul pants for you Oh God
My soul thirst's for God, for the living God
When can I go and meet with God
My tears have been my food day and night

While men say to me all day long
Where is your God?
These things I remember as I pour out my soul
How I used to go with the multitude
Leading the procession to the house of God
With shouts of joy and thanksgiving among the festive throng.

She led many to the house of the Lord to hear the Word of God the day of her memorial.

Donald and Sherry were driving down from Colorado for Christmas, and that would help Gale's spirits. She was trying to keep busy with Elisabeth and Renee's school activities, etc.

Angel was a friend and was kind to everyone, a good example of a caring Christian. God only knows how much her life made a difference in their lives after she passed away.

Vern's family—his mother, father, sisters and their husbands—came from Tucson to attend and give their condolences to Vern, Gale, and their children. His sisters helped prepare and serve food along with the dishes that were brought in from the church members and their neighbors. Gale was too upset to do help with anything, of course. Many people came to Gale's days after the funeral to give their condolences because they were unable to attend for some reason or another.

"It is hard to set a time that everyone is able to come. I understand," Gale told them.

Elisabeth and Renee was taking it hard, They cried a lot and kept talking about Angel. "Being so good to us, our big sister, she looked after us like a little mother hen looking after her little chicks. We are going to miss her a lot," Elisabeth said.

Gale and Vern kept blaming themselves for letting her go with Cal to the concert, and they had a hard time forgiving themselves, no matter what the preacher or Joy said.

"We never know when it is our time to go, only God knows, and we are not God, so please stop feeling guilty, it is not your fault. She was one of His angels, and it was time for her to return back to Him. Only He knows what would have been ahead for her life."

The kids at her school had a car wash and bake sale to earn money to help Gale and Vern with expenses; they raised $682.05. They would plant a tree in her memory in the spring.

# CHAPTER FOURTEEN

## *NEW ADVENTURES*

The holidays were not too far away. Celebrating Thanksgiving is so much fun going to Darwin's and Annabelle's for a big feast and fellowship with the children, grandchildren, and great-grandchildren. The all grow up so fast, finish school, get jobs, marry, and have a family—a cycle of life that goes on forever and ever, thanks be to God.

Donald and Sherry's daughter Lori had a little boy, Aaron, born on December 4. Lori and Terry live in Colorado close by Donald and Sherry. They also have a daughter named Shelly. Their families always get together on the holidays and celebrate. Brad, their son, lives and works in Canon City and drives up to spend time with them. They like to go horseback riding and just hanging out together, watching the football games and any sport that is on the television at the time, as long as their vacation lasts.

*Another year almost gone, one of many different events, happy ones as well as sad ones. Memories to file in our minds, to store and bring out whenever we need reminding of how life passes by, and we don't even realize how old we are getting, it doesn't seem possible. If we live until we are ninety or more, that is such a tiny little bit compared to eternity, and we will never realize it until we are older,* Joy silently thought.

She often thought of all her family whether near or far and prayed for them all to ask God for forgiveness and accept the Lord, Jesus Christ, as their Savior.

Forgiveness rolls in like the tide,
sweeping away all that would hinder us
from knowing God's peace.

The winter daylight hours were short—only four to five hours of daylight—yet beautiful with the snow-covered ground, and once in a while, you would see a moose pass by the house, looking for something to eat off the bushes and trees. It is another year to look forward to, the last year in the twentieth century. Who knows what this year, 1999, will bring?

"There is no place like Alaska, the mountain so high, the moose and bears roaming in the yards, like a picture painted by God only."

Joy was still working four hours a day for Lawrence. The routine each day wasn't hard to keep up with. Even though she tried a few times to retire, only to have Lawrence ask her to come and help him; he didn't want anyone else working on his books. He wouldn't own a computer and wanted someone to do his bookkeeping by the old-fashioned way.

After selling the last house Darwin had built, he started looking for property to build a small subdivision to sell lots. He searched the newspaper ads and called several, but they weren't what he wanted. While out at the Valley, he spotted a For Sale sign, and he inquired about it and made an appointment with the owner. There were views of the mountains all around, and on a clear day, you could see Mount Denali also. This was a challenge for Darwin, but that is the way he is, not afraid to try anything. He had the land plotted out for lots and then cut down many trees for a better view of the mountains.

He hired a man to build the road and remove many of the cut-down trees to save them, but Darwin didn't like the way the grader man was doing the job, so Darwin let him go, and he corrected and finished it. Preparing a lot to build another house to sell, a walk-in basement was the design to fit the lot. More cement work and all that goes with the building of a house.

Darwin stayed out there day and night, sectioning off a small part of the basement to keep warm and fix his meals. Framing, roofing, Sheetrocking, plumbing, wiring, painting, and more hard strenuous work that goes into getting a house ready to sell.

The borough told him to name the road, and he couldn't think of anything. The clerk saw his name was Darwin Daniel, and she suggested the name Dandy Circle. Darwin said, "That is a good name for it, I will name it Dandy Circle. Thanks for the idea."

He spent the fall and winter working on the house. It was a beautiful custom-built home on an acre of land, and it was beautifully landscaped. Another summer was almost here, and it was all ready to be put on the market.

Darwin suggested to Desare', his oldest daughter, she should go to school to become a real estate saleslady, and she did. After her courses were finished, she went to work for an agency. She listed Darwin's house with them and personally helped Darwin sell it.

She held open house dates and showed it to those who came and were interested in it. Desare' listed the rest of the lots in the subdivision also and had pretty good luck selling them to people wanting to build new homes out in the country.

Joy did all the office work that had to be done: recording, banking, mailing, faxing, phoning, and going to the title companies. She had power of attorney to sign any and all documents and to do the banking pertaining to the business. Her bookkeeping and secretarial experience came in handy to help Darwin in his business, and he didn't like to do that kind of work anyway. He said, "I will do the hard labor and think about what I will do for my next project."

Joy received word that one of her friends, Emma Tangs, from Florida passed away on February 20. She was the lady Joy and Clark stayed with in 1961 when they went to Florida to get away from Dean. They worked together at the Randal Radar Plant and had been friends for many years. Joy visited her many times through the years.

Alan, Joy's great-grandson, wrote her a letter and asked if he could come to Alaska. He had been impressed with what Joy told them about it. He is Debbie Marie's oldest son. Joy called Debbie Marie and made plans for him to come. He was almost thirteen years old and very active and inquisitive about nature, all the different kinds of animals, and their habitat. Joy booked a trip to the city of Seward, a city with a shipping dock and tour agencies booking cruises on large tour boats to see whales, puffins, many kinds of birds, the glaciers, and the Kenai Fjords, a beautiful sight.

Joy phoned and asked Larry, Darwin's youngest son, "Do you want to go along with Clark, Alan, and me to Seward, and next week we will go to Denali State Park? If you do, I will come out to the Valley and pick you up tomorrow, so plan on staying here with us."

Larry answered, "Yes, Grandma, I think that will be fun. I have never been on a big boat like that, I will be ready." Larry was a year older than Ricky. He was very shy and quiet.

The trip down the Seward Highway was beautiful; the inlet and the mountains seemed so close and large—wilderness for sure if you haven't ever seen it. Alan was astonished and couldn't stop remarking about how happy he was to come and visit and to see the sights he had never seen before, taking in all he could observe along the way. It is a long drive, and we would all be tired when we arrived, so Joy suggested to Clark, "I think that we should find a room to stay in for the night and be fresh to take the trip in the morning. What do you think?"

Clark replied, "Yes, Mom, I think we better, then we can go the Seward Sea Center, the boys will like that. It is so interesting looking at all the sea creatures in the water, swimming around. They also have people talking about them and explaining about where they live, their eating habits, and even about the hairs on their pelt, especially the seal."

After renting the rooms, they went to eat and then went to the Sea Center for a tour. It took about four hours to see everything featured, all kinds of water species and birds. By bedtime, everyone was really tired and didn't have any problem going to sleep.

Alan said, "Grandma, thank you, that was so much fun and interesting. I am so glad you let me come to Alaska. Good night."

Larry spoke up and said, "Thank you, Grandma, it has been fun. Good night."

"Good morning, everybody, it is time to rise and shine. We need to eat breakfast, then go down to the dock so we won't miss our boat," Joy cheerfully said.

They all jumped out of bed, got dressed, ate their breakfast, and packed their clothes and were ready to go to the boat. Joy had booked an early trip because they would be going home right after the cruise was over.

There were marine biologists on the cruise, explaining the details about the different chemicals in the water that they check every day and many other facts about the marine life in the inlet. Alan and Larry were very interested in the talks and paid attention to what was said and asked questions whenever they didn't understand. The boys surely did enjoy the ship cruise and the good dinner that was served aboard—a fresh salmon meal.

It had been a nice day and very enjoyable for everyone, and now they were on their way back to Anchorage. The boys slept in the backseat; they were tired. It was a busy day.

Joy was thinking about the trip they would be taking to Denali State Park in a couple of days and was happy she had reserved a camping spot for two days and nights. This was going to be a long trip up there, approximately two hundred miles.

The next day Clark and Joy took the boys to play miniature golf in a large building shaped like a fairy-tale castle. They played two games and had so much fun. Also that day Clark took them go-kart racing while Joy watched them laugh and have a lot of fun.

"Now we have to get things ready for our next trip to see Mount Denali," Joy said.

"Checking over all the gear we have to take, making sure we have everything to camp out at the park with, and the groceries we will be taking for breakfasts and lunches we will pack in boxes or put in the ice chest on ice, OK?" Joy announced to the boys.

Going north on the Parks Highway was so much different than going south on the Seward Highway. It didn't have a lot of curves and "no passing" zones as the Seward Highway.

"This is another gorgeous scenery to behold. Praise God for His grace given to us in the United States of America!" Joy shouted.

Awakening early, they ate breakfast and headed for the park headquarters where they showed their tickets and signed in for the bus ride. The bus took them miles through the park with a couple of stops for bathroom needs, and if anyone saw a moose, antelope, or bear, the driver would stop so tourists could take pictures. Many ooohs and aahhhs were said by the tourists as the animals passed by or stood in front of the bus.

The visitor's center was at the halfway point. For those who wanted to go partway into the park, they would be picked up later when the bus returned to go back to the campgrounds. They didn't seem to realize what was ahead as they drove closer to the mountain.

"Some of the people on the bus were friendly and wanted to get acquainted by asking questions about living in Alaska, 'How long have you been here? Do you like the cold weather? How did you happen to come up here?'" Joy remarked to Clark as they departed the bus and went to the campgrounds to get dinner ready. They were all hungry for some good hot food instead of sandwiches.

The next day they went farther north to see about renting a small boat to take a river ride. Reservations weren't made, and they wouldn't take them, so then they went back to the campgrounds and just relaxed the rest of the day. It felt good, and they needed it because they would be driving back to Anchorage the next day, and they would be stopping to see some of the historical sites on the way back so the boys could remember that too.

Arriving in Huston, Annabelle was happy they were back with Larry. She missed him because he didn't usually go away from home. He is so shy and quiet, and she worries about him. She asked him, "Did you have a good time?" He said, "I sure did."

Joy told her, "These boys have been having a good time. I am so thankful you let him come with us so Alan would have a buddy to talk to and get to know his cousin."

Arriving back in Anchorage, Joy received a phone call from Misty, her son Donald's daughter, who said, "Grandma, my baby was born on June 21, summer solstice day. We named her Destiny Sol after the day, we wanted her to be named with a special meaning."

"Congratulations, Misty, I like her name, it is unique and personal. I am anxious to see her. I will send something for her. How are you feeling?" Joy asked.

"I am doing just fine, and Destiny is a good baby, she sleeps good," Misty answered.

"I am so happy you called, it is good to hear your voice, Misty. I miss all my grandchildren that live so far away. Some are in Michigan, some are in Arizona. At least I get to visit when I can," Joy said.

"I know, Grandma, we miss you too, and it is always so good to see you when you come to visit us. I wanted to let you know about Destiny's birth," Misty said.

"Thanks for calling, tell everyone I said hello. I love you," Joy told her.

*I have missed seeing my grandchildren grow up, but I had made the decision to move to Alaska because of work. I couldn't find work in Michigan at that time, but I came to Alaska and found work and was thankful and enjoyed my job and Alaska. I thank God for leading me here. I have trusted in Him, and He supplied all my needs.* Joy thought.

Joy received a letter from her son Donald, with an article published in the *Rocky Mountain Bighorn Society Fall 1999* newsletter.

He said, "Mom, I have never written any kind of article in my life, but I decided to write this one. I have enclosed a copy for you to read."

# One Step Closer to My Life's Goal

## By Donald Godman

The count was 63 goats the evening before season opened: a few on the next mountain north. The mountain I had chosen to hunt held three different groups. One held 16 goats with seven bighorn sheep, ewes and lambs mixed. The second group had 10 goats. The largest and the closest counted 22 with a couple decent Billies worth a closer look tomorrow.

On July 14, 1998, I received a call from Dale Martin of RMBS informing me that I had won the annual raffle for a Colorado mountain goat tag. That was probably one of the best things that ever happened to me. It gets even better. With this tag, I could hunt any and all areas open to goat hunting.

The decision on where to hunt had been made years ago, I hunted sheep in the area a few years ago and seen a number of goats. After a couple of scouting trips, it was confirmed.

I happened to be lucky enough to have a wife that understands I need something more than monthly bills to work for. Hunting has always been that 'something else.' For as long as I can remember, my life's goal has been to take one good representative of every game animal in North America and do it on my own. This goat tag has put me one step closer to that goal. It's taken most of my 52 years to come relatively close. There are still a few critters I would like to hunt, something to look forward to.

When my brother-in-law, Bob Kellogg, also an avid hunter, heard about the hunt, he just had to come along. He flew out from Michigan to hunt with me the first week. My son, Brent decided to go along at the last minute. He had taken his vacation for bow hunting. The experience told him he would like to try for a goat someday. Every ones pack helped.

Opening morning finally arrived. Topping the first hill from camp, the 22 head were feeding along the next ridge, well out of range, yet close enough we couldn't move with out being seen. To our advantage, we only had to wait 20 minutes for them to move out of sight. Meanwhile, more goats came over a saddle at opposite end of the same ridge. Being closer to us and camp, we decided to have a closer look at these first. When we reached the saddle we spotted 10 goats, moving fast, away from us. We then dropped over the top, in order to stay out of sight and worked our way toward the first group. Topping the ridge on hands and knees, we could only see five or six goats lying down.

We set up the spotting scope and Bob said "The one you have the best shot at is a good one." After a look through the scope, I decided to try for him. We talked it over and figured the range at 300 yards. Using Brent's sweatshirt for a rest on the rocks, I lined up for the shot. The dirt flew just below him and without hesitation they were off. I quickly ran down the ridge, trying to get another look at them. Bob and Brent went left and swung right.

The goats were a half-mile out in front of Bob and Brent. The count was still 22. They seemed to have forgotten about the shot and were playing around. Now we are stuck out in the open with nothing taller than our boot laces to hide behind. It was about 200 yards to our left before we could reach the crest of the ridge in order to drop from sight again.

Topping the ridge once again, we could see only eight or ten animals, three or four were good clean shots.

I picked the one with the best horns and asked Bob and Brent to watch that particular animal. With the recoil of the 338 Winchester Magnum, the goat fell. While I chambered another round, it was back up, mingling with six or eight others.

"Which one is it?" I asked. Bob said "It's in the middle, facing left. There—it turned around walking to the right. It's going to go behind another one facing left."

At that instant I had the crosshairs on it and fired. Bob said, "It's down." As the rest of the herd ran off. We couldn't see it for the drop in the mountain. After the 200 yard walk, it lay there, as pretty and still as anything I've ever seen. At that moment an almost sadness over came me for a second or two. I wonder if killing such a beautiful animal is the right thing to do.

Although I don't believe everything the Department of Fish and Game does is for the good of the general public, save for a few ranchers, I do believe they keep a very good handle on the goats and sheep.

After all the pictures taking, hand shaking and back slapping came the task at hand. Bob and I started dressing and skinning the animal, Brent returned to our first position to retrieve our packs. Amazingly, the goats came back up the mountain and stood 50 yards from us. Most of them were watching Brent return. They must have stood there for a good five minutes while we took pictures,. We couldn't believe what we were seeing.

**Although our measurements were slightly longer with cloth tape, Fish and Game measurements at check-in, with a steel tape were 8-7/8 and 8-5/8. It won't make any record books, but to me is one of the best trophies I've ever taken: a perfect ending to a wonderful and rewarding hunt with two of the best people I know.**

**I would like to sincerely thank RMBS for this extraordinary chance to hunt a mountain goat. Also, to Bob and Brent for all their help and good company.**

As Joy read this article she thought, *My sons all love to hunt just like their dad. They like the sport of it, and it puts fresh meat on the table, keeping the grocery bills down.*

Laurie, Joy's niece, came to Alaska in 1999. She brought her bicycle with her because she was going to meet a group of people to travel many miles in Alaska. She came early so they could go some places together that Joy hadn't gone before. They drove to the coastal town of Homer and took a boat to Seldovia, a remote little town across the bay.

They had rented a hotel room for the night and toured the little town until it was time to go to the airport where they had a plane scheduled to fly them back to Homer. The lady pilot flew them over the glaciers so they could see what they looked like from above. It was a beautiful sight and thrilling in that little plane holding just three passengers.

After returning home and resting a bit, Clark took Laurie to the lake for a ride on his Yamaha Jet Ski, something she had never done before; she enjoyed the outdoors and loved to travel. They went out to the inlet along the Anchorage coast.

The next tour would be up the Parks Highway to the Denali State Park and the tour on the bus to see the animals and be close to the mountain. The first day they went to their room in the fashionable redecorated railroad car and freshened up to go to dinner before they went to bed. They had to rise up early to catch the bus. Laurie enjoyed the ride and took many pictures. She loved taking pictures, like her dad; he made a business doing it.

When they got back home, Laurie had to get ready to meet her group to start their long trip on their bikes. She had been preparing for this for months, so she wouldn't tire.

Gale called and said, "Mom, Bernie's ex-girlfriend, Wilma, Whisper's mother, called me and told me she was going to live with her mother, and she told Wilma, 'You can come here, but don't bring any of your children with you. I am raising your first son, Bernie, and I am not going to raise any more.' Mom, I asked her, 'What are you going to do with them?' And Wilma told me her husband would take their two little boys and go back to Jamaica to live, but she didn't know where Whisper will be going."

Gale continued, "I told her I would take her, and she said, 'Come and get her, I will tell my husband to get her clothes all ready for you when you come to pick her up.'"

Joy was astonished and said, "I just can't understand how any woman could leave her children like that, I almost killed for my children's safety. Are you going to get her?"

"Yes, Mom, I have some of the insurance money I received from Angel's death. I will go down and get Whisper and have Wilma give me a signed and notarized paper giving me complete custody of her, and I will bring her back here to Arizona. Mom, she is only four years old, that must be an awful emotional feeling for Whisper," Gale answered.

"I will keep you in my prayers for a safe journey and a good time getting acquainted with Whisper. You can go visit Clarice and Richard while you are in Florida too," Joy said.

It was time to book her flight to Arizona to go see Gale and her family at Christmastime. Rose Ann, Darwin's younger daughter, wanted to go along. Rose Ann and Angel were best friends as well as cousins; she liked Gale very much and could talk to her like a daughter. Rose Ann felt bad because she didn't get to go to Angel Marie's funeral, and she wanted to go and see the crash site where the accident happened the year before.

Gale had gone to the Highway Department and asked to be able to have a mile marker posted on that road in memory of Angel. They told her there was only one mile left on that five miles of road to have one of the signs. And thanks be to God, it was the same mile where the accident occurred—only God could have orchestrated that. Praise the Lord!

Gale cried and was amazed; it is a miracle. It read, "In Memory of Angel Marie." During the year, many relatives and friends would clean the mile and keep flowers and memorable articles on her gravesite; it was one of the cleanest miles on that road. During the summer, there were concerts in her memory to get her friends and family together for a happy celebration of her life and Christian influence there in Show Low.

A new century had begun—2000. This was the year people thought and feared when the clock struck 12:00 AM, there would be a lot of problems with clocks and metric measurements, etc., and about all things would come to a halt. People stored food and water, took their money out of the bank, and made many cautious choices, thinking the worst would happen. But it didn't; everything went on as usual, with no disasters.

It goes to show that men who try to play God and prophesy what will happen, they have to realize they are not God. Only He knows.

*A new century has begun. What will it bring, good memories and bad ones, as usual? Thanks be to God, He helps me cope with whatever comes my way,* Joy thought as she drank her morning coffee, waiting for the rest of the family to get out of bed. She was always an early bird; her body clock had been set many years before.

Friends came over for New Year's dinner. Dennis and Donna were fun to be around. Dennis did magic tricks and entertained the children and the adults as well on some of his tricks. He was very convincing and pretty good as an amateur. Joy enjoyed talking to Donna. She was the pianist at the church and enjoyed spending time with Gale and her family. She always helped cleaning up the table and doing dishes. She said, "It is always such a good meal, and I appreciate the invitation, so Dennis and I don't have to eat alone."

The time had come to go. Joy was going to spend a few days with Grace and Sean before she went back home. They came up to get her so Rose Ann could stay with Gale a few more days, then they would go down to Tucson to Grace's and pick Joy up and go to the airport. They loved to tell each other how much the Lord had done for them in their lives and experiences with their daughter, Doris, and her family. Doris was adopted, and she had found her biological mother, sisters, and brothers. They had a family reunion and visited each other many times before Doris passed away.

God works in mysterious ways, uniting them before she went on to be with Him in heaven.

Joy told Grace, "When Angel was only six years old, she asked me, crying, 'Why did those bad men kill Jesus on the cross?' And I told her, 'They took Him down and put Him in a tomb, but three days later, He arose and went to heaven.' And she said, 'Tell me that story again, Grandma.' And she stopped crying and was so happy to hear the rest of the story. When she came to Alaska at ten years old, I sent her to Victory Bible Camp, and she accepted the Lord Jesus as her Savior."

A total of three hundred or more people attended her funeral, and the pastor said it was the second largest funeral they had at the church. The largest was a dear saint that was a member. Grace said, "Our girls are with the Lord, and we can be thankful for that."

Joy told Grace about the mile marker sign, how God worked in that way for Gale and her family, reassuring them of His love for Angel Marie.

It was always hard leaving for home. Joy loved to be there and enjoyed the fellowship they have with one another. Now she had to go back to the winter cold and snow. Gale came to Tucson with the girls to get Joy to take her and Rose Ann to the airport. Grace was able to meet and get acquainted with Rose Ann and little Whisper while they all played some card games and had a snack.

Joy and Rose Ann returned back home still in sorrow over Angel Marie's death and yet happy to be back in Alaska with family and friends. Joy took Rose Ann back to her home.

The days went on as usual, and everyone went to work and carried on as if nothing ever happened yet questioning why all the hype and talk about it putting fear into their minds.

Joy continued to work four hours a day at the office and house-sit at Lawrence and Pearl's home while they were away on vacation for three months.

She wasn't feeling well. Her ribs were hurting, and she broke out all over her back and side. She decided to go see the doctor because she was worried. Nothing like that had ever happened to her. He examined her and asked, "Have you ever had the chicken pox?

She answered, "Yes, I did as a child."

The doctor said, "You have the shingles, they come later in life if you had chicken pox. I will give you a shot and medication for the rash, and you just rest until they are gone."

Obediently Joy listened to the doctor, and within two weeks, she felt much better and was able to go back to work. During that time, on Thursdays, some of the ladies from the Bible study and prayer group came to Lawrence's so Joy could participate until she was well and then she could join them at the church as usual. Prayer is powerful. With faith in God, you can "trust in the Lord with all your heart; and lean not on our own understanding. In all thy ways acknowledge Him and He will direct our path" (Proverbs 3:5-6).

Daily routines continued as the days rolled by fast, keeping Joy busy with work, Bible study, household chores, and secretarial work for Darwin and visiting friends and family.

Summer had passed, and the leaves had turned colors, so picturesque for a short time, then they fall only to be raked up. It wouldn't be long now, and we would see the termination dust, the first snow on the mountaintops, then later snow in Anchorage; winter is here.

Joy had been helping out with child evangelism and was elected to be on the board of directors. This was another responsibility she accepted as well as being on the board at church, keeping her busy working for the Lord, which she did willingly and joyfully.

Clark continued working for the school district and for Martin's Maintenance, keeping busy every day. Sometimes going ice fishing with Phil or four-wheeling when the snow melted. He liked to take Joy out to dinner about once or twice a month. They received two-for-one coupons in the mail, so the cost wasn't too bad.

Gale called Joy and said, "Mom, Vern and I are going to get married again in July 7, 2001, and we are planning a pretty-good-size outdoor wedding at a small park. The girls, Elisabeth and Renee, would stand up with us, Whisper would be our flower girl, and Bernie will be Vern's best man. Ruth, his mother, is making all of the dresses. They will be like Indian dresses, mine will be like an Indian princess. Isn't that great, Mom?"

"It sounds like Ruth has accepted you and Vern getting back together now, it is sure nice of her to do all that work. She has changed, mellowed, since Angel's death, hasn't she?" Joy answered, then added, "They see you and Vern are attending church regularly now and have changed your lifestyle for the good of the children as well as yourselves."

"Yes, she has. Vern's sisters are more friendly toward me now too," Gale agreed.

# CHAPTER FIFTEEN

## JOY AND SORROW

"Mom, I hope you can come down early so we can have some time together before the wedding. I am so excited about this, like a little kid. I hope and pray it will work better this time. I know I am really going to try harder, and with God's help, I believe it will. The girls are excited too. They want us to be a family, united and loving," Gale said.

"Gale, with God, all things are possible when you abide in Him," Joy advised.

"Yes, Mother, I believe that with all of my heart," Gale said.

Joy continued to pray for Gale and her family, asking God to keep His everlasting arms around them and may His gracious love abound with them from now on. God is love, and he that does not know God, does not know love, for God is love.

Springtime and Joy was asked to house-sit for the Goodings while they went on vacation. They had a cat and a dog to be cared for, and she knew the animals quite well.

The construction workers were doing some reconstruction in the house and were told to make sure the cat was in the house before they left. They did, but on Friday evening when Joy arrived, she couldn't find the cat. She looked and looked, going outside looking around, no cat! She called Barbara and told her about it, and Barbara told her to go to the animal shelter and see if the cat was there. Joy did the next day, because it was too late to go that night. No cat. She was getting worried. Barbara told her not to worry.

She could hear a *meow, meow, meow*, and looked all over and still couldn't figure where the cat was. As she sat at the breakfast table, she could hear a faint *meow, meow, meow*. She went down by the fireplace where the workers had been working and put her ear to the wall, and she heard *meow, meow*, again and again. She went and got a hammer and screwdriver and tore a piece of the Sheetrock off the wall (it hadn't been finished off yet), and *whoosh*, out came the cat in a big hurry, so happy to be free. Joy was happy to see her too and followed her up to the kitchen where her food was waiting for her.

The Goodings came home that same night and were so happy the cat had been found and said, "The workers probably didn't know the cat had snuck in between the wall and the fireplace before they sealed it back up."

Joy said, "She was getting very weak, she didn't eat for almost three days."

There is never a dull moment in Joy's life, always something to keep her going and happy as she goes along. God only knows what or when.

Spring had passed, and summer was here with all the beautiful flowers blooming, such a variety of colors and sizes galore for the eyes to behold and enjoy God's creations. It was time to get things ready to go to Gale and Vern's wedding in Show Low, Arizona.

*It will be hot there in July, especially outdoors, so I will need some short-sleeve blouses and light summer skirts, plus my sandals for sure,* Joy thought.

"Oh my goodness, it is hot here like an oven. How in the world can you stand this day after day?" Joy said when they left the airport and headed for the car.

Gale said, "It is better than that cold Alaska weather, Mom." And she added, "We are staying out by the park at a campground so we don't have to go back and forth getting things ready for the day of the wedding. We will take you to our house for a day."

"That is all right with me, I will have more room to move around in to get ready, and it won't be too hot there in the house," Joy agreed.

July 7, 2001, the wedding day was here, and the bride looked very pretty with her white Indian princess wedding dress, feathers in her long hair, and Indian moccasin boots on.

Vern wore a black shirt and Indian beads around his neck, white pants, a hat decorated with feathers, and Indian moccasin boots also. They were a stunning and loving couple. Elisabeth and Renee were like Indian maidens with their matching dresses and jewelry. Whisper's dress was white, and with her blond hair, she looked like a little angel. Bernie (Gale's son) was present to help usher the guests. All their children were there.

The food was prepared by Vern's mother, Ruth, and his sisters, Trudy, Karen, Janet, and Lee. They put on a tasty feast for all to enjoy, and everyone did, from the elders to the smallest child present. After opening their gifts, showing them, and thanking everyone personally, the musicians began to play the wedding waltz, and the bride and groom went to the area and danced. A little later on, other couples got on the dance floor and joined them, and then some took turns dancing with the bride. A good time was had by all that beautiful day.

After a week, Joy decided to go to Tucson and see Grace and Sean before she left to go back to Alaska. She had rented a car and was able to leave whenever she wanted to. She thought it was best to let the honeymooners have their place to themselves.

Vern's folks were still out at the campgrounds, and Gale's girls were staying with them for a while, playing at the park and going swimming—a real treat for them.

The drive down the canyon was a little scary for Joy. She always came or went back with someone else driving the car, but as she thought of all the miles she had driven back in 1995 when she drove all those miles by herself, she calmed down and kept on going.

Grace and Sean were happy to see her, greeting her with a big hug and kisses as she went into the house. She said, "I am so glad that drive is over, I prayed a lot going through that canyon."

Grace said, "We have dinner about ready, Joy, we knew you would be hungry when you got here. After we eat, we can play some card games, what do you think?"

"That sounds like a winner, Grace. I should be relaxed by then," Joy replied.

They played several card games, and Joy told them all about the wedding and her trip.

Grace said, "I wish you could move down here and be with Gale and her family."

"Grace, I am still working. Clark and I share household expenses, and I pay half of his mortgage, so I don't think I can do that. Maybe in years to come I might think about it. Clark needs me there to help him. He has a good job, plus a part-time job, and I take care of the house and do the cooking. I try to keep him from getting into those get-rich schemes and spending his money foolishly," Joy replied.

"Yes, I know, Joy, that is a problem. Gale told me about it, she said he was doing it when he lived in the little trailer by her house. He is weak and can't say no," Grace said.

They attended church services on Sunday and enjoyed the singing of the older hymns. Sean preached, and Grace led the singing. It's a small church with a few older ladies attending.

Sean said, "I try hard to get people to attend, but most people want to go to big churches and socialize rather than worship the Lord with all their heart, mind, and soul."

"Sean, you and Grace are doing the Lord's work. These saints need someone like you to keep their spirits up, and you are obedient to the Lord," Joy said, encouraging him.

"The time has come for me to go back to Anchorage, and I am going to miss you all until the next time I come. Keep me in your prayers for a safe journey home," Joy said.

After returning home, Joy had to open a pile of mail—letters, bills, and advertisements. She received a letter from one of her second cousins who lives in Germany, her cousin Dieter's daughter, Dany (short for Darwina). She was only sixteen when Joy was in Germany in 1979. Dany and her husband had been talking about taking a trip to Alaska in the future, and Joy was pleased to hear that and wrote back to her and said they were more than welcome to come and stay at their home in between tours around Alaska. It was a thrill to correspond with her family in Germany and get acquainted with them.

Bernie and Angel had a baby girl on August 11, 2001. They named her Angela Lee in memory of his sister. They lived on the same street as Gale and her family did.

Joy's cousins in Michigan were planning a big reunion and asked, "Joy, are you going to be able to attend? If you are, we want to know what date would be best for you so we can make the plans to reserve the park pavilion."

"Yes, I will leave here the first of September and go to Clarice's house first. Anytime after that would be fine with me, it should still be warm weather yet," Joy said.

Plans were made to fly to Chicago and then to change planes and continue on to Carlson, Michigan, and she was all packed and ready to go for two weeks to be with family and friends once again. She liked to fly because it takes so little time compared to driving. Joy left Anchorage approximately 9:00 PM on August 31, arriving in Chicago at 2:30 AM (5:30 AM Chicago time). She had to go to No.! airport terminal to Gate F1, then was routed to Gate F4 and finally boarded the plane, and they left at approximately 9:00 AM on United Express, a two-hour flight from Chicago O'Hare Airport to Carlson.

A one-hour time change, arriving at 10:00 AM. Before the door was opened, the pilot told us, "The Twin Towers of the World Trade Center has been bombed and the Pentagon Building also. I had to make a decision whether to keep on going or to return back to Chicago, I decided to continue on to Carlson. I wanted to let you all know before you left the plane and saw how vacant the airport was."

They were all shocked about it. This had happened from the time they left Chicago until they arrived in Carlson, Michigan. Joy wondered why there were no planes coming or going when their plane set down. It was because they were not allowing any plane traffic in or out of the airport. *I am glad our pilot received confirmation to continue on to Carlson,* Joy thought to herself as she gathered her luggage and exited the plane.

It was kind of spooky, no one around except those who just arrived. Joy looked for Clarice. As she waited for her, two TV reporters were interviewing some of the passengers who were on the last plane to arrive at the airport, and they interviewed Joy and asked, "What do you think about this terrible thing that has happened?"

Joy answered, "I was shocked that anyone would do such a thing, it is hard to believe it happened in America. I wondered why there were no planes around when we landed."

Joy waited and waited, and after an hour, she decided to telephone them and find out why they were not there to pick her up. She couldn't get through to them, so she called Christina, their daughter, and asked, "Why hasn't anyone picked me up?"

She replied, "Mom and Dad were there and were told no more planes would be landing and didn't stay. Their phone was shut off, it's why you couldn't reach them. They will be right there." They had to get clearance before they could drive in to pick Joy up.

Clark had called before they arrived back at Clarice's to find out if Joy had made it there. They heard the news and were concerned about his mother. Also Gale called and said, "I was so worried I was going to call the airlines to see if she could find her."

Joy explained what had happened and she was safe and sound at Clarice's, thank God. All afternoon they watched the television about the Twin Towers collapsing and burning. It was a terrible sight to see so many people's lives end and the destruction caused by this tragedy. And to think pilots flew their planes into those buildings and the Pentagon also.

Some brave men took over another plane full of passengers that was headed toward Washington, DC, and steered its course in another direction to keep it from hitting the capital, but it crashed in Pennsylvania, killing everyone. So many innocent lives lost.

Businesses, schools, universities, sports, and numerous other places were shut down, and the airports may be up in full schedule by noon of September 13. A plea for blood donations was announced, and many people responded to give willingly. Gas prices rose from $2.29 per gallon to as high as $5.00 per gallon in Detroit, Michigan. Price gouging was going on for about everything since the attack happened.

The reunion was held in the garage at Christina's home. They decided it would be a better place than going to the park. Many of the relatives were getting older, and it was hard for them to walk around on the park grounds, and it would be more comfortable for them also.

It is too bad her brother Louis couldn't make it. He had been unable to go anywhere except to the doctor's for a long time. Joy usually goes over to Battle Creek to visit him and Joan. She faithfully cared for him twenty-four hours a day. He had to have oxygen all the time, and his heart was failing also. This time Carlyle would go with Joy; he hadn't seen Louis for some time, and he wanted to go with her and spend some time with him.

So many people to see and so many places to go, there never seemed to be enough time to go around for everyone, but she tried to share her time and story about her trip and arrival to Michigan, this time, with as many that were interested.

Ester Street came over from Benton Harbor, Michigan, and the ladies from Indiana to meet with Joy again in Battle Creek. They caught up on all the yearly news of families and their children, spending all afternoon fellowshipping and laughing. These ladies were all schoolteachers and had many stories about some of their students.

A wonderful vacation was over now, and it was time to go to the airport and go back home. Friends and family asked, "Joy, aren't you afraid to fly after the 9/11 crisis?

She answered, "No, I believe God will keep me safe until it is my time to be with Him."

The merchants had their stores decorated in Halloween paraphernalia for the coming and observing of the All Saints' Day. The children dressed in costumes and played trick or treat. It was something else to see the variety of costumes the children wore and how they came in groups this day and age, for their safety, looking out for one another and sharing.

The fall months passed, and the holidays came along with Thanksgiving, always a special day for families to get together and share how God has been good to them so far this year.

Our God is an awesome God. He cares for everyone, even if they don't acknowledge Him in being thankful and praising Him for it. Here in America, from the beginning of this country, the pilgrims took time to be thankful and set an example for the rest of us.

Joy received a postcard from her cousin in Germany, Gilda, to wish her "Merry Christmas and a happy New Year!" She told Joy to stay in good health and to write, because she was always glad to hear from her. She had found some old pictures of Joy's mother, father, two brothers, and Clarice and wanted to know if Joy wanted them. This was written on November 8, and not much later after, she passed away. Gilda frequently corresponded with Joy, keeping up on the family news and because they had become good friends, and a loving friendship lasted between them ever since they started corresponding with each other and their meeting when Joy went to Germany in 1979. They were both the same age, and Joy felt sympathy for her husband, Eric.

Joy received a letter stating she had to be on jury duty in January 2002 for a trial. She signed the form and sent it back, acknowledging she would be present. In the meantime, Christmas season was upon them. Writing cards, shopping, putting up the Christmas tree, decorating the house, wrapping the presents, and planning for the big dinner kept Joy very busy and enjoying every minute of it while listening to the Christmas carols and thinking about all the previous years this same routine was carried out and the everlasting joy it brought to her. It had meant so much to her because of what Jesus had done, for whosoever believed in Him could have everlasting life.

Joy was thinking, *What a gift from God, Jesus Christ, His Son. This Christmas was one more for my memory book and a deeper love for my Lord and Savior.*

After Christmas, Joy went over to Barbara's to house-sit for a week, while Clark was house-sitting for their good neighbor Phil and watching his dog, Lady, for three weeks.

Joy received word that Donald's younger daughter, Misty, and Alan had another baby girl on January13, 2002. They named her Sheri Lee. Joy sent a gift for the baby and a congratulations card to Misty and Alan.

It was time to go to the courthouse and sign in for jury duty, and Joy was told to call in the evening to see if her group, number 3, would be called. She called the first evening, and her group had been picked to serve on the jury.

*Finally, I will get to know how the court system works, how they pick the jurors, and just listening to a trial in progress will be so interesting,* Joy thought.

Joy was house-sitting for Barbara again for another week while she was on jury duty, and it was closer to the courthouse from there, which made it nice for her.

First the lawyer and the prosecuting attorney explained to the jurors what the trial was going to be about and explained who the defendant was, who the one charged with the crime was, and what he was charged with—it was attempted murder. They interviewed each juror to see if they were acceptable or not to serve.

The teen charged had been harassed several times by the defendant, even going to his workplace and cornering him in the bathroom and threatening him. Plus many other times in public parking lots where the teen hung out in the evenings.

The defendant called and harassed the charged teen over the phone and said, "Let's meet and get this score settled, what do you think?"

Having put up with this harassment for so long, the charged teen said, "Said OK, we will meet at the same parking lot we usually hang out at, at the same time."

The charged teen went there, and there were several of the defendant's buddies parked alongside his car, and the charged teen started to walk over to the defendant teen and saw the others get out of their cars also. The charged teen went back to his truck and got a ball bat he had in his truck from playing softball previously. Then the fight started. The defendant was much bigger than the charged teen. He swore and said some bad things to the charged teen. This made the charged teen angry, and he hit him with the ball bat, and the defendant claims he was seriously injured and reported him to the police, and now he is in court being charged with attempted murder.

They questioned each juror about several things to see if they would be prejudiced.

When the prosecutor came to Joy, he asked, "What is your name?"

She answered, "Joy Godman."

"Joy, is there anything about this situation on trial here that might be hindering your serving on this jury?"

She answered, "Well, I was married to an alcoholic, and he was beating one of my sons, and I hit him over the head with a baseball bat, that might be something that would be against me serving."

The prosecutor said, "I have no problem accepting Joy as a juror, she was honest, and I believe she will make a fine juror. She is OK."

The lawyer for the charged teen said, "Joy will be fine to stay on the jury."

Joy thought, *Oh my goodness, I had to tell the truth, I thought that might prevent me from serving at this trial because the charged used a ball bat.*

It took most of that day for jury selection, and then they were excused to go home and were told to return the next morning.

The trial went on and on, first the defendant then the charged teen. Many witnesses testified for and against the charged. After two days of trial, the jury was about to go and decide whether the charged teen was guilty or innocent. There were thirteen jurors, and they put all their names in a barrel and swirled them around and around, and whoever was picked had to leave because there could only be twelve on the jury. They picked Joy's name, so she didn't get to go in and decide his verdict. She saw him in the hall as she was leaving and whispered in his ear, "I don't think you were guilty, he deserved what he got." He replied, "Thanks, I needed that."

Things were back to normal now, and Joy was back home, enjoying her easy chair and just being home with Clark and Darwin. Clark had been going to physical therapy. He was happy to see her back; they sure missed her cooking. They played card games and dominoes during the long, dark winter days instead of watching television all the time.

Joy received a letter from Clancy Martin, and he told her his mother, Madeline, passed away on February 11. He wrote, "She had gone to lunch at the cafeteria and went back to her room and sat down in her new La-Z-Boy chair and fell asleep and never woke up."

Joy said, "Oh my goodness, at least she went peacefully and didn't suffer. She was a fine lady. She reminded me so much of my mother, and we became friends a long time ago. She would call me and say she wanted to take me out to Kentucky Fried Chicken many times so she would have someone to talk to, and I would spend the day with her."

March 11, only a month since Madeline's death, Joy received a letter from Clancy, her son, informing her a check for $25,000 was enclosed, willed to her from Madeline. He thanked her for her intervention for two years with Royce, helping his mother, and Paul Kelly, an incredible lawyer to legalize her will. She immediately wrote to Clancy and thanked him for sending her the check and another sympathy card.

Plans had been made to go to Tucson the later part of March, and Joy was thankful she would have money to do more to help Gale and her family. Her family have been attending church services regularly and picking up neighborhood children to go also. The pastor, John, was mentoring Vern to teach the young people and maybe preach. During the week, Vern would help out cleaning the church. Thank God for their dedication and example for the girls, showing how God can change lives around and be obedient to Him.

Barbara called and asked Joy to house-sit for two weeks, and she told her she would gladly do it. She was still working for Lawrence four hours a day, and it would be closer to work. Barbara's cat had diabetes, and Joy gave her shots every morning after she fed her. That was quite an experience for Joy. They had the cat and dog for many years, and Joy got attached to them.

March 24, the time was here to go to Tucson. It was Palm Sunday, and Joy prayed for a safe journey. The last time she flew was when the Twin Towers were destroyed. Gale and Vern picked her up at the airport. They had to rent a car in Show Low because their van stopped running just before they came after her. After all the hugs and kisses, they headed back toward home but first stopping for something to eat at a good breakfast diner. On the way home, Joy told them about Madeline and the check she received from her son, Clancy. They were surprised, and Gale said, "Mom, you are always good to people, and it is about time you were rewarded for all you have done."

Joy answered, "Gale, that is the Lord working through me, helping whenever I can." She continued, "Vern, what are you going to do about your van?"

"I had an estimate for the work that has to be done on it from a repair service station, and they gave me a quote that was way more than I can afford," Vern answered.

"What about all of the neighbor children you pick up on Sundays?" Joy asked.

He said, "We won't be able to take them until I get it fixed, they all won't fit in my car."

"Maybe I can help pay for the van. I want to see those children continue going to church, what they learn about the Bible now will be with them as they get older," Joy said.

After the long scenic ride up the canyon, they arrived home, all tired and hungry again. The next day Vern took Joy to the repair shop to talk to the manager about the van.

On the way she said, "Vern, you have been faithfully picking these children up, and I believe you should continue, so I will pay the bill to have the van fixed. This is for the Lord's work for me as well as you."

"Thank you so much, Mom, I really appreciate it. I do want to continue what I started with these children as well as my own. We have known these kids for a long time," Vern said.

Easter morning, and the children were up early so they could look for their Easter baskets. Some were found very easily, and others were hard to find. After a while, they all had them. A good Easter breakfast was served, then it was time to get ready to go to church for the Easter service. Everyone got all dressed up, so pretty with new outfits and shoes. Faces were shiny clean, and their smiles were from ear to ear, happy to be going to church. The children were in an Easter program, singing and quoting scriptures. Gale was happy and so proud of them. She had tears in her eyes because she was thinking about Angel Marie.

Donna and Denis were invited to the house for dinner after church. Donna played the piano for the church services. They had befriended Gale and Vern when they first started to go to that church and continued to fellowship with them.

Bernie, Annie, and the children (she had three before she married Bernie) and little baby Angela Lee—they all came to dinner. It was good to have them all there as a family.

Ham, sweet potatoes, mashed potatoes and gravy, salads, squash, and all kinds of fresh vegetables and fruit slices, cheese, olives, and pickles—what a feast! Plenty for everyone.

Spending time with the family was fun. Going sightseeing or just sitting around talking was enjoyable for Joy. Being together was the main thing that brought contentment to her. She only got to come once a year to visit, and the time seemed to go by pretty fast.

With the van fixed, Vern was able to take the children to their Wednesday-night Bible study group along with Elisabeth and Renee. It seemed like Vern was happy now that they were back in the routine once again. This made Joy happy too, seeing that he was really faithful and responsible for continuing his little children's mission.

The month had gone by, and it was time to go back home. She had continued paying for the rented car for Gale, and they drove it down to Tucson because Vern had to work at the church, cleaning and getting ready for Sunday service.

Arriving back home, there was a pile of mail to open. She opened an Easter card from her brother Carlyle—it was a beautiful card—then she opened another card exactly like it from her brother Louis.

"What a coincidence, they live miles apart in Michigan, and they both chose the same card to send to me. Oh my goodness, that is so amazing to get two cards just alike from my brothers. Both thinking about me at the same time," Joy explained.

The rest of April was quiet, only board meetings and doctor's checkups and the normal daily routine one has to do. This month on the seventh was election time. Joy worked at a church were that precinct was held. She started at 6:30 AM and finished at 9:30 PM.

These seemed like long hours, because out of 787 registered voters, only 112 voted. That is a shame. Here in America we have the freedom to vote, and people don't come and vote, and they wonder why our country is failing in many ways.

176

# CHAPTER SIXTEEN

## *A VARIETY*

"April showers bring May flowers, how true this is. On Saturday, I received from my brother Carlyle an extra-large bouquet of flowers for Mother's Day. His card read, 'You're not my mother, but you have been like one to me ever since Mom died. I love you, sis.' How sweet of him to do this, he must have had someone help him ordering them," Joy said.

When the mail came that day, she received some Mother's Day cards. She opened the one from Carlyle. It was a beautiful card that read, "Sis, I am wishing you 'Happy Mother's Day.'" Plus there was a lovely verse inside, and he signed it "Love, your brother Carlyle."

After opening beautiful cards from both her daughter and son, she opened one from her brother Louis. "I can't believe it! This card is identical to the one Carlyle sent me, it has happened again, how many times in this universe would this happen? God only knows. They both must think the same about me. I am so thankful to have brothers like them."

She told Clark and Darwin, "This surely was a wonderful Mother's Day for me."

Laurie, Joy's niece, called her and asked, "Where would you like to go in Alaska you haven't been before?"

Joy replied, "I would like to take a trip to Seldovia, it is across the bay off Homer."

Laurie said, "OK, that is what we will do when I come to see you soon."

"I will get the information all about the boat going over there and the plane bringing us back from the gentleman that works in our office who lives over there," Joy told Laurie.

Laurie was looking forward to the trip going down the Kenai Peninsula to Homer and stopping along the way, visiting other small towns, looking for souvenirs. She had been in Anchorage before, going north, but she had never gone south of Anchorage before. The weather was beautiful for traveling, and the traffic was not too bad, especially this time of year when so many tourists come to Alaska with their motor homes and on tour buses. It is fun to look at their license plates to see what state they are from as they drive.

They rented a very pleasant motel room near Homer to rest before they took the boat ride, and they called and made arrangements for the plane ride back from Seldovia. Before they left on the boat, they had a halibut lunch that was very good and tasty.

Going across the bay, they saw many kinds of birds flying around. They were so pretty and graceful, freely going from place to place. It gives a person the wonderful feeling of how God has provided for every living creature on earth.

Arriving at the dock in Seldovia, they left the boat, going up a long staircase to the street. Looking at all the beautiful cottages built close by the shore seemed like stepping from one world on to another, so quiet and peaceful. They went to the room they reserved at the little inn. Looking out of the window, they could see the water for miles. The boats were coming and going, large ones and small ones, just cruising along.

In the morning they had their breakfast and went walking all around town, a very little town with a few interesting stores to shop in with artist displays. Many handmade articles were for sale, and there were many unique souvenirs to buy. Authors find this a quiet place to live while writing their books and novels. It has an inspirational presence about it being there.

It was time to go to the little airport and catch their plane to go back to Homer. They had a very nice woman pilot. She told them to just relax, it wouldn't take long, and she would fly over one of the glaciers so they could see it from the air how they are formed. *Oh, how beautiful everything looks when we can see it this close and not so high up.* Thanking the pilot for showing them the glacier, Joy and Laurie went to the car and started their journey back to Anchorage. The whole trip had been a good experience for both of them, and they were satisfied with the choice to go there, and the weather had been sunny and warm all the time they were on the trip.

Clark took Laurie for a Jet Ski ride out in the inlet off Anchorage, going up and down the coastline. Laurie had never been on a Jet Ski before and enjoyed the ride.

Clark asked, "Laurie, would you like to go out to Wasilla on one of the lakes and we could all go fishing on the same lake when we get tired of Jet Skiing?"

"Yes, that sounds like it would be a lot of fun. I love to fish up here, they are so big compared to fish in Michigan. Darwin took me fishing when I was here before, and we caught some real big fish, and we rode the four-wheeler way back to the lake," she said.

Darwin and Clark were surprised that Laurie liked the outdoors, fishing, Jet Ski riding, and four-wheeling because they thought as a retired schoolteacher she would be quiet and more straitlaced, so to speak, but she surprised them all.

After all the fun of fishing, boating, and touring, it was time for Laurie to go back home to Michigan. She is so sweet and fun to be with, and we all would miss her.

So far June had been a good, warm month, enjoyable being outdoors and soaking up some sunshine, but there were responsibilities and chores that had to be taken care of now. Joy was trying to spend more time at home, studying her lessons to teach Sunday school.

Pastor had asked her, "Would you like to teach the adult Sunday school class?"

Joy answered, "Do you think I am capable of teaching adults?"

"Yes, Joy, that is why I asked you to do it, Betty and I think you would be able."

Praying, Joy asked, "God, please help me with studying, and may the Holy Ghost guide me into all truth that I am to teach others to understand the Word you have given to the world to believe and receive salvation and everlasting life from you."

The TV nightly news was broadcasting about a big fire that was out of control in Arizona near Show Low, close to where Gale lived. Joy called her to see if they were in any danger or not. Gale said, "It is bad, and we will probably have to evacuate soon. We are boxing up some things now just in case. I will let you know if we have to leave."

"I have seen it on the news, and I was worried about you and the family, they announced it was close to area," Joy said.

It wasn't long before they were told to evacuate on June 22. They left the house and took their camper farther away on some friends' property. The smoke was so bad in their area it was hard to breathe. Eventually they got the fire under control, and people were able to return back to their homes. Gale kept in touch with Joy on how they were doing and how other people were coping with the situation around them. It was quite a long time before they could return because the smoke that just lingered didn't blow away.

Gale called and said, "Alice and Bernie had another baby girl, they named her Judy Ann Marie. She was born on August 7, 2002. This means they have six children between them, Alice had three, Nancy, Art, and Summer. Whisper's mother is Wilda. These were before they were married, and now they have the two little girls, Angela and Judy Ann."

Joy said, "What are they going to do? They can't afford to feed the ones they have now. If it weren't for her grandmother, Helen, they wouldn't even have a place to live."

"I know, Mom, we help them out as much as we can too," Gale replied.

Meanwhile back here at home, Clark was getting ready to go halibut fishing with Phil, their next-door neighbor, on a chartered boat docked in Soldotna, in the middle of August.

*August seemed like it had gone by faster than usual because it had been a busy month and with enjoyable weather to be outside in the fresh air and sunshine. It won't be long now before we will see the termination dust on the top of the mountains,* Joy thought.

Clark's birthday was on Election Day this year, November 7, the same day Joy worked at the precinct all day, and they celebrated the day after. She house-sat for Barbara for a week and continued her other responsibilities with church and child evangelism.

The year would be ending soon with Christmas on its way. There was shopping, writing Christmas cards, and getting everything ready for the celebration this year at home. During the last two weeks, Joy house-sat for Barbara until after the first of the year. On New Year's Eve, the dog, Sasha, came to Joy scared and wanted to climb on her lap. No matter what she tried to do to calm Sasha down, she kept jumping on Joy. She could not figure out what was the matter with the dog, so she called Barbara and told her.

Barbara asked, "Joy, are some of the neighbors shooting off fireworks?"

"Yes," she answered.

Barbara said, "Every time they shoot firecrackers, Sasha does that. The way to stop her is to put her in the garage and make sure she has water and just shut the door. She will be fine." Finally Joy could sleep. They quit shooting off firecrackers, and the dog had quieted down.

The new year of 2003 had begun with a *bang* for sure, and Joy was looking forward to another year of semiretirement and to continue doing about the same routine, volunteering and her chores as usual.

Clark got an inexpensive offer for a trip to Florida, four days and three nights in Orlando for two people, and he asked Joy, "Do you want to go with me on January 20 this year?"

Joy answered, "Yes, we could go visit Clarice and Richard while we are there."

Joy always liked Florida. She thought, *I thought someday I would move there, but I am as far away from there as I could get in Alaska.*

They boarded the plane in Anchorage and had a stopover in Seattle for an hour, then a nonstop flight to Miami. By the time they arrived, they were very tired. After renting their car, they decided to rent a room for the night before they headed to Orlando.

Joy's leg began to bother her; it hurt and it was hard to walk on, so she got ready for bed right away, while Clark went for a walk around the hotel.

After breakfast, they drove north because they had an appointment with the company that gave Clark the promotion. Joy's leg was getting worse; it was swelling and hurting. Clark wanted her to go to the emergency room to see what was causing the pain and swelling, and she finally agreed to go. They took x-rays, and the doctor examined it, and he thought it was a sprain and told Joy to keep off it as much as she could.

They went on their way to Kissimmee to Clarice and Richard's to visit them. Joy's leg seemed to be all right if she stayed off it. The swelling didn't go down.

The next day they went to the meeting about buying time-shares there in Orlando, and Clark and Joy thought that would be a good deal. They were beautiful condos and right in the middle of Orlando. They could go there once a year and visit Clarice and Richard, also go see her sister-in-law Sandra and Steve, her, husband. They signed the papers and were now time-share owners.

This package also included three days and two nights in Fort Lauderdale and various resorts close by. They decided to go and visit these places before they attended another meeting.

Clark was smitten on the lady who was trying to get him to exchange the Orlando time-share with one there in Fort Lauderdale, which cost more money. Although it had double-occupancy rooms, it would be so far away from their family in Florida and Disneyland. Joy told Clark she would not pay for half of the cost if he bought this one, and he said he was going to do it anyway, and he did buy it.

Joy's leg hurt and bothered her so much she stayed in the hotel for the whole time they were in Fort Lauderdale until it was time to go back home. Clark went to the beach and visited Boca Raton during this time to keep from getting bored.

After returning home, Joy went to her doctor to see if he could find out what was wrong with her knee. He sent her to the hospital to get a CAT scan of her knee. The young man who took the test said, "I think it is a Baker's cyst. Athletes often get them behind the knee, and they break and drain blood down in to the leg, causing the swelling."

Joy said, "You mean to tell me the doctors in Florida and my doctor didn't know what it was, yet you knew? That is something else."

He told Joy, "I was in medical school when several guys came in with Baker's cysts."

The doctor told Joy to stay off her feet for a couple of weeks, and it should drain off completely. It was hard staying off her feet; she was always busy doing something.

The rest of the year went by. First springtime came with the flowers peeking through the soil, and the trees were budding, getting ready to leaf out. A fresh smell after a hard rain, the air seemed to be cleansed of the dust particles floating about beforehand.

Mother's Day was pleasant. Donald, her eldest son, and Gale, her daughter, called and wished Joy a happy Mother's Day. Clark and Darwin took her out to dinner at a fine restaurant. It was a happy Mother's Day for Joy.

Debbie Marie had sent Joy an invitation to her wedding in May. She was going to marry Bill Parks. This would be her third marriage, and she was hoping he was the one for her. They had a Hawaiian theme for the reception; it was very pretty, with Hawaiian music.

Joy stayed in Michigan for about a month and visited friends and relatives. The ladies from LaGrange, Indiana, and Ester Street from Benton Harbor all came to see her and Laurie in Battle Creek. This was always a good reunion for them all, laughing, joking, and catching up on all their family news and about the new births in their families.

The Apollo chapter of the American Business Women's Association was having their annual Past Presidents' Night on June 3. Joy had an invitation to attend. Teressa was happy Joy was there at this time, and so were all the other past presidents.

Clark decided to have Darwin build a garage onto the house in June. The preparations were getting done for the footings and cement work. Darwin had measured the zoning variance of land use and applied to the municipality for an approval. There was about three feet of difference from one corner of the proposed garage to the required point.

A public hearing on property petition for variance was scheduled. Joy attended with plans for the garage and a description of the property for approval. The man who went in about his case before Joy did was asking for fifteen feet of variance for his airplane hangar, and they said OK.

Joy's turn came, and they asked her to tell them what she needed.

She said, "He got fifteen feet of variance, I am only asking for three feet for a garage."

They approved the ordinance for Clark's garage, and Joy was relieved and happy.

After the cement floor was dry enough, Darwin continued working on the garage, framing, roofing, and wiring. He put in a new hot-water heater and a new furnace in the garage. The old ones were in the crawl space of the house and hard to get at to do any repairs. New ones were needed; they had been in the house since it was built years ago.

Joy bought a computer and was taking free lessons at the AARP. She wanted to write a book of memoirs and needed to learn how to operate one. After the course was over, she proceeded to write her life story. She had kept a journal for many years to refer to.

After many hours and days, she was making progress, with Darwin and Clark helping with the meals and keeping the house in order for her. This was a whole new experience for her, but she wanted to do this for a long time. It was almost like living her life over again.

Gale and Vern were having marital problems. It seemed like Vern wasn't going to the church just to help clean—he was having an affair with the pianist, Donna, for some time. He asked Gale for a divorce, and she got mad and took Whisper and left. She got a ride to St. John and went to a Safe Shelter for women and children and stayed there for a while.

In the meanwhile, Vern was spending his time with Donna at her house and leaving the girls alone, not getting them to school when they were supposed to go. Donna didn't like the girls, so she wouldn't go to Vern's and stay. He took the girls to Tucson to live with his mother and sisters, but after a while, Elisabeth and Renee called Gale and told her they didn't want to be there and would she come and get them.

Gale called Joy. "Mom, would you rent a car for me so I can go to Tucson and pick the girls up at Vern's folks' house? They called me and want to come and stay with me."

Joy said, "Yes, I will, I will call and give them my credit card number right now."

"Thanks, Mom, they were crying when they called, this shows them who cares," Gale said.

The Garcia family tried to give Gale a hard time, but the girls told them they would run away if they couldn't go with their mother. So they agreed to let them go. Vern's parents and sisters thought Donna was a better choice for a wife than Gale was. They accepted her with open arms and treated her so much better than they did Gale.

Returning to Show Low, Gale found an apartment to rent. She moved in with the children and was able to get help with the rent from CPS and receive food stamps. Donald drove a Pinto car from his home in Colorado to give to her for transportation. She then needed to buy license plates and insurance before she could drive it.

This was October, and Joy thought, *I have to pinch myself to believe I am seventy-five years old, and I feel pretty good for an old lady.*

Her pastor said, "It is all in the attitude each of us takes in our lives and the gratitude of thanks we give to God for His Son, Jesus Christ."

December was here. Louis's friend called. "Joy, Louis passed away on the fifth."

"He hasn't been well for some time now, the last time I saw him I could tell he was failing and prayed for him. I will be there as soon as I can," Joy told Joan.

She was planning to go to Arizona on December 11, 2003, and she had to change her ticket to go earlier to her brother Louis's funeral in Michigan.

Joy's friend Jenny took her to the airport, and Joy asked her, "Would you read my manuscript and let me know what you think about it?"

She answered, "Yes, I would love to read it and will let you know when you get back."

Many friends and family members were in attendance at the funeral whom Joy hadn't seen in a long time, and they talked about what had happened through the years. Joy stayed for less than a week, visiting relatives and friends, because she was on her way to Arizona.

Sean and Grace picked Joy up at the Tucson airport because she was going to stay with them for a few days before she went to Show Low. She rented a car and decided to go to Phoenix on another route to Show Low. It was winter, and she was afraid the highway going over the Canyon Pass could have snow and ice.

It had been snowing just before Joy arrived, and she thought, *I left Alaska with snow and cold, and here I am in it again. Only difference is the snow melts by afternoon, and it is warmer here.* She was happy her trip was over, and she prayed and thanked God for her safe journey. Everyone was happy to see her; hugs and kisses were given by all.

It was getting close to Christmas, and Gale needed to go to the church and pick up some presents and a food basket for her family. Whisper had been attending Sunday school there every Sunday faithfully. Gale went to their food bank once a month for food for Helen, Alice's grandmother who was taking care of her three children, Nancy, Summer, and Art plus Angela and Judy, who are Bernie and Angel's girls. And Whisper is Bernie's. She is living with Gale now, and with all of them together, they ate a lot of groceries.

Christmas morning a knock came on the door. Gale answered, and there was a brand-new bicycle with a card that read, "Merry Christmas for Whisper," and no one was there; they had left. Gale was surprised, and so was Whisper. The gentleman that picked her up for Sunday school was the man who bought it for her. Gale learned later that it was him.

Everyone else received many presents, especially the children, with a variety of toys and new clothes. The three women—Gale, Greta, and Joy— prepared a big meal fit for a king. Kenny, Renee's boyfriend, came over for dinner and enjoyed it. Afterward they all watched the children play with their games and new toys, a very merry 2003 Christmas.

One of the children asked, "Why did Whisper get a bike and we didn't?"

Joy answered, "It was because Whisper got up and went to Sunday school every Sunday, they thought she deserved it, and a bike would be a nice gift for her faithfulness."

New Year's Day came, and it wouldn't be long before it was time for Joy to go back to Tucson to Grace and Sean's for a couple of days before she headed home. This apartment was crowded. Both Gale and Helen smoked, and it bothered Joy to smell the staleness of the air, and it was worse when others came in and smoked also.

After a couple of days with Grace and Sean in clean-air surroundings, Joy returned the rental car, and after arriving at the airport, there was hugging and their good-byes.

*Gale is trying to cope with the divorce, it is hard for her to think Vern would do this to her, but he is a man thinking of no one but himself,* Joy thought as she boarded the plane. *Another chapter of her life in my book when I write it.*

*Home, there is no place like home, no matter how humble,* thinking as she departed the plane in Anchorage and met her sons. She was happy to see Clark and Darwin.

Attending church the next Sunday, Jenny handed her the manuscript and told her, "I read your book and couldn't put it down until I finished it, it is really a good book."

Betty Lorden, the pastor's wife, asked, "Joy, can I read it too?"

"Yes, Betty, if you tell me the truth what you think of it," Joy answered.

The next Sunday Betty returned the book and said, "It is a good book, I couldn't put it down either, but it needs a lot of editing, you need to have this published, Joy."

Joy asked, "Pastor Joseph, have you read it yet?"

He answered, "No, but I will, it will take me a little longer to read it though."

The spring flowers were in bloom, and the trees budding with new life. It was always good to see, along with the longer daylight hours and more sunshine every day; it lifts one's spirit. Easter is coming, and that represents a new life risen with Christ to live forever, a wonderful promise from our Father, God.

Joy sent her manuscript to many publishers. Some wanted the whole book, some wanted just a few chapters, and others just wanted the first chapter. They all answered, "We are not publishing this kind of manuscript right now." All of them rejected it.

She was getting discouraged until someone told her there were publishers in Anchorage. Looking in the yellow pages of the phone book, she came across a publisher whose ad read, "Specialized in Memoirs." She thought, *Maybe that is the one I should call.*

She called and told the man answering about her book, and he told her, "Bring your book to me. My name is Ross, and my wife's name is Betsey, and we will look it over."

Joy took the book to Ross, and he said, "We will read it and get back with you."

Days later Ross called back and said, "We will publish it, come and talk to us about the procedures and cost if you want us to do it for you."

Joy listened to all they said and intended to do with the book and agreed to it. It took many months and trips back and forth to the office before it would be ready.

Gale called and said, "Mom, you won't believe it, Vern and Donna are getting married on my birthday, June 5. Boy, he sure knows how to hurt a person, doesn't he?"

Joy answered, "Gale, this shows just how low he really is, they just want to hurt you more than they already have. I wouldn't let it bother me, just pray and ask God to forgive them, they don't know what they are doing. God is their judge, He will repay."

Darwin had sold all the lots in the subdivision, and he decided to form a corporation before he started anything else. This he had done in April 2004. It would be in the name DDG & Co. All legal work with a lot of paperwork was done, and a meeting was set up. Darwin D. Godman was the director of the corporation, and Joy E. Godman was the corporate secretary. A State of Alaska Business License was issued to DDG & Co.

Darwin found an eighty-acre parcel and bought it to develop another subdivision larger than the first one. A lot of work had to be done with this heavily wooded piece of property, and Darwin was ready to tackle it because property was selling at high prices at this time. After having an appraiser look at the land and write up the potential worth it would be after developing it into a subdivision, Darwin took it to the bank to apply for a loan to pay for developing the property and improving the road joining another subdivision.

The banker advised, "You will need a president of the corporation. Your brother Clark will qualify, with you as vice president and your mother as corporate secretary."

The banker approved the loan for the subdivision. Darwin was very grateful. His next step was to get the gas company, the electric company, and the telephone company scheduled to install the utilities when Darwin was ready.

He bought a large dozer, rock trucks, an excavator, and a utility truck, planning to do most of the work himself. Bulldozing the trees, moving dirt around, and making a road in the middle of the first phase was the beginning, and it started to look like a subdivision. It was long hours and hard work. A large utility van was remodeled for Dan to live and stay in while he worked on the project.

# CHAPTER SEVENTEEN

## COMINGS AND GOINGS

Joy received word from Dany and Clark, her cousins in Germany, to let her know they would be in Anchorage the last two weeks of May and would call her from the airport to let her know when she could pick them up. They had to go through customs first, and it would take some time. Joy had invited them earlier to come and visit her in Alaska.

The phone rang, and it was Dany. She said, "Joy, Dany here, we are about ready for you to pick us up at the international airport. We will see you soon."

Joy replied, "Dany, it is good to hear your voice, Clark and I will be right there in about forty five minutes, it's not far from here."

"Hello, Joy, how are you? I want you to meet my husband, Clark. Clark, this is Joy, and this must be Clark, your son?" Dany asked.

"Yes, I am glad to meet you, Clark, we will have two Clarks," Joy answered and added, "I hope you had a good flight, and I know you must be very tired."

"My goodness, yes, we are tired. It was a long fight, it is good to be on solid ground and here in Alaska," Dany replied.

"Let's get you home so you can relax, you can tell us what you think of Alaska so far and what your plans are," Joy suggested.

"This is beautiful country, and we have rented an RV to take us all over the state. We will go tomorrow and pick it up at the dealers," Clark, Dany's husband, said.

"We are so happy you are here visiting us, we have looked forward to your coming. Darwin lives with us also, but he is working and will be around later," Joy said.

"Dany, how are your mother, father, and brother doing these days?" Joy asked.

By this time, they had driven in the driveway, and all the luggage was being removed from the trunk and carried into the house by Clark and Clark. Joy made coffee. They had a snack to hold them over until dinner while many questions were asked and plans made for the next two weeks they were going to be here.

"Good morning!" Joy said when they woke up in the morning. "I have the coffee all made, what would you like for breakfast this morning?"

Dany said, "What would you like to fix, Joy?"

She answered, "I will make some french toast."

"We have never had french toast before, what is it like?" Dany and Clark both asked.

"I dip a slice of bread in beaten eggs with a little milk and a little salt and brown it in the skillet. Then we put butter and maple syrup on it," Joy explained.

"Oh my goodness, this is so good, Joy, we have never had this before, we just love it," Dany said gratefully.

"My mother used to fix this for us when we were young children, I have fixed it for my children for years also, and now my grandchildren too," Joy said.

The motor home they rented was a nice one, just big enough for the two of them. They parked it in the yard for a couple of days because Joy and Clark were going to show them all around Anchorage and take them out to meet Desare' and her family in Wasilla. The weather was beautiful, and they enjoyed the scenery along the highway going to Desare's. Joy told them about Darwin's children and the kind of work they were doing.

Joy showed them the subdivision Darwin had built and sold lots on and one of the homes he had built and sold. Then they went out to the new property, the eighty acres where Darwin was bulldozing in the new road, getting ready to subdivide the property into lots.

Darwin took them one at a time on his four-wheeler all around the property to get a good look at how big the subdivision was going to be, and they could see the top of Denali mountain that day because it was clear and sunny. They enjoyed the ride and was getting to know Darwin and see how talented and what a hardworking person he is.

Joy brought them up to date on her brothers and sister while they drove back home.

She told them, "My brother Franklin passed away in 1996, and my brother Louis passed away in 2003, and now there are only three of the seven children left. Clarice, Carlyle, and I are remaining. Eric, the youngest, was killed in a train wreck in 1953, and Karl Junior, the oldest, died in 1969 of a heart attack. Karl Junior's wife, Darla, is still living. She is active at the school, the one she went to as a child, helping young children with their reading."

Their next-door neighbor, Phil, invited us all to a big picnic in his backyard. He wanted to meet Dany and Clark. Joy had told Phil they were coming from Germany. Phil had met and married his wife in Germany, and he wanted to talk to them. Annie, his wife, had passed away a few years ago, and he goes to Germany to visit her family once in a while.

Desare', Aaron, and their children, Amy and Anthony, came to the picnic also, a nice picnic with lots of food and soft drinks and good fellowshipping. The weather was sunny and warm, and they all stayed most of the day, eating, taking pictures, and talking. A good time was had by everyone. Phil and Dany exchanged addresses and phone numbers because Phil said, "I would like to call you the next time I am over there."

The next day, Dany and Clark were on their way to Denali Park in the motor home and were excited about the trip. After they come back, they would stay for a day and then will go down the Seward Highway to the Kenai Peninsula, which includes Whittier, Seward, Soldotna, and Homer. They would be going to Anchor Point, Alaska—North America's most westerly highway point. Seward Highway has been voted the "Most Beautiful Scenic Highway" many times. The mountain views reflecting on the water are breathtaking. Sometimes the whales and otters can be seen swimming in the inlet.

Photographing many scenes along their trip, Dany and Clark made several computer discs to give to Joy. They were scenes of all the places they had seen and visited. Joy was very thankful and enjoyed watching them many times.

*It has been so nice having them here visiting and sharing their time with us. It has been fun keeping the Clarks both answering to their names,* Joy thought.

The time was here for them to leave to go back home, and they all went to the airport to say their good-byes. Joy told them, "Anytime you want to, please come back and visit us again, it has been a rewarding time and a lot of fun, laughing and sharing."

They both said, "We are sure we will be back again to see you. We love it here, it is so beautiful and peaceful, and you have been very hospitable to us."

Joy answered, laughing, "When I was in Germany in 1979, I was treated like a queen, in fact, Gilda's mother-in-law said to me the only English words she knew: 'God save the queen.' All of the family treated me kindly and with love."

The garage was almost complete except finishing the Sheetrock and painting the inside walls. The office room had a few finishing touches that had to be done. It was nice to have the desks and computers in the new room and also to have the clothes closet so handy. Darwin wanted to get everything done because he would be working many hours out on his property, getting that ready to have the plotting done, sectioned into one-acre lots.

Gale called and said, "Elisabeth and Mitchell are getting married August 31. And they would be living at his mother and father's home for a while, then he would be joining the air force. His folks liked Elisabeth very much and are happy about the baby coming."

Joy replied, "I am happy to hear that. I like Mitchell a lot. He is a gentleman, and he treats Elisabeth like a queen."

"Yes, I know, Mom, she is very happy to be getting married and having the baby."

Jenny, Joy's friend, called and invited her to come down to Seward and spend the weekend with her just relaxing and driving around and sightseeing. Joy hadn't seen much of Seward and thought that would be a good idea. She had a busy summer, and it would be nice to just relax for a while.

Jenny took her to the Alaska Sea Center and spent part of the day leisurely observing the sea animals and reading about each one by their display. This was interesting and fun.

They went to a nice restaurant and had lunch, then went to see a couple at the Seaman's Mission, Paul and Ida Perkins. Paul was an ordained minister. Ida was a nurse and worked at the hospital. Joy had volunteered working with them some time before. Paul goes on the ships and invites the workers, who are usually from a foreign country, to go to the mission and learn about the Lord, and he gives them Bibles in their own language. Paul and Ida serve coffee and cookies and have sing-along sessions with guitar and piano accompanying them, a happy and cheerful gathering worshipping.

The seamen are permitted to make phone calls to their loved ones whenever they wish. Many of them come back whenever their ship is in dock there in Seward.

Jenny and Joy headed back to Jenny's to rest the remainder of the day. It had been a good day for them. Even the weather cooperated; it was nice and warm. On Sunday they attended church services and then rested the remainder of the day, listening to Gospel songs and sharing experiences with each other. Joy would be leaving in the morning.

The leaves have turned to their fall colors. The daylight hours were getting shorter now. It's September and still not too cold yet. There had been some nice days to get out and do the yard work before the snow falls. This is a good time to take a small trip to see the trees before the leaves all fall. The scenery looking toward the mountains is spectacular.

One doesn't realize the work that goes into developing property and getting it ready to sell. Clearing the trees and getting rid of them before winter, Darwin let those who burn wood take the trees that are cut down and haul them away in their pickup trucks. The rest he bulldozed into a pile and burned them, clearing each lot so the mountains can be seen without the trees being in the way of the view. It is amazing how he can see acreage like this and can envision ahead of time how the roads and landscape of the property would look.

> The book should be all printed and ready for sale by the first week in February. It has taken longer than we anticipated because it has to be sent out to the printers in the lower forty-eight. I never realized how much work it takes, to write and rewrite several times before it is ready for press. It has sure been a learning experience for me, and I am happy I found a publisher in Anchorage. They have been working with me personally, and I needed that. Ray said I needed a subtitle because of the content leading up to MY HOME SWEET HOME. So it is SURVIVING AN ABUSIVE RELATIONSHIP.

Joy wrote this in her 2004 Christmas letter to send to her family and friends.

Clark and Phil, our neighbor, went on another fishing trip down to Soldotna for salmon; they have been fishing buddies for some time now. They came back happy with their limit all cleaned and cut up, ready for the freezer and a meal that day. Alaska fishing is one of the finest places to fish. Tourists come from far away to go on chartered boats to catch salmon and halibut. They pay a lot of money for a license to fish. Although, the fishing industry isn't as productive as it was before the big oil spill near Valdez.

November 3, 2004, Gale phoned and said, "Mom, Elisabeth just had a little boy, and they named him Zek Stephen James Sanford, after Mitch's dad—that is a mouthful. Elisabeth and the baby are doing fine, and they are delighted of course."

Joy replied, "I am happy for them. Did she have a hard time delivering the baby? It is just two days before Clark's fiftieth birthday, he will be happy to hear that because he likes your girls. He was there when they were babies. He is my eleventh great-grandchild."

"This makes you a grandma now, doesn't it?" Joy proudly said.

"It sure does, Mom, it feels different than just being a mom, I feel special and believe I will enjoy it," Gale replied.

They celebrated Clark's birthday with all the special dishes he liked the best and a birthday cake and ice cream, although Joy didn't put fifty candles on it.

*This year has been another one with many different things that have happened that has affected the change in their lives for some time to come,* Joy thought.

Ronnie, Clark's friend from work, invited him to go to the Philippines with him to visit his family in January for three weeks, and Clark thought that was a good idea because he hadn't taken his vacation yet. Ronnie and his mother came over to meet and talk to Joy about Clark going and to let her know about the immune shots he had to have, plus to apply for a visa. He knew Clark had a memory problem and wanted to make sure it was done before he went. They were going to pay Clark's way over there and back.

Joy said, "I think that is kind of you to ask Clark to go with you, I believe it will be all right as long as he wants to go."

Thanksgiving had passed by, and Christmas, the Lord's birthday, was celebrated with family members and enjoying the time spent with each other as well as exchanging Christmas gifts and letting them know about Clark's trip to the Philippines.

The holidays had come and gone once again and brought another new year of living in the best way they know how for the Lord, doing His good work for others as they continued being His example as "doing unto others as you would be done by."

Clark was ready to leave with Ronnie and his family for the Philippines the first week in January, and he was very excited about the trip. They came to the house to pick him up.

Joy told him, "Please be very careful, I will be praying for you and Ronnie's family also. I will miss you." She was happy he had this opportunity to go to another country.

Gale had to find another place to live because the landlord didn't want so many living in the one apartment. Renee had to go back to live with their dad, Vern. Gale took Whisper to a friend's house to live until she could get help to rent an apartment. This didn't work out for them. She then went to St. Johns and stayed at a safe house, a place for women and children who didn't have a home. The managers were very kind and friendly to Gale and Whisper, supplying their needs and encouraging them. It was hard being so far away from her girls. Gale decided she would take Whisper and go back to Show Low and stay with another one of her friends, Buddy, until she was able to get a place of her own. This worked out for a while until personalities began to take over, and it wasn't a pleasant place to be with Whisper in the middle of it.

Calling another friend, she asked, "Ted, could Whisper and I move in with you and your son for a while? It just isn't working out here with Buddy."

"Sure, that is fine with me. Whisper can catch the school bus right out here in front of the house. Do you need a ride over here?" Ted asked.

"Yes, would you please come and help us? I will get things ready to go," she answered.

Gale had been working for a Stop and Go store and gas station where they also rented U-Haul trucks. She had charge of keeping track of all the customers using them, collecting the money, and recording the transaction, until she moved again and didn't have a car to get back and forth to work. She liked that job, and her boss was good to her.

February was here, and the printers were finished with her book. They were sending them to Joy, many boxes of them. Now she would have to get busy and sell them. This was all new to her. Ross was helping her with ideas for marketing them. She went to the bookstores and asked, "Could I have a book signing at your store? And would you carry the book to sell for me?"

Only one of the stores in Anchorage would carry her books and let her have a book signing; the others wouldn't carry the book but agreed to let Joy have a book signing at their store, which she did spend a day at that store and was able to sell a few books. A Christian store in a little town near Anchorage agreed to carry her book and also have a signing. This was encouraging to Joy and lifted her spirits even higher than before.

Many of Joy's friends bought her book. On Sunday, Pastor Joseph announced from the pulpit saying, "Our congregation has a member who is an author of a published book, and we would like to congratulate her today. Congratulations, Joy, we are all proud of your accomplishment and pray the book sells many copies."

Joy was surprised at the announcement and said, "Thank you, Pastor, I appreciate the announcement and am also thankful for you and Betty encouraging me to have it published."

After church service, many bought her book and congratulated her and asked her many questions like "How long did it take you to write it?" "Have you ever written anything before?" "I didn't realize you went through an abusive relationship, was it hard to write about it?" and many more questions and related subjects about her experience.

Joy's niece, Laurie, called and said, "Aunt Joy, Mother passed away on February 16. She has been ill for a while, and she went peacefully. I realized you won't be able to come to her funeral, but I wanted to let you know. You have always visited her whenever you come to Michigan. Mom was very active until she got sick, she volunteered many years in the Logan public school's HOSTS Program assisting students at Allen School, where she attended seventy years earlier. She loved helping those children with their studies."

"Laurie, I am so sorry, are you all right? Do you have someone there to be with you? I will come if you want me to, just let me know, will you?

"I am fine, Aunt Joy, Ann is here, and she will help me through this, we've been friends for many years, and we've been through a lot together. This is too far for you to come in the wintertime, just pray for us. Aunt Doris, Mom's sister, is here also. I will need to console her, they were very close sisters," Laurie answered with a quivering voice.

*Oh my goodness, another death in the family, the years have taken its toll on us all. I am seventy-five now. The Lord promised, "Three score and ten, makes seventy years and any time after is a blessing." I thank God I am living a blessed life,* Joy thought after she had talked to Laurie.

A friend, Randy Andrews, called Joy after she had e-mailed him about her book and told her, "You ought to come to Michigan to promote your book here because this is where it all happened, and I think many of your relatives and friends would buy a book from you. I could go to the library and see if they will stock it on their shelves and to some of the bookstores also."

Joy answered, "Do you think they will? I would be thankful if you did that for me, Randy, will you let me know? I will ship the books to Mary's house."

"Yes, I believe they would because you lived here for many years," he stated.

Gale called, "Mom, I have been arrested for having marijuana, and my bail is $1,500, can you pay it for me? I don't want to stay in jail because of the children."

"What happened? I will find out later. In the meantime, I will get a plane ticket and be there as soon as I can, it will be the later part of March," Joy answered reluctantly.

Arriving at the courthouse just in time for Gale's trial, Joy was anxiously waiting to find out the details of what had happened and what the outcome would be. The judge put her on probation, and she was free to go after Joy posted her bail. Gale met Joy outside of the courthouse and explained what had happened, and she asked, "Mom, will you take Whisper back to Alaska with you? I have a place to live, but I think it would be best if you took her home with you."

Whisper asked, "I am very happy to be going with you, Grandma, to Alaska, is it very far?

"Yes, it is very far, but by flying, it doesn't take that long," Joy explained.

Clark was surprised when he saw Whisper and asked, "How come she came home with you, Mom? Did they keep Gale in jail? Will Whisper be staying with us very long?"

Answering one question at a time, Joy said, "No, they didn't keep her. Gale didn't have a place to live where Whisper could go, and she will be here for about a year or so."

Joy enrolled Whisper in school and met her teacher, finding out the schedule she had to be there and when she could be picked up after school. The teacher was surprised that Joy was her great-grandmother; they have grandmothers enrolling children in school but not great-grandmas.

Proceeding on with her plans, sending boxes of books to Mary's, making arrangements with the airlines to fly to Michigan in June, and keeping her household chores done.

April and May passed by quickly. It was time to get ready to go to Michigan. Packing for two was different, making sure she didn't forget anything for her or Whisper.

Clark and Darwin took them to the airport on June 5, and they all said their good-byes.

"Have a nice trip and tell Gale we said hi. Good luck with selling your book, Mom."

Upon arriving in Logan, Joy and Whisper went to Mary's to get the details about the book signing and radio interview that Tom had set up. The books had arrived there earlier.

Joy had babysat for the Andrews children when she was their next-door neighbor many years ago. Their father, George, had passed away, and their mother, Lois, went to work in a factory close by, close enough she could walk to work. There were four children: Randy and three girls, Mary, Martha, and Darlene. They were good and did as they were told.

The next day Joy went to the bookstore and talked to the manager and set up a time for her to display her books and sign them. The manager was very friendly and interested. She asked, "When did you live in Logan and why did you move to Alaska?"

Joy answered, "I lived here for fifty-five years and went to Alaska to visit two of my sons and to find work in 1983. I got a job and moved there, and I have been there since."

"I have assigned you the Sunday-afternoon shift, starting at one o'clock. Another author will be here in the morning, he booked earlier," she told Joy.

"That is just fine, I am thankful you had time for me. I can go to church in the morning before I come," Joy said.

The radio program *Announcements for Activities Going On in and Around the Town* was scheduled for Joy to appear on the Thursday before the book signing. The announcer called Joy and asked her many questions about herself and the book so when he interviewed her live on radio, he would be aware of why he was presenting her.

Visiting relatives and friends the first of the week, Joy was able to tell them the time of the program. They could watch if they wanted to.

Mary accompanied Joy when she went to the radio station on Michigan Avenue, downtown Logan, for spiritual support, because she was nervous about the interview. They waited until others were finished with their announcements of coming activities and the advertisements in between. Finally it was Joy's turn to be interviewed. She sat on their very comfortable couch next to the reporter and waited for his questions.

He asked, "When did you live in Logan? How long have you been in Alaska? Where did you work? Your brother Carlyle lives at the George Johnston Home, and he is watching this show with all the residents and staff, I know who he is." And many more.

Joy answered, "I lived here for fifty-five years and have been in Alaska since 1983, twenty-two years. I used to work at the Green Brier, right down the street from here, for three years for Mario. The book I wrote is about my life and takes place here in Logan County. I am having a book signing out at the bookstore in the West Mall." These were the answers to his questions, and she went into more detail with some of them. She thanked him for having her on his program and gave him one of her books.

Sunday afternoon Joy was setting up her display of books, when a lady came up to her and said, "I'll bet you don't recognize me, do you?"

"No, I don't," Joy answered.

"I am Jean. Bartlet was my maiden name," Jean said.

"Oh my goodness, Jean, it is so good to see you, is your mother still living?" she asked.

"Yes, she is, she is the one that saw you on TV Thursday and called and told me about it. I decided I would come and see you. It has been many years since I last saw you. Nanicy passed away a few years ago," Jean explained.

"I am sorry to hear that, Jean, she had children, didn't she?" Joy asked.

"Yes, she did, we all miss her and do everything we can for her children. Mother still lives in the same home out in Sand Lake, will you get time to go and see her? She will be happy to see you, she is feeling pretty good," Jean asked and said.

"Yes, I sure will, in fact, I will go out there tonight after I get done here. I am so glad to see you, Jean, it raises my spirits sky-high. This is one of my great-granddaughters, Whisper, she is my daughter Gale's granddaughter," Joy happily said.

Many people that Joy hadn't seen in years came. She recognized some of them, and others she couldn't, until they let her know who they were. This was so uplifting for her that so many who knew her and Dean, her husband, came to see her and buy a book.

The bookstore manager asked, "Joy, will you leave a dozen books? When they are all sold, I will send you a check and order some more."

"Thank you! This is great, I will give you my address and phone number to keep in touch, and I will ship the books to you," Joy said.

Gale's best friend, Amy, stopped by to buy a book and visit with Joy. It was good to see her and catch up on her family news and about her job and son. Whisper was getting restless, and Amy asked, "Whisper, do you want to go for a walk and window-shop?"

"I sure do, I am tired of just doing nothing here," Whisper answered.

Relatives and friends continued to come and greet Joy with hugs and "Hello, how are yous." Joy was thinking, *I am so thankful Tom arranged this for me. I didn't know anything about marketing my book, this is all new to me. Thank You, Lord, for all of my friends.*

Driving out to see Rose, Jean's mother, Joy told Whisper, "I used to babysit her two girls when I was a teenager too. They would come and pick me up on Friday evening. I would stay with them for the weekend and babysit on Saturday nights. In the summertime I was the Andrews's babysitter, these were my first jobs."

Arriving at Rose's, she came to the door and hugged Joy and said, "I was surprised to see you on TV Thursday, I had to call Jean and ask her to go to the mall to see you."

"Rose! It is so good to see you, I was surprised to see Jean, after she told me who she was, I remembered. I am glad you saw me on TV, this is great seeing you again," Joy said.

"This was like the icing on the cake, seeing so many people I haven't seen in years," Joy told Whisper on their way back to Mary Andrews's home.

Most of the books Joy had sent there were sold to friends and relatives, and she was happy to be in Logan where her life had begun seventy-seven years ago. It brought back many memories—some she had written about, and so many she couldn't fit them all in.

It was about time for her to go visit Teressa, her friend, in Michigan Center. Joy usually stayed with her at least a couple of days. It was very peaceful and quiet there.

Whisper was staying with Misty, Joy's granddaughter, and her two girls, Jo Ann and Sheri, cousins whom she just met. They live out in the country and have many toys, a trampoline, and bikes to ride. She was getting bored around so many older people.

Teressa took Joy out to dinner at least once while she was there. She asked Joy, "Where do you want to go to eat? I think I know, but you tell me where."

Joy answered, "You know, Teressa, at Coney Island for hot dogs, there is no place that makes them like they do. I know I can eat at the finer places, but I want hot dogs."

The Apollo chapter of the American Business Women's Association was meeting on that Tuesday evening, and Teressa and Joy planned to go. It had been two years since she attended and was anxious to see all the members.

Teressa said, "Joy, you better take some of your books with you, the ladies might want to buy some. It isn't every day we have a real author-member come and visit."

"Oh, that is a good idea, I will get them ready to take right now," Joy answered.

The ladies were happy to see Joy and to know she had a book published, was on the television, and had the book signing. They each bought one and had Joy autograph them.

"Teressa, I am glad you told me to bring these books here tonight, the ladies were happy to buy them. They will learn about the life I lived with Dean," Joy said.

The evening meal was very good and enjoyed by all as they fellowshipped with one another. After the meal, the ABWA meeting was brought to order, minutes were read, and committee chairmen each discussed their concerns and voted. These were women in many different types of jobs and responsibilities, volunteering their time to help raise money for scholarships.

After the benediction, they were excused, and everyone stood around for a while and talked. Many came to Joy and asked her many questions about her book and Alaska. Answering as many questions as she could, Joy let them know she missed them all.

After breakfast the next morning, Joy told Teressa, "I need to go out to Misty's and spend some time with them and to see how Whisper is getting along with her cousins and if she is enjoying herself. I am sure she is, Jo Ann and Sheri are good little girls."

"I believe I will go out to Rives Junction and visit my husband's sister Alane and her family before I go to Atwood. It's been a long time since I have seen them," Joy said.

She called to see if they were going to be home, and they were. She told them she would be there soon to visit for a while.

Alane, Lou, Lee Ann, and her son, Nate, were all happy to see Joy, and they asked her many questions about her children and grandchildren. They served her lunch while she told them about her book and how the boys and Gale were doing in their jobs. It was a good visit catching up on everything that had happened throughout these last years.

# CHAPTER EIGHTEEN

## *A FAMILY SECRET*

Driving on her way over to Atwood where Misty and her family lives, Joy was silently thinking, *Teressa is ninety-two now, and I don't know when I will get back here again, I pray she will be here for a long time. This has been a busy time trying to visit everyone.*

The children all came running out to the car yelling "Grandma!" and hugging Joy.

She said, "Let's go in the house now, OK?"

"Grandma, we've been playing on the trampoline with the hose squirting water up at us, it is fun," Whisper yelled.

"It looks like you are having a good time here with the girls," Joy said.

Sheri said, "Yes, Grandma, it has been fun with Whisper here, we've been playing with our dolls, bike riding, and jumping on the trampoline. Can she stay?"

"I am going to stay for a couple of days with you, so that means she can stay too, right?" Joy told Sheri.

"Misty, it is so much fun with you and the family, I enjoy being here in Michigan with you all. I miss you all, the girls are growing up so fast and are so smart," Joy said.

The weather was warm, and the adults sat out on the back porch, watching the girls play, getting wet with the hose sprinkler. This was a break for Misty. She works and is also going to college to become a social worker, plus taking care of the household chores, getting meals, and keeping the girls busy and out of trouble.

"Time flies by when we are enjoying ourselves. It is time for me to be on my way. I want to stop and see Debbie Marie for a while before I go to Carlson to see my sister. Relatives are planning a reunion at Clarice's so I can see them all in one place," Joy said.

"Whisper, tell the girls good-bye, we are going to leave now to go visit Debbie Marie and her son, Rodney, for a little while. I know you're having fun, but Grandma has more places to go and people to see," Joy told her.

"Misty, I hope you enjoy my book, it had been a lot of work getting it done and trying to market it. I am a greenhorn at this business," Joy said.

"I am sure I will, Grandma, I will try to find the time to read it between work, school, and everything else," Misty replied.

"Good-bye, thanks for letting Whisper stay for a while, she needed to be with other kids for a while, and that gave me a chance to do what I had to do," Joy said.

"Bye. Grandma, I miss you, it was good to see you again," both of the girls said.

"Well, Whisper, we are on our way to see Donald's older daughter, Debbie Marie, and her son, Rodney, then we will be going over to my sister's in Carlson," Joy explained.

Debbie Marie had divorced and was alone again, living in Logan. Joy and Whisper arrived and spent the evening with her and Rodney. This was on Saturday. She worked the second shift during the week, so this was a good time to catch her home.

"Hello, Grandma, it is good to see you. Is this Whisper?" Debbie Marie asked.

"Hello, yes, it is, Whisper, this is Debbie Marie, Debbie Marie, this is Whisper,"

Debbie Marie said, "Whisper, this is Rodney, Rodney, this is Whisper, your second cousin."

They spent the evening catching up on all the family news. Joy signed and gave her one of her books to her. She said, "I hope you can find time to read this, it is my life story up to 1966. I am going to write another book later to finish the years beyond this time. Debbie Marie, I kept a journal to help me to remember most of the things that happened."

"Thank you, Grandma, I will try to find the time to read it, it looks like it is interesting with all the pictures you have in it," Debbie Marie said.

"Yes, I started out writing it as my memoirs, then the first lady, Jenny, a retired schoolteacher, read it, and my pastor and his wife also read it and told me it should be edited and published. So I did as soon as I could find a publishing company that would do it for me."

Joy added, "It has been quite an experience for me. Writing it brought back many bad memories of deep hurts and a broken heart, in between the different times of the abuse. I had to go in my bedroom and get on my knees and cry my heart out several times. Then God gave me the peace to go on and write more. This was a cleansing period that had to take place in my heart because there was still a lot of hatred toward my husband I didn't realize was there, plus the hurt of abandonment and abuse. Debbie Marie, God cleanses our hearts from all of our sins and heals us, filling our heart with His love. He knew I had the hatred in my heart, and it had to come out in order for me to have peace. Love and hate both can't occupy our hearts."

"Grandma, I never realized you had to go through so much," Debbie Marie said, amazed.

"I wrote this book, and I hope and pray that it will help some young girls who read it, realize that what they think they want isn't always what is best for them and they should seek God's will be done, not their own will."

"How come you never married again, Grandma?" Debbie Marie asked.

"First reason is, I had four children and I didn't want anyone telling me how to raise them. Second is, I could never love another man as much as I did my husband in the beginning. Third is, I believe I hated all men and wouldn't give them a chance to even touch me. Fourth reason is, I turned my life over to the Lord, Jesus Christ, and He is my husband. He loves me and leads and directs my life now, where He leads me I will follow."

"I guess you have plenty of reasons, Grandma," Debbie Marie said.

"Well, my dear ones, I think it is time for us to be on our way, it is getting late, and I am very tired, Debbie Marie," Joy said.

Good-byes were said along with hugs and kisses given by all.

While driving back to Mary's, Whisper said, "Grandma, Rodney is fun to play with. We will both be ten years old this year, my birthday is in August, and his is on Christmas day. Boy, I wouldn't want my birthday on Christmas, I want a separate day for mine."

Joy remarked, "Whisper, we don't choose which day we are born on. That depends on God's timing."

Returning to Mary's, Joy told her about her visits and her plans for the next few days.

"Mary, I am going to call Carlyle tonight and let him know the time I will pick him up to go to Carlson tomorrow. Are you, Mary, Randy, and Martha still planning to go to Clarice and Christina's for the picnic?" Joy inquired.

"Yes, we are, it will be so nice to be together again after all these years," Mary said.

Joy called Carlyle and asked, "Can you be ready about ten o'clock in the morning?"

"I sure can, are we going over to see Clarice and Richard in Carlson?" Carlyle asked.

"Yes, Mary, Martha, Randy and his wife are going there too, I thought you would like to know that because Randy is good to you," Joy replied.

"Good. He always talks to me when he sees me out at Myers, and he buys me coffee," Carlyle happily said.

In the morning after breakfast, Mary, Whisper, and Joy were ready to leave. They picked up Carlyle and stopped by Martha's house to get her. It was a beautiful day for the trip to Carlson, and Mary said, "It will be nice with three of the Andrews family and three of the Wise family getting together after so many years have passed by."

Joy said, "I am so happy you all decided to go. It will be a nice reunion, and you will get to meet Clarice's family also. Laurie will be going there from Battle Creek."

Greetings and introductions were taking place as soon as they arrived. Catching up on all their family news and personal experiences throughout the past years, everyone was enjoying themselves very much before the dinner was served. Joy helped out in the kitchen, getting the last things that had to be done so they could sit down at the table.

One of their cousins, Jason Winters, and his wife, Kate, came; usually they came to all the reunions. Clarice's daughter, Heather, and her family; Phillip, Clarice's son, and his wife, Nancy; and Christina and her son Arnie were among those the Andrewses hadn't met before. They got acquainted and enjoyed conversing.

Carlyle was happy to be with family. He didn't get to very often, only on holidays. Randy took him over to his house for lunch once in a while to get him out and about. Carlyle has a bike with a big basket, and he picks up empty cans and bottles until he has a lot of them, then he turns them in for ten cents apiece. He uses the money to buy a hamburger, french fries, and a soda because he spends his time at Miner's counting all the large semitrucks going by on the highway bridge, seen from the window. He said this was his hobby.

During the winter, he rides the bus back and forth to the store. The manager is very friendly and allows him to sit in the lunchroom because he understands Carlyle's handicap.

Many photographs were taken with families and friends that day to remind them of the great fellowship they had that day. Later when they look at them, it will bring back the joy in their hearts they felt that day being together.

Joy thought, *The time has gone by so fast, and now it is time to go back home to Alaska and start selling some more books. God help me market these books, I can see now I bought too many of them.*

Mary and Martha took Joy and Whisper to the Detroit Metro Airport on June 27 to go back home. They had a good time laughing, singing Christian hymns, and conversing about their visit while driving on their way to the airport.

"Whisper, bye! We had a good time, will you come back again sometime?" Mary asked.

"Yes, if Grandma wants to bring me, I will," she answered.

"Good-bye and thanks for everything, Mary and Martha, I love you gals for being my friends and being here when I need you," Joy said with gratitude.

"We're heading home now, Whisper, I hope you had a good time, I certainly did," Joy stated.

Independence Day was coming, and there were many people driving motor homes and campers taking their four-wheelers and boats, heading for the lakes and parks, picnicking and celebrating in the beautiful surroundings. The wildflowers (weeds) were blooming, making the landscape look like a floral carpet on the hillsides.

Joy thought, *I remember when we used to go camping and boating every summer on the weekends and holidays. Water-skiing was so much fun for the whole family. These were some of the good memories that helped me get through many of the trials.*

Joy received an e-mail from her cousins Dany and Clark who lived in Germany. They wrote, "We are planning our next trip to Alaska; we will arrive on September 12 in Whittier and plan staying at Martin and Rena's for a week and tour the Kenai Peninsula. We will be in Anchorage to see you and your family for a few days. It will be good to see you all; we enjoyed ourselves so much the last time we wanted to visit again."

Dany and Clark met this young couple the last time they were in Alaska. They met on one of the tour boats and struck up a conversation because both of the men were wearing caps that read Coast Guards; one was with the American Coast Guard and the other one was from the German Coast Guard. They became friends, and Martin told Clark his grandparents lived in Germany and he would like to go there and visit them someday. Clark told him if he did decide to go to let him know, and they could get together over there.

The next year, Martin and Rena did visit them in Germany. His grandparents lived in a small town close to Clark and Dany's home, and they continued to keep in contact.

August was here, and Joy had a big birthday party for Whisper. She turned ten this year, and many parents from the church brought their children. Cousins from the Valley came, and many friends who had children came to celebrate with Whisper. She was a happy young lady with all the children that showed up and brought presents for her.

Whisper had been abandoned by her mother when she was only four years old, and her grandmother, Gale, picked her up, and Whisper had lived with Gale until she came to live with Joy. It was nice having the garage to be able to have the functions out there where there was plenty of room for card tables to sit at and the table for the food. Whisper and Joy thanked everyone for coming and for all the presents.

Joy's friends Will Ivy and his wife, Doreen, had taken Whisper under their wings. They enrolled her in ice-skating lessons and helped tutor her, and they bought her a new bike so she could go trail riding with them. They never had children and took a lot of interest in children who need extra loving care.

"Joy, would you to let her go to our summer cottage in Seldovia for the weekend?"

Joy said, "Yes, I think that would be good for her, you have been good to her. It helps me because I am too old to try to keep up the activities she needs."

Summer was over, and the school was in session now, and Joy took Whisper to and from school every day. It wasn't far; it was the same school that Elisabeth and Renee attended when they lived in Anchorage in 1995. Whisper had ice-skating lessons twice a week. Joy took her to the college campus ice rink and watched, remembering, *How I loved to ice-skate and roller-skate too.*

Clark liked to take Whisper to play miniature golf, and sometimes on Sunday, they all played a few games, trying to see who could win the most games. Then once in a while, Clark would take her to the bumper-car track so she could drive the cars. She had a hard time learning how to drive them, but once she caught on, she didn't want to stop.

It was fun having Whisper stay with us; it was keeping Great-Grandma young and happy.

Clark and Dany arrived. It was good to see them. They told much about their family in Germany. "Aunt Gilda was in the hospital and has cancer and has a hard way to go, we are hoping she gets better, but it doesn't look good," Dany said, and she added, "My father and brother are doing all right. Dad likes being retired, and my mother is living in France now. I don't get to see her very often."

After a good night's sleep, everyone arose to a nice, sunshiny day, one they could enjoy doing things outdoors. They talked about going out to see how Darwin was coming on his subdivision and to visit Desare and her family, but first they needed to eat breakfast.

Joy asked, "What can I fix for you for breakfast this morning?"

Dany answered, "Joy, can we have french toast again? We just loved it the last time we were here, we had never had any before."

"Really? My mother used to fix it for our family quite often, and I did for my family too," Joy replied.

"Thank you for the book you sent to me, I enjoyed it very much. It's really great to have and know the wife who made it by herself in so many years of work at it," Dany said.

"When I started writing, I thought it would be my memoirs, but my friends said I should have it published, it would be a good book for young girls to read," Joy said.

The trip to the Valley was fun. They stopped and looked over the subdivision to see how much Darwin had accomplished since they had seen it two years before. Then they drove over to see Desare', Aaron, Amy, and Adam. Desare' had a nice lunch fixed for them.

They all sat around the table, each one talking about their experiences they have had in all kinds of situations, like some of Darwin's hunting experiences when he encountered a bear and his bighorn sheep hunts on the cold snowy mountains. Dany and Clark were thrilled to hear about his hunting and fishing stories. They had never known anyone that hunted moose, elk, sheep, and goats before.

Aaron told them about his job as a car salesman, and he asked Clark about the German automobile business. Clark told him, "Dany's uncle Franklin owns a car dealership."

Joy said, "His wife, Gilda, is my cousin, she is the same age as I am, and when I was in Germany, they took me to see his place of business, and every year, they send me a large calendar with his advertisement on it, with beautiful pictures. I think it is so neat that Dany and Clark are here to visit us and get acquainted with their American family."

As usual the time came for them to leave. Time waits for no one; it passes by especially when everyone is enjoying themselves and doesn't even think about tomorrow until they realize it's time to go. Clark had taken many pictures of their gatherings to give to them.

*It would be nice if we could freeze time, then thaw it out when we want that experience to happen again,* Joy thought.

Joy had signed up to go to a continuing education conference in the middle of November to display and sell her book. This was the Second Annual Conference on Trauma cosponsored by the Central Psychological Association.

The meeting was very interesting. They talked about abusive situations in all walks of life and how these affect all those around. After many spoke about their way of thinking, they asked the audience if there was anyone who had any questions they would like to ask.

A few people asked questions they wanted to know the answer to. Joy raised her hand to speak, and she told them a short version of the cruelty she endured for a long time and how she kept taking it until the children were being abused then the "old mother bear instinct" came to her and how she hit her husband over the head with a ball and knocked him out cold, and then she had the bat on her shoulder again, thinking, *You can hurt me but leave my children alone, kill him, kill him.* Then Darwin yelled, "Stop, Mom, you will kill him."

"Then my mind just snapped, and I thought, *Oh my god, what have I done?* How do you explain the psychological trauma reasoning in this real situation?"

None of the speakers had an answer to her question.

After the meeting was over, they announced that there was a table with many varieties of lunch meat, fresh vegetables, chips, and desserts for those attending and for the speakers.

While standing in line, a gentleman behind Joy said, "Your question must have been a hard one to answer for the doctors, they couldn't think of an answer."

Joy said, "Doctors? You mean I said that to doctors?"

"Yes, didn't you know these are all doctors of psychology?"

"No, I didn't. I thought it was a continuing education and information about trauma. Oh my goodness, I said all of that to psychologists and psychiatrists," Joy answered.

He said, "I think you told them your story of being the one abused is the other side of the equation, they talked more about the abuser and their psychological reasoning, and it was an entirely different focus on who was being abused than what the abuser was thinking."

Joy ate her lunch and then went in where her books were displayed. She sold ten books, and she got to talk to some of the speakers about her book and how writing it was a healing process for her.

The director, a PhD, presented Joy with a continuing education certificate saying,

This is to document that Joy Godman has attended in its entirety a
Continuing Education Activity Cosponsored by AWRC and the Central
Psychological Association.
AWRC Second Annual Conference on Trauma
November 14-15, 2005

AWRC's definition is Alaska Women's Resource Center.

What a big surprise it was when Joy received this certificate in the mail.

A wedding invitation was sent to Joy and Clark; her friend Barbara's daughter, Sharon, was getting married December 18, and they decided to go. They had been friends for a long time, and Joy loved Barbara's children, Arnold and Sharon.

The invitation explained all about the ceremony. It is a Jewish wedding, full of meaningful rituals, giving the deepest significance and purpose of marriage. These rituals symbolize the beauty of the relationship of husband and wife, as well as their obligation to each other.

Chuppah: The wedding ceremony takes place under the chuppah (canopy), a symbol of the home to be built and shared by the couple.

Ketubah is the marriage contract stating the marital responsibilities of the couple. The document is signed by two witnesses and has the standing of a legal contract.

A blessing with wine is a symbol of joy and sanctification of a man and woman to each other.

Breaking the glass: A glass is now placed on the floor, and the groom shatters it with his foot. This act serves as an expression of sadness at the destruction of the temple in Jerusalem and identifies the couple with the spiritual and national destiny of the Jewish people.

Mazel tov marks the end of the ceremony with shouts of "Mazel tov," an enthusiastic reception from the guests as the bride and groom leave the chuppah together as a couple.

Joy and Clark sent their RSVP to Sharon, acknowledging they would be attending. This would be a ceremony that neither of them had ever experienced before, and they were both anxious to attend and see all of Barbara's family once again.

The last week of November, the arts and crafts Christmas sales at the Anchorage Museum was being held, and Ross, Joy's publisher, rented a table in the publishers' section to sell books for the authors that he published their books and to advertise his publishing business.

Ross asked Joy, "Would you like to attend this sale and experience the marketing of your book and to meet other authors? Also you can look around and see many other publishers and the kind of books they publish."

Joy answered, "Yes, I would, I need to do that."

The first floor of the museum was full of arts and crafts articles, jewelry, pottery, oil paintings, knitted hats and gloves, and many more different kinds of handmade items. The mezzanine floor was occupied with all publishers displaying many different kinds of books, especially books about Alaskan experiences like boating, skiing, hunting and fishing, touring, and a variety of native stories and survival.

Joy told Ross, "I am happy you asked me to join you here selling my book. This is a good experience for me to meet people and tell them about my book, thanks."

The day had come to attend Sharon's wedding, and Clark said, "I have something to tell you that is important about my trip to the Philippines."

"What is it?" Joy asked.

"When we were in the Philippines, I married Ronnie's sister, Suzie, on January 25. I think that is why he wanted me to go with them, so she would have a way to get to the United States by marrying me," Clark confessed sheepishly.

"Why did you wait so long to tell me about this?" Joy asked.

"Because Ronnie and his family didn't want anyone to know it. I had to fill out a request and proof of our marriage before she could get an immigration visa to come," Clark said.

"In other words, that is the reason Ronnie asked you to go with them, that is so deceitful, and he calls himself a friend, yeah right, some friend."

"Mom, she wouldn't even let me get near her while I was over there, she was a cold woman, that's all she wanted, a way to get here to be with her family," Clark said.

Clark added, "Now I have to get all the paperwork filled out to send to the immigration department. Ronnie said he would help me do it."

"They didn't even want you to tell me about it?" Joy asked.

"No, they didn't want anyone to know it," he answered.

"That is probably the reason why Ronnie was so friendly with you, he thought you would be a good one that would fall for their scheme to get her over here," Joy said.

"Mom, I didn't realize what I was getting into, he said he had a sister that I might be interested in, because I had been looking for a girlfriend. That's when he asked me to go with them to the Philippines to meet and marry her, and I said I would," Clark explained.

"We better get going to the wedding, I don't want to be late," Joy advised.

The wedding was a beautiful ceremony. It was good to see Barbara's family and to celebrate with them. Clark was dancing and enjoying himself being with young people.

On the way home, Joy mentioned, "It would have been nice if you had a wedding like that, not Jewish, but a Christian wedding, wouldn't it?" Joy asked.

"I have realized my mistake, now I have to keep my promise to Ronnie," he answered.

Christmas dinner was held at Desare' and Aaron's home this year. It is good to see the grandchildren here in Alaska all together at one time. Everyone's lives go in different paths and time schedules. Thanksgiving and Christmas are always good times to get together and enjoy each one's presence. We can thank God for these holiday celebrations, the pilgrims thanking Him for their bounty of food to them and Christians thanking God for His Son who died for us and our sins to set us free from sin, guilt, and shame. We honor Him by acknowledging and praising Him for what He has done and will do.

Whisper had been practicing her ice-skating and her part in the program *Little Orphan Annie*. The Anchorage Figure Skating Club was going to present Oscars on Ice for the Fur Rondy celebration that takes place in February every year in Anchorage.

*Another busy year has come and gone, with memories galore to reflect upon in my quiet moments. I wonder what 2006 has in store for us,* Joy thought.

Clark had received the paperwork permitting Suzie to come the America. He went over to Ronnie's in order to get help filling them out. Ronnie had filled out this kind of form before. And he knew what to do and what not to do.

There was an affidavit of support form, a form of verification of employment and earned income, bank accounts and tax reports, and many more forms to be sent to the US Department of Justice, Immigration and Naturalization Service. This took months to get all the information together; some Ronnie couldn't help Clark with.

Clark told his mother, "I will never make a promise to anyone again like I did to Ronnie before I know what I am getting myself into."

"Do you think she will change her mind about you and try to be a good wife?" Joy asked.

"No, she told me she was going to live with her mother," Clark answered.

# CHAPTER NINETEEN

## *VISITORS GALORE*

During the Fur Rondy celebration, they have a dogsled competition. A Miner's Ball is where everyone dresses up like they did in the old days—women in hoopskirts and big hats, men in miner's outfits—and they have a variety of activities to participate in. The ice-skating program Oscars on Ice was held at the University of Alaska ice rink for two nights.

They all skated a wonderful program. Children from three years old were in *Little Orphan Annie*. A variety of ages presented their programs throughout the evenings.

Whisper was a little scared to be in front of so many people, but she did fine and enjoyed watching the rest of the program. Will and Doreen came to watch her also. They had paid for all her lessons and were pleased she was doing so well.

Desare' and her family decided to move to California to be in the sunshine and get out of the cold, snowy winter driving. They put their home up for sale, had a yard sale, and packed up everything and shipped it all down to California. The rest of the family hated to see them go. They would surely miss them all. Aaron's sister and her family live there.

*We never know what our children or grandchildren are going to do next. We can't live their lives for them. They have to experience life and its ups and downs for themselves,* Joy thought as she drove away from their home for the last time before they left.

Gale decided to come to Anchorage for a visit in May to see how Whisper was doing. She missed her and didn't like living alone. Clark was happy to see her; they were always close and liked doing things together. He took her on a fishing trip. They also went to Denali Park and then canoeing down the river by the National Park. Gale needed that; she had been under stress for some time. She came back from their trip a new person.

June is a month of long daylight hours and plenty of sunshine until after midnight, with beautiful sunsets. The flowers were all in bloom, the city has large hanging baskets full all along the streets on light poles, various types and colors, and the parks have flower beds full also. The flowers get so big here because the sun shines so many hours a day.

*This year Donald will be sixty, and Gale will be forty-five years old,* Joy thought.

Gale went out to stay with Rose Ann, Darwin's daughter, a few days, and they visited with friends and family in Wasilla. Joy didn't go much because she liked her retirement and just being home, with contentment. Many years of working and responsibility were passed now, and she just wants to do what she wants to do when she wants to do it.

When it was time for Gale to go back to Arizona, Whisper wanted to go back with her. She had missed Gale and didn't want to stay in Alaska anymore. She had been with Gale since she was four years old, and Gale missed her also, so there was no question that she wouldn't be going back. Joy felt bad because she had grown to love her and wanted her to stay, but she knew Whisper would be unhappy if they made her stay. They left for Arizona on July 18, a beautiful sunny day outside but a heart full of sadness for Joy to see them both get on the plane.

Clark continued to correspond with Suzie to keep up the appearance they were happy and he was looking forward for her to come. The immigration department sent forms for Clark to fill out telling them about his correspondence to and from her.

Every once in a while, Ronnie would invite Clark over to his house or take Clark out to breakfast to keep the friendship alive. Ronnie didn't know Joy knew about Clark's marriage to his sister.

Friends from Michigan were coming to Alaska in August, and Joy was looking forward to seeing them. Rose was one of the friends from LaGrange, Indiana, that always came to Battle Creek when Joy was in Michigan.

They came with a land-and-cruise tour starting in Fairbanks then driving on the Top of the World Highway, traveling south, touring many cities and museums along the way, stopping in between at hotels to rest, and sightseeing the territory.

They visited the Denali National Park and then on to Talkeetna for the night before they left to go to Wasilla, a few miles from Anchorage. Their tour bus would be in Anchorage for three days parked at one of the trailer parks near Joy's, and they would be visiting them. It was good to see Rose and John and show them all the interesting places in and around Anchorage.

216

They had been enjoying their trip so far and were amazed at the size and beauty of the mountains in Alaska and the miles you have to travel in between cities.

*It is always nice to have visitors come to show them around our state and entertain them here at the house, feeding them and talking about friends and families,* Joy thought.

It wasn't long after Rose and John left when Laurie and her friend, Ann, came to stay for a few days. Ann had never been in Alaska before; it was going to be a whole new experience for her. Laurie will be a good guide to show her many of the places she had already been to and would take her there also.

After a good night's rest and breakfast, they decided to go out and see how much Darwin had accomplished on the subdivision. He was on the bulldozer, leveling the high places of dirt when they saw him. Laurie said, "I have always wanted to drive a bulldozer, do you think Darwin will let me, Aunt Joy?"

"I am sure he will if you ask him," Joy answered.

Getting out of the car, they waved at Darwin to come and talk to them, and he did.

He said, "Hi there, Laurie, how are you?"

"Hello, Darwin, I want you to meet my friend, Ann, she came here to see Alaska because I told her all about it and how much fun I had with all of you," Laurie explained.

"Hi, Ann, I am happy to meet you, and I am glad Laurie brought you to meet her crazy cousin," Darwin said, smiling.

"Hi, it is nice to meet you, Darwin, she did tell me about you, but she didn't say you were crazy, just how hard you work and how much talent you have in the building trades," Sue replied.

"Darwin, Laurie would like to drive your bulldozer, she said she has always wanted to drive one, can she?" Clark asked.

"You sure can, come on, get up there in the cab, and I will show you how to operate all the levers, it is really easy to do," Darwin told Laurie.

She stepped up into the cab and waited for Darwin's instructions and yelled at Ann and Clark, "This is something else. I am nervous, but I am going to do it because I will never have another chance to drive one."

Ann got her camera out and took many pictures of Laurie driving the bulldozer. She did look a little scared while she was driving. She didn't go very far before she decided to stop it and get off. She told Darwin, "Thanks, I do appreciate you for letting me drive it."

This had been a fun time looking over the landscape to see how Darwin developed the subdivision, with the rolling hills of the whole area, for one-acre lots to build homes on. Many more pictures were taken of everyone. Laurie always brought her camera with her and took a variety of pictures for everyone. After a good visit, they decided to let Darwin get back to work and would go sightseeing while they were in the area.

The days slipped by before we knew it, and it was time for Laurie and Ann to go south to Seward and Homer for the remainder of their trip before they had to go back home.

Clark asked, "Laurie, have you ever been to a farmer's market? There is one downtown in Anchorage. If you and Ann would like to go, I will take you, they have a good selection of handmade souvenirs."

Laurie answered, "Yes, we would like to go, it sounds like a fun place to shop."

Clark had enjoyed having Laurie and Ann here. They were a lot of fun to be with.

He told them, "I am happy Ann came with you, Laurie, it has been fun being with you. I do hope you will come back again sometime, maybe I won't have to work so many hours the next time you are here."

Clark and Joy took them to the airport, and Clark told them, "It has been nice to have you ladies come here. We enjoy entertaining guests from the lower forty-eight, they always appreciate our information about the best places to go."

The next three weeks were busy. Joy had book signings at two different bookstores in Anchorage and also at the Book Fair of Alaska Authors at the library. Keeping up with her church responsibilities and training for the next election was a must whenever she worked at the election precinct.

Finally after months of filling out paperwork, verifying Clark's ability to take care of Suzie, she was able to come to America. After stopping at the Immigration Department for clearance, she was able to continue on to Anchorage.

Ronnie's family, his mother, and Clark were at the airport to meet Suzie when she arrived with open arms and fond embraces. A little hug and "Thanks" she had for Clark. The family gathered at Ronnie's home and celebrated Suzie's safe arrival.

Fall season was here, and the leaves had fallen from the trees. The daylight hours were getting shorter, and it was getting colder. It seems like the summers go by fast, and before we know it, is winter again, then we wear our winter coats and boots to keep us warm and cozy. Joy was thankful for the garage Darwin built to keep the cars from the snow and cold, icy windows, which she had to do before for many years. Gratitude is the attitude of having a happy life and enjoying life each and every day.

Ronnie invited Clark over to his house once in a while so he could get acquainted with Suzie and get to know her better, but she never stayed in the same room with him.

Clark had told him, "We didn't get to spend much time together when I married her. She wouldn't even let me get near her so we could get acquainted."

Ronnie said, "She is a shy person and doesn't make friends easy."

"So I married her so she could come here to America, right? You knew that when you asked me to go to the Philippines with you and your family, didn't you?" Clark asked.

"What will happen if they check up on us and we aren't living together as man and wife?" Clark asked.

"You will have to bring some of your clothes over to Mother's and make it look like you live there with Suzie, in case they do investigate," Ronnie answered.

"Ronnie, you have really put me in a bad situation. I am married to a woman who won't have anything to do with me, and in the meantime, I can't date other women," Clark said.

Ronnie said, "Clark, I thought you understood this is what we were doing."

"I feel like you used me because I am easily led, and I was hoping she would like me. I guess I am the one who got fooled," Clark replied.

Joy was very upset about this manipulation, and she discussed it with Clark after Suzie had been here for a while. Suzie was ignoring Clark and wouldn't give him a chance to take her to dinner or on a date with him so they could get to know each other.

Clark continued to work both jobs and keep busy, so he didn't have time to worry about it.

Once in a while, their family invited Clark and Joy over for a barbecue dinner they had in the house, and they were friendly. Joy believed they were trying to get on her good side, and then she wouldn't cause any trouble.

"Just in case there is any problem about your assets, you should have a prenuptial agreement typed up and signed by both of you and notarized to be assured she can't take everything you have, Clark," Joy suggested.

"Mom, you are right, I don't want to take any chances after getting myself into this bad marriage. I don't think she would try to take me for what I have got though," Clark said.

Joy typed up a prenuptial agreement that each asset and each liability acquired before marriage will still be on each own in case of a divorce. No demand from each of them will be made in case of a divorce and that they will file the income tax jointly.

Suzie read the agreement and was willing to sign it. Then both of them signed, and it was notarized, and copies were made for both of them.

It was the time of the year for the book fair to be held, and Ross asked Joy to join him at his booth so she could sell more of her books to people for Christmas gifts.

"This is a great opportunity for me, and I will be there," Joy told him.

After that, life went on as usual, for everyone was working, doing everyday chores, filling the hours of the day keeping busy now, and looking forward to the holidays that were coming soon, with shopping and meeting friends to wish them "Merry Christmas."

The holidays were filled with many festive activities with the families getting together for dinners and gift exchanges at Christmas. They all missed Desare' and her family, who were still in California, enjoying the sunshine. Annabelle, her mom, called them on the telephone to ask them, "How are you all doing? We wish you all a merry Christmas."

Lo and behold, the first week of 2007, on the seventh, Rose Ann had a little baby girl. Lee Ann is her name. She is Joy's twelfth great-grandchild; there were seven girls and five boys now. Elisabeth was expecting another baby in February, who is a boy, so that would make it even, six and six. His name was going to be Zack Nicholas.

Joy needed new eyeglasses, and after the examination, the doctor told her, "You have cataracts, and you need to have them removed before I can fit you for new glasses."

The doctor made an appointment for Joy to have this procedure done, and she kept the appointment, and the removal of the first cataract went very well, and she couldn't believe how much better she could see with just one eye done. Then after the second was removed, she could see even better. The colors were more vibrant and distinct. She was amazed how much better her sight was. She went back to the eye doctor to get fitted for new glasses, and after the examination, he told her to go down to the Meyers store and buy some reading glasses, 325 strength.

"You mean to tell me I don't need a prescription?" Joy asked.

"No, your eyes are fine for those, you will see good with them," the doctor stated.

Joy said, "Thank you, Doctor, I appreciate your telling me about them. I thought I would have to buy prescription glasses. That will save me some money."

Gale called and said, "I am in the hospital, I had gallstones in my liver removed, and I am awfully sick. I will be here for a couple of days, Mom."

"I am sorry, Gale, are you feeling better now? I will have the ladies Bible study group pray for you, and I will e-mail the prayer-chain group and have them pray," Joy said.

"Thanks, Mom, I need all of their prayers. I am still sick, but better than I was," she said.

There was going to be another election, and Joy worked at the polls all that day in April, and she also worked for Lawrence a few days this month, helping him at the office. It seemed so good that everything was so clear and brilliant since her cataract removal.

From then on, the next months were filled with keeping the bookwork done for Darwin's business, recording sales of each lot, filing, faxing, paying the bills, and balancing the checkbook, etc.

In October there was a domestic violence conference being held by Alaska Women in Crisis Organization, and Joy set up a display table in the lobby of the Loussac Library. Many tables displayed various kinds of books relating to domestic violence and help resource information for the victims of domestic violence.

Many people stopped and looked at Joy's book and asked her many questions about it, like "Why did you decide to write about your life and publish a book?" "How long did it take you from start to finish?" and "Does this take place in Alaska?"

The program was held in the auditorium, with many speaking about how domestic violence affects many people and those living with them and around them. The mayor of Anchorage, the governor of Alaska, the chief of police, the fire chief, the superintendent of schools, and a lawyer were the speakers, talking about different cases they have attended to and the destruction of innocent women and children that have been violated and left homeless. Witnesses of the violence spoke and gave their testimonies.

After the program was over, the director of AWIC Organization said, "The speakers will be lining up at the foot of the stage, and if there is anyone who wants to ask them questions, feel free to come down and speak to the person you would like to."

Joy thought, *I am going to give Governor Palin one of my books.*

Joy went out to the lobby and got one of the books and wrote, "To Governor Palin." She then walked down the side of the auditorium and waited her turn to speak to the governor. Finally it was Joy's turn to talk to her, and she said, "Hello, Governor, I am Joy Godman. I wrote a book about the domestic violence I went through, it is *My Home Sweet Home: Surviving an Abusive Relationship*, and I would like to give you a copy that I have already signed for you."

"Thank you, Joy, I hope to find the time to read it," the governor said.

Joy was shaking and nervous after she went back to the display table. She had to say a prayer to calm down. "Lord, thank you for the courage You gave me to do what I just did. Without You I am nothing, but 'I can do all things through Christ Jesus who strengthens me'" (Philippians 4:13). She put the books in her bag and said good-bye to the other ladies who had displays and then left the library.

Another November was here, and it was again time for the book fair. It was fun for Joy to attend and sell her books. Friends she knew stopped by to chat with her and catch up on any news about what was going on in their lives, and she did the same.

"I never knew there were so many authors in Alaska. The variety of books written and all of the publishing companies that are here is overwhelming to me," Joy told Ross.

"Yes, Joy, I have a lot of competition in this business, but I specialize in memoirs, and many of them do not," Ross explained.

It was time to leave the museum and go home. Opening the door, Joy saw the snowflakes floating down and covering the ground. It looked so pretty with the streetlights shining in the background through the flakes.

Joy thought, *Winter is here officially now. With the temperature so cold, this snowfall, it will probably stay on the ground and won't melt.*

This Christmas was another joyful time with the grandchildren and great-grandchildren playing with their toys and the parents getting the food set on the table, ready to eat, and enjoying each other's company. Little Lee Ann was almost one now, and she was getting most of the attention. Rose Ann had dressed her so cute in a frilly little red dress.

Desare called and wished everyone "Merry Christmas, and I miss everyone, and I wish we were in Alaska too, it doesn't even seem like Christmas without family around."

Annabelle, her mom, said, "Merry Christmas to you all, and we miss you too."

She let Grandma, Rose Ann, Donald, and Larry speak to Desare', Amy, and Adam for a while also. It was good to talk to them and hear their voices say "Merry Christmas."

Continuing to work part-time, Joy prepared the information for the accountant to figure out the taxes for Lawrence's company and get the journals and files ready for the new year. Joy had been working for him for twenty years and had tried to retire three or four times, but the women he hired wanted him to use the computer for doing the records of business, and he refused to. Lawrence ended up calling Joy to come back in to work.

Renee and Michael had a little baby boy, Jacob Patrick, on January 27, 2008.

*Now the total of great-grandchildren is seven girls and seven boys, fourteen. Thank You, God, You have blessed me with this many great-grandchildren,* Joy thought.

Plans were made to go to Arizona to see the new baby and visit all the families there. A reservation at the Roundhouse Resort in Pinetop for two weeks was made for Joy to stay along with Gale. All the grandchildren enjoyed staying there because they could go swimming and do other inside sports at the recreation building.

Donald and Sherry came down from Colorado to stay with them for a week also. They brought their horses along to go trail riding, and Gale went with them several times.

Renee invited everyone to come to her home for a cookout and to see the new baby. Donald and Sherry took the horses with them and let the children ride them, plus some of the adults also. It was a very pleasant day, warm and sunny to be outside and enjoying the children playing and the adults visiting and taking turns holding little Gannon.

Donald had found a place to board the horses that was close to the resort, and it was nice for them to get the horses whenever they wanted to go riding. The stay at the resort was so much fun for everyone, especially Joy; being with her family made her happy and content, realizing and thinking, *Just think how much Dean* [her deceased husband] *has missed over all of these years with his children growing up, their accomplishments, and now the grandchildren and great-grandchildren.*

Elisabeth and her two boys, Zeek and Zack, Renee and Jacob, Whisper, Angela Lee, and Judy Marie were all there to go swimming. Grandma took care of Jacob. He was only two months old. *God is so good. He continues to bless me over and over again. Life is a wonderful gift from God, and it goes on forever for those who believe,* Joy thought as she held and hugged little Jacob in her arms.

"The wages of sin are death but the gift of God is eternal life" (Romans 6:23).

The latter part of Joy' vacation was spent at Grace and Sean's home, resting and enjoying many card games and dominoes.

"Elderly people like us live a different pace of life than the younger ones do, we don't move as fast, think as fast, and need more rest," Joy told Grace and Sean.

"Tell us about it! We've been in that stage of life for some time now," Grace replied.

"Joy, we hate to see you leave, we enjoy you being here so much," Grace told her.

Springtime was here, and Easter was just around the corner. It seemed like this year was on a fast pace already, Joy thought as she returned home.

Working only one day a week made it easy for Joy to be able to go and do other things during the week, like studying her Bible lessons she taught for Sunday school class, working at the food bank, going to lunch with friends, and doing her household chores.

Joy received word that her friend Teressa Harrison had passed away at the end of March. She was ninety-four years old, a wonderful Christian woman. Joy had worked with Teressa for sixteen years before moving to Alaska. They had been good friends for many years.

Clark saw Suzie at least once a year during income-tax time, and that was about all. Ronnie took Clark to breakfast once in a while to see how he was coping with it all.

Darwin's lots in the subdivision were selling, but the borough wouldn't accept the road because the road builder didn't do his job correctly and it wouldn't pass the inspection. Darwin was furious and took the owner of the road-building company to court for not abiding by the signed contract they had between them. Darwin spent a lot of money and many hours and days at the courthouse with his lawyer, testifying his case against this man. Leroy hired a highly paid corporate lawyer group to defend him, and they manipulated many points in Darwin's favor to look the opposite of what it should be to defend Leroy.

The judge was a woman whom Darwin had before in a driving-while-intoxicated charge, and she didn't like him; although she said at the beginning of the trial she wouldn't let that influence her judgment of the case. Well, it sure did. Darwin lost the case and had to pay a portion of Leroy's lawyers besides all he had already paid his lawyer.

This experience was devastating for Darwin. It took away the enthusiasm he had in the start of this project to the end of it, and he didn't have the willpower to continue, and he decided to sell the remaining acreage as one piece of property and continue rebuilding the boat he had started. He would buy a couple of motors and a new boat trailer to pull it. Then he would retire by staying on the boat most of the year before it got too cold.

Clark and Phil went down fishing again and had good luck catching them, and when they were not fishing, they had fun staying in Phil's motor home, playing chess. Lady, Phil's cocker spaniel, usually went along. She was getting old, and it was hard for her to get up and down the steps, but Phil and Clark both loved Lady. Clark house-sat and took care of Lady for Phil many times when he went out of town and couldn't take her. Phil was a very good and thoughtful neighbor who was always there when they needed him.

The summer was a quiet, peaceful one, not much work at Lawrence's office. Most of the lots in Darwin's subdivision were sold. Joy took a break and just took it easy.

Joy received word that her brother Carlyle was in the hospital and wasn't going to live much longer according to the doctor. and the nurse said he kept asking for Joy.

"Is it possible that you can get here soon, Joy?" the nurse asked.

"Yes, I will call the airlines right now, and I will be there as fast as I can, just tell him that I am on my way," Joy answered.

Joy was able to get a flight right away, and Laurie picked her up in Chicago, and they drove to the hospital in Logan to see Carlyle. Clarice and Richard were with him. Joy gave her and Richard a big hug and said, "Hello, how is he doing?"

Clarice said, "He is in and out of sleep and isn't saying much, but he can still hear us when we talk to him. I told him, 'Joy is on her way with Laurie,' and he shook his head."

Joy told Carlyle, "This is Joy, I came to see how you are doing, do you hear me?"

He smiled and nodded his head yes a little, enough she knew he heard her voice. They stayed with him for a few hours and tried to converse with him, but he just slept.

The nurse came in and said. "The doctor would like to speak to Clarice and Joy about Carlyle's condition, could you both come with me?"

"Yes, we will," they both said in unison.

"Being his sisters, you are his closest relatives and will have the last decision made for Carlyle. He is a very sick man and is not expected to live without life-support systems. I would advise that he be disconnected from them because there is no hope because of the condition Carlyle is in. His legs are raw and bleeding, gangrene has started to set in, and we would have to remove them soon. Will you let me know what you decide?"

Clarice and Joy agreed that this decision was the right thing to do for Carlyle's sake. They went back into his room, and he wasn't responding to their voices.

Clarice said, "Joy, I think we made the right decision, don't you? He is seventy-eight years old."

"Yes, I do, I can't stay here and just watch him slowly die, it is not right," Joy replied.

Funeral arrangements had to be made and relatives called and informed of his passing. Carlyle had a good heart. He loved animals and little children and was kind to everyone. He had the heart that no one sees. Some people made fun of him because of his handicap.

"Clarice, this leaves you and me out of seven children our mom and dad had," Joy stated.

"Yes, I know it," Clarice answered.

The funeral director recognized Carlyle. The funeral would be on Monday, September 8.

"Was he the man who rode his bicycle around collecting cans to sell?" he asked.

Joy said, "Yes, he was, he went rain or shine collecting so he could have extra money."

Laurie said, "Aunt Joy, there is a plot next to your mother's grave for Carlyle to be buried in, we can go out to the cemetery and let them know we need it excavated for Carlyle, and also there is money for a headstone for him. A bank account was set up when Grandma Wilson died, for Carlyle's portion of her estate. My father set it up, and now I have charge of it since mama died."

Carlyle had a lot of friends who attended his funeral and paid their sympathy and respects to all the family. The funeral home was in the same neighborhood as they grew up in.

After the funeral, the George Johnston Home staff prepared a luncheon for the family and friends. This was at the facility where Carlyle had lived for many years. Many tears were shed, and condolences were expressed by those who couldn't attend the funeral.

Rather than rent a car, Wendy Anderson offered to let Joy drive her van while she was in Michigan. Laurie took her to meet Wendy and pick up the van. This way, Joy could go visit and stay with friends without inconveniencing Laurie driving her all over.

Joy stayed with Wendy for a few days and visited. Her daughter, Lucy, prepared a lovely dinner for them as they visited with one another. Wendy had called Ester, her niece, and told her, "Joy is staying here, and you are welcome to come and stay also."

Ester answered, "Oh, that is great. I will call Rose and Jerry and ask them if they want to come also, OK?"

Wendy said, "That will be nice to see those ladies again, it has been a long time since I have seen them. We will see you soon."

The day was filled with happiness and friendship among this group of ladies getting together as friends love to do, even if it was only once a year or so. They stayed overnight and had a good night's sleep, and Wendy made a delicious breakfast in the morning.

Renewing old friendships is rewarding. It fills the heart with many good memories to blot out some of the bad ones that won't go away.

After all the ladies left to go home, Joy decided to go to see her granddaughter Misty and her family to spend a couple of days with them. They lived close to Wendy. After finding out how to get there, she called Misty and let her know she was on her way.

Joy said, "Thanks, Wendy, it has been fun being with you, Ester, and her friends."

Misty had called Debbie Marie and asked, "Will you and the boys come over for dinner and spend some time with Grandma?"

"Yes, we would love to see her before she goes back to Alaska," Debbie Marie replied.

"Hi, Great-Grandma," Jo Ann and Sheri said as they came to hug Joy.

"Hi there, girls, how are you?" Joy asked.

Misty hugged Joy and said, "Hello, Grandma, how are you doing? I know it must be hard losing your brother. Another brother died a short time ago, didn't he?"

"Yes, that was Louis, he passed away two years ago. Yes, it is hard, Clarice and I are the only ones left out of seven children now," Joy answered.

"Here comes Debbie Marie, Alan, Cody, and Rodney, now we can eat," Jo Ann said.

"Hello, Grandma, how are you doing?" Debbie Marie asked.

"As well as can be expected after Carlyle's death. It is hard because Clarice and I had to make the decision to stop the lifelines to him, but the doctor recommended it because he didn't have much more time to live," Joy explained.

The dinner was delicious and fun with all the children around teasing each other whenever they could. That's little boys and girls—they are differently made by God. Family pictures were taken in the evening before Debbie Marie and the boys left to go home.

It was getting late, and Joy was very tired, so she went to bed after the girls did. They had to get up and go to school the next day. They were very smart girls; when they entered kindergarten, the teachers passed them on to the first grade right away.

Joy stayed another day with Misty and had a good long talk about how the girls were doing in school and how Misty liked her job she had now, just some girl talk.

# CHAPTER TWENTY

## CONTENT

Clarice, Richard, and Christina were happy to see her and to know she was going to stay there. The days were quiet and restful there in Christina's lovely home. They caught up on all their families' news, new babies, graduations, weddings, and travels—many subjects to cover. Clarice's son Phillip, his wife, Heather, and their children came over on Sunday.

Heather, Clarice's daughter, wasn't able to come with her children.

Joy said, "I got to see her at Carlyle's funeral."

The next day they went to visit Kate, their cousin Jason's wife. He passed away in June the year before. Joy wasn't able to attend his funeral. She had sent a sympathy card to the family at the time. They had a good visit and talked about all the family, how so many were passing away and there weren't many of them left. "We are the older generation now, our children are going to be the elders when we are gone," Joy said.

Then she added, "It doesn't seem possible so many years have passed by."

They all agreed with Joy's statement.

Returning back to Christina's, they prepared a lunch, then rested in the tilt-back chairs, each taking a little nap, typical retired people.

"We deserve it, we all worked hard for so many years," Richard said to Christina.

Clarice and Richard were both eighty-two, and Joy would be eighty years old in October.

"We have been blessed. The Lord said life will be three score and ten years, and anything past that is a blessing," Joy stated with a big smile.

"You are right, Joy, it sounds good to me," Richard confirmed.

The next stop was to go to Mary's house in Logan for a couple of days to spend some time with her, Martha, Randy, and his wife, Martha. They had planned on her coming.

*It is nice having many friends and family to stay with while I am in Michigan. I lived in Logan for fifty-five years, then I moved to Alaska and have been there for twenty-five years this month,* Joy thought as she was driving Highway US 27 from Carlson.

The Andrewses were all at Mary's home, waiting for Joy to come, and they all said their hellos and gave her hugs—what a wonderful greeting from them all—as she went into the house. "It is just like home, being here next door to where I used to live," Joy said.

Randy said, "We have planned to take you out to dinner tonight, Joy, to the buffet, all you can eat for the one price. It is very good food there, we all like it. OK?

"It sounds good to me. I like buffets because you have so many choices. My goodness, I am going to gain so much weight this trip, everyone wants to feed me," she replied.

"You don't come that often, Joy, and we like to eat out. That way, the ladies aren't on their feet cooking all day," Randy said.

"By the way, how are your book sales coming?" Randy asked.

"I am not selling many now, one once in a while. I give more of them away than I sell. I ordered too many of them. I still have two hundred left at home," Joy told them.

"I just haven't had the will to finish the second book. I have six chapters done, and I stopped, I just can't seem to get in the mood to write," she added.

Leaving the restaurant, they went their separate ways, each to their own home for the night. They planned to get together the next day to play some games and visit some more.

Joy told Mary on the way home, "You don't know how much this means to me."

"Joy, it means a lot to us that you take the time and come to my house and stay. We know you have many places to go, and we appreciate you sharing your time with us," Mary replied.

Martha, Randy, and Martha came over and had lunch with Mary and Joy, then they got the card game out and proceeded to play the game Phase 10. They liked this one. After many games were over, the time was getting closer for Joy to leave. She had to meet Laurie at Wendy's friend's home to return Wendy's van, and she didn't want to be late.

Joy arrived before Laurie did, and she let Wendy know she was there. They were having a Bible study and asked Joy to join them, and she did. It was almost over, but she listened to the questions and answers that were given to learn what they were studying. After the study, they said a prayer for their friends and church members.

The lady of the house served a lunch and invited Joy to eat with them. As the lady talked about her school classroom in Concord, telling about some of her students.

Joy asked her, "Which grade do you teach?

She answered, "Second grade."

Joy asked, "Do you have a little girl in your class named Sheri Curtis?"

"Why, yes, I do," she replied.

"She is one of my great-granddaughters," Joy told her.

"She talks about her great-grandmother who lives in Alaska all the time. So you are the one she talks about," she said in astonishment.

"Yes, that is me, Great-Grandma Godman," Joy said.

"Sheri is the smartest student I have in the class, she skipped kindergarten," she said.

By this time, Laurie had arrived, and Joy introduced her to all the guests, then she proceeded to tell Laurie about the lady being Sheri's teacher. It's a small world, isn't it?

Joy thanked Wendy for letting her use the van and also thanked the lady for the lunch.

Laurie said, "That was quite a coincidence that being Sheri's schoolteacher, wasn't it?"

"Yes, when she said she taught at the Concord school, I remembered Misty's girls went there, then I asked her if she had a student named Sheri Curtis," Joy explained.

This was Wednesday, and Joy had two more days left before she had to leave to go back to Alaska, and she thought, *This has been a busy three weeks for me. I will need to get home to rest up after all this fun, food, and emotional strain.*

Clark was at the airport to pick Joy up on Saturday about midnight, and she was very tired. On the way out, Clark stopped to let a man cross the crosswalk, and when he did, the man in the car behind them smashed the taillight on Joy's car. Clark got out to talk to him, and he tried to give Clark a hundred dollars to fix the light, and Joy told him no. Because the week before, Pearl, Lawrence's wife, had a taillight replaced, and it was two hundred dollars, and her car is just like Joy's. So they got his insurance number and license number.

232

"Boy, can't anyone see this big car? This is the third time someone has rear-ended me," Joy said. Joy's car is a 1988 Mercury Marquis.

"Hello, thanks, Clark, for picking me up, you did the right thing stopping for that man. Thank You, Lord, I am home once again, my home sweet home," Joy said as they drove into the garage and she entered the back door of the house.

Darwin said, "Welcome home, Mom, it is good to see you. I missed you a lot."

"Yeah, welcome home, Mom, I hope you had a good trip," Darwin said.

Joy came home about the same time Rose Ann had to go to the hospital. Rose Ann and Chris had another baby girl. They named her Diana Marie; she was born on September 22, 2009.

"Rose Ann is doing fine, she wanted a little boy because I did," Chris said.

Chris had a daughter by a previous marriage, Ellen. She was eight years old. Chris e-mailed pictures of little Diana Marie right after she was born for Joy to see.

Clark informed Joy he had met a lady named Janice, whom he was dating. She was older than he was, but they didn't let that bother them. They enjoyed each other's company very much. They made plans to go on a vacation together in the lower forty-eight states to visit some of her relatives and also to visit Donald, his brother in Colorado, and his sister Gale in Arizona. It was many states and miles of travel, and they had a good time together.

Janice was very friendly with Joy, and they enjoyed being together. Joy invited her to all the family gatherings to get acquainted with the rest of the family, but usually, she had her own family celebrations together with her son.

Desare' and Aaron decided to move back to Alaska because of high prices in California. He wanted to find a job, and they wanted to be near the family. It was good to know they were back and to be able see them from now on.

Working for Lawrence, the daily routines, doctor's appointments, luncheons with friends, and all the normal responsibilities were carried out with the anticipation of the holidays ahead, Joy's birthday in October, then getting ready for Thanksgiving and Christmas.

These were joyful celebrations with all the family and Rose Ann's new baby, Diana. She was new life in the midst of all problems and responsibilities the adults all had.

*The holidays are over now, and a new year begins with looking forward to whatever God may have in store for me and my family,* Joy meditated.

She continued studying her lessons to teach on Sundays, working part-time, and relaxing in between other activities.

The women's retreat was held the first part of February at the Victory Bible Camp, many miles north of Anchorage. Some of the ladies at church planned on going because they learn more about God's spiritual indwelling. They have fun fellowshipping with ladies from other churches as they get to know them. It is a relaxing time, no cooking—the meals were provided—and it is high in the mountains with magnificent scenery.

One of Joy's Christian friends she had known since she arrived in Alaska passed away in March this year. She was the greeter at the church, and her name was Joy also. Joy told her it had been a long time since she met anyone named Joy.

Joy received an invitation to her sister's grandson David's wedding in May but had to tell them she wasn't able to attend. Her finances were low at the time and couldn't possibly make it. She sent a beautiful wedding card with a gift card enclosed for them.

This summer was a beautiful one. Everything went smooth and, so far, no major happenings, just a quiet peaceful time. The flowers were in full bloom with their array of sizes, and the colors were breathtaking—what a picture they make for the eyes to behold.

Clark and Janice were still dating and spending time together. They both seemed to be very happy and contented with each other so far.

Rose Ann came to town every once in a while and stayed overnight with Joy. The girls were growing so fast. Rose Ann said she was pregnant again and was expecting in December.

Joy continued to work for Lawrence once a month, and the normal responsibilities of each month were going along smooth without tension or surprises to cope with.

Clark and Janice took Joy to a very nice restaurant for her eighty-first birthday. It was a delicious dinner, and there was a big piece of cake and ice cream just for Joy. The man at the restaurant took a picture of all three of them at the table, celebrating—a nice memory.

Clark and Suzie's divorce was final on November 1, and the Decree of Dissolution of Marriage was granted to them. Now Clark was free once again after four years and nine months of this life, and she really never got to know Clark; all she wanted was to use him.

Joy had Thanksgiving for her family: Darwin, Desare, Aaron, Amy, and Adam. Clark invited Janice to come also for dinner. Everyone had plenty to eat, a variety of desserts also. Janice enjoyed the dinner and the visit, getting to know the family better. The holidays are so important to their family, getting together and renewing the love they have for each other, and the children grow up and have different stages they go through.

What a big surprise—Rose Ann had twins, a little boy and a little girl born on the third. They named them Ziden and Zina; they were born so little and petite. Rose Ann and Chris were so happy one of them was a boy. Now they have four girls with Ellen and one boy. Rose Ann has made sure she will not get pregnant again. She said that was enough, no more.

After all the Christmas shopping, wrapping packages, writing and sending Christmas cards, and preparing for another Christmas family get-together, the time was here to go to Annabelle's (Darwin's wife) house in the Valley for another delicious meal. She always fixed two prime rib roasts because everyone eats an extra-big portion of it, plus the gravy is out of this world, good on mashed potatoes. Ymmm.

There were eleven adults and seven children present. Janice came with Clark and enjoyed herself very much. She fit in with the family as a part of it. The new babies were good; they slept a lot of the time, unless someone was holding and loving them. Lee Ann and Diana were still wondering all about their mama bringing home two babies instead of one.

The children opened their gifts, and the wrappings flew all over as usual. They were all happy for their new presents and thanked everyone individually for them. Rose Ann was doing a good job raising the girls; they mind and are polite to one another.

Joy thought, *My family is having such a good time together and loving each other. It is a shame Dean* [her husband] *couldn't have lived to see and be a part of this. Thank You, Lord, for all You have done for me and my family. Another Christmas to remember.*

*The years fly by so fast. It seems like when a person gets old, it goes by faster because, I guess, they have more time behind them than they have ahead of them.*

The early months this year had been routine with some part-time work at the office for Lawrence, training for the election coming in April, and Darwin was still busy with his legal case with the road builder throughout March. Clark had an operation on his knee in April and was laid up for a while and wasn't able to work. He had several appointments with the doctors for over a month until they released him to go back to work.

"Donald, one of Darwin's sons, girlfriend had a baby girl, Carol, on April 15.

Joy received word from Gale that she was having problems with Whisper. She was skipping school, going out with older boys, and wouldn't mind. Gale called the police to help her find Whisper, and when they brought her home, the policeman told Gale, "What she needs is a good spanking."

So Gale did spank her with a belt, and the buckle hit Whisper and left a small bruise on her thigh. Whisper went to school and reported Gale to the authorities, and they took Whisper away, and Gale lost custody of her. Gale wouldn't be able to leave her trailer at the place she had rented for it.

Gale was very upset and said, "Mom, I don't know what I am going to do. I can't stay here anymore, I have got to move very soon."

Joy said, "Let me talk to Clark, maybe you can come up here with us. He is fishing with Phil but will be back in a couple of days. I will call you at the phone number you are calling from, is that OK?

"Yes, I will start packing my stuff up to take over to Renee's, thanks," she said.

Clark and Phil went on their yearly halibut-fishing trip on the Kenai in Phil's motor home and were successful catching their limit and were happy campers all the way back home. Clark and Phil were good buddies, and their friendship was important to both of them.

After helping Phil get the fish in his freezer, Clark brought his share of fish to put in their freezer, then he helped Phil clean the camper out and take care of the trash.

When Clark finally came in the house to clean himself up, Joy told him, "Gale has been having problems with Whisper running away. Gale called the police and told them about it, and when they found her, they brought her back to Gale and told her that Whisper needed a spanking, well, Gale spanked her, and she reported it to the authorities the next day at school."

Joy continued telling him about the situation and asked him, "What do you think about letting Gale come up here? She could stay with us, and you have two cars, she could use one of them. I have enough airline miles she could use to fly up here. Clark, she is so depressed and has nowhere to live, we are her family and we have to help her."

"You better call her, let her know, Mom, and get her ticket to come up here," Clark said.

Joy called Gale and told her, "Gale, Clark said you could use his car and stay here with us. I have called the airlines and reserved a seat for you. You can pick the ticket up at the airport. It is all arranged. The ticket is for the fourth of July."

"Thank you, Mom and Clark, I will get Renee and Michael to take me to Tucson. I love you, Mom and Clark," Gale said humbly.

Summertime was busy for Clark; he mowed lawns for several people besides his work at the school district and for Martin's Maintenance. Clark had ambition galore. Besides, he enjoyed working outside in the summertime. He also liked to go to the car auctions early Saturday mornings while the grass was still too wet from the morning dew to mow.

It was time for Gale to come. Clark, Darwin, and Joy went to the airport to pick her up. She was so happy to see them. She brought her little dog, Molly, with her. She had Molly for a long time and couldn't give her up. She needed something to cuddle and love.

"Hello, Gale, it is so good to see you, how was your trip?" Joy asked.

"Hello, I am fine, even Molly enjoyed it. I had her little cage under the seat, and she was good," Gale answered.

They left the airport and headed home. It was still light outside, and Gale said, "It is kind of good to see so many green trees, we have mostly desert and not many trees. I am so glad to be here with you all, I didn't know what I was going to do."

Joy said, "Gale, that is what families are for, to help when you need help."

"Oh, it is so good to be here with you, Mom, Clark, and Darwin, my family," Gale said.

"The Fourth of July, freedom from the old life into a new life blessed by God," Joy said.

"Later when you have been revived from all of your turmoil and sadness, you can look for work now that you have a car to get around," Joy added.

Clark took Gale to different places to get her mind off what she had been going through, visiting family and Janice, his friend whom Gale had met when Clark and Janice went to her house in Arizona on their trip.

Through counseling, rest, and many friends loving Gale, she began to relax and enjoy herself without taking a lot of medication she had been taking. Security is an important fact in a person's life; it is the foundation that holds one firm without collapsing in a heap. God's love is understanding and forgiving. Forgiveness rolls in like the tide, sweeping away all that would hinder us from knowing God's peace.

*It is good to have Gale here and to know she is feeling well and has a new outlook in life. I don't have to worry about her anymore. Clark will help her through it,* Joy thought.

Gale found a job working with a man she met, Bert, who had a business washing windows in all sizes of buildings. She worked with him for a while until she found out his business practices were unethical. She quit and wouldn't have anything to do with him.

"Experience is the best teacher, and that taught you to make sure who you are working for is an honest businessman," Joy reminded Gale.

"Yes, Mom, I didn't want anything to do with him when I found out," she replied.

"Thank God, you don't need any more problems in your life," Joy said.

During the summer months, Gale helped Clark with his mowing jobs to relieve him a bit.

Rose Ann and her children came in to visit. The twins were eight months old now and so cute. Joy was in the height of glory whenever the children were around, and Gale poured her love out on them also. She missed her grandchildren. She stayed at Rose Ann's once in a while in order to help her and give her a break. The children were so close in age. Lee Ann was three, Diana was just two, and the twins were eight months old. That is four children three years and under; boy, Rose Ann had her hands full.

Darwin and Clark had been talking about going moose hunting the last part of August, and Clark was looking forward to going. It had been a long time since he had been hunting. Darwin told Clark to start practice shooting at the gun range before they went hunting. Clark asked Phil if he could borrow his gun to use hunting, and Phil gladly said yes. For almost two months every Sunday, Clark took the gun and a paper target to practice shooting. As the weeks went by, he was hitting the target closer to the bull's-eye, showing Darwin his aim was much better now and he had accomplished what he started out to do.

Now it was time to get everything ready for the trip: a tent, sleeping bags, ice chest, sharp knives, ropes, large plastic bags, and plenty of nonperishable food. A lot to remember—Clark was thankful Darwin knew what they needed going on this hunting trip. They tied the canoe they would need going down the river on the top of Clark's car.

The hunting spot where Darwin knew would be good for moose hunting was by going a long ways down the Delta River to reach. They were all packed and ready to start they journey up the highway to the place where they would put the boat in the Delta River.

Clark was excited about going; he hadn't been hunting for many years.

"Good-bye, Mom, we are on our way," Clark said and kissed his mother.

"Good-bye, Mom," Darwin said and hugged her too.

"Bye, Clark and Darwin, you boys be careful, I love you," Joy said with tears in her eyes.

The trip down the Delta River would be a tedious job: first packing the boat full of all their supplies and the tent, then rowing miles until they came to the right spot. After setting up camp, they looked for and chose the spot they would be hunting in the first day.

Darwin directed Clark to hunt in a good location where he had seen many moose when he had been there before. After some time had passed, *BANG!* Clark shot a big moose.

He was so happy he jumped up and down, waving his arms, saying, "I got him, I got him."

Darwin went where Clark was and said, "We have got to start getting it gutted and cut up, ready to haul out of here." They proceeded and started the task, skinning, cutting it in quarters, and putting the parts in plastic bags. This was a very tedious and time-consuming job lifting the heavy quarters of the moose and putting them in the plastic bags.

Darwin was running out of bags. He asked Clark to go back to the campsite and get more. Darwin told Clark to go in a certain direction, and Clark said, "I know the way." And he started going in a direction he thought was the right way.

Darwin waited and waited and thought, *I wonder if Clark got lost.* A short while later, he heard a gunshot and thought, *I guess he found the campsite and let me know.* Darwin continued to wait, and Clark didn't return. Finally he decided to go see where Clark was. Leaving the moose parts all sprawled out and cut into pieces, Darwin headed through the thicket toward the campsite, wondering why Clark didn't come back.

Coming upon the campsite, Darwin saw Clark. He was dead from a gunshot. "Oh my god, Clark!" Darwin screamed and lost control of himself and cried, "Why? Why?" It took a long time for him to get his composure. He was stunned by this tragedy no one brother should have to come upon; he couldn't believe it. Hours later, he finally got control of himself and realized he had to go to report this to the police. His cell phone wouldn't work that deep into the wilderness.

Darwin packed the gear into the boat and started back down the river, asking hunters who were camped along the way if they had a cell phone. They all answered no. He continued rowing the boat and finally came to a bridge where there was a little store. He went in and asked if he could use the phone to call the state police. They let him call, and Darwin explained to them just what had happened.

They came in a helicopter and picked Darwin up so he could show them the way back to the site where Clark's body lay.

Darwin explained what had happened. They asked him many questions and investigated the scene fully. They put Clark's body in a body bag and left in the helicopter. They took Darwin back to where his boat was; he had to finish the trip alone. Arriving back where the car was, Darwin unloaded the boat and put it back on the top of the car and headed home.

He was devastated and still couldn't believe this had happened, and all the way home, all he could think about was, *How am I going to tell Mom?*

As he got closer to Anchorage, he decided to go talk to Joy's pastor at the church she attends. Pastor James and his wife, Tracy, comforted him after he explained what had happened to Clark. After Darwin settled down, the pastor told him, "My wife and I will go and tell your mother, you wait a while before you go home to see her."

Just before they came to see Joy, Martin, Clark's friend who employed Clark part-time, stopped by to see Clark, and Joy told him, "Clark isn't home from moose hunting."

Martin said, "I just saw his car with the boat on top, and Darwin was driving it, I thought Clark must be here."

"No, he isn't, are you sure it was Clark's car?" Joy asked.

Martin answered, "Yes, I would know Clark's car, and I recognized Darwin."

"Excuse me, Martin, someone's knocking at the back door, I will be right back," Joy said.

"I am going to leave, Joy. I will talk to you later," Martin said.

Joy was surprised when she went to the door and saw the pastor and his wife, Tracy.

She said, "We bet you are surprised to see us, aren't you?"

Joy answered, "Why, yes, I am, please come in and sit down. I'll get you something to drink, would you like coffee, water, or soft drink?"

"No, thank you, please sit down, we have got something to tell you," Tracy said.

"What is so important you came here to tell me?" Joy asked.

"Joy, there has been a tragic accident, and Clark has died where they were hunting."

"Oh, no, oh my god!" Shocked and devastated, Joy was speechless. She just stared into space and heard, "Joy, I gave Clark back to you after his bad accident when he was seventeen. You have had him all of these years, and now I want him here with me."

Joy knew that it was God speaking to her, and she had such peace believing what God had promised: "I will give you peace that passes all understanding."

James said, "Darwin was so upset he couldn't come and tell you himself. He came to the church and told us all about it, and we told him we would go tell you about it."

Joy looked up, and Darwin was standing there with tears in his eyes, and he said, "Mom, I couldn't come home and tell you, I was so devastated and upset. I needed someone with spiritual capabilities to talk to before I could come home."

He went over to her and hugged her, and they both cried, and he said, "Mom, I am so sorry this happened, I should have never taken Clark hunting."

"Darwin, it is not your fault, it was an accident. God only knows why. We don't," Joy said, trying to console him, and she explained her relationship she had with the Lord and how He spoke to her about Clark going to be with him.

"I had to drive the car back. I told the state police my license was revoked, and I didn't have insurance to cover an accident, and he told me to go ahead and drive it back home."

Darwin decided to go out and unload the boat and get the supplies out of the car while the pastor and his mother were having a discussion about the plans for Clark's funeral.

Pastor James said, "We are familiar with a good funeral director we could contact for you and set up a time to meet with him if you would like me to, Joy."

"Yes, James, I would appreciate it and think that would be the best way to go. I don't know any funeral directors up here. I have got to notify all of my family, this is hard for me, and call the school and let them know too. Please pray for me," Joy asked.

They all prayed with Joy for her and the family during this time of grief and sorrow.

"God, give Joy the strength and mercy to see this through and be with the family, help them all to be comforted and have faith to believe Clark is with the Lord. Amen."

Pastor and Tracy left after they knew Joy would be all right. They knew Darwin was here with her, and he would be able to talk to her more about the accident.

As they were leaving, Martin returned and asked, "Where is Clark? I saw Darwin unloading the boat, but I didn't see him, is he in the house?"

Joy told him what had happened, and he said, "No, not Clark!"

"I am afraid it is true, Martin."

"I thought it was funny when I saw Darwin around the corner, sitting in Clark's car. I knew it was Clark's car. Remember I told you when I stopped here, you didn't know about it then, did you?" Martin asked.

"No, I didn't. Darwin felt so bad he had to go to my pastor and tell him, and they came over. He was waiting a while for them to tell me before he came home, that must be where he was waiting," Joy explained.

The next day the funeral arrangements were made, and when Joy got home, she had company. Thelma, the lady that was Clark's head at work, came over and talked to Joy and told her to go to the school district's office and fill out papers for his insurance.

She stayed nearly all day with Joy while many others came and gave their sympathy and told what a good person Clark had been. Many sympathy cards were sent as well as long-distance calls. Many brought casseroles, desserts, and all kinds of meat dishes for them.

Joy received word the death certificate was ready, and she went to the church and picked it up. She read it, and it said the cause of death was "suicide."

"Oh, no, that can't be, Clark would never do that, he loved life too much, and he was so happy when he shot his moose. I will not accept this death certificate. I will call the coroner right now," Joy said with anger.

This was a battle she was going to fight to the finish, and she did. After calling the office, she told the coroner, "I will not accept the certificate as it is."

He told her, "Call the police officer who was the inspector at the scene of the accident and who wrote up the report."

She called the officer and asked him, "Why did you mark 'suicide' on the report of my son Clark's cause of death?"

"Mrs. Godman, because that is the conclusion of how it happened," the officer stated.

"Sir, my son wouldn't take his own life. He was extraordinarily happy after he shot his moose, and I found a list of what he had planned to do in the future on his dresser, that surely doesn't sound like a man who would commit suicide, does it?" Joy exhorted.

Joy added, "I am going to e-mail you several copies of the sympathy cards I received from coworkers, teachers at the schools he worked at, friends and relatives, and many more, you will read what they say about Clark and what a good and cheerful guy he was. Clark had a steel hip and wasn't very steady on his feet, and he just had surgery on his knee."

Scanning, copying, and e-mailing about twenty cards and letters to the officer, Joy was bound and determined to succeed in correcting this error. Eventually a report from the trooper to the coroner's office was mailed to have that wording removed and changed to "There was not conclusive evidence to show that the shooting was intentional, it was however, accidentally self-inflicted."

"Unknown how decedent got shot. Cannot be determined" was the final decision.

Upon reading the full report, Joy discovered a huge mistake in the explanation of the shot's location, they said "*Darwin's* head," and in the next paragraph, they said, "We placed *Darwin's* body in a body bag."

*Whoa, there! Clark was the one who died, not Darwin,* Joy thought.

Joy wrote to the trooper and told him about the mistake, and it took months to get a corrected report. It wasn't enough going through the grief of Clark's death—all of these mistakes had to be dealt with and corrected. This had to be done for the insurance company that demanded this report.

Clark's memorial service was held at the church on September 18, at 4:00 PM. Many relatives and friends attended. The gathering at the dinner was to join the family and fellowship, and they let the family know they were there anytime if they needed them. Joy was thankful for her church family; they stood by her through thick and thin and held her up in many prayers. The Holy Spirit comforted her with promises, such as "I will never leave you nor forsake you, I am here forever."

The next day, Joy received word from her brother-in-law. "Joy, Clarice has passed away. She was in the hospital and soon was gone."

"Oh no! Now I am the only one left of the seven children in our family. I don't think I will be able to go to her funeral, I have been through too much to go now. I am too overwrought and need time to be revived," she stated, then added, "I will send flowers now and come to Michigan later to visit with you, Jim, and the children and spend some time with you all," Joy explained.

After hanging up the phone, she had to go in and get on her knees and pray to relieve her heart of the burdens she had experienced these past days. This was her quiet refuge among the storms she had been in lately, the only one she could go to now, her Lord and Savior, Jesus Christ.

The rest of the year seemed to go by so slow. Joy's spirit wasn't the same; she couldn't forget about Clark, and Darwin was having problems, blaming himself for taking Clark hunting, and was depressed also.

*Thank God for the holidays when the family gets together and celebrates, it helps knowing I have a big family and God has blessed me abundantly,* Joy thought. *I am so thankful for my life. Sometimes it was a rocky road, sometimes there was grief, sometimes there was disappointment, sometimes abusive treatment, most of the time there was happiness, and through it all, I had my Savior, Jesus Christ, guiding me.*

My life was committed to Christ, and I am
contented with Christ.
This is the story I wanted to tell.
And God gave me the years to be able to do it.
Thank You, Lord.

God's will is that no man should perish but shall come to the knowledge of our Lord and Savior, Jesus Christ.

Edwards Brothers Malloy
Thorofare, NJ  USA
December 27, 2013